Praise for the novels of

RONA JAFFE

"Reads like Maeve Binchy with an edge...."
—*The Buffalo News*

"A minor genius."
—*New York Times Book Review*

"Rona Jaffe's deft storytelling is irresistible."
—*Los Angeles Times*

"Jaffe comprehends the ambivalence of women in love
like few other contemporary novelists."
—*New Woman*

"Diverse characterizations...entertaining."
—*Booklist*

"Rona Jaffe has her finger squarely
on the pulse of the times."
—*Washington Times*

"Vivid and trenchant...wry and very readable."
—*New York Times Book Review*

RONA JAFFE
THE
ROAD
TAKEN

MIRA®

ISBN 1-55166-825-4

THE ROAD TAKEN

Visit us at www.mirabooks.com

Printed in U.S.A.

Research for a novel is an arduous task. Many people gave generously and graciously of their time and expertise so that I could learn the things I needed. Some were experts, others were people who directed me to these experts, others lent me otherwise elusive research materials, a few "just" gave me moral support. All of them were important to my journey, and so I am listing them as chronologically as I can remember.

Robert L. Sherman, Mark Bregman, Marc Neal Simon, Dr. Martha Friedman, Leonard Finger, Lynne White, Deborah Lowen-Klein, Ellen Wolf, Michael D. Shadix, Roger Bilheimer, Dorothy Bilheimer, Rozanne Gold, Dr. David Weinberg, Steven Gaines, Joseph Olshan, Helen Horowitz, Joan Dim, Dr. Jean-Claude Bystryn, Dr. Rache Simmons, Dr. Alan Copperman, Anne Sibbald.

ONE

It was 1910, a time of medical mysteries, of family tragedies, of faith in a God who swiftly took away loved ones for reasons unknown, and who almost as quickly brought replacements. But for Rose Smith, who was ten years old and sitting in the church at her mother's funeral, it was impossible to imagine a replacement, ever, *ever*. In the pew, holding her breath so she wouldn't cry, she let her older sister, Maude, stroke her hand abstractedly and her little brother, Hugh, clutch at her other hand, and she knew that they were all alone. Grief and fear washed over her in waves that sent her skin tingling and made her feel sick. What would she do without her mother? Who would teach her how to grow up? Their father, William, was there of course, a solid presence on the other side of Hugh, a good and kind and strong father; but he was not a mother, he would never answer a little girl's questions, he would never be her best friend. William didn't even know why his wife had died.

Rose had asked him, after the men came and took the body away to the funeral home, when the shrieking and bustle and craziness had stopped and there was, finally, a motionless moment. She had stolen up to him quietly and tugged at his coat.

"Papa, how did Mama die?" What was that strange glance he gave her?

"Peacefully," her father said.

Rona Jaffe

"No, I mean, from what?"

"God took her. It was her time."

"Did she have diabetes?"

He looked at her in that way male adults often did when female children tried to have a conversation of any importance with them, and Rose knew he would have liked her to go away. "Why would you think that?" her father said.

"My friend at school…"

"No, your mother did not have diabetes."

"Then what, Papa?" Children were not supposed to nag their parents, but she had to know, if only to make this horrible thing more real.

Her father shook his head, gazing off into space. "Heart…lung," he said finally, vaguely.

What about heart lung? Heart lung *what?*

And then Rose realized, irrevocably, that either he didn't want to tell her any more, or, more likely, he didn't really know either. No one would ever tell her. "Don't annoy your father, child," her Aunt Martha said, and led her away.

Rose had wanted to ask him if her mother's death was her fault, but now she couldn't ask him anything.

Today, in the church, she looked at the coffin with the pink roses on it, her mother's favorite, and felt guilty for all the times she had been angry because her mother was sick. Her mother had been sick so often. Why were those memories coming back now to hurt her? It seemed her earliest mind picture was of standing in her parents' bedroom next to the bed, knowing her mother was lying in it but unable to see her. The wooden frame of the bed was as high as Rose's head; it seemed enormous. The armoire in the dimmed room was enormous too. All the furniture seemed to loom at her, as if it could tilt and fall if it wanted to. She had been told her mother was not well, and that she could visit the room to reassure herself, but she must be quiet and could only stay for a moment. Her mother was there, under the hump of sheet.

"Mama?" Rose said, quietly.

"Yes, dear," her mother said, and coughed. Her voice sounded strangled, different. Rose knew this person was her mother because her father had told her it was, and because her mother had disappeared from the rest of the house, and from her daily life, so she had to be here.

Come back, Rose wanted to say, but she was still so young that she didn't have so many words yet. She had tugged at the blankets, and was filled with infant rage. She remembered it, that rage, filling her mouth and eyes, pressing on her chest. After a while Maude or someone else came and got her.

At the funeral the minister was saying what a good person their mother, Adelaide Smith, had been. Oh yes, Rose thought, and the tears overwhelmed her, even though she had been trying to act grown-up. She didn't care what her father said, it wasn't right that God would take away a good person whose children needed her. "We have the gift of happy memories," the minister was saying. "They will comfort us." Easy for him to say.

Rose thought back to the happy times in between her mother's illnesses when her mother could take her for a walk, just the two of them, while Maude was at school or playing with her friends. Her mother was a pale princess, almost borrowed, Rose had always felt. Bristol, Rhode Island, the small, beautiful New England town where they lived, was surrounded by water. It glittered in the sunshine, the air smelled of its presence. You were never more than a block away from water of some kind. Rose had never complained when she got tired on these walks, because being alone with her mother felt like a privilege. The two of them would stroll down Hope Street under the huge, arching elm trees, avoiding the Rubber Company plant with its smokestacks pouring black smoke, and make their way to the harbor to breathe in the fresh breezes and look at the activity. The harbor was very busy with imported goods being unloaded from the boats: molasses, and coal, and other things that made life go on. Her mother's long skirts swirled around the tops of her dainty buttoned shoes. All summer long her mother dressed in white, and when they went out she always had a little parasol.

Sometimes they went to William's butcher shop, to pick up something for dinner. Standing there inhaling the moist, sweetish smell of raw flesh always made Rose a little queasy. Her mother would get a thick, rich steak, marbled with fat and oozing juices, or a roast, or sometimes, for variety, Linguica, a spicy sausage the Portuguese people in town liked to eat, which her mother fried in their way with onions or peppers and then added a thin tomato sauce. When Adelaide was well she was a good cook. She made salted cod cakes with cream sauce, or mealy Johnny cakes with salt and pepper, which she served with a piece of fish. In summer she baked apple or berry pies, their buttery crust crumbling under the sweetened fruit.

Everyone was standing; it was time now to go to the cemetery. *I didn't kill her,* Rose told herself. *God killed her.* In order to "take" her he had to kill her. I'm not so stupid as not to know that. Of course she could never tell anyone how she felt; you were supposed to love God, even when he killed your mother.

At the cemetery the family stood beside the grave in their family's plot. Rose looked around, anywhere but at that open grave, and tried to think of other things. *Mama won't mind if I don't watch,* she told herself. *Mama loves me and she doesn't want me to suffer any more than I do already.* There were the two tiny headstones of her older brothers, who had died before Rose was born.

One had died of diphtheria, the other of pneumonia, a year apart, when they were not even three. Those were things people knew about, that were not mysteries. How badly her father had wanted another son, Rose knew. He had probably been disappointed to have had her. When Hugh was born, when she was five and Maude was ten, he had been thrilled.

She remembered that day. While her mother was in the bedroom with the midwife preparing to have Hugh, the door tightly shut, Rose and Maude were sent to help their father boil water. People always boiled water when a baby was being born, although Rose could not imagine why.

"What's the water for?" Rose asked Maude.

"To keep Papa's mind off what's happening in there," Maude said authoritatively.

"They boil water for no reason?"

"That's the reason. So he won't be nervous."

"Why can't they just cook?" Rose said, thinking how stupid customs were.

After this birth their father opened a bottle of champagne, to toast his new son.

And why shouldn't he celebrate? Hugh was an attractive, charming child, beloved from the beginning and totally unspoiled by the attention and hugs and kisses he received from his sisters and mother, and the proud looks and smiles he got from his father. Most families weren't demonstrative with children, except to beat them when they misbehaved, but no one ever needed to spank Hugh. Even as a toddler he was considerate, in his babyish way. He not only shared toys, he offered them. Before he had started school, he could already read. Rose looked over at wispy little Hugh, hiding behind his sturdy father. I still have my family, Rose told herself. We'll stick together.

Maude had not let go of her hand, not in the church, and not now. Rose had always adored Maude. Maude was big and pretty and blond, with healthy, luminous skin the color of lamplight, and, because she was five years older, she could do everything better than Rose ever could. Maude brushed her long, thick hair a hundred strokes every night, and in the daytime she put it up in a pompadour in front, the rest tumbling down her back; half girl, half woman. She and her girlfriends looked at boys and whispered about them. Will Maude be my new mother, Rose wondered, and she tried not to cry again, because Maude was only fifteen.

Suddenly she wondered if anyone would ever love her as much as her mother had. She wasn't the oldest, nearly a woman, like Maude, and she wasn't the baby, like Hugh, whom everybody loved. She wasn't the only boy and she wasn't even the only girl. She was too skinny to be pretty—she'd heard that often enough—her hair was not golden like Maude's nor raven dark and shiny like Huey's, but simply an ordinary brown, and although her mother sometimes told her she had beautiful eyes, the color of cornflowers, she also knew that everyone in their family had eyes the same color. At least her mother had tried to make her feel special.

After the burial everyone went back to the Smith family's house to eat covered casseroles the neighbors had brought over, and the adults drank whiskey. Their house was crowded with friends and relatives; even people they didn't know very well seemed to be there. Although it was a sad occasion, eventually some of the little boys began to play tag among the heavy, dark furniture and were sent outside. Rose lost Maude, but several of her own friends from school were there. The adults were patting her and clucking over her, trying to cheer her up, and some were asking her to bring them glasses of lemonade as if giving her a chore would make her feel better, or maybe, Rose thought, they really just wanted her to wait on them.

"Here's Rose, our town's New Year's Baby!" some

of the grown-ups greeted her. She had been the first baby born in Bristol with the new century, on January first, 1900, and had gained a kind of celebrity from it as if it had something to do with her own accomplishments. Rose didn't like it when people talked about when she had been a baby, but she smiled at them as if she did.

There by the food table was Tom Sainsbury, the older brother of her school friend Elsie, the one who had died of diabetes. Rose had recently developed a little crush on him, but being three years older and already a teenager he never seemed to see her, and she didn't know what to say to him anyway. He was handsome and self-assured, with a winning grin that made people feel happy. Beautiful teeth, she thought, beautiful hair. You just had to notice him.

Now he came over to her. "I'm sorry about your mother," he said. "It feels so terrible now, but it will be easier for you later. I know."

How kind he was. Boys were hardly ever kind. "Thank you," Rose said.

It was sad, she thought, that it took a tragedy like this for them to speak. She felt wicked even thinking about a boy at a time like this, and besides, she told herself sternly, she was much too young to think about a boy at all.

She wandered into the kitchen. There, in the cupboard, forgotten, was Hugh's birthday cake from three days ago, from the day their mother had died. The sight of that box brought back more painful memories. Rose opened the box and touched her finger to the icing and tasted it, wondering if the cake was stale. It did taste old, a little, but not too badly.

On Hugh's birthday their mother had been feeling ill again, upstairs in her darkened room, and could not bake the cake, so Rose and Maude had gone to Kisler's bakery to buy one. The yeasty, sugary smell of bread and cookies baking made Rose's mouth water. Mrs. Kisler was a widow whose husband had been the baker. He was a much older man and he had died suddenly a few years ago, leaving her the shop to run and a young son to raise. She had hired a baker to do the work her husband had done, and she ran the front of the shop and kept the books. She had no choice. People said she was lucky to have the bakery and still to be relatively young so she could work hard and not have to clean other people's houses or depend on relatives to take her in.

Mrs. Kisler was a pleasant, fair-haired woman with bright pink spots of color on her narrow cheeks, and after the girls bought Hugh's cake—chocolate with white creamy icing—she gave them free lemon cookies to eat while the baker put Hugh's name on the cake with a pastry bag. "5," he wrote, after Hugh's name, and wreathed it with soft chocolate leaves.

"Do you think we should have made the cake ourselves?" Maude asked on the way home. "It would have seemed more thoughtful."

"Oh, he won't care," Rose said. "This one is gorgeous. We could never have made anything that looked this nice."

They entered their house and put the cake in the kitchen, hiding it in the cupboard so it would be a surprise. Then they heard men's voices. One was their father's—what was he doing home in the middle of the day?—and the other, they realized when they saw him come down the stairs, was the doctor's.

They were used to seeing the doctor, but they had never seen this grim look on his face before. He gave a little shrug and left.

"What?" Maude screamed. Rose was frozen.

"Your mother is dead," their father said.

Rose burst into tears. She had never felt so lonely and afraid. "I want to see her," she gasped and ran up the stairs into her parents' bedroom. Her mother was lying in bed the way she always had, but this time she didn't look like their mother. Without life, she was a completely different person.

"Mama," Rose cried, "come back."

"Come away," her father said, taking her by the shoulders.

The rest of the day was frantic; relatives coming, Hugh crying, Maude trying to comfort him. The cake was forgotten. They didn't have the heart to even mention Hugh's birthday, the words *Happy Birthday* too ironic now. The blown-up balloons floated above the banisters like a reproach, and the wrapped gifts looked trivial.

Poor Huey, Rose thought now, and took the cake into the dining room and put it on the table with the rest of the food. She saw Mrs. Kisler and her son among the people who had come to console the family, and recognized the more elaborate cakes on the tables as ones from her bakery, which other people had obviously brought. But even now, the mourners wouldn't eat Hugh's birthday cake. It seemed just too morbid. Eventually, when everyone had left, the family ate it, so it wouldn't go to waste. Rose had been right; it was stale.

After that the family went on as best they could. There was a hired girl to take care of Hugh during the day while William was at the shop. Maude took Hugh into her bed at night to comfort him when he cried out from nightmares, and Rose spent extra time with him too. Ever since he had been a baby, whenever their mother was sick she and Maude had given him his bath, and still did, even though by now he knew how to do it himself. They loved the look of his silky little limbs covered with soap bubbles, his damp hair, his happy giggle when they tickled him. He had become their charge, their child toy, and now he was all theirs.

He clung to his two older sisters perhaps more than he should, but he was comforting them too. Their father didn't criticize this because he didn't even notice. He seemed in a haze somehow, distracted. Rose attributed this to grief, but she didn't know how to make him happy, any more than she had known how to make her mother well.

That summer her sister, Maude, had bloomed overnight into a beautiful young woman. The boys who had been her childhood playmates were now uncomfortable with her, liking her too much—although some of them had the courage to ask her out for a walk. How tense and confused and romantic these silly little afternoon dates were! A glimpse of ankle under a long skirt, the light brief touch of a gloved hand on an arm, and a boy's neck could redden in a blush. Rose thought they were all idiots.

But the other new development was that she herself had a boyfriend of her own, or sort of. In her fantasies Rose thought of him that way, even though she knew they were make-believe. Now that he had broken the ice, Tom Sainsbury smiled at Rose whenever he saw her in the neighborhood, and gave a little nod of recognition, and the thrill of that, of feeling chosen and grown-up, lasted for hours. She felt he was the best-looking boy in town. Tom Sainsbury was different from the boys who chased her sister, Maude; he was adult, casual, comfortable, a boy who had known sorrow, who understood girls.

His father worked at the local boatyards, the Herreschoff Manufacturing Company, which made sailing yachts, steam launches, and U.S. Navy torpedo boats, and that summer Tom got a job there to learn the trade he intended to follow when he graduated from high school. He was helping to work on a yacht for the America's Cup race. Sometimes Rose walked to the waterfront hoping to catch sight of him. He was fourteen now, and Rose supposed that in a few years he would have girlfriends his own age, and then he would eventually fall in love with one of them and get married. But for now, she kept on dreaming; it didn't hurt anybody, no one knew. Sometimes she let herself dare to hope that he would wait for her.

And now her father, Rose was beginning to notice, was no longer grieving. In fact, he was looking cheerful, and sometimes hummed a little tune under his breath. He had seemed to adjust to getting on with his life more quickly than Rose thought was proper.

In the warm spring and summer evenings, after he had closed the butcher shop, and Mrs. Kisler had closed her bakery, their father would stroll down to her shop and walk her home. After a little while he began to take walks with her in the evenings after supper too, and then on Sundays after church. It was clear to everyone, even his children, that William Smith was courting Celia Kisler. And why not, people said. Celia was young enough to work hard, although of course she would prefer not to, and young enough to remarry and have more children, and certainly William's children needed a mother; a man couldn't do it all himself. Rose was horrified. She considered her father's behavior a betrayal of their mother, and even of them.

Mrs. Kisler's son, Alfred, was the same age as Huey. The two boys knew each other from the neighborhood, but they had never been friends. Hugh played with the "good" boys, the docile and timid ones, and even, sometimes, with girls. Alfred played with the leaders. Even at their age, children were mean to each other. Rose knew that when the boys teased Hugh, Alfred sometimes did too. But now, because of their parents' courtship, it was inevitable that the two families began to do things together: sometimes a Sunday dinner at Mrs. Kisler's house, or a day at the beach having a picnic.

"You mustn't tease Hugh anymore," Celia told Alfred. "Now you must defend him." Alfred made a face and shrugged.

Rose moped along the water's edge, feeling gravelly sand in her stockings and pain in her heart, and wishing she could go home. Alfred and Huey couldn't have been more unlike, and she didn't know why the grown-ups forced them on each other. Alfred was self-righteous, his widowed mother's "little man," a cocky miniature adult; while Huey was still a cuddly, vulnerable child. Alfred was athletic and coordinated, his older cousins had taught him how to swim, and he was already diving off the "high wall" into the water with the other kids; Hugh just wanted to spend hours dreamily looking for shells. When the families were together Alfred was the leader and Hugh the follower. But at least they got along.

"How nicely they play together," Celia Kisler said. "They will be good brothers."

Papa looked smug, as if he had made an excellent choice. That's what you think, Rose thought, and glanced at Maude in despair. Hugh, however, gazing at Alfred with big eyes, looked ecstatic.

And suddenly it was fall and their father married Celia Kisler. Everyone they knew came to the wedding, and seemed to think it was a happy ending for both the bride and the groom. Celia Kisler, now Celia Smith, sold her bakery to the baker, and her house to a Portuguese family, and moved in with her new family.

"Now you'll call me Mother," she said to the children.

How could Celia dare to say that, Rose wondered. How could she call this woman Mother? But at least she didn't have to call her stepmother "Mama." There would be only one Mama.

People got married and then they had children; that was a fact of life whether you liked it or not. Quite quickly, Celia had a baby girl, whom they named Daisy. Alfred and Hugh now had to share a room. Hugh didn't mind, but Alfred wasn't happy about it, although he got used to it. Alfred had also gotten used to Hugh following him around, and finally even seemed to like it. Whenever Hugh got on his nerves Alfred could send him away with a simple command, and only Rose saw the hurt in Hugh's eyes.

Rose still didn't like Alfred very much—there was a tough wildness in him—but she loved the little baby, Daisy, right away. How could you not love a baby? It wasn't the baby's fault that she had been born to this family. Daisy was soon followed by another girl, Harriette, and Rose loved her, too. Both her little half sisters were pretty and healthy. It was a boisterous household now with six children so close in age. If Papa regretted not having another boy he didn't say so. Celia, of course, was always pointing out to him how wonderful Alfred was, as if to make up for the lack of another son of his own.

Celia was smart, Rose began to realize at fourteen; Celia knew how to handle a man. She could probably learn from Celia, who might show her how to grow up since her own mother wasn't here to do it. But Rose still couldn't feel close to Celia, and she didn't think she wanted to learn anything from her. Maude would be mother enough.

When Rose had her first menstrual period she was terrified at the sight of the blood, but it was Maude she went to, not Celia. Maude explained to her what it was, said she was not to exercise or bathe while she was unwell, and then with a little embarrassment Maude told her that now that she would be menstruating every month she was grown up enough to have a baby of her own, and therefore to stay away from men.

But of course she would stay away from men! She was a nice girl. Men made you pregnant, Rose knew, but she was not sure how the babies got in there in the first place. Maude was so evasive Rose was sure she didn't know either. Rose knew it had to do with the marriage bed, although from whispers and gossip she'd overheard she knew that sometimes it happened out of it. People always gave you warnings, they never gave you details. People did not discuss these things, and they had no mother. It was inconceivable to talk about it with their father. Rose would rather have cut out her tongue than ask her stepmother such a personal question, particularly since it had something to do with Celia and her father.

Rose still missed her own mother, although her father seemed to have forgotten all about her. It was as if her mother's existence was drifting farther and farther away, just as her brownish photograph, which Rose hid in her dresser drawer under her ribbons, was slowly fading. Ever since his remarriage her father had unaccountably stopped mentioning her mother, not a word. Didn't he care anymore? It was as if Adelaide Smith, the departed, belonged in her own compartment, her own era, and that era was gone. Celia liked to say life went on.

Rose never learned what her mother died of. Many years later, when she had children of her own and the world had changed a great deal, and everyone knew about things like tuberculosis, cancer, emphysema, coronary artery disease, she realized her daughters thought it very strange that she had lived docilely with such a mystery, but that was the way things were when it happened. Everyone had only wanted to protect her.

What good did it do for a young child to know the name of something so terrible that there was no cure for it?

TWO

Growing up in a household where the women outnumbered the men, in a society where men were considered better than women, and where everyone loved him, Hugh had always felt special, chosen. After his beloved but distant mother died, his older sisters took care of him, trying to make him feel safe. And his father, Hugh knew, would protect him too. For a time after Hugh lost Mama, he had nightmares in which he was chasing her through an ominous wood full of lowering trees, choking with anxiety and never able to catch up to her, but after a while the dreams went away, and by then his father had married Celia and Celia had brought into the family his stepbrother and new best friend, Alfred.

Hugh could hardly believe his luck that this popular boy, who had ignored him and sometimes even made fun of him when they were only neighbors, now shared his actual bedroom, and his table, and his house. While Alfred never actually defended him, in the neighborhood and later in the school yard, Alfred didn't take sides against him anymore either, and because they were now brothers Hugh was treated with a little more respect from the bullies, just in case Alfred did decide to hit them.... To Hugh, Alfred was perfect. Alfred was confident about everything, he treated his mother as politely as if he were an adult, and he usually treated Hugh (quite rightly, Hugh thought), as if

he were backward. And as if this were not enough to
impress Hugh, he also liked Alfred's clothes.

Hugh could sense right away that they were more
fashionable than his own, because Alfred's mother, Celia, cared about clothes a great deal. The fact was,
Hugh liked her clothes even more than he did her
son's. She was often at the dressmaker, and even her
two pregnancies didn't stop her from looking *à la mode*,
a French phrase Celia often used. As a small child
Hugh had not paid much attention to Celia, the baker's
wife, except to think of her as a kind woman who gave
him cookies; but when she became his stepmother and
moved into his house, he began to see that not only
was her son different from him but that she was very
different from the women he had always known.

Because his mother so often was sick, Hugh had not
been allowed to spend much time in her bedroom, but
Celia was frequently away from hers on all kinds of
household errands, so he was able to sneak around and
ferret out the secrets of this strange newcomer, and
also through her the mysteries of adult women in general.

Celia Kisler Smith was extremely neat: Her silk
stockings, in small rolls, were laid in rows in her
dresser drawer, and her bloomers, petticoats, and cam-
isoles were folded into large, flowered, silky envelopes
that she had sewn herself. Her corsets, long and sleek,
in the shape of a woman, lay folded flat and tied with
ribbon. Hugh let his hands slide over them, feeling
their texture and wondering how it felt to be laced into
these things. The color that gave her those blooming
cheeks was contained in a pot beside her brush and
comb. He dipped a tentative finger into it and put pink
spots on his own cheeks and then his lips, looked at
himself in the mirror for a long moment, and then
wiped the rouge away because he knew boys were not
allowed to do these things. He investigated further.

Her long fair hair, which he had thought was so naturally abundant, he discovered was not; she apparently wrapped it over and around a hair-colored thing that looked to him like a small dead animal. She kept lavender sachets in her bureau drawers too, and scented mouthwash in the bathroom. His own mother, as he remembered her, had often smelled medicinal. Celia kept her jewelry in a porcelain box, and when Hugh looked in it he found her wedding ring from her first husband. Their father had given their own dead mother's wedding ring to Maude, who wore it on her right hand, even though Celia had suggested several times that she stop.

His stepmother was determined to replace his mother in every way. Because his mother had died on Hugh's birthday, at first the family had not had the heart to celebrate his actual birthday; instead they had a party on whichever day nearest to it fell on a weekend. This was not unusual; weekends were better for parties. And that way you wouldn't be both happy and sad. But then, finally, Celia had insisted they celebrate Hugh's birthday on the day it came around.

"You can't change the boy's age," she had said briskly. "He's entitled to his real birthday. The past is over. He must get on with his life. We all must."

Rose had given Celia a strange look, but had said nothing.

Although Hugh called Celia "Mother," by her request, he thought of her privately as simply Celia, or sometimes as "Alfred's mother." Although she was kind to him, even generous, he sensed somehow that on her list of favorites he was somewhere near the bottom. And he knew he really didn't need her. He had Maude and Rose, for unconditional comforting; and his father, for pride and acceptance; he also had Alfred, who was good at everything, for his idol; and his two little half sisters, Daisy and Harriette, who were only babies yet and knew nothing, as smiling or wailing bundles of background noise, as pure Baby, something every home he knew had.

Maude and Rose loved to give plays, dressing themselves and him in costume, even dressing the toddlers, sometimes even the family cat, and acting out their own abridged version of historical events at home. They did a tableau at Christmas (Hugh was the stand-in for all three Wise Men), and on Thanksgiving, after dinner (he was an Indian), and on July Fourth, after the annual town parade (he was a Founding Father). Alfred looked down on the whole idea of family plays and refused to join them, which disappointed them very much, but Hugh was not only accommodating but eager. Sometimes they made up their own scripts, and a few times, if it was a comedy, they put Hugh in a dress. He would never admit it, but he liked that best of all. Somehow it made him feel closer to his sisters, as if he could understand them when he put on their clothes. He had heard people say: "If I could get into your skin..." He felt their clothing would do just as well, as if it were magical.

"What a good sport!" everyone said gaily, amused, when Hugh stood there coyly posing, dressed as a milkmaid. "What a little character, what a little clown!"

Everyone said it but Alfred. "What a sissy!" Alfred said, turning away in scorn. Hugh didn't know what to do. He wanted Alfred to approve of him, but he also wanted to pretend to be someone else. Perhaps that's what it is, he thought.

"I'm not a sissy, I'm an actor," Hugh said. He looked at Alfred pleadingly, wanting him to understand.

"If you say so," Alfred said. "But *I* would never do it."

Of course you wouldn't, and that's why I like you,

Hugh thought. He knew he was forgiven and once again felt suffused with love.

He was eight now, tall and slim, a reed next to the muscular Alfred. They had been a family for three years. His father and stepmother shared one bathroom, and all the children shared the other one. Three years ago when Celia had come to live with them, she had told Maude and Rose that Hugh was too old to be helped with his bath anymore. He had not been disappointed; actually he had begun to feel shy and uncomfortable having to take his clothes off in front of them, even though they were his sisters. And now that he was older he felt even more differently about them. Suddenly he was curious; they were familiar yet unfamiliar. He had begun to spy on Maude, as he had on Celia, because now she was a woman too, another member of the mysterious species. She had graduated from high school and went on walks all the time with boys who liked her, and soon, everyone knew, she would pick one and get engaged.

One day he really lucked out in his spying. It was a hot afternoon, and Maude was taking a bath. Because she thought she was alone in the house, she had left the door ajar. Hugh crept down the hall, and looked in.

Her arms and shoulders and breasts and knees, visible above the soapy water, were plump and rounded, almost edible-looking; her bare skin was cream and peach. Her blond hair, piled high, had escaped in tendrils that stuck to her damp neck. He gaped, fascinated, at her nipples. They were large, and as pink as her lips. He caught his breath, and could feel his heart pounding, and a kind of stirring down there in the part he sometimes secretly played with. As Maude moved, he could catch just a glimpse, through the bath water, of her blond patch of hair. How soft it looked. He felt both excited and repelled.

This is not a girl, he reminded himself, struck with

guilt, *this is my sister.* Whatever feeling had passed through him a moment before now seemed wicked, shameful, and—he knew—forbidden. And, as suddenly as the excitement had come, it went away, and the naked girl in the bathtub no longer seemed fascinating and erotic, but pink and rubbery, a swimming cow. He couldn't even bear to look, and went to his room and lay on his bed, exhausted and confused.

Later he forgot everything but the disgust. He knew what was under Maude's layers of clothing, and he knew those boys who chased her wanted it, but he could no longer imagine wanting to undress a girl.

Years later, when Hugh looked back at those early childhood years, spoiled and taken care of in a houseful of women, he thought of them nostalgically as the happiest years of his life. The mind works that way, sifting out. He remembered the happy times and the comradeship, but he forgot the guilt and fear. He knew that growing up he had never been attracted to girls, and that also he had been, in some way, in love with Alfred, in love in a way beyond what you could express or admit. He forgot that his sister Maude had been his first love; he remembered only that Alfred had been. When he reviewed Alfred's wonderful qualities through romantic hindsight, Hugh thought anyone would have felt as he did. Or perhaps not.

THREE

Celia was a pragmatist. She had always been one, since she was a little girl and saw her brothers getting everything she wanted and couldn't have by virtue of the simple fact that they were male. It had been made clear to her and her sister that if they wanted anything they would have to marry it, and that the career of marriage would be hard work, which they would have to be very good at. So when Celia was eighteen she married Joseph Kisler, the baker. She wasn't in love, but he was a good-looking man, and a generous one, who would give her the material comforts she needed. She wasn't sure if she had dreams of a more exciting life; perhaps she'd had them once, but by the time she was married and had her son, Alfred, Celia realized she would probably never go farther from her town than on the train trip to Providence or the ferry to Boston, and that these trips would have to provide her with conversation for a long time.

When her husband died of a heart attack, Celia was surprised, shocked even, to find herself so suddenly bereaved; but what surprised her even more was how quickly she got over her grief. It took her two weeks, although she wore mourning for a year. She realized that reminding everyone that she was a widow would make her seem more mature, because now she had to manage the bakery, a woman in commerce.

She had seen her husband keeping his ledgers and

accounts, and she knew he ordered and paid for supplies, but no one had taught her how to run a business, just as no one had taught her the business part of running a home. She discovered she was levelheaded, and she learned these male duties quite quickly, realizing the alternative was disaster. When Joseph had been the baker and the bookkeeper no one could steal from him, but now Celia mistrusted everyone, even the new baker, who everyone said was honest as the day was long. What would they care if they were proven wrong?

She was twenty-three years old, a widow in black with a child to support. Little Alfred was her joy, her blood, and she knew he was the only person she had ever really loved because he *knew* she was important. To him, she was. The vulnerability of children goes a long way toward making their parents love them. Celia taught him good manners, respect, and confidence, and after a while she was thankful she'd had only one child, because providing for more would have been too much for her to handle all alone.

She knew that eventually she would have to remarry if she could, because a part of her wanted a normal family life and more children, with a father to support them; but for now she enjoyed meeting the people who came into the shop, giving them free cookies so they would think she was generous, chatting animatedly with the women and commiserating with them on their domestic troubles. Sometimes she thought she knew more news and gossip than was ever in the local newspaper.

Her brothers worked in the rubber factory, which made belting, packing, covered wire, and footwear. Now, for the first time, despite her constant anxiety, Celia felt that she had come to a better kind of life than her brothers had after all, because the bakery was clean and pleasant and quiet and smelled good, she didn't have to do repetitive physical work since the baker actually made the bread and cakes, and she was making her own money, just as they were. Of course, it was hard to support a child and herself and pay a woman to look after that child, much more difficult than it had been for her husband when she had taken care of their home as unpaid labor. But she was her own master now, and it had its moments.

When Celia came out of mourning there was another expense: pretty clothes. Celia loved clothes, and she was aware that she had never been beautiful, so how she put herself together was extremely important to her. She began to realize there was another reason she was so attentive to her appearance; she missed and wanted the company of an admiring man. That meant only one thing: remarriage. She didn't want to give up her new and hard-earned freedom, but, pragmatic as always, she knew that if she didn't find another husband before she and Alfred were too old, she would be alone forever, working forever, worrying forever about expenses and about people cheating her, long after being a businesswoman was not fun anymore.

There were certain things to do if she expected to attract another man to marry. She attended church regularly, in case there was a God-fearing bachelor she had overlooked, she went to every town social event, and she went to the funeral of everyone in Bristol she had ever met, particularly if it was the funeral of a wife.

She had known William Smith for several years because she bought her meat at his butcher shop, and when she heard that his sickly wife had died on the very same day she herself had attended to his son's lovely birthday cake, Celia thought it might be an omen. He was an older man, which she liked, he was healthy and good-looking enough, and he had young children who would need a new mother. The fact that the oldest of these children, his daughter Maude, was fifteen while Celia herself was only twenty-five, didn't bother her. People were old and died at fifty; twenty-five was middle-aged. His girls would need a trusted older friend, which she would be. In all the time she had been listening to gossip at the bakery, Celia had never heard a breath of scandal about William Smith—despite his wife's frail health he had never been known to look at another woman. That was good. He would be a faithful husband.

Celia not only went to Adelaide Smith's funeral, but she wrote William a sympathetic note. It was on expensive stationery she really couldn't afford, but she didn't want him to think she needed his money. Her letter was formal and old-fashioned, the way she had been taught to write before she left high school. "I hope you do not feel offended that I take the liberty of saying that I know how you must feel," Celia wrote, in her painfully neat penmanship, "as I myself am recently bereaved. But it must be so much worse for you because you have three heartbroken children to comfort, while I myself have only one. Life goes on, yes, that is true. Believe it. If you need anything please do not hesitate to ask me. Your friend and neighbor, Celia Kisler."

Not long afterward he came by the bakery at closing time and asked her if she would like to take a stroll with him.

He opened up on these walks, seeming glad to have another adult to speak to who was not a relative. He talked of his worries about his children, how hard it was to be both father and mother to them. He said he felt awkward with his daughters, and that they needed a woman's touch in their lives. Their aunts were not enough, he knew, and besides, their aunts had families of their own to take care of. Celia, of course, agreed. William also told her, several times, how beautiful his wife, Adelaide, had been, and how much he missed her.

Beautiful? Celia thought. That pasty-faced creature? He really must have been in love.

She looked at this masculine man, of respectable old Yankee stock, with his own business, and thought what a good catch he would be. He was lonely; she listened to him, and complimented him, and sometimes gave him the sort of domestic advice only a woman could give. She made herself as attractive and feminine as possible, scented, softly murmuring, but also practical. She often gave him cakes or cookies to take home to his children, a sign of caring, and a treat. She invited him and his children to Sunday dinners and arranged outings. She wanted him to see her and Alfred as a part of his family. William Smith needed her, and Celia was aware that the need he felt would, in time, convince him that he had to have her. He couldn't keep living with just the memory of a woman; he deserved a real one. Eventually, he proposed.

When they were married everyone said they were both lucky: Celia because she didn't have to work anymore and he would take care of her, and William because she would take care of him and his orphan children. Whether or not the newlyweds were in love didn't matter. They loved each other enough.

The truth was they did love each other enough: Celia no more or less than she had ever loved anyone, except for Alfred, and William more than he had expected.

Celia set to work getting her new household in order. She had a hired girl who worked several hours a day cleaning and doing the wash, while she herself attended to the meals. Soon she had two more children of her own. William was generous and she had as many new clothes as she wanted. Although Alfred was only ten by now, Celia was already dreaming of sending him to college some day. She put aside some of her household money privately every month for this, even though she had persuaded William to do the same. He was saving for Hugh's college, so he would save for Alfred's too. That was the way it had to be, they both agreed. Brothers. Education, betterment, the American dream.

But what odd brothers, she thought. Alfred was everything a young man should be, a serious, manly young man, old for his years, while Hugh was like a puppy. Hugh always played with his sisters as his first choice over other friends; his few neighborhood friends were pathetic little creatures, and she had seen him often playing with several girls, as if he were one of them. What a poor little sissy he was, Celia thought. His father should have paid more attention to him. But now that Hugh had Alfred, she hoped her son would be a good influence on him, if not right away, then eventually. Hugh obviously adored Alfred, as well he should, and he seemed eager to learn from him, although Hugh never seemed to learn enough. Not that I care, Celia thought. It's for William.

That year Celia asked William to give Alfred his name, so that all the children could feel more alike. William was glad to, and Alfred Kisler became Alfred Smith. Hugh was delighted, more so, Celia noticed, than Alfred was, even though Alfred didn't remember his real father.

Maude finally became engaged, at twenty. "I hope it's not going to be a pattern in this family, marrying late in life," Celia said. Maude had been so popular with the young men in town, so pursued and flattered and courted, that she claimed she couldn't make up her mind. But Celia felt it was more because Maude was so tied to her family, and that all three of the older children were too dependent on each other in that curious way.

Celia and William gave Maude a beautiful church wedding, and afterward a garden party reception at home. Rose was the maid of honor, and four of

Maude's girlfriends from school were bridesmaids. Daisy was an adorable, toddling, absentminded flower girl, but Harriette was still too young to be a part of the ceremony. Hugh, the ham, had begged to be the ring bearer with the satin pillow, even though in Celia's opinion he was too old for that, and she was glad when the groom decided the best man was going to hand over the ring. Hugh and Alfred were made ushers.

The groom, lanky, red-haired Walter Miller, worked at the local bank. He was not at all the one Celia would have expected Maude to choose, neither the wealthiest nor the most handsome of her numerous suitors, but Maude was obviously in love with him.

"Walter is the funniest man I know," Maude said. "He makes me laugh all the time."

You'll need a sense of humor to survive marriage, Celia thought unexpectedly, surprised she had thought it. But she didn't say it; she just smiled. At the dinner after the wedding Celia looked at her own family at the long table—the sisters and brothers all blended now, Hugh and Alfred side by side, Rose feeding little Daisy, baby Harriette in her mother's arms, William the proud patriarch—and felt secure.

Maude and Walter went to Niagara Falls for their honeymoon, and when they returned they moved into a small apartment near the family while they saved up for a house of their own. Celia helped Maude decorate on a budget, something Celia was good at and enjoyed.

While Maude was looking forward to having children, Celia didn't want any more and told her doctor so. A device called a pessary was available at the pharmacy as a womb support for women who had given birth to so many children that their uterus was prolapsed or distended, a commonly diagnosed condition in these days of large families, and Celia's doctor told her quietly that since it covered the entrance to the womb it also worked as a contraceptive. He also told her that it was unsanitary and would probably give her an infection. She got one anyway. She would have been as happy to use abstinence as the way to prevent babies, but she knew William would never agree, and she didn't want to jeopardize their good relationship.

It occurred to her, almost as an afterthought, that during all the fevered wedding plans she had never sat Maude down for a womanly heart-to-heart talk about sex in marriage; but now that she was married, of course Maude had already learned everything she had to know. Sex was an instinct, wasn't it? People bumbled through. It was more fun for the man than for the woman, but each carnal encounter (as Celia thought of it, wincing), was so brief Celia sometimes wondered how much fun it was even for the man. Yet, William, although certainly not young anymore, still wanted to do it several times a week, so she knew he really enjoyed it. She herself didn't particularly like it, but she liked that her husband was so virile. Virility, masculinity, power, were important to her.

There was war in Europe now. Everyone was concerned, some people wanting the United States to strike against the Huns and others wanting to stay out of it. President Woodrow Wilson was doing his best to keep the country at peace and maintain an impartial neutrality. But when a U.S. ship, the Lusitania, had been sunk by a German submarine that past spring of 1915, feelings ran high and there was a storm of public protest. Celia kept up with all of it through the newspaper that William brought home each evening. She knew there was a possibility that their country would send troops abroad, as they had done previously in Latin America, but she was sure there would never be fighting on American soil.

The family had bought a motor car, a Ford, with a gasoline engine, and Celia made William teach her how to drive. She drove it to the grocery store, even though she could as easily have walked, choosing one or another of the children to sit beside her in the other seat, waving hello to everyone she knew on the street. Alfred begged more than any of the others to have a turn; he could have sat in that car all day long if she'd let him, and he wanted William to teach him how to drive, even though he was only ten. Of course, what Alfred wanted, Hugh did too, and William told them both quite sternly, hiding his laughter, that they'd have to wait until their feet reached the pedals.

On these days, during these car trips, Celia allowed herself a rare burst of optimism, unusual for such a pragmatist as she was; she counted the pluses and minuses of her life and decided it was a success in every way; and best of all she knew she had been a part of making it that way. She didn't feel middle-aged anymore, she felt young. She saw herself entering gracefully into middle age, with Alfred at Harvard or Yale and then becoming a professional man—the son of the butcher and the baker becoming a doctor or a lawyer, or, if he preferred, Celia imagined in these daydreams, the president of the local bank.

Their garden bloomed beautifully that summer, bees drifting through the rose bushes, cut flowers brightening the house. And when Alfred came back from playing in that garden and ignored a scratch he had gotten on his face from a thorn, Celia didn't think anything of it. Boys played roughly, and they were always getting cut and bruised. At dinner he felt feverish. When she told him to go to bed early and to be sure to wash his face, he didn't try to make excuses to stay up later.

In the morning when Alfred came downstairs to breakfast she didn't recognize him.

His face was hugely swollen and red, with ruby blotches on it. She touched his forehead and felt fever. His cheek, where he had been scratched, was hot, the skin tight. She felt a wave of panic, and sent Hugh to get the doctor.

"Blood poisoning," the doctor said, and sent Alfred back to bed.

How quick, how frightening, to become so sick from such a little thing! Although there were methods to try, everyone knew there was no cure for septicemia; it either cured itself or it didn't. The doctor had given Alfred aspirin for the pain and fever and gone away. Celia tried to put cold, wet compresses on his painful face, but he moaned and turned away from her. She was shaking with fear, holding back the tears. By that evening his eyes were swollen almost shut.

The family prayed, and waited, and slept at last, but Celia couldn't leave her son's bedside. She had told Hugh to sleep in Rose's room, in Maude's old bed, but a moment after she had sent him away he came back.

"I want to be with him," Hugh said. His eyes were full of concern and fear. He sat next to Alfred's bed and took his hand. "I'll stay with my brother," he said.

He had always referred to Alfred as his brother, and she had always encouraged it, but suddenly a voice deep inside Celia screamed silently: *He's not your brother. He's nothing to you, he's mine.* Then she as quickly realized the thought had been unkind... although she had meant it, and felt it still. Alfred was the joy of her life. No one but a mother could know how strong their bond was.

"You may stay, but don't disturb him," she said.

Early in the morning Rose and William came in to Alfred's sickroom. When she saw him, Rose gasped.

"I'll take care of the little girls," William said. "Should I get the doctor again, should we take him to the hospital?"

The doctor came, and said again, gravely, that nothing could be done for blood poisoning. "If the aspirin doesn't help, I can give him something stronger for the pain."

"Cure him," Celia said. "I don't care what you do, but do something."

"Ah, yes, something," the doctor said. "There are things we know now in medicine and much we don't. You know, when people are shot or stabbed it's often the septicemia that kills them, not the wound itself. I can try strychnine, eggs, and coffee enemas to strengthen him…"

"You must bleed the boy to get rid of the poisons," Celia said.

The doctor looked grave. "I think bleeding is old-fashioned and barbaric myself, and I've never seen it work. People think it works, but it's God who does the healing. I will try the other things, and above all, let us pray."

"We *did* pray!" Celia cried.

She kept a vigil for four days, nursing him. Sometimes she slept a bit from exhaustion. The girl who cleaned their house brought her food, which she couldn't eat, and water. Alfred, refusing the eggs, drank a little water, but by the second day he was delirious, his distorted face oozing pus. He thrashed in his bed and moaned from pain. When he became unconscious it seemed a respite. Perhaps now he could get some peaceful rest, and that would strengthen him.

Oh, my brave, beautiful boy, Celia thought. All the times you played and hurt yourself and I thought nothing of it. What terrible thing was in the garden, on that thorn, to make you so sick? What germs were there that weren't there before when you fell, when you tore your skin? Was it something on your hands? A little boy's dirty hands, carrying fatal disease? You were *just playing*. You were only having a happy childhood! What weakness of your system made this the time when you were cursed?

Just before dawn Alfred died.

Celia screamed like an animal and would not be consoled. She didn't want to let go of her son so he could go to the funeral home. At his graveside, William and her son-in-law, Walter, had to hold her up so she wouldn't faint or throw herself into Alfred's grave to join him. She had never been so emotional, and the family was alarmed.

In the days after the funeral she held her two little girls so constantly and so tightly that she frightened them so much they cried and tried to pull away. No one knew what to do with her. She didn't care; she just wanted everyone to leave her alone.

After ten days Celia slowly began to pull herself together. She looked into the mirror, and was upset at the sight of her drawn and grieving face. She forced herself to go into Alfred's bedroom for the first time since he had died, and realized with a kind of sick shock that without any instructions to the contrary Hugh would have been sleeping there—since it was his room, too— ever since they had taken her son away. But Hugh's bed was untouched.

And Alfred's bed had been slept in—the sheets wrinkled, defiled by someone who had tried to take his place, for what selfish and morbid purpose she had no idea.

Hugh had been sleeping in his dead stepbrother's bed. Was he crazy?

"You must stay in Rose's room—just for now," Celia told him. "I'm closing off this room for a while. Until I feel better."

"I loved him," Hugh said softly.

"We all did," Celia said, with no kindness in her tone.

William watched helplessly, quite concerned, when she turned Alfred's room into an untouchable shrine.

Her implacable mourning went on and on. He didn't know how to deal with Celia's seemingly endless grief.

"But it was you who always said that the past is the past and life must go on," William said.

"When did I say that?" Celia snapped.

"A boy of eleven should not sleep in a bedroom with his sister," William said. "Hugh is too much with women as it is."

"All right, he can stay in my sewing room."

"Celia…"

"Then let him go away to military school," Celia said. "It will be good for him. He is too much with women." She simply wanted Hugh out of her sight, but she wasn't sure why.

"No military school," William said, appalled. "He's just a child."

"You said he wasn't."

"I won't discuss it," William said. "He's my son."

Celia burst into tears.

It had been her hubris, she knew, that had killed her own son. She had taken too much pride in him, and loved him too much, and had been too confident that she had made her life a success. And while she tormented herself for her flaws, Celia began to realize something else. She realized that she resented Hugh because he was alive, when Alfred was dead, and because Alfred had been perfect while Hugh was so lacking in all the masculine qualities she had admired in her son. Yes, she resented him, even though he was a little boy.

And after a while she almost began to hate him. Everything he did annoyed her. She had to hide this feeling from her husband, and from the others in the family. When the girls fussed over Hugh, too much she thought, Celia had to bite her tongue. It had never bothered her that she didn't love her stepson. No one knew or cared, and she had always been scrupulous in treating the two brothers alike. But she now realized something flawed but unavoidable about her own character, and the future of the household's only surviving boy.

Even if she never did anything about it, she realized she had become his enemy.

FOUR

Rose was sixteen now, and the boys she had known in the neighborhood as simply friends, or sometimes just as pests, were starting to look at her differently. The older ones, who had thought *she* was a pest, were coming to call on her. She liked the attention, but she didn't like any of them, because she couldn't help comparing each one to her longtime secret love, Tom Sainsbury, and it was perfectly obvious that none of those boys was as good-looking, or as charming, or as nice as he was. When she was with them she felt nothing at all. She was sure that in some way her soul and Tom's were joined, and that was why she wanted him and nobody else.

He had asked her to dance at Maude's wedding reception, and when she was in his arms for the first time, unbelieving, nervous, and somehow safe, he had looked down at her with his wonderful smile and told her she had grown up to be "a beauty." A beauty! Tom thought that! Suddenly she, who had always thought of herself as nothing special, began to think of herself as more, as a young woman with promise.

But he didn't come to call on her. She watched him occasionally walking with other, older girls, and felt an actual pang of pain. What did he see in those girls that she didn't have? Could she ever have it?

She missed Maude, who was living away from the family in her own home, a busy married woman starting on a life of her own. Rose went over there more often than Maude came to see her. Maude seemed so adult, so finished now, knowing the mysteries of sex (although Rose was too shy to ask her about anything so personal), owning her own household things—sheets, dishes, silverware, pots—and with a husband to please and share things with. Rose wondered if she would ever have a home of her own. What if she couldn't fall in love with anyone? She knew she would never marry without love. She was adamant about that. She would be a spinster if she couldn't have Tom, so it looked as if she were doomed to be alone, living with her father and Celia forever, a pathetic figure.

When Rose told this to Maude, her sister just laughed. "You're too stubborn," Maude said. "You need to open your eyes and look around you. There is never only one man."

"For you, maybe," Rose said. "You couldn't make up your mind for ages. I'm not like you. You liked them all."

"No I did not like them all," Maude said. "I picked the man who had the qualities I *wanted* to live with for the rest of my life. The others, some of them, had qualities I would have been *able* to live with. If Walter hadn't come along I could have fallen in love with someone else eventually, but I'm glad he did come along. I know Celia never understood why it was Walter. She was always partial to looks and money."

"Aren't most people?" Rose said.

"Apparently not you. Tom has looks but he'll never be rich."

"I don't care."

"Well, I don't care either. Walter will make a good living in the years to come, but what's more important is that he's my friend, he's kind and honorable, and we have so much fun together. No matter what our future brings, I like him just the way he is."

"How lucky you are," Rose said, feeling a little sad. "And I'm lucky to have such a smart sister." She knew that in the past six years Maude had been as much a mother to her as her own mother had been, and sometimes she wondered how she could possibly have grown up without her help. She liked Celia, who was fun-loving and modern and often generous, but there was a core of coldness in Celia, even when she was being kind, that made Rose wary. She didn't know why she felt that way about her stepmother, but she did.

"If Tom doesn't notice you then you need to get over him," Maude said. "It's just not fated to be. What does he have, anyway, that no one else has?"

How could she define it? She had heard people say, as a compliment about certain young men, that they represented the best part of America, and she had always felt it applied to Tom in particular. He seemed both solid and glamorous. He had a certain glow about him: that handsome, open face, his optimistic look, his health and strength and cheerfulness, his muscles from working in the shipyard. If they were to put someone on a patriotic poster symbolizing the brightness of their country, it would be Tom Sainsbury. People always referred to America as "the New World," while Europe, where the war raged, was the old one. Half their town consisted of people who had come from other countries, from that old world, with different faces and different customs, all looking for a better life, and finding it, Rose was sure. Anyone would be proud of Tom—as she was, as she would be if he let her become a part of his life.

"I want him," Rose said.

"Well, all right," Maude said. "I'll tell you what I'll do. It's about time I entertained at home, so why don't I give a little dinner party? I'll invite a few couples, and Tom, and you, and another fellow to make him jealous.... I know, Ben Carson is home from Yale, and his sister is a good friend of mine; I'll ask the two of them. I'll sit you between the two men."

"Tom will like the sister," Rose said.

"No, he won't; she has a fiancé, and of course he'll come too. You'll be the only eligible young woman at my dinner party, and both Tom and Ben will have to pay attention to you."

"Thank you, thank you, thank you!" Rose cried, jumping up and down with joy.

"Now, no shrieks and squeals or leaping," Maude said, smiling. "You have to act like an adult."

"Oh, I will."

"Demure, but not too shy. Friendly but not forward. Mysterious but not too aloof."

How could she ever be all of those things, Rose thought. "Of course," she said, as if she knew just how to do it.

She wore her good white dress, and Celia helped her put her hair up and lent her violet toilet water, which Rose dabbed on her wrists, neck, and handkerchief. When she arrived at Maude's apartment the others were already there: Maude's four former bridesmaids and their fiancés (was everyone in the world over eighteen engaged?), the eligible Ben Carson with his sister Gloria and *her* fiancé, and her beloved Tom Sainsbury. They were fifteen in all, hardly a "small" dinner party, as Maude had described it, and Rose realized that if she got married she would have to learn how to entertain. But Maude and Celia would help and advise her, as Celia had Maude.

Ben Carson was twenty, a year older than Tom. During dinner he announced that he was going to go on to Yale Law School after he graduated from the university, and Maude cast Rose a significant look. Rose couldn't have cared less about his future brilliant career. She glanced at him dispassionately. He was of slightly above-medium height, of medium build, with

dark hair, and dark eyes that she supposed burned
with intelligence, well dressed—by any standard a
nice-looking young man, a good catch for someone
else. When they finally sat at the table and Tom was
next to her, she felt the heat. He smelled faintly of soap
and tobacco. If Ben Carson smelled of anything she
didn't notice. But she was very careful to divide her
time between the two of them. Demure but not too shy.

Maude served cold cream of cucumber soup, a
standing roast of beef from Papa's butcher shop, juicy
and rare, with crisp roasted potatoes, and buttery
beans and carrots, and then a wonderful moist cake in
a large glass bowl with fruit and whipped cream between the layers. She said it was called a trifle, and was
from a recipe in her new cookbook. Of course Rose
could hardly eat a bite, but she pretended.

"And what sort of law will you specialize in, do you
know yet, Ben?" she asked, not caring.

"Wills and estates," he said.

How perfectly morbid, she thought, but smiled
brightly. There was probably a lot of money in wills
and estates. She had heard that certain old people who
felt neglected by their children and grandchildren pro-
vided handsomely in their wills for their attentive lawyers.

"Have you set a date for your wedding yet, Gloria?"
Maude asked.

"September," Gloria said. "You'll get an invitation,
of course."

"I didn't realize that you had turned into a young
lady overnight," Tom said quietly to Rose, accepting
her, young as she was, as a part of this more sophisticated group. Weddings, careers, first dinner parties,
and she was still in high school.

"Hardly overnight," Rose said flirtatiously, trying to
appear mysterious but not aloof. "You just didn't notice." Was that friendly but not forward?

"I did notice," he said.

"Oh?"

"You look very pretty tonight in that dress."

"Thank you." He hadn't noticed; she always wore that dress to festive events, she had first worn it as Maude's maid of honor, and afterward it was her good dress for this year.

Well, at least he had noticed now.

When the evening was over Ben Carson asked her if he could walk her home. "Oh, I was going to do that," Tom said. Rose couldn't look at Maude because she was afraid she would break into a triumphant smile.

On the way home Tom asked her what she wanted in life. "A happy home," Rose said. "Lots of children, well, at least five; love, of course, and to laugh every day, and to spend my whole life right here in Bristol. I feel safe here."

"That's just what I want," Tom said. "I come from a big family, as you know, and everyone helps each other. I want to keep working in the boatyards like my father did. It's exciting to see a beautiful yacht rise up out of nothing and to know I was a part of that. Wherever it goes, it will take a piece of me with it. And, later, when I'm too old, maybe I'll work in the office."

"I'll bring you your lunch," Rose said lightly.

"Would you?"

"Yes, I would."

"That's very sweet."

When they reached her house they stood together for a moment on her front porch. "Would you like to go to the beach with me tomorrow?" he asked. "We can dig up quahogs."

"I'd love that." He was asking her out, at last! She hoped she wasn't blushing. Oh, thank you, Maude, Rose thought.

"I'll pick you up at four o'clock, when it's not so hot.

Bring a big basket. I've found some really good ones this summer."

"All right."

"Maybe afterward you can come over for supper. My mother will steam them. You haven't seen my family for a long time."

"I know. I'd like to see them," Rose said.

She felt his breath on her cheek, and then he kissed her. It was her first kiss. His closed lips were warm and firm, and when she looked into his smiling eyes she saw the children they would have together.

"We mustn't go too fast," he said. "You're very young."

"We've known one another all our lives," she said.

"I know. So we don't have to be chaperoned. No one will think anything of it." They both laughed.

They went to the beach the next day, and after that day they saw each other regularly. He was cautious because she was only sixteen: He thought she might change her mind, or that someone might talk her out of her feelings about him. To protect their privacy they tried to pretend to everyone else that they were still just friends. Rose even went out with other boys occasionally, just to keep up appearances. She and Tom didn't know if they were fooling their families, but everyone went along with the game. As for Rose, she was so in love, so afraid of losing the best thing she had ever had after all the losses in her life, that she wanted the two of them to stay on this private island of romance for as long as they could.

The only one she told was Maude, of course. She told Maude when Tom said he loved her, and when they decided they would become engaged in two years when she was eighteen, she told Maude that too.

"I haven't told Papa and Celia," Rose said. "They think I'm still a child. Well, maybe Celia wouldn't think so; when she was eighteen she was already married; but still, you're the only one who knows, and I want to keep it that way."

"That's probably wise," Maude said. "You'll find out that everyone has an opinion."

Rose nodded. But why would anyone have the opinion that Tom Sainsbury was not the perfect man for her? She couldn't imagine it.

She wished her mother could have been here to see how her life had turned out. It seemed such a short time ago that she had lost Adelaide, even though it had been six years. And then there had been Alfred's death. Rose had been stunned by that. She had never really warmed up to Alfred, but he had been a part of their family, and after he was gone there was a great gap. Sometimes she wished she had been nicer to him. She had so many questions about what was fair and what was not, and why people had to suffer so much, and she had never been able to answer them. Here she was, so happy with Tom, but it seemed there was always a reminder that something bad could happen, as if life were a balance, a kind of scale.

And yet, it was curious how even in the face of such unpredictable and tragic events as they all had undergone, and probably would again, people clung to thoughts of future happiness with such obstinate optimism: love, marriage, children, careers. When she looked around she saw that they just kept going on. People buried their dead and made plans. No matter how helpless they were in the face of fate, they kept trying to make things better.

Rose began to think there was something about human nature that was admirable. Or perhaps stupid. Or perhaps, simply innocent. But what else could you do?

FIVE

In the spring of 1917 America entered the war. Feelings were mixed about United States involvement in a place so far away, in a conflagration that seemed to have so little to do with this country. Many people still didn't want to send American doughboys to Europe to fight, but because the Germans were so openly hostile to the U.S., and France and England were in such danger, President Wilson (who had won his first term on an election platform of "no war") had finally decided war was unavoidable. The propaganda machine cranked up to make the war into a noble cause. Antiwar demonstrators were dealt with harshly; some were lynched in the streets by angry mobs.

On the other hand, this war to rescue the "decadent" Old World seemed romantic to a lot of young men. They felt they were knights from the novels they had read in school. None of them had ever known a war, much less one three thousand miles away. There were grizzled veterans of the Civil War still living, with their tales of violence and death, but that was the past. These optimistic, eager, strong young American men felt they were Ivanhoe.

"Over there," the popular song went, "Over there…the Yanks are coming…the drums rum-tumming… And we won't come back till it's over over there."

Along with the other healthy local young men, Tom

Sainsbury was drafted. Therefore, because they would be separated for what might be a long time, he and Rose decided to become officially engaged a year earlier than they had planned. She had a tiny diamond to wear on her left hand before he left for Fort Riley in Kansas, and she wrote to him every night. Tom had been lucky enough to be kept stateside, in the Quartermaster's Corps, building and repairing things, but as the war effort escalated Rose worried that he might be sent overseas. She knew he wanted to go, that he had requested it, and that frightened her most of all.

Her letters were passionate and effusive, since you could say what you wanted to a man as long as you were far away. She pretended to be strong, but she wasn't, and some nights, after she had sealed her letter with a kiss, she was unable to sleep at all.

Their small town had turned into a boom town because of the war. The war effort had increased the demand for products from the local rubber factory, and that in turn led to fifteen hundred people being employed there, in that one place, a quarter as many people as had been living in the entire town in the year of Rose's birth. They were mostly immigrants—from Italy, Portugal, and the Portuguese Islands—who had joined the original Yankee settlers and the Irish, the blacks, and Native Americans, to make Bristol a kind of mini country itself, or so it seemed to Rose.

"Dearest Tom," Rose wrote. "I hope and pray every day for you to be well and safe, *here* in the United States! You wouldn't recognize what has happened to our peaceful little hometown. I wonder what it will be like after the war is over. Meanwhile, last summer, when we were so happy, seems like another world. We are all trying to be brave because you are so brave. I know you're doing your part and the Army is proud of you. Your skills are needed on the home front, and you mustn't think you aren't just as vital to the war effort as the men who went to Europe. Please try to write to me if you can and reassure me…." Then she crossed out "and reassure me," because she didn't want to whine. "The only news I have since yesterday is very good news—Maude is expecting a baby! She is so lucky that Walter, as a husband, has been deferred. Now that he will be both a husband and a father he is even safer."

She often thought that she and Tom should have gotten married too, then he wouldn't be in the Army. But she didn't say so in her letters. He had been patriotic, wanting to do his part in the war, and he might even have enlisted, married man or not. Why did men think war and danger were so exciting? Didn't they know what could happen to them?

"I'm so proud of you, dearest Tom," she wrote, keeping her feelings to herself, hoping she didn't look like a future nagging wife. "And our country is proud of you too. I think about you, I dream about you, and I imagine our future marriage and its private moments with so much longing." Of course, she did not know what those "private moments" were, but she relived his kisses, and was sure that he would know even if she didn't. "All my love and a thousand kisses, Rose."

That winter was unusually cold, with shortages of fuel, especially coal. People bought Liberty Bonds, and there was food conservation, with wheatless and meatless days, because so much was needed to feed the troops. Celia and Maude rolled bandages for the Red Cross, and Hugh collected scrap metal for the war effort. While the women were busy he also volunteered to take care of his two younger sisters; he had the patience to play with them for hours. William complained because the income tax, which had only been around for four years, had already been heavily increased. He said it penalized the middle class and the poor, and that the rich were "getting away with it." No one could stand the income tax; it was a kind of shock. But money had to be raised for the war.

"People hate the Germans so much," Rose wrote to Tom, "that they are actually kicking dachshunds in the street!"

Conscription speeded up. There was compulsive universal draft now, and military training for the hundreds of thousands of new recruits.

Ben Carson, who had received military training at Yale in the Student Army Corps, was going to be shipped overseas. He came back to Bristol on leave before he left, and Maude took Rose to the tea his sister Gloria (whose new husband was now a serviceman in Europe) gave for him.

He looked very official and serious in his uniform. "I'm so eager to join 'The Great Adventure,'" he said.

"The great adventure?" Rose said, surprised.

"That's what Theodore Roosevelt called it," Ben said, "and I think that's very apt and inspiring. This will be the most exciting thing that has ever happened to any of us."

Rose didn't answer. She didn't want to insult or discourage him when he was about to go off happily to save freedom, although she had to turn her face away. How naive these soldiers were to think it was only an adventure when their lives were at stake, she thought, upset. All her life she had been taught that men were more practical than women, that they were more intelligent; but now she was beginning to think that women were the ones capable of rational thought, while men, with their uniforms and guns and marching songs, were the instinctual ones.

"How is Tom doing?" Ben asked.

"He's well, thank you," Rose said.

"Still at Fort Riley?"

"Yes. They need him there."

She was glad when she and Maude left. "You could

have had him," Maude said to her while they were walking home.

"Ben?"

"Yes. He's always had a soft spot for you."

"But I hardly know him," Rose said, insulted. "And besides, he knows I'm engaged."

"Yes, he does. And I think he's very sorry."

"So what?" Rose said. "Why are you telling me this?"

"Why are you so angry?"

"Everybody thinks that because his family has money and he's going to be a lawyer, that Ben Carson is a good catch," Rose said. "To me he's only the man you sat next to me at your dinner party to make Tom jealous, and it worked, so for that I'll remember him."

"I thought you'd be flattered, that's all," Maude said mildly.

"I'm worried about Tom. In every letter lately he mentions that he wants to go overseas. I don't know what to do."

"It's not in your hands," Maude said. "In the end, the Army will decide."

But in the end, there was something worse than the Army.

The influenza epidemic started at Fort Riley the following winter, in 1918, when a mess cook complained of a sore throat and achiness. It spread through the troops, and to the general population, and was taken abroad to France, and then to all of Europe, by soldiers. It was said that a person could start out for work, feel ill on the streetcar, and be dead before he got to his destination. If you were not dead in three hours you were certainly dead in three days. There was no cure, unless you had a mild case and simply got well. Entire families were wiped out. The flu particularly struck young, healthy people at the prime of their lives. People were hemorrhaging, dying as literally "bags of blood,"

drowning as their lungs filled with fluid. At Fort Riley
the dying kept up at such a pace that finally beleaguered morticians stacked the bodies outside where
they froze like cordwood. Schools, churches, and busi-
nesses closed, and a call was put out for women to
nurse the sick in the barracks that had been turned into
hospitals. In all, half a million Americans, and twenty
million people worldwide, would die.

Tom Sainsbury, "safe" at Fort Riley, was one of
them.

If it had not been for the enormity of the epidemic,
and the daily evidence of it in front of her eyes, Rose
thought she might not have survived the death of her
beloved fiancé and the end of her dreams. But by the
time she received the news that she would never see
Tom again, she was already in such a state of numbed
shock that she could hardly comprehend it.

"We have walked into hell," she told Maude.

Maude, nursing her firstborn baby son, Walter Junior, only nodded. She brushed her lips across her
baby's head, grazing his soft red hair, the color of his
father's. For now, her husband was well and safe. But
there would be no Tom Junior for Rose.

Rose suddenly felt old. She was eighteen years old
and she had lost her youth. After Tom's funeral she
pulled into her family and withdrew from the world,
like a widow. Because Celia forced her to she did her
schoolwork, but like an automaton; and when she was
free she played with her little half-sisters, Daisy and
Harriette, and with Hugh—who tried uselessly to console her—and rocked her baby nephew, Walter Junior,
as if the sight of these still living children could bring
her some sort of comfort, the way soft, green spring
leaves calm the spirit.

When the war was over and Rose graduated from
high school, their yearbook listed as many students
who had died of the Spanish flu in the Army as had

been killed in the Great War itself. Rose didn't know what she would do with her life now, and so she did nothing.

Ben Carson came back from France and came to see Rose to pay a condolence call. He was in his civilian clothes, his eyes different. He asked her to take a walk with him, but she didn't want to, so he sat there in her family's parlor and sipped at the lemonade Celia had offered him because Rose hadn't thought of it, and talked about the war.

"We were so stupidly happy," he said. "Men together in a man's world. We were knights on a crusade. Our company went off to the battlefield all marching together, singing, with flowers we had picked by the road tucked into our helmets. The fields were so beautiful. The wheat was yellow, there were so many flowers, different kinds of flowers and trees than we'd ever seen at home; France was like an enchanted garden. The cathedrals were so ancient and historical. Even the people were old; perhaps that's because the people we saw were all that were left to do the farming. Believe it or not, they still used scythes. We were just gaping at everything. For some of us it was the only chance we would ever have to see the big world, to get away from our dull little lives. It's hard to believe, but we were delighted to be there.

"And then the other part of it came. The real war, the shooting and killing. It was raining; there was mud in the trenches, sucking us in; so much mud that men were actually drowning in it. They had swollen feet, they had maggots, the wounded were screaming in pain. There was nothing to kill the pain. There was so much blood...." He stopped for a moment and his eyes filled with tears, then he controlled himself and went on.

"Those French fields were black and fertile, and men were dying in them of blood poisoning. They were wounded and they either bled to death or died of septicemia. We were summer soldiers, Rose, and we didn't know a thing."

"I'm sorry," Rose murmured.

"I was so young then," Ben Carson said. "We all were. Do you know Alan Seeger's poem: *I Have a Rendezvous with Death?*"

"We read it at school," Rose said.

"We thought it was romantic. We thought being doomed was romantic. We had no idea."

How could you? Rose thought. You're just a man. And you were young, besides. But at least he's apologizing for having been so arrogant. I will give him credit for that. She liked him better now.

"The worst part is," Ben said, "that although the war changed me, I don't feel it changed the world. It was too far away and too short. Even now, people don't really care about the returning veterans."

Really? Was that true? She didn't know because she hadn't read the newspaper in months.

"Your family does," Rose said. "That's all that matters."

"Is it?"

"It is to me. But I've lost so much."

"I know, and that's why I came here to see you."

"That was kind," she said. "Thank you for telling me about the war."

"Thank you for listening."

She sighed. Now she wished he would go.

"Perhaps I could come to see you again," he said.

"Why?"

"Just to see you."

"I'm still grieving," Rose said. "I have nothing to say to someone who visits me."

"You could use a friend."

"I have friends." She didn't want to be impolite, but he was being too pushy. Could Ben Carson possibly, in a million years, think that since he hadn't been able to rescue the world that he could try to rescue her?

"I'm going back to law school soon," he said.

Rose held out her hand to say good-bye. "Then I wish you luck."

When he had gone Celia came in, looking as if she had eavesdropped on the entire conversation, and what was more, as if that was perfectly acceptable. Ever since Rose had started acting like a wooden doll, Celia had treated her as if she were stupid and had no rights, as if she were a real doll, to be placed in position, to be spoken for. "You didn't have to be rude to him," Celia said.

"I wasn't rude," Rose said.

"He's a good young man, he's kind, he's very intelligent. How well he expresses himself! You could do worse than have Ben Carson for a friend."

Rose didn't answer.

"You'll get over Tom some day," Celia said.

The way you got over Alfred? Rose thought. His room a shrine, his brother treated like a temporary guest? But of course she said nothing. She couldn't be either a friend or a conscience to Celia even though now they had something in common; she had no energy, she didn't know how to talk about such painful things; their lives were filled with secrets that everyone knew and everyone avoided mentioning.

"Ben could console you," Celia said.

Nothing can console me, Rose thought, touching her engagement ring, thinking of Tom and the loving, peaceful, simple life they had dreamed of having together. But again she said nothing, and finally Celia left the room. The silent often scream inside, Rose thought. I hear you, Celia, why can't you hear me?

SIX

Celia was at her wits' end. She had been looking forward to seeing Rose married, living in a home of her own, so she could put Hugh into Rose's room and reclaim her sewing room for herself, so she could relax and take care of her own little girls, who were getting bigger and more interesting every day, and attend to her husband, who was getting older and more difficult; but instead Rose was moping around the house like a constant rebuke. Did Rose think she was the only one in the world who had suffered a loss? You went on, you kept busy, you kept up a brave front. Tom Sainsbury had been dead for three years now, and Rose was twenty-one, on her way to becoming a spinster.

Exciting things were happening all around them. Last year the women finally were given the vote, after the terrible ordeals of the brave suffragettes being force-fed in prison. It made Celia choke just to think about force-feeding, those tubes down their throats. As an adult, Rose would be able to vote for the first time this year, a historic occasion, but she didn't even read the newspaper to see who and what she wanted to vote for. She needed either a husband or a job, but she was equipped for very little. Celia tried to keep her up to date, but their conversations at breakfast were more like a monologue.

"Rose," Celia said today, rattling the newspaper like a gentle reproach. "Didn't you have a playmate named

Elsie, Tom's younger sister, who died of diabetes? We used to call it the sugar disease, and we thought it came from having eaten too much sugar as a child. The doctors would make the parents starve their children, but it didn't work. Well, it says here in the paper that a doctor named Banting has discovered the cause of diabetes, that it comes from not having enough of something called insulin, and he has found the cure too. It's called Banting's Extract, and it's made from the ground-up pancreas of animals. They say it will be available in a few years. Isn't that wonderful! So many people will be saved."

"A miracle," Rose said, but her look said that it was too late. Her look always said it was too late, whatever you told her. She was drowning in self-pity.

A few men had come to call on Rose, but she drove them all away. Even William was concerned, and Celia didn't want him to get upset because he already had pains in his heart when he was agitated, and sometimes he couldn't catch his breath. But today she was going to get Rose headed toward a life, whether Rose liked it or not.

"I've been thinking, Rose," Celia went on firmly. "They're looking for an intelligent woman to work in the office at the shipyard. You would just fit the bill. You were always good with sums. Why don't you and I go down there today and talk to them?"

"That's a good idea, Rose," her father said. "You'll certainly meet strong, healthy young men at the shipyard. I would like to see you go out. You're alone too much."

Rose looked at them blankly and went on serving the oatmeal, stirring big spoonfuls of butter and sugar into it the way her father liked it, and topping it with heavy cream. She handed it to him as he pushed aside his finished plate of bacon and fried eggs: bacon crisp, eggs over light, yolk slightly runny. "Don't you need me here?" she said.

"We can manage," Celia said brightly. She smiled at Daisy and Harriette. "These little hands are ready to help me now, aren't they, girls?"

The girls nodded enthusiastically; they loved to help like big girls, playing house, playing their future lives.

"Rose, do you need a job?" Hugh asked.

"I didn't know I did," Rose said. She sipped her coffee. She hardly ate lately, and was too thin, Celia thought.

"I think you could be a teacher," Hugh suggested. "You're lovely with children."

"She would need a teacher's certificate," Celia said. She looked at William. "You could send her to school for that."

"Teaching is good," William said. "A good career for a woman to fall back on when she's older and everyone in her family is gone."

Rose glared at him.

"I won't be gone," Hugh said cheerfully. "I'll take care of you, Rose."

"Oh, of course," Celia said sarcastically. "Drawing sketches of ladies' dresses and hats all day. What kind of living will you make?"

"He'll be a designer," Rose said, coming to Hugh's defense, as she always did.

"A seamstress?" Celia asked, and laughed.

"No, a haberdasher," William said, and laughed too. He always defended Hugh too, his only son, playing along with Celia because he wanted to keep peace in the house, but getting his own way in the end.

"Maybe I'll be an artist and draw Gibson girls," Hugh said.

"I don't think you'll replace Charles Dana Gibson," Celia said. It was true, Hugh's drawings were nothing special, and he really didn't care.

"Of course I won't. They'll be called Smith girls," Hugh said with a smile.

"Enough nonsense," William said. "We all know Hugh is going to go to college in two years, to Brown University, and he won't be in trade, or an artist; he'll be a doctor or a lawyer or a banker. It's important for a son to do better than his father."

"You do perfectly well, Papa," Hugh said.

"But I never went to college. Wouldn't you like to learn how to be a secretary, Rose?"

"No."

"Typing and shorthand?"

"No, thank you, Papa. If you want me out of the house I can get a job helping in a shop."

"I think you'll go to school and learn to be a teacher," William said. "That's settled. Celia will find out how to go about it." He held out his cup. "More of your delicious coffee, please." He lit a cigarette and leaned back, enjoying it, content that he had solved their problem.

So, despite her objections, Rose began to teach first grade. Actually, she liked it, and the children liked her. Celia felt Rose made an appealing picture there in the schoolroom, surrounded by nice little faces: an advertisement for a future wife and mother, should any young man care to look. Unfortunately, most female teachers didn't marry, either unwanted or too independent, Celia didn't know, but she still kept up hope for Rose. She was an attractive young woman—fresh-faced, well-groomed and neat despite her depression—and it was a shame, Celia thought, that Rose still believed she was living *Romeo and Juliet*.

What if the boy had lived, for goodness' sake? Did Rose think that life was so perfect they would never have fights, never lose their radiant good looks, not have money troubles, not get sick and old and fat, not lose children? Did she actually think they would still be holding hands and kissing when they were fifty? She could tell Rose a thing or two about the stupidity of love and the practicality of companionship, but what was the point? Celia had never thought Rose liked her very much. Oh, Rose was polite and did all the right things, never forgot a birthday, even gave her a card on Mother's Day, but Celia felt that no matter how many of the right things she did to ensnare Rose's affections, Rose's dead mother was still there, keeping her ghostly hand on her possession, holding Rose back, even though Rose didn't know it.

Well then, so be it. Celia had her own bank account.

A woman had to secure her independence in any way she could, even if she did it secretly. William was much older than she was, and not very well. When he was gone (of course she hoped that would not be for many years, but one had to be realistic), she would inherit some money; but he was not a rich man, and when she was a widow again she would have to take care of Daisy and Harriette until they found good husbands. Certainly none of William's children would take care of *her*. Rose was useless, Hugh, unless college shaped him up, was on his way to becoming useless too, and the only one with money was Maude, but she had two children now, and the way things were going she and Walter would happily have a dozen. No, Maude couldn't be depended upon either. Celia quietly took some of her household money each week and deposited it in her own account. No one asked, no one knew. Many shrewd women did that. It was not as if she were saving the money to run away, she simply wanted to be comfortable for the rest of her life.

Ben Carson had graduated from Yale and was now at Yale Law School. He came home for vacations, and whenever he did, he came to visit Rose. Celia couldn't imagine why he continued to do that. Now that Rose was teaching, and surrounded by lively, living people, she seemed much less despondent, but she had no interest in being flirtatious or charming. Apparently they were friends. Celia knew it was only a matter of time before he met someone else, if he hadn't already, and then Rose would have lost her best chance, if in fact Ben Carson was a chance at all anymore. I would have done it so much better than you, Celia thought, if it had been *my* life.

Now there was a psychic in town, and some of Celia's friends had gone to see her and enjoyed it. Although Celia prided herself on being a rational modern woman, she was also superstitious and liked the occult. So one afternoon she went to see Madame Pauline, as the psychic was called, and took Rose with her, Rose of course protesting all the way about how silly it was.

Madame Pauline was dressed like a gypsy from a carnival—for all Celia knew, she was one—so Celia held tightly to the strap of her pocketbook while she sat down. The psychic had rented a storefront with two rooms, one of which was a small waiting room. The main room was draped in jewel-colored velvets and paisleys, and on the round table behind which she sat, there was a crystal ball, a deck of soft and rather filthy Tarot cards, and an equally unappealing deck of ordinary playing cards that had seen a great deal of use. Rose waited outside for her turn.

Madame Pauline asked Celia to shuffle the first deck and then laid out a hand. "Someone in your family is ill," she said. "Your husband?"

"That's true."

"I wouldn't worry though, he has many years yet."

"I'm glad to hear that," Celia said.

"And someone dear to you has died, some years ago."

Celia felt a lump in her throat. "Yes, my son."

"He's happy. You must let him go and attend to the

present. You still have three daughters at home to
guide to lives of their own."

"Two," Celia said.

"I see three. Two young ones and an older one. Is she
a niece, perhaps?"

"My stepdaughter."

"Ah…" Madame Pauline laid down some more
cards. "What an extraordinary life she has before her!"

"Rose?" Celia said in surprise.

"Yes. Do you see this card?"

Celia nodded.

"Sometimes destiny has nothing to do with what we
do or what we choose. It simply happens to us. Each
event leads to something else. I don't think you believe
that."

"I do, but I don't really understand," Celia said.

"There is nothing to understand. It is."

Celia nodded. Madame Pauline asked her to shuffle
and then laid out another hand. "There's another boy
in your house," she said. "Still living. He needs you."

"I'm sure he does."

"No, I mean he needs your love and support. He's
very vulnerable. Very sensitive."

"Oh, he is that," Celia said.

"I don't know why you don't like him."

Celia said nothing.

"And you yourself are in excellent health and will
have a long life," Madame Pauline said.

The session was over. Rose took Celia's place. Celia
sat in the waiting room, amazed. How could this
woman know so many things? On the other hand,
everyone had several children, and it would be a good
guess that some were girls and others were boys, that
one of them might have died, and that there was another one who didn't fit in. Certainly she had given
away enough clues about how she felt about all of
them, if not actual information. And Madame Pauline

had been wrong about Rose. Nothing would ever happen to Rose. I could be a fortune-teller myself, Celia thought, sorry she had spent the money. She tapped her foot, waiting impatiently for Rose to be finished.

"Oh, what fun!" Rose said cheerfully, stepping through the curtain. "Thank you for taking me."

"You're welcome. What did she tell you?"

"She did the cards and my horoscope!" Rose said. "Because she said I was interesting." She read from a little piece of paper where she had taken notes. "I'm a Capricorn with the moon in Libra and Aquarius rising, and I'm well-balanced and thoughtful and extraordinarily adaptable. I have a dignified, humane, law-abiding nature, and a good disposition, and my combination of signs is favorable for marriage, partnership, and friendship."

"That's what I keep trying to tell you," Celia said. She was a little jealous that Madame Pauline hadn't found her interesting enough to do her horoscope too. "And what else?"

"That I would be rich and have a surprising life," Rose said.

"Well then," Celia said, "you'd better get on with it."

Rose laughed. "Not that I believed it, but it's nice to hear," she said. "What did she tell you?"

"Don't I get to keep some secrets?" Celia said coyly. She supposed their adventure had not been such a waste after all. She smiled at Rose. It was nice to see her cheerful again; it had been a long time.

SEVEN

It was 1925. People gossiped and speculated about Rose Smith and Ben Carson, although it was old news by now. He came around faithfully to see her on all his vacations back home. She was twenty-five, no longer considered young and dewy enough to be so picky as to turn him down, if in fact he had even asked. The town consensus was that her engagement to her poor dead soldier had counted for her as enough connection to love and romance for her lifetime, and that she would wear her memories instead of a wedding ring to her grave; and so for this she had become a kind of symbol, a casualty of the Great War, even though Tom had not died in battle, or even in Europe.

Rose seemed resigned to whatever life would bring her. In place of babies of her own she had the first-graders she taught so contentedly. She had her close and affectionate family, her lifelong friends (who were all married by now), and her friends' children to play with. She went to the motion pictures every week, and she read novels voraciously. Hugh had given her the two books by the new young author F. Scott Fitzgerald, whose world, so foreign to her own, she found romantic and glamorous, and after that she had begun to go to the library and bring books home. She listened to music, and in the early evenings if you passed the Smith house and the windows were open you could hear her phonograph.

Her early grief had given way to a center of calm; she had a look about her that was surprisingly arresting. She seemed self-confident, self-sufficient, self-contained, and this in a woman who should have been pitiful was mysterious and admirable, if not actually provocative. People were a little jealous of her, and that was why their interest in her private life persisted. No one knew what the relationship was between her and Ben, the good catch. Were he and Rose just good friends, or was he a man obsessed by unrequited love? The truth is that Rose herself didn't really know, since she chose not to think about it at all.

What she did think was that these days the center of her loving family had scattered. Maude and Walter had four children already, red-haired and blonde, and Walter had bought an automobile so large that their entire family could ride in it. She also missed Hugh, even more than she missed Maude, because he was really away, at college—gone off to become an adult, majoring in English Literature and Art History, coming home dressed in a dapper white jacket and a straw boater, praising his roommate to the skies.

"Well, you must ask him to come to visit us," Celia said.

"We'll see…," Hugh said vaguely.

"Perhaps we're not good enough for this paragon," Celia said, with a raised eyebrow.

Hugh just smiled.

Rose had begun to depend on Ben's visits more than she used to. They would sit in her family's parlor for hours talking about the world outside, where he spent his time, and sometimes she was just a little envious. She served him lemonade and sandwiches if it was summer, or cider and cookies by the fire it if was winter, and he brought her small gifts: a record of Caruso singing, postcards of Impressionist paintings he had seen in a museum, a beautiful platinum negative photograph of a New York street, and he even brought her a lavish gift for her birthday—a table radio of her own. It was almost too generous to accept. Many homes had radios today, but now the Smith household was the only one in town with two.

So far, he had not brought any young woman home to present as his fiancée, nor had he become serious about any of the younger women in Bristol, many of whom would have been glad to have him. He had graduated from Yale Law School, and served an apprenticeship in a New Haven law firm, and then, to no one's surprise, because he was known as a go-getter, he had been offered a position in the prestigious New York City law firm of Delafield, Cross, and Ward, in their wills and estates department, and he had accepted it. He had sold some of his rapidly rising stocks, and, due to a propitious estate sale, he now owned a town house, on West 10th Street in New York, where he would live when he went to work there. It was natural and apparent that in only a matter of time he would fill up that large house with a wife and children, and if things didn't clarify between him and Rose then she could bid her one and only suitor (if that was what he was) good-bye.

"New York!" Celia said. "Oh, I would like to see New York before I die! Rose, if I had your life I would know what to do with it."

It was boom time in America. The stock market kept rising, and even Celia had bought some stocks, with money William gave her. Because of Prohibition, people who had never drunk at all wanted to drink, and the ones who had enjoyed a cocktail before now became voracious about it. Skirts were shorter, so was hair. Curvy women were out, and Rose's slim figure was finally fashionable, thanks to the rage for flappers. Men wore debonair wristwatches instead of the heavy, old-fashioned pocket watches they used to carry. Time itself seemed to be going faster, in some strange way, as if people had suddenly come awake. The new music was jazz. From Rose's open windows you could hear Duke Ellington's rendition of "The New East St. Louis Toodle-oo."

It was spring, the time of nostalgia and changes. Ben had come to call on her before he left to start his new job. She looked at him admiringly in his sober but fashionable suit, his carriage erect, his dark hair neatly parted in the center, his eyes always interested in what she had to say.

"I want to have a talk with you, Rose," he said.

"Don't we always talk?" she said, smiling.

"I mean, a serious talk."

"All right."

"I enjoy being with you. I know I'll miss you very much when I go away to start a different life."

"But you'll visit me, won't you?" Rose asked.

"No. No, I don't think so."

"But why not?" she said, shocked and hurt, although it should have been apparent to her that this development had been inevitable. It was over; their relationship had run its course.

"Because I want you to come with me."

She was more than startled. This had really not occurred to her, perhaps because she hadn't let herself think about it.

"I want to marry you," Ben said. "I don't know if you have similar feelings for me."

He wanted to marry her? She didn't know what to answer. Did he love her? If "similar feelings" meant fondness, friendship, even generosity of spirit, always wishing him well, yes, she had those. She had always had those feelings for him, and obviously so did he for her. But she didn't love him...at least, she wasn't in love with him, if that was what he wanted, what everyone else wanted for her, to be in love with him—what they all, while trying to be tactful and stay out of it, had nevertheless made abundantly clear. She supposed she was dead inside, that she would never love anyone again. There had been too many losses. She had accepted that disappointing realization a long time ago. So she said nothing for what seemed like a very long moment, while she hoped she wasn't being unkind.

"You don't have to love me," he said calmly. "You would be the right wife for me, and I would be a good husband to you. We would have intelligent and beautiful children. I would give you an interesting and comfortable life, better than you would have here, I think. We would discover New York together. It's the most exciting place in the world right now. You would help me rise in my career, help me entertain, and I would give you anything you want. My mother will give you the ruby ring that belonged to her mother."

He hadn't even said he loved her. He didn't care if she didn't love him. She was being punished for having believed in everlasting love, in passion, having believed in it so much that she had used it all up; and this business deal was what he was offering her instead. She knew she should be practical—she was the suitable mate for this practical man—but she felt as if some little thing had torn in her heart.

"How can you marry a woman who doesn't love you?" she asked.

"I don't mind."

Because you love me so much or because you don't love me at all? Rose thought, dismayed. Even now, she had not been ready for his casual answer; she had been expecting—or at least hoping—that he would tell her at last that he was in love with her, that he had been hiding it, and that he would *make* her fall in love with him, that she would learn to love him because he would be so kind.

"You should mind!" she said. "You're entitled to more."

"I would be happy to be with you. Think it over."

So this was her choice: Lose her friend or marry a stranger, the stranger she knew, but a stranger all the same. After all these years, the man doesn't know me, she thought. I suppose I have been so cold that this coldness is what I get in return.

"Yes, thank you, I'll think about it," Rose said.

"I have many things to do before I go," Ben said, rising. "I would like to come over the day after tomorrow. Then if you say yes we'll make plans for the wedding, and if you say no we'll say a proper good-bye."

Marry me or lose me, Rose thought; it's what people have been threatening their lovers with for years, and it often works. Or not. Doesn't someone always lose? She had been selfish to think everything would go on unchanging forever.

"All right," she said. "Until then," and showed him to the door.

Her family was ecstatic when she told them about Ben's proposal. She didn't tell them the businesslike way in which he had described their future lives together. She did tell them that she had not decided if she should accept. "Why can't you marry him?" Celia demanded. And her father, and Maude. "Why not? What's wrong with him?" The question, of course, was rhetorical. There was nothing wrong with him.

Could she tell them he didn't love her? No, because it humiliated her. Could she say she didn't love him? No, because they obviously didn't care. She had spent so much time with him that how could she claim she wasn't attached to him? What was love anyway?

Only Hugh, when she telephoned him, was somewhat on her side.

"Ben would be a good husband for you," Hugh said. "I like him. But it's you who has to live with him, not any of us. You must decide what will make you happy."

"I thought I *was* happy," Rose said.

In their excitement about this offer of a wonderful new life, none of them even said they would miss her. "Oh, do you remember that psychic we went to a long time ago?" Celia said. "Madame Pauline...she said you would have an extraordinary and surprising life! And now you will."

"You've waited so long," Maude said. "You deserve this happiness. Take it."

"What's holding you back? It's not still that Tom Sainsbury?" Celia asked suspiciously..

"No," Rose said. And in fact it was not. Tom had been the love of her childhood. He had been gone for longer now than the two of them had been together. She didn't expect to find that kind of love again.

When Ben came to ask her what she had decided, Rose told him she would marry him. He had his mother's ruby ring in his pocket, and put it on her finger. It was only then that he kissed her for the first time.

Rose was neither attracted nor repelled when Ben kissed her. She felt a kind of pull to him, a nascent sexuality, partly from her fondness for him and partly because he had an attractive male presence. She thought perhaps in time she could lose herself in physical love. But first she had to find out what it was.

She went to visit Maude. The four children were pulling on her sister until the woman who worked for her took them away, and Rose was finally free to ask what she had on her mind.

"I know next to nothing about sex," she said. "I don't want to go on my honeymoon so ignorant."

"Of course you don't," Maude said. "I have a book for you." She went upstairs and came back with a thick volume called *Ideal Marriage* by Dr. Theodore Van de

Velde. "This will tell you everything. I must admit, I couldn't understand most of it until I was married."

"Thank you. Will you want it back?"

Maude laughed. "Not anymore."

"You and Walter are so well suited to each other, aren't you," Rose said, rather wistfully.

"And you and Ben will be too."

She had another question, although when she thought about all those children of Maude's, Rose wondered if she knew the answer. "I need to know about birth control," Rose said.

"You know it's illegal, and most of it is dangerous," Maude said.

"Yes, and that's why I don't know anything about it."

"But that woman in New York, Margaret Sanger, the one who keeps getting arrested for running her clinic, she's going to change that, I think," Maude said. "You will be in New York soon. It's the modern place where everything is happening."

"Don't you know how to do birth control?"

"Oh, I suppose every married woman with an education has her ways," Maude said. "There are condoms; Ben will know about those because he was in the Army. There are things the woman can use: cervical caps, or pessaries, or suppositories made of Vaseline and cocoa butter that you put inside yourself..."

"Ugh!" Rose said.

"Well, you can't do it right away anyway because you're a virgin. And of course, there's douching with Lysol."

"What we use to clean the house?" Rose said, queasily.

"But I'm sure you've seen the ads in the woman's magazines, with the fountain syringes, for 'fastidiousness.' "

"I thought that was for hygiene."

"Hygiene is a euphemism for birth control. Lysol will kill anything. You need to dilute it, though, or you'll get burned."

"I didn't realize this was going to be so much trouble," Rose said.

"If all else fails, there's abortion, but it's illegal, violent, dangerous, and very nasty, and I hear it hurts a great deal. You could easily die from it if you go to the wrong person. Better safe than sorry. And, of course, there's always the old faithful, withdrawal."

"Withdrawal?"

"Before he…don't you know anything, Rose?"

"How could I?" Rose said. "Who was there to tell me?"

"Well, you'll know all you need to about sex when you read the book," Maude said.

Rose read her way through *Ideal Marriage* for the first few nights, locked in her bedroom, confused, embarrassed, and titillated. The marriage act seemed so acrobatic. She was fascinated by the description of an orgasm, although she didn't really understand that either, although it was described in detail. Apparently the wife and the husband were supposed to have them simultaneously for the best marital sex. She found that concept somehow both erotic and romantic. Whenever she had finished reading for the night she hid the book under the cushion of her bedroom armchair. Of course she never said a word about this secret education to Ben.

They got married rather quickly because Ben needed to start work in New York and he wanted her to help him complete furnishing the house. They decided to do that first and take a delayed honeymoon at Christmas, when he would have time off. Rose had expected that they would spend their wedding night at the Hotel Belvedere and then go to New York the next day, but Ben said they should spend it in New York in their own home. She wondered if he was nervous, and if he knew what to do. But of course he *had* to know; he had been in the Army, he was nearer thirty than twenty.

She gave her notice to the school. At least the school year was over so she wouldn't be deserting her children. The new class would have a new teacher. She would miss the children, but she would have children of her own…when she was ready, when she and Ben were settled, when they knew each other better in this new way.

Maude was her matron of honor, and her two teenage sisters, Daisy and Harriette, were her bridesmaids. Ben's brother-in-law was his best man.

"Poor me," Hugh said merrily, "an usher again."

"Then you'd better find a girlfriend so you can get married yourself," Celia said, not kindly. Hugh had never been seen with a girl, except for his few childhood friends, which meant nothing.

"I'm only twenty," Hugh said. "Much too young." It was true, of course. He had recently been eating live goldfish at college with his friends, the new silly fad, and one could hardly see him as a family man.

After the ceremony, at the reception, everyone started hugging Rose and saying how much they would miss her when she went to live in New York. Now that her departure was real, Maude wept a few tears.

"You must all come visit us," Rose said. "We'll have a guest room."

The immediate family went with her and Ben to the railroad station, to see them off. They were Mr. and Mrs. Carson now, with a great deal of luggage. On a whim, she had waited to throw her wedding bouquet from the steps of the train. Daisy, shrieking, caught it.

And so, without ever having expected or even wanted it, Rose exchanged her middle-class small town life for a town house in Greenwich Village, in New York City, and a different life about which she knew nothing except what she had seen in the movies.

EIGHT

From the moment she saw New York, Rose was stunned and enamored. In the fresh and crystalline air the tall buildings rose, sharply etched in the pure light; their streets were shadowed canyons. A block or two away, in this city of progress and contrasts, were small, old, and gracious homes, many like the town house where she lived with Ben. Farther downtown, beyond the Arch in Washington Square, were twisting little streets, crowded slums, immigrants, life and noise. There were Italians, Germans, Irish, and Jews, making a lively old-world street life, but it didn't seem strange to her because the town where she had grown up had also been home to many different nationalities.

And the noise in this city! Something new was always being built, and the sounds of jackhammers and trucks and the honking horns of cars and taxis in traffic jams were sometimes unbearable. The new El had just been put up on Sixth Avenue, linking the Village to the rest of the city, and there was another train line under construction, farther east, opening her formerly quiet little enclave to tourists who wanted to see the Bohemian life a few blocks from where Rose lived her normal one.

There were almost seventy theaters in New York, showing over two hundred plays a year. She begged Ben, who was sometimes more old-fashioned than she wanted him to be, to take her to see Mae West in Sex, the hit show on Broadway, and he finally did. "Is that a pistol in your pocket?" Mae West asked a man, "or are you just glad to see me?" Ben looked over to see if Rose was blushing, but she wasn't.

Clara Bow was the "It" girl, Edna St. Vincent Millay wrote proudly of burning her candle at both ends, Woodbury Soap advertised "the skin you love to touch." This new world, it seemed to Rose, who had recently discovered sex, was obsessed with the pleasures of the body, and she refused to be embarrassed. When she read in the newspaper that a doctor they called Goat Gland Brinkley was implanting goat's sex glands into men to make them more virile she only shook her head and smiled.

She was glad to entertain Ben's clients in their new home, as he had requested in his marriage proposal, and sometimes they went out—to restaurants, or to tea rooms, which were only a disguised way of saying speakeasies, where bootleg liquor or wine could be had, served in coffee cups. Rose herself had never much liked alcohol, particularly that disgusting bathtub gin, but she liked discovering this new city. Uptown in Harlem, where most of the black people lived, was the Cotton Club, where a client of Ben's took them to hear jazz and blues. The exotic part of Greenwich Village, only two blocks below their house, was full of winding little streets, and the ubiquitous tea rooms, and nightclubs. There were strange people in plain view in the clubs and even on the streets: long-haired men who looked like women, and short-haired women who looked like men. That made her a little uncomfortable, but she didn't dwell on it. She learned to dance: the Charleston, the Black Bottom, the Lindy Hop, and the Turkey Trot, the Grizzly Bear, the Fox Trot, and the Monkey Glide. "Is this a club or a zoo?" she asked Ben, laughing. There was such a spirit of fun in New York.

Women smoked here. Everyone wanted a tan. They discussed weight, calories, and vitamins. After Rose and Ben returned from their belated honeymoon, to humid and exotically scented Florida, where they spent all day lying on the beach, she bought the recently patented Detecto home scale, and weighed herself every day like everybody else did, glad that food was not very important to her even now when she was happy, and so she was as slim as any flapper wanted to be. She couldn't think of herself as a matron, even though she was married and settled. Perhaps when she had a child she would, but not now. She felt she had wasted a great part of her youth in mourning, and now she had regained it. In New York a woman in her midtwenties was not considered old.

Margaret Sanger, whom Maude had mentioned when she told Rose the facts of life, had opened a birth control clinic not far from where Rose lived, where poor immigrant married women with too many children could obtain information and contraceptives. Birth control was still illegal, birth control information branded "obscene," and the police were still giving Mrs. Sanger great trouble. Rose's own private doctor, while grudgingly giving her the messy, gooey, and not very trustworthy supplies she needed, told her, "The diaphragm that woman is trying to have imported from Europe will give a woman cancer."

Was this true? It seemed, now that she was a sexually functioning woman, that everything either went in or went out. It had been bad enough when she only had the curse to bother her. All those secretions, those potions, what Ben put into her and she tried to get rid of, the worry, the counting. When the Bohemian women in the Village bragged in public about the pleasures of free love, Rose thought they must have a lot more energy than she did.

Ben was affectionate, sometimes even passionate,

but there was still a sort of formality about him that had never changed. Marriage and sex had not changed it, their honeymoon had not changed it, and Rose wondered if it was because he knew she was not "in love" with him. But she couldn't imagine another companion, or one she would prefer. They were lucky they got along so well. She knew couples who were very unhappy, some of whom didn't even know they were unhappy. The Bohemians got divorced as often as they wished, but people of her background did not. If it didn't work, you put up with it.

She had made a new best friend here in New York, the sweet-faced young woman who lived next door with her businessman husband and two small children. Her friend's name was Elsie, the same as that of her long-dead friend from childhood. The moment Rose met this new Elsie, Elsie Wilder, she had exclaimed, "This is destiny!" If they had not been the same age and of similar background they would have been friends anyway. As it was, they visited each other every day, just dropping in, and sometimes, even though she had no children of her own, Rose went to the park with Elsie when she took her children there.

They sat on benches with the other young matrons, in the shadow of the Arch, and talked. Right now the hot topic under discussion was the Monkey Trial, where a teacher named Scopes had been trying to teach Darwin's theory of evolution to his schoolchildren in Dayton, Tennessee, and had been arrested. It was the first trial ever to be broadcast live on the radio, and Rose and Elsie were fascinated.

"Of course men are descended from monkeys," Elsie said. "Just look at my husband."

"Oh, how could you!" Rose said, and they both laughed, because her husband, if truth be told, did look like a very clean, well-dressed, member of that under species.

"I can't wait until he's older and his hairline recedes," Elsie mused. "Of course, it might not! Now, you mustn't tell him what I said."

"I wouldn't dream of it."

Was Elsie "in love" with her husband? Or was she like Rose? They never discussed it.

Every Sunday Rose telephoned her family. She worried about her father, who sometimes complained of aches and pains and shortness of breath; but that had been going on for a long time and the doctor said he was strong as an ox, Celia reassured her. "I'll tell you if anything happens," Celia said. "Don't worry. Enjoy your new life." If Rose didn't know better she would think that Celia was trying to get rid of her.

Celia, of course, was well. Daisy and Harriette had recently become boy crazy. Poor Maude had suffered a miscarriage and was very upset. Too many children too quickly, Rose thought, but said nothing. Why couldn't Maude just enjoy the children she had? Large families were so old-fashioned.

Hugh had refused to apply to law school, which had greatly disappointed Papa and given Celia new ammunition to use against him. His marks were not good enough for him to have been accepted anyway. He had not yet decided on a career. Rose could sense the tension when she spoke to any of them. In his family's eyes he was a disappointment, but never in hers. She loved him, she wanted to protect him, and she worried about him.

He had completed his final year at college. His exams were over, and he announced that he was finally coming to visit Rose in New York during the free time he had before graduation. He would be the first member of the family to come. She was overjoyed, because, for one thing, since she and Ben had missed Christmas in Bristol because of their honeymoon, and Easter because Ben had insisted she see the famous Easter Parade, she had been feeling a little nostalgic and neglected.

"I'll stay for a week," Hugh said. "Can you stand me for a week?"

"For longer," Rose said. "Stay forever."

"Don't say that so lightly, because I might."

When he came she took him everywhere, showing him this city she loved. He loved it too. He looked like someone who had awakened from a bad dream and was relieved to find he was safe in his own bed again. He was a tireless tourist, and wore her out. At night, after he had eaten dinner with her and Ben at home, he would go out alone to explore, and even if they had all been to a restaurant or a club, Hugh was too restless to go back home with them.

"I'll just take a walk," he would say. "Don't wait up for me."

"Oh, to be young," Ben said. They both knew Hugh sometimes stayed out all night.

The day he was to leave Rose decided it was time to have a talk with her brother about his life. She took him to Washington Square Park and they sat on a bench in the sun. "If you could do anything you wanted, anything that suited you," she said, "not what suited other people, but just you, what would it be?"

His eyes filled with tears, and then he composed himself and smiled. "Anything I want?"

"Yes."

"I would move to New York the moment I graduated, and live with you if you'll let me, and I would work in Greenwich Village in an antique store."

An antique store? "All right," Rose said, trying not to seem surprised. "Is there a living in that?"

"Of course. I've already found the place. They said they would hire me as soon as I get back here. And I'd contribute to the household expenses, of course. Rose, I can't live with Celia and Papa anymore. She hates me. She always has."

"Oh no, she doesn't hate you."

"She does," Hugh said. "She can't wait to get me out of there so she can redecorate again."

When Rose thought about Hugh living here with them she realized how happy it made her. It was customary for an unmarried sibling to live with a married one if it was not possible to live with one's parents, and she knew Ben wouldn't object. They would have a real family again, the family of her childhood. And their house was large enough so that Hugh could live in the guest suite on the first floor, away from them, enabling everyone to have enough privacy.

"I've changed my life," she said. "There's no reason why you shouldn't have the same chance."

How his face lit up when she said that! It was almost as if she had rescued him, although she could not imagine from what.

NINE

For most of his adult life now, although he seemed to fit in more at college than he ever had before, Hugh felt he was probably the loneliest person on earth. His family, of course, did not, *could* not, be allowed to know his tumultuous inner thoughts, and neither, of course, could the few new friends he had finally made at Brown. His first year he had been secretly and miserably in love with his roommate, George, a brilliant pre-med student, athlete, and dark-haired Adonis, who went out with girls and didn't know that every night the young man in the next bed was listening to his breathing and timing it to his own. Whatever his roommate did Hugh copied; he wanted to dress like him, talk like him, have that practiced ease with people. But he knew he never would. And in sophomore year, George went off to share a suite with three other young men, all of whom were normal, and left Hugh behind. He didn't even ask Hugh if he wanted to join them. From then on Hugh roomed alone.

He was invisible…or perhaps too visible. He knew what he was. Sometimes he thought Celia knew, or at least suspected, because she had a cruel tongue where he was concerned. He was afraid she would tell his father and turn his father against him, although his father seemed endlessly forgiving and oblivious. His father didn't want to know, and perhaps he wouldn't have understood what being a "fairy" meant even if he did know. His father came from another world, where things were ordered and simple. If Hugh could have forced himself to go to law school to please his father he would have, but he could barely stay at college because he felt like such a misfit.

Having his own room in the dorm had two advantages. He could cry secretly when the feeling that his life wasn't worth living came over him, and he could buy and wear women's clothes. He had makeup too; rouge, lipstick, powder, and a black liner for his eyes. At night when everyone else was having a good time doing all the things that normal college students did, having a social life, studying together, going out, Hugh would be in his room with the door locked, engulfed in fantasies.

He had no idea who he was or what he was, but he knew that the makeup and the tea gowns made him float off into that invented world where he was lovely and everyone liked him. He even had a secret name for himself, Camille. The lady of the camellias, the tragic one who coughed herself to death. His style of clothing was eclectic. He did well as a flapper because he was lean and without breasts (real girls had to bind their breasts to look right in those dresses), and he also favored an old-fashioned look. For a while he had thought of calling himself Lillian Russell, but discarded that. He tried different hair styles, and let his hair grow a little longer than was usual for a man, so that he could have more latitude. It was not that he wanted to be a woman, because he knew he was a man. It was the clothes he liked, the masquerade. It made him feel free, even while it chained him more and more to guilt and self-hatred, because he knew it was wrong.

No one would ever understand, because he could hardly understand it himself.

Freud was hot; people talked about complexes even when they didn't have any. It was all too easy to be an armchair psychiatrist. But they didn't talk about Hugh's predilection, and he suspected it would only appear in much more ominous books; the works of Kraft-Ebbing or Havelock Ellis, which the psychology majors read. He found these books in the university library, but after reading a few pages he was so upset at the pain and torment people inflicted on innocent little children that he had to give them back, feeling nauseated. Who knew there were so many evil people in the world? There were words people had for him and his kind—pervert, invert, and androgyne were the more civil ones—but he was an angel compared to some of those parents and governesses in the textbooks. Yes, he knew it would hurt his family terribly to know how strange he was, but he wasn't really *hurting* anyone. I am kind, Hugh told himself. I am good. I am lost. I am doomed. What will become of me?

And then came the miracle. When he went to see his sister Rose in Greenwich Village, everything fell into place. He went from damned to saved in a few short days. There were people here like him, who would accept him. It was not hard to seek them out. When he went out on his own at night he discovered a world so magical, so outrageous, so comforting, that it seemed not only an alternate reality but the only real one. Men wore makeup—they called it paint—and styled their long hair. They shrieked and giggled and joked, and they were so funny. They were open about everything: They talked about their dates, their boyfriends, the sexy and sometimes available men from the Brooklyn Fire Department, their engagements and broken hearts. For the first time in his life Hugh made friends immediately.

His friends had women's names as he did: Lady Clifford, Nazimova, Zazu. It was all in the spirit of high camp. He found a private gay club on Christopher Street, where the admission fee was a steep five dollars, but well worth it, and his new friends took him to another gay club, more a restaurant, not private—but who else but a fairy would want to go there?—called Paul and Joe's. These clubs were small and always packed. Gus, the "hostess" at Paul and Joe's, was friendly to him. Hugh brought his makeup with him from home, and put it on in the bathroom. He always wore a man's suit, but he carried a compact for touch-ups. His friends told him there would be a costume ball soon at Webster Hall, the huge old meeting hall, and told him not to miss it; they were all going to be in drag, and there would be half-naked men in togas, made of bedsheets, to swoon over.

There was the Everard Baths if you wanted willing, anonymous sex, even orgies, or perhaps to find love. He learned what a glory hole was. Fairyland, as he thought of it, even had its own language.

"Dearie," the rouged and lipsticked men in the gay clubs called each other. "Dearie, people who live in glass houses should undress in the dark!" "Dearie, if you associate with garbage you'll get flies!" "Dearie, just look at that pathetic old queen!"

In the clubs after eleven o'clock the Broadway chorus dancers would arrive from their shows at the Winter Garden, or from Vanities, or the Music Box Revue, flouncing, effeminate, and happy. Some of them had sugar daddies, just like girls did. And then after midnight everyone would go uptown to 58th Street and Fifth Avenue, to Childs restaurant, the largest of the famous chain, for coffee and breakfast. In the small hours of the morning, here in New York, Bristol seemed as far away as if Hugh had never lived there.

As soon as he graduated from Brown, Hugh packed up all his things and took the train to New York. His father looked bewildered, and Celia, fixing him with her gimlet eyes, looked smug. His job at the antique store, Montezuma, was waiting for him. His friend Zazu, from the clubs, an older man who looked better without makeup, was the proprietor. Hugh settled into his comfortable bedroom, with adjoining bath, on the ground floor of Rose's house. His brother-in-law Ben, who was a generous man, made him feel welcome because he knew how much it meant to Rose. Hugh thought again, as he often did lately, that Rose was lucky to have such a nice husband.

Hugh unpacked his women's clothes, and his lingerie, and his makeup, and put them away. He knew no one would spy on him. When he went out he would dress at a friend's house so Rose and Ben would never know. Lots of drag queens who lived with their families did that.

Greenwich Village was full of small single rooms to rent, for bachelors, gays and lesbians, and Bohemians, people who had left the stultifying or forbidding life of their small towns to gravitate to New York; but he wouldn't dream of living in a rooming house when he had a family. He was safe here, as happy as he had been when he was a child, when the world was good and he had a place in it, before he knew anything.

TEN

In 1928 Rose and Ben joyfully welcomed their first child, their daughter Peggy Ann. She was a placid and beautiful infant, with blond curls, and the blue eyes that ran in Rose's family. Rose weighed her every week and dutifully inscribed each weight in Peggy's pink baby book. The baby book also gave helpful hints, which followed the child-rearing edicts of the day, and Rose followed them.

"Don't let Baby suck finger, pacifier, etc. It causes irregular teeth, etc., later. *Never* play with Baby till over six months—then, seldom. *Excitement harms*. Baby Must Have: Regular Hours for Sleeping, Feeding, etc. Good habits are as easy to form as bad ones. Protection from Contagion—No Kissing on mouth or hands! 'Colds' or disease never allowed near. Keep off floor—Dirt, Germs, Danger! Whooping-cough is often fatal to infants."

Peggy's first words were *Dada* and *Tick-tock*. She said Mama much later. Rose felt a little hurt. She wondered if it was because she, the reluctantly strict mother, let Peggy scream for food or attention when it was not time to give them to her, and that Ben, the kindhearted father, couldn't bear to hear these cries and went into the room to pick her up.

"She's a Daddy's girl," Ben said, pleased.

But of course he couldn't nurse her, so Rose knew she was still number one. Now when she went to the park with Elsie and the other mothers, she had her own baby, and was now a true member of the club.

Hugh brought little Peggy a Victorian English highchair from his shop. You could take it apart when the baby was older and put it together again to become a small chair and table for meals. He was devoted to his niece, and loved to play with her during the brief periods when the book said it was allowed.

Since travel was not recommended for small children because of all the threatening and unknown germs that might be encountered, William and Celia made their first trip to New York to see their new grandchild. Rose and Ben took them to a few nice restaurants, but not to any speakeasies, and Rose took them to see the sights. The economy was booming, the city was prosperous, and all sorts of new tunnels and highways had been built and were being built, so Manhattan was no longer in any way an isolated island. The Smiths were only two of a stream of tourists. Celia was thrilled with everything, but Rose had the feeling that her father was only being good-natured when he smiled as she dragged them around. She could see he had lost so much of his energy in these later years, and when they left he said, "New York is too busy for me."

"Not for me," Celia said. "I could live here easily. We'll be back."

"I hope not," Hugh said when she was gone.

But whether or not they would come back was not an issue, because in the fall the stock market crashed. People were jumping out of windows. Fortunes, that had only existed on paper because they had been bought on margin, were now lost. Since wills always had to be written and executed, Ben did not lose his job, but he had to take a cut in pay. There was only enough money for essentials now. Hugh's antique shop became more of an upscale secondhand store, as people were forced to sell their cherished belongings to eat and pay the rent. Maude and Walter, with four growing children to feed, sold their car, and Maude tearfully told Rose on the phone that she'd had an abortion. In fact, illegal abortions soared, and the disguised birth control ads became more specific, if you knew what you were looking for. Lysol now promised "Complete freedom from fear."

People who knew how simply stopped having babies. An only child was the norm, two was the sign of a family with some money. But in the midst of these dark days Rose decided she had to have another child before she got too old. She didn't want Peggy to grow up alone. She'd had a wonderful family to grow up with, and what if something happened to her the way it had to her mother? Peggy would be all by herself. If Ben remarried, who knew what the woman would be like? Rose couldn't help worrying. It seemed she worried about everything lately, and who would not?

Their second child, another girl, who looked just like Peggy, was born in 1931. They named her Joan, one of the most popular names of the year. There were four other Joans in the hospital when Rose was there. She liked giving her child a modern name; Joan would be a modern woman.

But in the hospital when Rose looked at the new baby she was disturbed by a small red blister on the child's forehead. "What is this?"

"It's a hemangioma," the doctor said. "A blood blister. When she grows older and combs her hair it will bleed. Better to get rid of it right away, while she's a baby and doesn't feel much pain. We have a new medical miracle these days, thanks to Madame Curie. You've heard of radium?"

"Yes," Rose said. "Of course."

"I will put a small piece of lead on the baby's forehead with a hole in it where the blood blister is," the doctor said, "and then I'll put a piece of radium over the hole and it will simply burn the hemangioma away."

"Radium must be so strong," Rose murmured, alarmed.

"Isn't it wonderful? The same thing that watchmakers use to paint luminous numbers on dials can also cure disease. I'll do it when she's a month old."

After the procedure, Joan cried and screamed for days and nights. It was obvious that the doctor's idea of not feeling much pain was totally subjective. Then the site ulcerated, and whenever Rose had to clean it Joan screamed more hysterically, and Rose was near tears herself. Finally it healed, leaving a round, shallow, indented scar, which made Joan's forehead look as if the soft baby head bones had not closed—but of course they had not closed yet because she was so young. Rose wondered if they would.

"What have I done to her?" she said to Hugh. "The doctor worried about her combing her hair, and now he just says, 'She'll wear her hair in bangs, she'll be fine.'"

"Is he a doctor or a hairdresser?" Hugh asked. He was furious. His love for his two nieces was as fierce as if he had been their father.

As for Ben, he seemed not to want to deal with it at all.

But then, eventually, the indented scar stopped looking so raw, and finally turned a mottled white, although it never went away. Madame Curie died of radium poisoning after all her years of touching it and working with it. The watchmakers, who had licked the tips of their brushes to make them pointed before they dipped them into the luminous radium paint, were dying of leukemia. Radium, although it turned out to have other uses and to be very valuable, had been, like so many other cures and panaceas, elevated into a firestorm of overenthusiasm for just a moment, a mistake. At school, Joan charged her friends a nickel each to look at her "horrible scar." Whether or not she was living with a bomb inside her body no one knew, and after a while, because she seemed normal in every way, they more or less forgot about it.

During the Depression the thing that seemed to save everyone was going to the movies. The plots were fanciful, the movie theaters even more so, their interiors resembling exotic palaces. In summer the movie theaters were the only places that were air-conditioned—a large sign outside promised: *Cooool.* On dish night you would get a free plate, if you wanted it, along with your entertainment—a further incentive for struggling families to part with their money. Talking pictures had been around for a while, but the technology was still primitive enough so that everyone on the screen had a high-pitched voice. After a while you believed they really did. Many of the actors had been trained on the New York stage, so they had accents that were almost English. You could also believe that all upper-class people spoke that way, and maybe they did.

America's darling was blond, curly-haired little Shirley Temple, with her fat cheeks and tiny mouth, tap-dancing up and down staircases, pouting and singing her way into everyone's heart. Peggy and Joan begged for tap-dancing lessons, and finally Rose found a woman who was willing to teach them for very little money. No matter what, you gave your children the best you could, whether it was piano lessons or dance, and you sacrificed other things that weren't so important, like new clothes for yourself.

Although the girls liked Shirley Temple, Rose's fantasy was Ginger Rogers and Fred Astaire. The top hat, white tie and tails, the twinkling feet, the impossibly glamorous chiffon tea gowns with the trailing hems that never tripped dancing Ginger…and what were these places? Who lived in these mansions? Who went

to those parties? You believed they existed, somewhere.

Outside in the real world, hungry families with
worn, lined, prematurely old faces and missing teeth
left the Midwestern dust bowl in battered trucks to try
to find work in California. Rose had never seen eyes so
bewildered as those in the photographs of the migrant
workers. Their lives were a tragedy of nature's whim
as well as the Depression. She knew she and Ben were
lucky to have all the good things they still had.

A special treat for the Carson family was to go out to
eat at the Automat. They did that once a week. Rose
and Ben and Peggy and Joan, and often Hugh, would
take the subway uptown to West 57th Street, to their
favorite Automat (the flagship one, the best and bright-
est, they felt), where they would get a fistful of nickels
to put into the coin slots. Behind small clean glass windows, in compartments, were perfect slices of apple
pie, little pots of baked beans with a square of bacon on
top of each one, sandwiches, roast beef, clam chowder,
cake. Coffee flowed from urns with animal heads for
spigots. The children loved to choose their food; they
might have been buying art. There were condiments:
catsup, mustard, and hot water for tea. Poor people
would make soup from the free catsup and hot water,
and Rose would warn the girls not to stare. Then the
family would sit at a table, sometimes with these same
strangers, sometimes with people who looked rich,
and eat.

Rose was thirty-eight now, and Hugh was thirty-
three. He was still a bachelor, still living with them, as
he most likely would forever, unless he surprised them
with a life of his own. Not that he didn't have a life of
his own; he went out late in the evenings and sometimes stayed out all night, he had friends, obviously, he
was busy. Rose assumed he dated women, although
she never met any of them. But Hugh was so attractive

and lively she was sure women liked him. There were many bachelors in the Village, "confirmed bachelors," and sometimes they actually did marry in middle age, but more often not. Secretly, Rose would have liked Hugh to stay with them forever, with things just as they were. Uncle Hugh's position in the household was so entrenched, so valuable, that by now Rose couldn't imagine their family's life without his presence, and neither could her girls, who had never known it any other way.

That year, to her surprise, Rose became pregnant again. She had thought it was less likely to happen at her age and hadn't been as careful as she might have been. Although there wasn't much money, not for an instant did she and Ben entertain the thought of not bringing this child into the world. She had grown up in a household with many children and this new one made her feel she was recreating her childhood. She and Ben were hoping for a boy this time.

But it was a girl. Ginger Carson, named after Rose's idol, Ginger Rogers, was a January baby. Of the three children, she was the one who looked like Rose. Straight brown hair, the family's blue eyes, and a sober nature. When Rose looked into those little blue eyes she saw sunshine, though, and a fierce intelligence. Ginger would be a child with secrets. Rose could tell.

Peggy was the most like her aunt Maude: rounded and glowing, a caretaker to her dolls and probably later to everyone who needed her. Joan, in the middle as Rose had been, a child who had known pain early, was the rebel. Sometimes Rose thought Joan looked for trouble in the search to find her identity. She got bad marks in deportment at school and then made the teacher laugh and forgive her. She could write an excellent note of apology, and often had to. "Please let me come back to Shop. I promise not to 'gab.' This year if you let me come back I would like to make bookends in the shape of a horse. I enclose a drawing of my plan." This at seven years old.

In Europe there was an increasing threat of world war. Hitler's army was devouring little countries, and it had become apparent, despite America's continuing policy of noninvolvement, that he was going to be dangerous. Jewish refugees, the ones who could escape and were allowed in, told stories of Nazis and anti-Semitism, of yellow stars and pogroms, of the night of broken glass, but few people listened. America was cracking down on the arrival of immigrants; there were quotas, and then it was as if a door had shut. But finally, in 1939, Hitler invaded Poland, and England and France declared war against the Axis: Germany, Italy, and Japan.

English children appeared in American schools, a few in Peggy's class, sent away from the shrieking buzz bombs that were falling on their country. "What a short time ago it seems that we had the Cavalry," Ben mused, "and those frightening zeppelins the Germans used—and our little planes. Now the airplanes and bombs we have make them seem like lethal toys."

Celia had been back to visit New York several times, usually bringing Harriette, who now had a job as a secretary at a small local law firm, but remained resolutely single. It seemed no one was good enough. William, who really disliked traveling, allowed himself to be brought once to see each of Rose's babies, and then stayed home and let Celia enjoy herself, while he waited contentedly for everyone's Thanksgiving and Christmas visits.

Under Celia's tutelage Harriette had become an attractive and fashionable young woman, but Celia was worried about what would become of her. She wasn't worried about Daisy anymore: Daisy had married a lovely local young man, who worked at the bank with Walter, and she had given birth to a baby boy. But now

Celia had decided that Harriette would have a better chance of meeting a successful, interesting husband if she looked for him in New York, and so whenever they came Rose got all her friends to bring around brothers and cousins and friends, and gave a cocktail party.

Alcohol had long since become legal again, and everyone had a silver cocktail shaker and a book that gave recipes for all sorts of fanciful mixed drinks, and they smoked cigarettes nonstop because it was sophisticated. Luckys, Camels, to break the ice, to keep you thin. These parties were an entertaining change from their usually austere lives as responsible parents, and Rose and Ben enjoyed them. Celia, who liked parties, had fun too. But Harriette, although some of the men later asked her out, never seemed happy at all.

"Will you do something with her?" Celia asked Rose. "Talk to her. I don't want her to be like me—too independent. I want her to be like you."

Rose was not sure if that was to be taken as a compliment or an insult, but she invited Harriette to a nearby restaurant for lunch so they could talk, away from everyone else. "What's wrong?" Rose asked. "Tell me. You can trust me."

"You won't understand," Harriette said.

"Well, try me."

"There *is* someone in my life."

"But?"

"My mother will never stand for it. My father will have a heart attack. This would kill him."

"What would kill him?"

"My friend…the man I'm in love with…he's married," Harriette said.

Married! No wonder she was so sad and never looked at any eligible young men. And of course Harriette couldn't tell anyone; it would be a scandal if the story came out in their close-knit little town. Rose was very surprised and deeply sorry, but not as shocked as one might have expected her to be. She considered herself a rather worldly woman now, who lived in Greenwich Village, in New York City, where anything could happen and did, and she supposed Harriette thought so too, which was why she had been chosen as the confidante. "Who is he?" she asked.

"One of the men I work for. I'd rather not say."

"Oh, Harriette. Is he going to get a divorce?"

"He can't. There are children."

"But this will lead nowhere," Rose said.

"I don't care."

"You will ruin your life."

"That's what my mother would say."

"And she'd be right."

"I thought you would understand."

"I won't tell anyone," Rose said. Harriette looked relieved. "Are you...?" Rose began, and stopped. It wasn't her business and she had no right to pry.

"Sleeping with him?" Harriette said. "Yes."

She was only fourteen years older than her half sister, but suddenly Rose felt old. She herself had been so pure, such a virgin when she got married, and it had taken a while for Ben with his patience and kindness to show her that sex between a man and a woman could be a powerful thing. Once you understood that, you were tied to the man who had shown you, in a way you were tied to no one else. Yet even now, after all these years, when they were out of the bedroom she and Ben never discussed what happened when they were in it. What occurred between them was a part of the night, as if he thought it was a part of their darker natures.

"Are you upset?" Harriette said.

"A little. But it's a fact, and I can't change it." She wondered if other men were like Ben, or if Harriette's lover was lusty and romantic. "Do you...I hope you...take precautions?" Rose asked.

"French letters?" She saw Rose's bewildered look and smiled. "Condoms, Rose. And yes, I do."

Rose knew she could not even tell Ben. In his own way he was more old-fashioned than she was, and she knew he would think much less of Harriette. The truth would come out eventually, she was sure of it, and who would marry Harriette then? Her married man would abandon her, or he would not, and in either case her reputation would be ruined.

As they walked back to the house Rose looked long and hard at Harriette: her slim body, her relaxed walk, her now cheerful face. How could she be so happy, so nonchalant? In the presence of this fallen woman, her "little" half sister, she was suddenly, shockingly, filled with all sorts of erotic thoughts and fantasies. Rose had once thought she was tragically in love forever, but she now knew that she herself could never throw everything away for love, or sex. Did that mean the love or sex she had experienced in her life fell far short of what was possible? She would never know. She had a family of her own now, she was happy. But she could understand why other women would hate the "home wrecker," and why other men would want to seduce her. Whether or not Harriette and her illicit lover knew things that would always be hidden to her older sister and her courtly husband, and to their more conventional neighbors, was not the issue. They made people doubt their own sense of peace.

ELEVEN

Despite everything that was happening in Europe, the American people did not want another war, whatever the cost of staying out; they remembered too well how the Great War that had ended over twenty years ago had taken its toll. They continued with their ordinary lives, in a kind of half restless fantasy. Meanwhile, President Franklin Delano Roosevelt, tied down by strict neutrality acts and aware that the danger of the aggression abroad would eventually harm the United States, campaigned, argued, and warned the country to wake up. Isolationists and interventionists argued hotly through 1940 and 1941, but then there was nothing to argue about because on December 7th the Japanese bombed Pearl Harbor. America was at war again.

This was the good war, the virtuous war, and finally, even a popular one. Hitler and Mussolini and Tojo were clearly evil and the Allies were clearly good. A struggle between good and evil is always virtuous, heroic. And furthermore, unlike the Great War (which was now called World War I), this war was too close for comfort. The enemy was capable of flying over our soil, bombing our cities. There were air raid drills, air raid shelters, blackouts. Almost all the nation's men under thirty-five were drafted, and many who could have been exempt because of family obligations or age enlisted. You had to be pretty sick to be classified 4-F, because you could always do a desk job. Women enlisted too. Other women went to work in factories and war plants to take the place of the fighting men who were away. Rosie the Riveter, in her turban or snood, making bullets, was suddenly no longer denigrated as the weaker sex.

"They're either too young or too old," the song went. "What's good is in the Army, what's left will never harm me."

Rose covered the glass doors that led to their dining room with black packing tape, in case a bomb would shatter them. Ben was an air raid warden, who watched on top of their building every night, flashlight in hand, to make sure the blackout was complete. Hugh, who had been saved from the draft by one year because he was now thirty-six, surprised everyone by enlisting.

"You don't have to," Rose said.

"I do. I want to do my part."

Somehow she could not imagine Hugh in the Army, certainly not in battle, and perhaps the Army felt the same way because Hugh was sent to Newport News, Virginia, to be in charge of uniforms. "Perfect for him," Celia said when Rose told her. "He'll probably try to redesign them."

"Why are you always so mean about Hugh?" Rose said. He had come home on leave, his hair cut short, his chest filled out from doing push-ups, and he looked proud and patriotic. He seemed unexpectedly masculine, the actor in his new role, his great, world-class, costume drama. Perhaps, Rose thought, the war had brought out the best in him. She was proud of him and she loved him.

Peggy and Joan wrote to him regularly, and he always wrote back, cheerful, funny letters, which they saved. Rose remembered herself, so long ago, writing to Tom at Fort Riley, deluding herself that he was out of danger, and she prayed for Hugh to be safe and well.

There was gas rationing now, and food rationing: hardly any sugar or coffee, meatless Tuesdays and Thursdays—Papa, the butcher, was so popular lately, everyone trying to get on his good side to buy what little meat there was—and there were plastic bags of strange-looking white margarine with a little blob of yellow coloring in them, which the housewife would knead until it was all yellow, although it still didn't look or taste like butter. There was clothes rationing and shoe rationing. The flapper skirts of the twenties had dropped to a dowdy mid shin length in the sad Depression thirties, but now they were short and narrow again because the Army needed the cloth. The military look was completed by large shoulder pads.

Once again, Celia and Maude rolled bandages for the Red Cross, while this time Peggy and Joan, age thirteen and ten, collected the tinfoil wrappers from packs of cigarettes and chewing gum, for the war effort, hoping to hand in enough to rate a pair of wings from the AWVS uniform, since collecting enough scrap metal for an entire uniform was out of the question because you had to get so much. In addition, the girls had chores to do at home, because the family's cleaning woman was welding parts for bombers. And Rose was in the park again with a baby stroller, for lively three-year-old Ginger, comparing notes with her friends, worrying about feedings and discipline, confused and annoyed that child psychology rules seemed to change with every baby, as if the doctors themselves had no idea.

The medical miracle of the war was penicillin. First discovered in 1928, a bacteria-killing mold made from bread, it became the first successful antibiotic, refined and used on the battlefields for the wounded and then becoming part of every doctor's arsenal for infectious diseases. Pneumonia and septicemia were no longer death sentences. *Alfred would still have been with us,* Rose thought, and was sure Celia was thinking the same thing, although they never mentioned it. No one ever spoke of Alfred; the subject was just too painful for Celia, even now after all these years.

And there were other medical strides into the future. Blood plasma could be stored to transfuse the wounded instead of whole blood. A new generation of doctors was improving plastic surgery through reconstruction. And the Strang Clinic in New York City was the first to introduce the Pap test, a vaginal smear test for the early detection of cervical cancer, which, like penicillin, had been discovered in 1928 but only now in the 1940s was able to be used. It was a routine test, and Rose and Elsie and several other women in the neighborhood were sent for it; after their initial nervousness at the very idea of such a procedure, about even having to think about such a terrifying thing as cancer, they were relieved to be diagnosed normal.

That summer, at the beach, a friend of Rose's and Elsie's in the neighborhood was struck on the breast by a medicine ball, and the doctor, when examining the bruise, found a lump. Their friend had a mastectomy, the first person Rose had ever known with cancer; or perhaps there had been many—the stomach pains, the coughing, the broken bones, the weakness and bleeding—whom she had not known about. In the park while they sat with their children, the women friends all talked about it nervously. Breast cancer, they were sure, came from a blow to the breast, among other things. Everyone knew that, and this was proof of it. You had to be careful. Never stand too close to a door; someone could open it and hit you.

Surgery for cancer, they were all convinced, was sure to spread the malignancy by exposing it to the air. Better to leave things alone. Uterine cancer, which was what they called everything "down there," came from having your babies at home.

"Diaphragms give you cancer," Rose said.

"Really?"

"My doctor told me that years ago."

"But people use them," Elsie murmured.

"People don't know."

"Is it because they're dirty or because they irritate you?" another woman asked.

"I guess both," Rose said. They spent another moment in silence, thinking about the lethal foreign object.

Elsie lit a cigarette and inhaled deeply. "It's awful that they would give us something like that and not tell us," she said. "Isn't it?"

"Dreadful," the other women agreed.

The more you thought things were easier, the more confusing they became. Birth control was legal now, birth control information having been ruled by the Supreme Court no longer obscene. The scandalous tampon had been introduced, causing religious leaders to claim it destroyed virginity and encouraged masturbation. When Rose was a girl she hadn't thought women *could* masturbate; they didn't have what boys had, so what would you touch? The year before, when Peggy turned twelve, Rose had decided she couldn't wait any longer to tell her two older daughters the facts of life. Peggy was ready to become a woman, while Joan was still a tomboy, but Rose thought it best to tell them both at the same time, so the older one wouldn't get the younger one confused.

There was a booklet called "What Every Girl Should Know," put out by one of the makers of sanitary napkins, and Rose got one for Peggy and Joan. Besides the usual story of the birds and bees, there was a drawing of a uterus in the booklet, and she thought how lucky her daughters were to have the sex education she had missed.

Peggy already knew.

"How could you know?" Rose said sternly. "Have you been talking in the gutter?"

"If school is the gutter, yes."

"Who in school?"

Peggy shrugged. "Most of us know, that's all."

Rose sighed. She felt a little bit of a failure. She had been so pleased to think she was a modern mother, and it was too late. She wondered if years ago some of her own friends at school had known about these things and simply hadn't told her.

She was relieved that in some ways Peggy was still a little girl. When she got her periods Peggy was too shy to buy sanitary napkins in the drugstore, because there was a male clerk, so Rose got them for her. Rose then discovered Peggy was even embarrassed to ask the clerk for deodorant, and had made Joan buy it. Joan didn't mind; she was eager to grow up.

Ben was making money again. Peggy entered a private, progressive high school; when it was Joan's turn she would go too. Peggy's freshman year, when she was fourteen, her school gave her class sex education (a bit late, Rose thought), the boys and girls separately, of course. A female nurse, in a white uniform, came to address the girls. As Peggy related it later, after telling them the names of the male and female private parts, the nurse drew a large V on the blackboard. "V stands for Victory Girl," the nurse said. "A Victory Girl is a teenager who goes down to Times Square and sleeps with sailors because they're going off to war. Don't be a Victory Girl."

The girls had rolled their eyes and stifled their giggles. They had heard of Victory Girls, of course, the farewell gesture had become a kind of craze; but they didn't know any and certainly wouldn't think of becoming one. Those girls were a joke. How could anyone dream *they* might do such a thing? Who would want to sleep with *them* anyway? What kind of prize would this acned teenager with braces and rubber bands on her teeth be for a sailor's last stateside memory?

Rose did not know whether she should be concerned because the nurse was so out of line, or relieved that Peggy thought the whole thing was hilarious. Soldiers and sailors, after all, were teenagers, too. The war had made everyone wild.

TWELVE

In the second year of the war, Peggy Carson's social studies teacher suggested the students might want to boost the morale of their fighting men overseas by writing them letters with encouragement and chatty news from the Home Front. They would be like pen pals, the soldiers young and single and lonely, people from far-off places—in even farther-off places now—whom they would not have known in real life, where things would have been settled and preordained. Peggy thought that would be fun, as well as worthy, and volunteered. She was given the name of Private Ed Glover, age eighteen, formerly from Iowa, current address censored. She was only fourteen at the time, but she decided not to tell him. He would have a much better morale boost if he thought she was his age.

Peggy had so far not had a real boyfriend, the boys in her class too immature and too short, the older ones uninterested; and, except for her unrequited passion for Frank Sinatra, she didn't even much like men, except at an unavailable and therefore romantic and sexy distance. Private Ed Glover, she decided after they had exchanged a few letters, his slashed through with black lines from the censor, was just that distant figure. Without meaning to be diabolical, she began making her letters more personal.

Her letters to him were the stuff of fantasy. His, what hadn't been censored, brought that same sense of fantasy to her. Alone, separated, symbolic to each other, they told one another things they probably would never have told anyone else. Some of the things she told him were true; her opinions and feelings about all the issues of life that were beginning to be interesting to her. Their letters to each other arrived in clumps, with gaps, and they read and reread them as if they were chapters of a novel.

Since he didn't have a photo of himself in the middle of a war, he had his mother mail Peggy a copy of his high school yearbook picture. He had written that he was five feet eleven with blond hair and blue eyes; his photo also showed that he was clean-cut and handsome. Looking at this gentle, somehow naked, face, Peggy now felt responsible for him, her own soldier, fighting to keep the world safe for her, and she began to care about him very much.

She had read in the *Reader's Digest* that a four-year age difference, the man older of course, was ideal for marriage. When the war was over she wouldn't be fourteen anymore.

When Ed Glover asked for her picture, which was inevitable, Peggy bought makeup at the five-and-ten and made herself look older, stuffed her bra with Kleenex, and went to one of those photo booths with the curtain where you could take a strip of photos of yourself for a quarter. Lips closed to hide her metal braces, her smile was the Mona Lisa's. She even looked sultry.

He wrote back that she was beautiful and that he was longing to meet her. Of course that was what she had wanted, but the concept made her heart lurch, partly with romantic anticipation, partly with little-girl fear because this was going too fast, and partly with the knowledge that he would know her for a fraud. She was relieved that nobody was getting a leave, and that even if he did, he wouldn't have one for long enough to come home. She prayed that he wouldn't be wounded, not only for his sake, but because she didn't want him here until she was older. How fast could she get older? How long would the war last? How could she be so vile and wicked to wish a war to go on because of her selfish interests?

At moments like this Peggy wondered if she was this way because she was immature or because there was some basic flaw in her nature. She suspected the latter. People were getting killed. No one wanted the war to go on even a single hour longer than necessary—only until the Allies won—and to desire this because of love, no, infatuation? She was glad she was powerless, that she had no control over the war.

Her family, of course, was incredibly nosy about the letters she was exchanging with her serviceman. Her sister Joan was impressed and thought it was grown-up. She begged Peggy to let her read the letters from Ed, and sometimes Peggy did, until they became too personal to share. Of course Peggy showed no one what she wrote to him. Her father was amused about the whole thing. He assumed it was completely inno-cent, rather sweet, and even cute. But her mother, hov-ering and worrying in her wispy way, made it clear that she had her doubts.

"Why would a soldier in combat want to hear from a fourteen-year-old girl?" her mother asked.

"I'm like a sister," Peggy lied. "He's an only child."

"I can't understand your teacher giving you an as-signment like that," Rose went on.

"Everybody's doing it!"

Nag, nag, nag. Her mother was so old-fashioned, such a prude. She had been married late in life, and not only was she proud that she had been a complete in-nocent, but she was even prouder that she had let her own daughters have some information, as if she had done them a marvelous favor. Too little too late, Peggy thought, but what could you expect from someone that old?

It was 1944 now, she was sixteen, and Ed Glover was still alive. Or at least she thought he was, because the most frightening thing about the situation was that you could receive a letter from someone after he was dead. She told herself that if he had been killed his mother would have written to tell her, since she and Ed had been pen pals for two years; but perhaps, it occurred to her, his mother would be too grief-stricken to write to her at all. Whenever Peggy went to the movies and saw the Fox Movietone newsreels of the latest battles, she wondered if any of the soldiers shown might be him. They looked so tired, so dirty. She loved all of them, but especially him; yes, she was in love, she was sure of it, and the fact that the letters were so few and far between now because of his situation, and the fact that she could be getting a letter from a ghost, lost forever, only made her want him more.

In the real life she lived, she was dating now, although none of the boys meant anything to her. They seemed so young and boring. Anyone old enough to be interesting was in the Service. These pathetic contemporaries took her to the movies, where they held her hand until theirs began to sweat; or to school dances, where they became embarrassingly aroused and she pulled away; and at the end of the evening they kissed her good night and she was polite and unmoved. She went to Sweet Sixteen parties, and had one of her own, where the boys and girls danced and drank punch, and her parents hovered, missing everything, thinking they were missing nothing.

When she was little, Peggy had loved being Daddy's girl, but now that she was older she found it suffocating; however, her mother was worse. Her father would back off if you approached him sweetly, but her mother never would.

Although she had more adult privileges these days, she still wasn't getting along with her mother. Rose said it was normal—adolescent rebellion—and added firmly that didn't mean she would put up with it. They had discussions about life and disagreed about everything. Peggy had already decided the best policy was to shut up before it turned into another argument.

That spring, her grandfather had a heart attack. Not knowing if he would live or die, the family went to Bristol so Rose could sit by his bedside. He was in the hospital, with an oxygen tent around him, and everyone was distraught. Peggy was sorry for him, because he seemed frightened, and sorry for her mother and the others who were choking back tears, but as for herself she was uncomfortably aware that she felt little because she hadn't known him that well. Of course, that was another secret she would have to keep. The only person she confided it to was her sister Joan, who felt the same removed blankness. He had always been old and tired, it seemed to them, in his own world: if he wasn't stubbornly at work he was lying on the couch, talking little, letting Grandma run everything. Luckily no one asked them to act upset; it was assumed they were as grief-stricken as the others, and that their calm was simply bewilderment.

Uncle Hugh had gotten a leave because of the family emergency. The family was bunking in the Smith house, in their usual visiting sleeping arrangement: Peggy and Joan sharing the room that had once belonged to their mother and their Aunt Maude, years ago, when they were girls; Uncle Hugh making do on the living room couch, although there was an extra, empty, room upstairs; while curious and feisty little Ginger, occasional sleepwalker, shared a room with their parents. Their Aunt Harriette, nervous talker, fashionable dresser, thirty now and still unmarried, still working as a secretary, lived there too. When they weren't visiting the hospital, Aunt Maude and Uncle Walter, with at least one of their four children, came by the house every day, and Aunt Daisy with her husband and son came too.

There was a certain kind of tension in the house, Peggy noticed, that had nothing to do with the imminent death of their grandfather. It was more complex, but she couldn't figure out what it was.

Ben's parents had died when Peggy was young, so Rose's parents had to do double duty as grandparents. Now, Peggy thought, she would only have Grandma Celia, who in any case was her favorite. Despite what Grandma was going through, she managed to act normal, which Peggy thought was brave. She was trim and lively for a woman of her age, which had to be at least sixty, and she was generous. "Come in," she said, the very first day, leading Peggy into her bedroom. "You're a big girl now, you'll be wearing earrings soon. Here." And she gave her a pair of small clip-on pearls surrounded by gilt. "Take them, I don't wear them. They'll look pretty on you."

"Oh, thank you, Grandma!"

In this chaotic situation Peggy was free to roam around as she wished, invisible. She saw, from her position in the hall outside the hospital room doorway, her Uncle Hugh standing solemnly by his father's bed. "Papa, can you forgive me for disappointing you?" he asked quietly.

Whatever her grandfather answered, Peggy couldn't hear him, but Uncle Hugh wiped away tears.

Later she wanted to ask what Uncle Hugh had done to disappoint his father so sorely, but she couldn't, because she was not supposed to eavesdrop.

Their grandfather had his second, and final, heart attack a few days later. After the funeral everyone came back to the house to eat and drink and console each other. Peggy had never been to an event like this before, and found it surprisingly festive. When the party, because that was what it seemed, broke up it was midnight. Uncle Hugh, restless, had gone out for a late walk. Her parents and Ginger were in bed, Joan was asleep too. Peggy helped Grandma and Aunt Harriette wash the dishes and put them away.

"I've been thinking," Grandma said, "that it's high time I moved to New York."

"For good?" Peggy asked.

"Yes."

"That would be wonderful. Would you live with us?"

Grandma laughed. "Of course not. Ben can find me an apartment near the family. I've been thinking about Washington Square. There are some lovely town houses there with floor-throughs and apartments in them. He knows who's dying; I'm sure he'll find something nice like the house he bought years ago where you all live, Peggy dear. If I wait until the war is over there will be nothing. Now is the time. And Harriette, of course, you'll come with me."

"I don't want to go to New York," Harriette said, looking horrified. "When did you have this insane idea?"

"A while ago."

"Then good-bye," Harriette said.

"Oh no, you're coming with me, and that's that."

"I am not," Harriette said. "My life is here."

"Exactly why you have to leave."

"I am not having this discussion," Harriette cried. She slammed down her dish towel and ran to her room.

"My goodness," Grandma said calmly. "Where does she think she's going to live if not with me? On her salary she'd be in some tiny rented room someplace, in the worst part of Bristol. She can't live with Daisy or Maude. I'm selling this house, of course. The proceeds will get me something very satisfactory in New York. Harriette is so stubborn. I can't imagine how she'd get along without me."

"Why wouldn't she want to move to New York?" Peggy said. "It's a great place to live."

"She's just a little surprised," Grandma said.

Later, when Peggy went to bed, she heard them fighting. Joan was a lightly snoring lump under the covers, so Peggy got out of bed and tiptoed into the hall so she could hear them better.

"My father isn't dead a day and already you're pulling everything apart," Harriette was saying. She sounded hysterical. "This house is my home, I grew up here. The man I love is in this town. You want to destroy everything I care about. Go, I don't care, but I'm staying."

"What kind of life do you think you'd have here all alone?" Grandma said. "You're a scandal and a pariah. The only reason people are kind to you is out of respect for me. It's not enough for you that his wife knows, it's not enough that his children know and you ruined their lives. He will never marry you and neither will anyone else. This town is too small. I'm taking you to New York where you'll have a second chance."

"No!" Harriette said. "I will not be dragged around like your property."

"And whose property are you then, his?"

"No one's."

"You don't act it."

"You know nothing about it."

"I know too much about it," Grandma said. "I don't ask myself where I went wrong with you, there's no point. I'm putting the house up for sale next week, after a decent interval for respect. Your father left it to me, I know that. He left everything to me, understanding that I would provide for the others if need be. I should let you stew in your own juice, but I can't, I'm your mother. But I'm tired of worrying about you. Where will you be when I'm dead? Who will take care of you?"

"I'll take care of myself," Harriette said.

"Just try it," Grandma said. "You can't take on the world."

Peggy heard Harriette slam her bedroom door, and then there was silence. She crept back to bed.

So Aunt Harriette was having an affair with a married man and everyone knew! How glamorous and extraordinary to have something like this happening in her own family! Peggy smiled. She was not the only adventurous one after all. What would the poor thing do, give him up? Aunt Harriette could certainly find another married man in New York if that was what she wanted. If this was a movie she would be played by Joan Crawford. She looked like her, a little.

They went back to New York, and a few weeks later Grandma succeeded in selling the house in Bristol and leased a rent-controlled half-floor-through apartment in a beautiful old stone town house on Washington Square, not too far from the family, with a view of the park. Harriette did not come with her. To everyone's astonishment, Harriette enlisted in the WAVES, to see the world, to have her second chance on her own terms. Perhaps she knew how hopeless it was with her married man, but she also knew it would be another kind of hopelessness in New York, in mourning, with her mother controlling her. She was stationed in Washington, D.C., a busy and chaotic city filled with Service people. The war had changed her life too. Grandma bought a dog.

THIRTEEN

It was 1945, and the war was over. The two fascist dictators, Hitler and Mussolini, were dead; Mussolini shot by Italian partisans, and Hitler dead by his own hand in his burning bunker. The Allies had won in Europe. And three months later, the new atomic bomb, rumored at first to be the size of a golf ball, melted into fire and ash two Japanese cities full of innocent civilians. It was, in fact, just chance that made the Americans choose the first city, Hiroshima; the planes had been headed for a military target, but the weather had not allowed it and they had decided not to turn back.

The mushroom-shaped cloud signaled the end of the war in the Pacific and the beginning of doubt and fear about the morality of science. Like it or not, this was the dawning of a threatening new age. The bomb could end all wars or end all civilization. It was the first time that human beings had had so much power, and so much responsibility. The bomb brought peace, and infinite guilt.

At the movies, on the Fox Movietone news, Peggy and her family saw pictures of the liberation of the Nazi concentration camps. The discovery of the death camps, which people had not known about or had not wanted to believe existed, astonished and horrified everyone. Unbearable photos were in the newspapers too: the crematoriums with their ovens, the piles of bones, clothing, shoes, shorn hair, teeth, and skeletal bodies, the mass graves, the barely living prisoners in their striped uniforms, their terrified and defeated eyes enormous in their starved faces, peering out from the tiers of wooden bunks where they lay in rows like animals in some wretched pen. Peggy had never seen adult men with expressions like that, and it shook the center of her confidence in an unforgettable way, because grown-ups, especially men, had always seemed so in control.

Hitler had killed more people than was imaginable, six million of them Jews, systematically wiping out entire families, entire villages—and also exterminating Gypsies, dissidents, homosexuals, the sick, the different. Josef Mengele, the Nazi "angel of death," had performed unspeakable medical experiments on prisoners. For amusement the Nazis had made lampshades out of human skin, bearing the numbered tattoos from the prisoners' arms. As each new atrocity became known people became more appalled. But it didn't make them like the Jews any better. There was still anti-Semitism in America, just as there was prejudice against the blacks.

Peggy was seventeen, and the war was over, so she went on with her life. She bought her first pair of stockings, three pair actually. Before the war she had been too young to wear them, and then during the war there had been none, and women had put dark makeup on their legs and penciled in a seam. She went shopping with Grandma, who did not try to keep her in silly preteenage clothes the way her mother still did, and bought a form-fitting angora sweater and a pair of high heels. She got a new cold wave permanent. Her sister Joan, who was jealous, called her "Brillo head," but Peggy thought she looked great. Her braces were off, revealing white, perfect teeth, and her skin had cleared up completely. Her bra was a very respectable 36C. Every girl wanted to be as big on top as possible. And one day, as she had been expecting, the phone rang with a long-distance person-to-person call.

"Peggy?" the caller said. "This is Ed Glover."

His voice was sort of gravelly, not as she had imagined it, and incongruous with his innocent face, but after a few words she decided his soft, gravelly voice was sexy and made him even more interesting.

"I'm back home," he said. "Safe and sound. I really want to meet you."

"I want to meet you too."

"I was thinking of coming to New York. I've never been there. Someone said I can stay at the YMCA and it's not too expensive."

"Yes, that's right."

"Could I come next week?"

Next week! "I have school, but…"

"I'll go sight-seeing. What college are you going to? You didn't say."

College? Of course, she was supposed to be twenty-one, she should be a senior in college now, or even have graduated. "Hunter," she lied.

"Do you know anything about NYU? I'm thinking of going there on the GI bill, take a degree in accounting. If I like New York."

"Oh, I hope you do," Peggy said. "It's really odd to hear your voice after all this time; it makes you a real person."

"Yours too. You have a very warm voice. I knew you would. Your letters meant a lot to me, you know, all through the war."

"And yours to me."

Maybe I'll never have to tell him, she thought. Maybe I can get away with it. By the time he has to meet my parents he'll like me already, and then if I tell him he'll forgive me. After all, it was my mind he liked, not my age.

But she knew he would be humiliated to discover he

had poured his heart out to a little kid, and she had the feeling none of this could end well at all.

Uncle Hugh was back from the Army now, ensconced again in his first-floor hideaway, working at his beloved antique store. He had let his hair grow immediately. Ginger was seven and in the second grade, and loved school, and they all agreed that she was turning out to be very bright. But she still sleepwalked occasionally, and once appeared in Hugh's room in the middle of the night, waking herself and him up and asking, "Who are you?"

"I've asked myself that many times," he told her. They both thought that was funny.

Rose and Ben were concerned because she had never opened a door before in her sleep. They were afraid she would fall down the stairs, even though she seemed able to execute complex movements with ease. So after the Hugh incident they locked her in her room at night, to keep her safe, and left her a potty to use because she couldn't get to the bathroom. Ginger hated it, this humiliation and loss of freedom, and cried and howled so loudly that finally after two weeks that were unbearable for everyone they relented and left her bedroom door open with a ribbon tied across it, so she would wake up.

"I used to let you scream for hours when you were a baby," Rose told Peggy. She sounded sad. "They told us to."

"I don't remember," Peggy said.

Peggy wondered whether Ginger was only pretending to sleepwalk. Ginger, of the three sisters, was the one who most needed adventure. She was curious and opinionated and willful, sober and fierce. When you looked at Ginger's little face you could see just what she was going to look like as a grown-up. Maybe it was only her big nose.

"Beaky," Joan sometimes called her. Ginger and

Peggy were Beaky and Brillo head. Why was Joan so mean, so taunting, so angry? Their mother said four- teen was a difficult age. Peggy thought that was so. At fourteen she had found everything wrong with her mother. But she had been nice to Joan then, hadn't she? Well, maybe not. She didn't remember that, either.

Ed Glover called again, making plans. "Who is that?" her mother asked.

"The boy I wrote to during the war. He's coming to New York."

"Then you should have him here for dinner."

"All right," Peggy said. "If he isn't too busy."

"He's not too busy to see you," Rose said.

Peggy shrugged.

She met Ed Glover under the clock at Grand Central Station. He had just gotten off the train, and had civil- ian bags and civilian clothes and a crew cut. He was as handsome as she had expected, but so much more ma- ture than his high school yearbook photo had shown him to be that at first she almost didn't recognize him. "Peggy?" he said, doubtfully.

"Ed?"

Then they flew into each other's arms and hugged. "You're even prettier than I imagined," he said.

"And you're so much more…grown-up."

"Well, so are you." The first hurdle had been crossed.

They went to the YMCA in a cab, and she waited downstairs and read a tattered magazine she had found in the lobby while he put his bags in his room and took a quick shower. Then they went to Times Square, and walked while he gaped, and then they had coffee and he talked about the future, about peacetime, and all the things that would be available now: money and freedom and schooling and cars and loans for houses and, above all, just not worrying that in one in- stant you might die. It was a beautiful fall day, the sky clear, the air pleasant and breezy, yet crisp; the kind of day that occurs from time to time in the fall and spring in New York, and is so magical it makes you want to do things you never did before.

"I could move to New York," he said. "I like it."

"You haven't seen it yet."

"Does that mean I won't like it?"

"No, it just means you have to know a lot about something before you decide you want it."

"Oh, I agree."

They smiled at each other. The strangeness had easily worn off and Peggy felt comfortable with him. "Should we get theater tickets?" he asked. "Should we go to dinner? Do you want to go dancing?"

She had to be home at ten o'clock. "Aren't you tired?"

"No. I'm too excited to be tired."

"Well, let's have dinner and talk," Peggy said.

She showed him around Greenwich Village and then they went to a restaurant in Little Italy, which he found picturesque and fun. Over plates of spaghetti and a bottle of Chianti—of which she had only a few sips because she had hardly ever even tried a drink—they told each other about their families. He was an only child and had a stepfather who was a successful farmer. His stepfather didn't care that Ed didn't want to work on the farm, even as an accountant, because he had two much older sons of his own from his first marriage and they were working there already.

"What does your mother think?" Peggy asked.

"I can do what I want," Ed said, smiling. "I'm her spoiled only son."

"Are you spoiled?"

"Yes."

She looked down at her hands. She hadn't bitten her nails since she heard he was coming, and yesterday she'd had a manicure. It occurred to her suddenly that an engagement ring would look very nice on that finger. Why not? The war was over and people were eager to get on with their lives. But in their letters she and Ed had never talked about ongoing significant relationships with others, and she thought she should make sure he was free before she gave in to her fantasy.

"Do you have a girlfriend back home?" she asked.

"A girlfriend?" He looked surprised.

"That's not so unusual."

"No. Before the war I didn't want to get involved and then go away, and during the war I found someone."

Her heart sank. There was an unexpected lump in her throat and she wanted to cry. She couldn't speak. It had not occurred to her until this very day to protect herself from the possibility of someone new. He had only come here for a vacation, and to satisfy his curiosity about his longtime pen pal, and to look at schools, and then he would go away. Whom had he met, an Italian? Would he be at NYU studying accounting while his war bride was studying English?

"What?" he said.

"I didn't say anything," Peggy whispered.

"You look so upset. Maybe I'm pushing you."

"Me?"

He took a little box out of his pocket, opened it, and took out a gold ring with a tiny diamond. "I couldn't wait," he said. "I was going to give it to you after a few days, but I know we're right for each other, Peggy."

"Oh," she gasped. "Oh…."

"Don't tell me you have someone else?"

"No."

"Then just try it and see if it fits."

She put the ring on her third finger left hand, her heart pounding, more with apprehension than excitement. She might as well take it right off before she got attached to it, she thought; he would want it back when he discovered who she really was.

"The war made people do strange things," she said, unable to look at him. "I mean…"

"What *do* you mean?"

"I really got to love you when we wrote to each other. It's not that…"

"But it's what? You don't want to get married? This is too sudden? All right, I can see that. I'm an impetuous person. But you and I understand each other so much more than people who only went out on a few dates and necked and then got engaged because the war was coming. Those people are getting married and they'll have to get to know each other now. We know each other already."

"You might think…I'm too young," she said.

He looked perplexed. "You're twenty-one, the same as I am. Is it your parents? You're afraid they'll disapprove? You don't need their permission anymore."

"I do want to marry you, Ed. But…"

"But what? Tell me. Did I do something?"

"No, I did." She tried to breathe deeply to calm herself, but she felt as if she were choking. She took a big gulp of her glass of wine, but that only made her choke more. She had never felt more unsophisticated and childish. "I'm seventeen," Peggy said.

There was a pause while he considered this. "Then you were…"

"Younger when we started writing."

"You were *fourteen*?"

She nodded.

He considered this further. Then he smiled. "Well, heck, it works in the Ozarks," he said. "No reason why it shouldn't work here."

"You don't mind?"

"No."

"Oh, Ed!" She bounced out of her seat and ran over

to him and sat on his lap, and they kissed and hugged, laughing. She thought she could kiss him forever. His lips aroused her the way no one else's had. She inhaled him. His hair smelled of shampoo and his skin smelled of Old Spice aftershave, and under that was his own personal odor, rather musky.

People in the restaurant were looking at them, smiling and laughing, but with approval because it was romantic. Peggy waved her left hand in the air so they could all see her ring, see that she was engaged to him, that theirs was a love story that had come true.

Of course, she would still have to deal with her parents.

On the walk home to make her ten o'clock curfew Peggy told him how much she disliked high school. "I can't wait to grow up," she said. "I want to be an adult, a married woman, and have a real life. I want to take care of you, and have kids."

"We'll wait to get married until you graduate," Ed said. "Meanwhile I'll start next term at NYU so we can see each other. Then we'll get an apartment here while I finish getting my degree. You could work while I'm at college, it will be good for you. I don't want you to think you missed anything, because afterward you'll never have to work again."

I could be a secretary, Peggy thought. Everybody's a secretary. "What will I do this whole year?" she moaned.

He ran his hand lightly over her breast. "Maybe I'll get an apartment *this* year," he said.

Her parents and her sister Joan were waiting up when they got to the house. Peggy introduced them, showed them her engagement ring, and told them she and Ed had no secrets. Her parents looked a little shocked, but Joan was thrilled. She looked as if she had half a crush on Ed already. Her father offered him a drink. During the expected routine of Ed's telling her parents what a stable and good catch he would be, and their trying not to pry rudely but asking things anyway, Peggy sat there demurely, thinking about the apartment he had said he would get, and what things the two of them would do there. With all those high school boys she'd had no inkling she was so sexual. But Ed's hand on her breast had aroused her and she was still aroused.

I'd go all the way with him, she thought. I will. He's a responsible person, he'll get condoms. And if I get pregnant, so what? We're engaged anyway. She smiled like the Cheshire cat. Everyone there took this to be the contented grin of a girl whose future has just been settled, who never has to worry again about getting a date or being an old maid or getting her heart broken. They had no idea that all Peggy was thinking about was Ed Glover between her legs.

FOURTEEN

It was rather a shock to Rose to realize Peggy's future was about to be settled. Good, in a way, but also not so good. She was not sure how she felt about having a seventeen-year-old daughter who was already engaged to be married. She reminded herself that she had been that young when she got engaged to Tom Sainsbury, but that had been in a more innocent time, in a smaller place, and she had known him almost all her life. Peggy didn't know this ex-soldier at all. Oh, she'd been writing to him for years, but was that enough? Ed Glover seemed like a nice young man, and he was certainly as handsome as anyone you would want your daughter to meet, his family had some money, and he had ambition. Being a CPA was a safe career. But it was a good thing they were planning a long engagement.

The other strange thing was, Rose realized, that the whole situation made her feel as if she had come to another place in her life where she hadn't expected or wanted to be so quickly. Her oldest daughter would get married, and move away, and have children. She would be a grandmother. What a strange idea, she realized, herself as a grandmother; but if not now, when?

Celia, of course, was delighted. "She would marry them all off at twelve," Ben said wryly. In some way he seemed to understand Celia better than the rest of them did. She amused him, but he kept a slight distance. Rose wondered what Ben would have thought of her real mother, if she had lived, and what her mother would have thought of him. It had been a long time since she had thought about her mother. She still did on Hugh's birthday, of course, which was the day Adelaide had died; and she had thought about Adelaide when she had given birth to each of her own children; but her mother and her childhood were so far away. Yet when Peggy had a child that would make Rose a grandmother and Adelaide a great-grandmother—Adelaide, not Celia. The bloodline.

Rose wondered again what Adelaide had died of, and realized again that she would never know. That part of their family medical history was closed to her, and to the rest of them. She supposed it mattered now more than it used to, now that doctors routinely wanted medical information, to see if you had inherited anything. But luckily the doctors asked about grandparents, not great-grandparents. Peggy would have all the information she needed.

Ed went home to Iowa, and then he moved to New York, where he rented a studio apartment in the Village, near NYU, and Peggy helped him paint and furnish it. He and Peggy were inseparable. She hardly ever saw her friends anymore. Instead, she took her homework to his apartment and they studied together. Peggy seemed to be much more serious now, as if he were a good influence on her. She had changed in another way too; overnight she had turned into a woman, although Rose couldn't put her finger on the exact reason she thought that, unless it was the almost embarrassing attraction between them. You wanted to turn your face away. When Ed came over to dinner, the sexual bond between him and her daughter was so powerful Rose could almost see it, like a warm, damp fog. Even Ben noticed, although he compartmentalized such things as feelings of the night.

"They're so young and so full of sap, aren't they?" he said, trying to make it safe, normal, healthy, natural, like spring.

"I'm worried," Rose said to him.

"They'll be married soon," Ben said to reassure her. Perhaps he was worried too.

"Peggy," Rose asked her finally, "are you…doing anything…with Ed that you shouldn't?"

"Such as what?" Peggy asked coolly, to annoy her. Peggy knew what she meant.

"You are still a virgin, aren't you?"

"Of course I am," Peggy said. "What an offensive thing to ask your own daughter."

Rose backed off. It *had* been offensive, but she wasn't going to apologize. She still wanted to know, but she was afraid to know. "You haven't got that wedding ring yet," she said, trying to sound wise but only sounding stern. "Just don't ruin your life like you know who." Peggy smiled.

Harriette, honorably discharged from the WAVES, had decided to stay in Washington, she wrote Celia. Her life there made her feel free, she said, and she was going to work for the government. Celia, walking her little golden spaniel in Washington Square Park, had met a gentleman her age who also had a small dog, and now he sometimes took her out to dinner, or they played cards with his friends. Celia said she had no interest in marrying again, but she enjoyed having a date.

"A date!" Rose said to Hugh. "Would you have imagined Celia on a date?"

"There's hope for me," Hugh remarked wryly.

Rose wondered about Hugh. She knew he had friends; he was out very often, and sometimes mentioned a few names, and he went to the theater and movies and art galleries, the museum, restaurants, parties, with these friends whom she never met. Some were men, some were women. Some were even royalty, apparently, the lady this or that. But his life was a complete secret to her in many ways, and she supposed that was what it was like with a middle-aged bachelor in the house. Hugh was forty. She didn't think he should be a bachelor forever, but time was going by. He seemed happy enough. When he was with the family he was wonderful: a good uncle, a good brother, a good brother-in-law, interested in everyone's doings no matter how unimportant, pulling his weight. He took his own clothes to the cleaner, or to the laundry. He brought presents, cake and flowers, like a guest. He even made most of his phone calls from the antique store. He still insisted on paying rent. He was completely independent. And Rose couldn't help feeling as though their house was merely a dock, and Hugh a ship.

She wanted to know him better, this man whom she had known since he was born, whom she had even bathed when he was little, and she didn't know how to start.

Although she had never done it before because it was unacceptable, she went into his room, his special place, while he was away at work, and under the pretense of putting something away she began to snoop. Not that she hadn't been in his bedroom before, but always when he was there and only to see him if there was a reason that couldn't wait. In a crowded household with several adults in it, privacy and respect were particularly important to everyone. In fact, Hugh often kept his door locked, and no one but the somnambulist ever went in without knocking and asking permission. The other girls almost never went in. Rose knew what she was doing now was an invasion, but her curiosity, although she had no idea what, if anything, she would find, spurred her on.

Hugh's room was always quite neat, and he had a lot

of things around: pretty antique brocade cushions piled on the bed, strange fussy lamps, paperweights, rare books, a silver-backed comb and brush set he never used. He often brought things back to the shop and sold them, and replaced them with other things. This made him seem even more transient, somehow. The room smelled faintly of his cologne: vetiver, a nice fresh manly scent that women sometimes wore too. There was a big bottle of it in the bathroom.

The top bureau drawer, she noticed, had been locked with a key, but the key was still in the lock. After only an instant of guilt Rose opened the drawer. There was the usual man's clutter, but there was also, she saw to her surprise, a half-open soft black case full of women's makeup, and there were several lipsticks loose and rolling around in the drawer too. Her first thought was that without anyone in the family knowing it, Hugh had invited a woman to his room, and this was her makeup. After all, he lived alone on the street floor, with his own entrance. Was there a secret woman? She inspected further. There were several snapshots lying in the drawer, of an attractive, hard-looking woman with a great deal of blond hair, a bit too much makeup, and wearing a tight, dressy black dress slit up the side like a tramp. The blonde was also wearing, and flirtatiously playing with, a feather boa, looking seductively at the camera and smiling.

Hugh's secret love? No wonder he had never brought her home.

It had never occurred to Rose that Hugh liked flashy women, and she realized how little she actually did know about him. The woman in the photograph looked familiar somehow, and she wondered if she were an actress. She tried to open the second drawer, but it was locked too. The same key opened it. Behind the usual piles of men's underwear, arranged neatly as was Hugh's nature, she noticed the edge of something red and frilly. It was a piece of woman's underwear. She looked further and discovered there was more lingerie: white, pink, black. This was increasingly bizarre. It was as if he had an invisible roommate none of them had ever known about. Rose headed for Hugh's closet and opened it.

There were Hugh's fashionable suits, in a perfect row, and beside them were two quilted garment bags, with squared-off edges and long zippers. Rose opened the garment bags. Inside them were a number of evening gowns and cocktail dresses, one of which was the black dress from the photograph, and hanging on a hanger was the feather boa. It was purple. On the shelf above the clothing were some men's natty hats, which she had seen him wear. Behind them was a large box, like a hatbox. She took it down. Inside it was a wig block, and set on the wig block, as if "the actress" had been decapitated, was a voluminous blond wig. The familiar-looking woman had been wearing a wig...

It wasn't a woman, it was Hugh.

Of course, Rose thought. Hugh, the little actor. It was not beyond comprehension. But where and why would he wear those clothes, that disguise? She figured out the answer after a moment. It was very simple. He was in a show, or he had been, and he hadn't mentioned it to them. She felt hurt, knowing they had become so estranged without her even realizing it that he had simply cut her out. She would have gone to the show, they all would have gone, like in the old days, and cheered him on. She put back the wig box and sat on his bed waiting impatiently for him to come home so she could straighten out the situation.

When Hugh walked into his bedroom and saw his sister sitting there waiting for him he looked surprised and not pleased. "Rose?" he said, as if he were waiting for an explanation of her presence, as if one were needed, and of course one was.

"Oh, Hugh," she said, "it's been so long since you and I had a talk."

"Is it?" He didn't seem angry; his tone was meek. But he was looking at her in an odd way.

"I apologize for snooping, but I saw your costumes," she said.

"My costumes?"

"The dresses...the other things."

"You went through my things?"

"I was curious," she said. "I felt left out. You never share your life with me anymore."

"Well," he said. He lit a cigarette. "And what would you like me to share?"

"Tell me about the play you were in. Why didn't you invite us?"

"The play? Ah, yes, the play."

"Where was it?"

He paused for a while, as if the answer escaped him. "Webster Hall," he said.

"And when?"

"Oh..." He shrugged. "Halloween."

"You must have had a big part to wear all those costumes. Were you the lead?"

"Hardly," he said.

"Don't you want to tell me about it?"

He paused again. "I don't know," he said finally. "I don't know if you would understand."

"What in the world is there for me to understand, Hugh?" Rose asked. "You and I were always so close, but now..."

"I was different then," he said. "A long time ago. Or perhaps not so different. Just unaware. You shouldn't have been in my room, Rose. You turned a key. That's forbidden. People can't live in the same house when keys are turned behind other people's backs."

"I'm sorry. Please don't lock me out of your life. That would be worse than anything."

"Than anything?"

"Yes."

"All right," he said. "It was more than just Halloween."

"I was sure of it."

He smiled, a strange little smile without mirth. "I've
been waiting for this, in a way," he said. "Let's see
what your love is made of."

She looked at him, puzzled, letting her love shine
out of her eyes so that he would believe in it. "What
could be so wrong?"

"I'm queer, Rose. Didn't you ever notice?"

Queer? A fairy? But of course everyone had said
Hugh was a sissy, for years, forever, it seemed. Still,
you could be a sissy and not be a queer, as far as she
had seen it. She had believed what she had wanted to,
and so had the others. Perhaps not Celia; Celia had always made those unkind remarks, but everyone else in
the family had just let them pass. Celia had an ax to
grind, they thought. Ignore her.

"But you were in the Army!" Rose said.

"There were a lot of queers in the Army," Hugh said,
amused at her. "They were patriotic, just as I was.
There was a world war on, remember?"

"But you were masculine then!"

"Rose. I'm queer. I've always been queer. I am a particular kind of queer who likes to wear dresses. And
paint. And the occasional wig. With my closest
friends." He was peering at her again. "What do you
think about that? Are you horrified? Do you hate me?
What are your feelings?"

"I don't know," she said. And she didn't. She had no
idea what she thought. It was all too big to grasp. She
was not an ignorant woman, she lived in New York
City, near Greenwich Village, she was out in the world.
She knew about free love, Bohemians, bisexuals, lesbians, homosexual men; but none of that had anything to

do with her and her life because she chose to ignore it. A few blocks away from Bohemia, Rose might as well have been back in Bristol, or in the heartland of America. In that innocent heartland no one ever wanted to admit anyone was queer, not even when they saw the movies with those fussy effeminate men in them— wasn't it usually a prissy desk clerk in a comedy?— and people were just amused at those actors and thought nothing.

Most people probably were ignorant, she realized. But she supposed what she had been was in denial. She had never given the other side of life any thought at all. And in your own family was the last place on earth you would want to look for something aberrant. You ignored it. As you ignored Celia when she decided to be cruel.

"I don't know what I think," Rose said. "I have no idea."

"That's a step in the right direction," Hugh said. "Nonjudgmental."

"I didn't say that. I don't want you to be the way you are."

"There's nothing you can do about it. I am who I am."

"That woman in the photo…you dress as her…with your friends?"

"Sometimes. Her name is Camille."

"And do you go out with other men?"

"Do you mean on dates?"

"I suppose I do," Rose said.

"When I can get one," Hugh said. "I'm not so young and pretty anymore. It's difficult for any woman past a certain age, or so you keep telling your girls."

"Oh, Hugh!" Despite herself, she smiled.

"Usually, though, I go out with my dates as a man. I'm better-looking as a man."

"Oh, Hugh!"

"Stop saying, 'Oh, Hugh!' "

"We must never tell anyone in the family about this," Rose said.

"*Au contraire.* We must tell them all. I want to be loved and forgiven. I want to teach the girls how to put on makeup properly. I want to be restored to the bosom of my family. The only one we will never tell is Celia."

"Of course not. Never Celia."

She was still in shock, but instinctively, as always, she was protecting him.

As it happened, Hugh's secret life didn't change. He never dressed in women's clothing in the house, unless he was behind locked doors, and who knew then if he did or he didn't? No one ever saw a tall, voluminous-haired blonde who looked of dubious reputation leaving their building in the evening, or coming home in the early hours of the morning. Hugh prepared, and restored, as always, at his friend Lady Clifford's house. But somehow, after that night when he had revealed himself to her, Rose was not able to tell anyone in the family, except for Ben.

Ben was not as horrified as she had worried he would be. He only seemed a little bewildered. The queer part he accepted without argument, and the women's clothing part he chose to forget. But he didn't mention it to anyone either, and when Hugh began to advise Peggy and Joan on their hair and makeup the girls simply thought of him as a higher authority, like a hairdresser, or makeup man on a movie. They knew about the third sex; Rose had heard them talking about their gym teacher, who they suspected was a lesbian. And she thought they probably knew about Hugh without being told, but because they had known and loved him since they were born they never made an issue of it. Perhaps, Rose thought, they were more sophisticated than she had believed. Certainly they were more so than she was. It was what you expected of the younger generation, whether you liked it or not. In this case, at least, she was glad.

FIFTEEN

Prosperity had returned to America. Christian Dior's the New Look swept fashion, with tiny waists, long flowing skirts, crinolines, ballgowns. Hair was short, or pulled back. Hats were small and perky. Heels were high, on narrow pumps. Lips and nails were bright crimson. Sophisticated femininity led to the fulfillment of nearly every woman's wish to be mom in an apron. The favorite gifts were perfume and a large appliance. The returning veterans married, had babies, and moved to the burgeoning suburbs. The running joke about these identical suburban tract houses was that sometimes the husband would come home at night and get so confused that he went in to the wrong house, not discovering his mistake until he saw someone else's wife and children there.

The War had decimated; the young couples were re-populating. The husbands commuted, on trains, or in cars that had become huge because there was gas to run them again. The wives stayed in the suburbs, baking cookies and tuna fish casseroles, raising neat, well-behaved children, driving them to activities in station wagons, so called because you used them to pick up the husband at the station. The license plates of these cars and station wagons often bore the initials of the kids.

Peggy had graduated from high school, and now she waited impatiently for Ed to finish college so they could get married and start their adult lives. Once they had thought they would marry as soon as she had graduated, but then they discovered there would be no money, or at least not enough to support them both if he wasn't working, so it would be best to hold off until he had a job. Neither his parents nor hers offered to support them, which Peggy thought was cruel. After all, their parents were supporting them now, separately. What was the difference? She wondered if his parents didn't like her enough, or if hers didn't like him enough, and it made her frustrated and sulky.

Her parents had asked her if she wanted them to send her to college while she was waiting, but she said no. She found a job as a secretary (a typist, really) in a boring law firm, gotten through her father's influence, and she couldn't understand why Ed had told her working would be interesting and that she would need to experience it so she could get it out of her system and not think she would be missing something. She hadn't thought that since her first day on the job. Even worse, she made so little money that she might as well have been working for free. It was clear that she would not be able to support Ed and herself, that he would have to do it, and that they would have to hold on and suffer until he could.

Her parents asked again, this time, if she would like to take some extension courses instead of working, but again she declined. If she had ever been a scholar, and she doubted it, all that was gone now; she lived in a haze of romance and sex, of anticipation and irritation, collecting dishes and towels piece by piece, naming and renaming her unborn children, clipping recipes from women's magazines, meeting Ed in his apartment and going all the way.

Sex with him was everything she had imagined, and then some. She wondered why no one noticed how different she looked now, how glowing. Well, maybe her mother did. Peggy couldn't decide if her mother was suspicious and questioning because she was paranoid, like all mothers, or if she could tell. They were engaged, after all, and Ed was an adult. If her mother was so worried about her precious virginity, the coin of the realm, she should help them get married.

Little Ginger was taking ballet, and had already read all the Oz books. Joan slept all the time. It was said that teenagers needed their sleep, because they were nervous and growing, but Joan could drink a cup of coffee and then lie down and take a nap. At one point her mother, thinking Joan might have something wrong with her metabolism even though she was slim, took her to the doctor for tests. He had Joan breathe into a bag to test her metabolism and said it was fast if anything. There would be no need for her to take thyroid, which was fortunate, since they had heard thyroid tablets could make a girl grow a mustache. Let her sleep if she wanted to. When she had something she really wanted to do, Joan could manage to wake up fast.

At Christmas Ed took Peggy home to Iowa to get to know his family better. She had met his mother and stepfather only once, when she and Ed announced their engagement and his parents had taken the mandatory trip to New York, partly as tourists, partly to size up the Carson family. Peggy felt as though his family didn't really take her seriously. She was just the fiancée, and there were no phone calls, no friendly letters, except for the thank-you note his mother wrote to Rose. To tell the truth, Peggy didn't care about Ed's parents all that much either. Her own family was both satisfying and annoying, a force to fend off when you wanted to grow, and to embrace when you needed their warmth and support, and the idea of taking on a whole new set of parents at this time in her life seemed odd.

At Christmas in Iowa, that year, in a house that

smelled old, surrounded by snow, Peggy was home-sick. Naturally she and Ed had to sleep in separate rooms. Why was it, she wondered, that she always wanted to cry? Her closet smelled like camphor and her mattress of mildew. She had never been away from New York, where she had been born, and now she counted the days until she could go back, with Ed. Sur-rounded by well-meaning strangers, including the two large men who were Ed's stepbrothers, Peggy only felt vulnerable. She knew she couldn't tell Ed. A grown-up wouldn't complain. These people were doing the best they could, and they thought they were being nice to her. They pretended to like their Christmas presents (or perhaps they did, who could tell?) and she pre-tended to like hers, a bunchy bone-colored sweater with multicolored rosettes on it, which his mother had knitted herself, and which Peggy wouldn't be caught dead wearing.

"It's so special, I'll save it for a party when I go home," Peggy said, feigning awe and delight.

Ed had given her a link bracelet, to which he would later gradually add charms—the first piece of jewelry except for her graduation watch from her parents that Peggy had ever had in real gold. That is, unless you counted her engagement ring as jewelry, but she did not; that ring was a bond, a troth, something of such emotional value that calling it jewelry would be like calling the Taj Mahal a house. Her own gift to him was a leather album for the photographs and memories they would amass together. It was personal and yet not so intimate it would threaten his mother. Already she could sense that his mother was far from thrilled that Ed had decided to marry a girl who lived in New York, a stranger he had met through letters, and that he would be living far away from his dear ones.

"It's wise," his mother said, "that you two children are going to have a long engagement, to get to know one another." By now it was thoroughly clear, if it hadn't been before, that if she and Ed got married before he was self-supporting, his parents wouldn't want to help them.

On their way back to New York on the train, released from their mandatory charade, Peggy and Ed necked and petted for hours. Breathless, her lips sore and swollen, wishing they were in bed and he was inside her, Peggy finally felt like herself again.

Their own little studio apartment in New York, his "student apartment," was their haven. It was tiny compared to her parents' house, or his parents' house, but to Peggy it was big. It was sophisticated. It was paradise. It occurred to her that if she and Ed got married and had a baby before he graduated from college, the baby could fit in there fine. The baby had become a part of her fantasy ever since she came back from Iowa. The baby, a pregnancy, was how she could get married. No one would want her to be a disgrace, a slut. A child out of wedlock? Unthinkable! A six-month-long pregnancy resulting in a chubby full-term infant would be bad enough. If she got pregnant, Peggy knew, her mother would make her get married immediately.

She had a diaphragm now. Engaged, she had been able to go to a gynecologist and be fitted for one with no embarrassment except for the doctor's expression of surprise when he discovered she didn't need the novice's size. She and Ed had been careful, but one time they had been carried away, and Peggy knew it could easily happen again. She didn't like the idea of tricking him, but she was afraid to tell him that she planned to have an accident, in case he tried to talk her out of it, or worse, got angry. She allowed herself a few moments of guilt and fear over being manipulative and then decided what she planned to do was good.

It seemed a long time ago now that she had lied to him about her age, and it had turned out all right after all. This second little deception would turn out all right too, she knew it. Everyone who would be trusted with the news she was pregnant, and there would be few, would be upset at first, and then would rally around her and Ed to cover it up and make a happy ending. Peggy knew she wouldn't be the first girl to get pregnant in order to hasten a marriage, and she wouldn't be the last.

She knew that a girl her age who was healthy could conceive with no trouble at all. When her period was three weeks late she went to her doctor, who confirmed the good news. That night she told Ed. He looked dismayed for only an instant, and then became adorably excited at the thought of becoming a father. "I guess we have to get married sooner than we thought," he said.

Peggy told her mother there had been an accident, that she and Ed had only done it once. She didn't know if her mother believed her, but Rose got to work on the wedding plans right away. Luckily Ed's midterm vacation was coming up. He and Peggy would have a small church wedding, with a white dress for her while she could still fit into it, and her sister Joan as maid of honor, and the couple would spend a few days in Bermuda, where everyone went for their honeymoon because it was a beautiful and peaceful place to do what she and Ed had been doing all along anyway.

"Ed is an honorable young man," Rose said. "He could have backed out. He could have deserted you. These betrayals aren't unheard of."

"You don't know him at all, do you, Mother?" Peggy said. She was really annoyed at such lack of trust. It had recently occurred to her from what she saw and heard around her that many women didn't think of men as people. A man was a prize to be won, an animal to be tamed, a rescuer, a status symbol, a villain, or a fool. The woman had to go through all the right steps and then maybe it would work out and she would catch a husband. If a woman really knew the man she loved, Peggy thought, the way I know Ed Glover, she wouldn't have to play tricks to keep him from running away.

Ed's mother and stepfather and two stepbrothers came to the hastily planned wedding. They all knew, and Peggy could see that whatever love could have developed between her and his immediate family had been nipped in the bud. At the reception Ed told her that his stepfather had told him he would lend them some money. Her father was contributing too, but he was making it a gift, not a loan. That was like her father, Peggy thought: generous and kind. It was sweet to see how thrilled Ben was at the thought of his first grandchild.

"I know exactly what that child will look like," Joan said to her. "You and Ed look so alike you could be brother and sister. That's probably why you fell in love with each other. And baby makes three."

"Someday, Joan, you'll be nice," Peggy said.

"I am being nice."

Aunt Maude was at the wedding, down from Bristol with Uncle Walter and Peggy's four cousins, two of whom were bridesmaids; and Aunt Daisy was there from Bristol too, with her family; and even Aunt Harriette, the adventuress, was there from Washington, D.C., alone but looking chic and content. One of Ed's two stepbrothers was best man. Uncle Hugh and Ed's other stepbrother were ushers. Ginger was a perky flower girl, allotting her petals so seriously and precisely that she almost stole the show. None of Peggy's or Ed's friends had been invited, in order to keep the wedding small. Secret, almost. Later there would be a mailed announcement.

Peggy thought her wedding was magnificent and moving. She had dreamed of this day, and her dream had come true. Even though there was an unavoidable subtext of embarrassment and haste, it was felt by the others, not by herself. The wedding didn't have to be a big production. What mattered was that she was marrying the man she loved and would always love, united forever in the sight of God and her family. Her ring was a plain gold band, and Ed had one too. That would keep the women away from him! Her mother, in the front row, cried.

After their honeymoon the couple moved into Ed's studio apartment. Peggy quit her job so that she could devote herself to cooking for Ed and cleaning their little paradise and making everything nice for him. She actually liked being pregnant, up until the last month, when she couldn't wait for it to be over. She was getting along with her mother better now than she had in a long time, because they were more equal. The baby, born in New York Hospital six months after the wedding, was an eight-pound twelve-ounce boy with blue eyes and blond fuzzy hair. They named him Peter.

A new baby, Peggy soon discovered, was a lot of trouble, but she didn't care. She felt like a part of life, of the universe. Whenever she saw a mother wheeling a baby she basked in the warmth of sisterhood. She felt important. Soon she was sitting on a bench in Washington Square Park with her contemporaries, the young mothers who were only a few years older than she was, talking about formula versus breast feeding, sleeping patterns and behavioral problems, and future nursery schools, just the way her own mother had with her and her sisters.

When Ed graduated from college Peggy brought Peter, who was a toddler, to the ceremony. There were a lot of veterans in Ed's class, older and more mature than the usual college boys, and many of them had wives and children too. Peter was a placid child, and he was well behaved. "I wonder if he'll remember this," Ed said.

They moved to the suburbs, finally, to Levittown, a new development on Long Island on the site of what had once been potato fields. The identical neat little houses with their peaked roofs stretched into the horizon as far as the eye could see. Their area hadn't been landscaped yet, which gave it a strange, military feeling. Peggy got a driver's license and drove Ed to the train every morning so he could go to work in the city, and picked him up at the station at night.

At college Ed had decided he didn't want to be an accountant anymore, that he wanted to go into advertising instead, because it was the new glamorous thing to be an ad man; and he had taken English composition courses, although they hardly seemed necessary in order to write a slogan. Still, it turned out he had a knack. So now he was at an ad agency that promoted air travel and cigarettes and cars—some of the things America wanted in this new era of prosperity—and making people want them more. He was earning a lot of money—ten thousand dollars a year—and paid off his family's loan. Once a week Peggy got a baby-sitter and met him in New York, and the two of them went to a good restaurant, or to a play. They were still so in love they were perfectly happy seeing no one but each other.

In the next two years Peggy had two miscarriages. The first one consisted of sharp pains, a terrifying amount of blood, and finally a clump of blood and human tissue—the end of what she had planned to make her destiny complete. But the second time the baby was six months old, a girl, born dead. She and Ed were devastated. Her doctor told her to wait a while before trying again, in order to be as strong as possible.

She knew she wanted everything too much, too soon; that had always been her nature, and she had always gotten what she set her mind to. For the first time she had to pause and think about life. She realized how lucky she was that she'd gotten pregnant with Peter, her sweet, beautiful son, without even thinking any part of it might be difficult. She and Ed were determined to have another child. Everyone wanted at least two children, most people three or four. But two children, a boy and a girl, Peggy thought, would be perfect without being greedy or tempting fate. Then they would move to a larger house in a better suburb, perhaps in Larchmont: an oasis close to the city, with growing green things around it, an ocean of green, peaceful and fresh. She would be able to sit at her bay window and look out, and not see anybody's house. Although she would have privacy, the other houses would be right there, of course, so she wouldn't be afraid or feel isolated, and so that her children could play with the other children in their neighborhood. The sound of little kids playing, she thought, their high voices calling to each other in the dusk just before they came in for dinner, was one of the prettiest sounds in the world.

It was not that she was bored or unhappy here in Levittown, or that she had nothing to occupy her. Even now, living so close to the city, she hardly saw her family anymore except on the big holidays, unless she and Ed made a real effort so that Peter's grandparents could see him. There was so much for her and Ed to do around the house on weekends. There were chores, things to be fixed, Peter's social activities. They had bought the new Weber grill that had just been invented, so now they could cook out-of-doors, and they had barbecues, for themselves, or, if they wanted to be festive, for another couple or two with their children. On weekends there was a plume of fragrant smoke coming from everyone's yard. The husbands were tired from commuting during the week, and this suburban life was what they were working so hard to have. She was twenty-three now, and she considered herself in the prime of her womanhood.

When Peggy became pregnant again, and gave birth to another dead baby, her doctor ran blood tests. Resentfully she thought he should have done it in the beginning, so all these tragedies wouldn't have happened, but you never criticized your physician. There were new discoveries all the time, and the ramifications of this one, affecting infant deaths, were fairly recent. Her doctor told her that her blood was Rh negative, while Ed's was Rh positive, which meant that if she carried an Rh-positive baby her blood made antibodies against the child, her body thinking it was not part of her but something alien to get rid of. Ed, her trusted love, whose body she shared in passion and hope, his blood was dangerous to her. She was struck by the irony, the ridiculous unfairness of it.

Peter, her first child, had been safe because her body didn't know that the blood crossing from her to him through the placenta was different. But after his birth, it did—for ever after. Now, only if she carried an Rh-negative baby, its blood like her own, would the child be all right. Unfortunately, negative was rare. But her doctor told her she didn't have to take the gamble. There had been a vaccine developed, to be given to the mother within seventy-two hours after a miscarriage, and he gave it to her now.

A year later Marianne was born. Completely perfect, six pounds twelve ounces, and beautiful, with the blue eyes and blond hair of both her parents and her brother, she looked like a fantasy baby in an ad. In fact, Ed wanted to take her photos to his office and get her a job doing a commercial, but Peggy wouldn't let him. "All I want from now on is for us to be normal," she told him.

As normal as you could be with the Cold War on,

and the war in Korea, and everyone afraid of the Communists, hating the Russians, worrying about the atomic bomb. Duck and cover, the little kids in school were told, hiding under their desks, falling facedown on the playground, eyes shut, in their bomb drills. Peter started wetting his bed again after Marianne was born, and Peggy didn't know if it was because he was afraid of the bomb or jealous of the baby. In any case, she didn't make a fuss. Kindly Dr. Spock was the child and baby authority now, his book every sane parent's bible, and it was official that children were to be treated with benevolence and understanding. It was the first time.

SIXTEEN

Joan knew that if you were to describe in one phrase what each person was in her family, she would be the black sheep. Except for knowing that disconcerting fact about herself, all of her life she had been unsure of who she was, or even of what she wanted to be. She knew about her sisters. Peggy would be a contented wife and mother, and Ginger would be a genius or a star of some kind. But what would Joan be? She felt that not only did she not know herself, but other people hadn't a clue who she was either.

When she complained, her mother said that being the child in the middle was difficult, that she had been one and understood. Her mother also told her, too often and in a guilty way, that Joan had been subjected to great pain as an infant, the reminder of which was the scar on her forehead. Joan didn't think her scar was as ugly as she led people to think, and making her friends pay to see it was a bit more of a joke than a way of turning around embarrassment. But she had also discovered early that if you told people something bad about yourself they were less likely to discover it and throw it up to you later.

There was plenty that was bad about herself. Although she was smart, she didn't work hard because she had figured out she didn't have to. She dreamed or whispered in class, but when she read the books they were given for homework she remembered everything, which annoyed her teachers even more than if she had actually been stupid. Her teachers sent notes home with her report cards, the gist of them being that she was her own worst enemy. Joan was not sure what that meant, but she knew it was scary; it implied there was a malevolent creature inside her that might jump out and destroy her some day. She would have to be prepared.

In her personal life, she hoarded money, always had. She hated to help around the house and do chores if she was told to, and often managed to get out of it, but if not asked she would do anything to be helpful. She teased her sisters and made them angry, when she really hadn't meant to and didn't know how it had started. She had nothing against them, she loved them; in fact, when she was young she had followed her older sister, Peggy, slavishly because she thought Peggy knew everything. Peggy had wanted tap-dancing lessons, so of course Joan had begged for them too. Then they both got bored and quit. Peggy didn't feel guilty but Joan did, because they both knew there wasn't much money and their parents would do anything for them.

When Peggy fell in love with her soldier and actually married him, Joan wasn't jealous for an instant. She knew her own adventures were coming, although she had not the faintest idea what they could be. What she did know was that every girl's ambition of being a young wife and mother as soon as possible was not for her. It seemed like a dead end and too much responsibility. She was aware this made her a kind of misfit in the world, and what was worse she didn't keep her feelings a secret, so other people thought she was odd, selfish, flighty. Not want to get married and have children? But what would she do with her life?

Joan's good marks got her into college; she went to Radcliffe, which was a triumph. The family gave her a going-away party and a new typewriter. Then she flunked out after the first year because she was so tired she couldn't get out of bed in the morning to go to her classes. That was a disgrace. Back at home with her confused and disappointed parents, bored and a child again, she let her mother talk her into taking some extension courses at NYU. She went only because Peggy had not and she wanted to appear better than Peggy—in some way, any way, what way? Peggy had deserted her, and she had no inclination to follow.

At NYU Joan took art appreciation and French, in case she ever went to Paris. Everyone who could afford to was going to Paris now that the war was over; college graduates went as their graduation present, always with a friend. Joan wasn't a college graduate celebrating, and she didn't have a close friend to go anywhere with. Her friends from high school were away at college, or married and going on trips with their husbands. Most of the time it was just easier to sleep than to think about any of this.

In New York, people were reading Freud, and going into psychoanalysis—a sentence of five days a week for five years. Something minor, like sibling rivalry, or rage, was enough to send you off to the couch, on that lengthy, expensive journey toward normalcy. But luckily, in her family, eccentricity was accepted. You only had to look at Uncle Hugh. He was gay and no one seemed to care, except for Grandma, who was something of a perfectionist.

There were beatniks now in Greenwich Village, wild-haired young people who always dressed in black, who read strange poetry aloud in dim, smoke-filled little coffeehouses, or converged in bars like the Limelight, the Cedars, Joan's favorite coffeehouse, Figaro, or the White Horse—where they talked for hours, made friends, found lovers, understood each other (or admitted they understood nothing, which made them feel better). There were drugs, and furious marathon writing sessions, and experimental plays, and artists who had no money.

Uptown, in real life, theirs was the generation that would soon be called the Silent Generation because they didn't object to anything and wanted to conform, but downtown they were the Beat Generation. Uptown, people watched *I Love Lucy* and *The Honeymooners* on television, where it was made clear that husbands had the control and wives had to connive. The heroic working women of the war years had disappeared. Every girl had to be a virgin, although you couldn't say the word virgin in the movies because it was too sexual. Everyone was having babies, although you couldn't say the word *pregnant* on TV, because it, apparently, was too sexual too. Hollywood's and TV's married couples slept in separate beds with a night table between them. Downtown unmarried couples slept in the same bed, often a mattress on the floor, and if they had a night table at all it was an orange crate. In suburbia, Peggy and Ed were collecting Danish Modern; that life was light-years away from Joan's.

Did "Beat" mean beaten down? Joan didn't know, but she started hanging around in the Village too, started dressing all in black like the others, let her hair grow: blond, long and straight, with bangs. She met people. She felt that finally she had friends who were just like her, who believed in individuality and freedom, who questioned the establishment, who understood that anger was an acceptable emotion. Although she had not thought of herself as having any literary talent, eventually she started writing her own free-form poems, and reading them aloud from time to time. She drank red wine and smoked pot. She discovered pills that people took for a marathon evening of fun, though for herself they merely helped her stay awake. She went to parties in people's apartments—

pads, they were called—where the bathtub was in the kitchen and the toilet in the hall, and where people who weren't married to each other lived together anyway and sometimes even had a child.

Paris could wait for a while, Joan thought. She was actually having a good time here. However, she still lived at home.

Her parents didn't like the way she looked, the way she dressed, or that she stayed out late and came home smelling of cigarettes. If they had known the rest of it they would have liked it even less; perhaps, despite their tolerant nature, they would have made her stay in the house or sent her to the dreaded Freudian psychoanalyst. But they didn't know, and there was not even anyone for her to tell, although sometimes she thought of confiding in Uncle Hugh because his life was unconventional too, and he might understand.

What Joan wanted to tell him was that she had a lover now, her first, Henry Collins—at the same time her sister Peggy, the good one, had a new house in Levittown with her successful husband and their adorable little son—and that her secret lover was black and he was an aspiring painter. Of course, she could never bring him home.

Joan and Henry even had to be careful in the street. It was one thing downtown, but ten blocks uptown, where her family lived, people would stare at the interracial couple. She and Henry could never hold hands or look as if they were interested in one another. There were restaurants they could not go to, even if he had the money to take her. They never went further uptown, although sometimes she splurged and bought them standing room tickets for a Broadway play. Joan thought how ironic it was that Peggy and Ed sometimes went to see Broadway shows too, but that the four of them could never double-date.

The place she felt safe was in Henry's tiny apartment, with his unframed paintings stacked up against the brick wall and one in progress always on the easel surrounded by a spattered drop cloth. He was beautiful, with skin the color of milk chocolate and as soft as that of a girl. His lean and muscular body was so admirable that he often worked as an artist's model when his paintings didn't sell and he needed money to eat. Joan found sex—with him, and in general—fascinating. If anything, she thought her friends didn't appreciate sex enough because it was too easy to have, too accessible. They got drunk, they got stoned, they just did it. But not her, she took it seriously.

Love, of course, was a different matter. No matter how much you made fun of the transient and hypocritical nature of love, it could still wound you more than anything. She and Henry were fascinated with each other, with each other's bodies, with each other's looks, with each other's differentness and the few things they had in common; but they weren't in love with each other, although they told each other they were because that was part of an affair. She knew that, and so did he, but they would never admit it. They were very fond of each other, they had fun together, they were well suited physically. So they said they loved one another, and later, Joan knew, when they grew bored with each other or the relationship, one of them would say that the love was over, and the one who was told would be hurt. That was the way it was; she knew it already, just starting out on her road of life. She had seen it with her friends. Even if you thought you really weren't in love, when the love was taken away you would feel hurt. The sex, of course, could be replaced.

She had started keeping a diary, hiding it in her dresser drawer. It was more like a manuscript than a diary per se, since she thought she should make some use of her college typewriter for something besides the occasional poem. In this sheaf of papers she noted her discoveries about human nature. For example, there were so many young women downtown who had run away from their traditional, conformist, middle-class families, and who were now living with abusive men who pushed them around, put them down, and expected to be waited on—allowing themselves to be turned into just the kind of wives they had sworn they would never become. And they were not even married! They considered themselves muses. Was that what love did to you? Why didn't these women even notice what they had done to their lives?

I will always control my destiny, Joan thought. No matter what happens, there is always free will. Later she would look back and wonder how she could have been so arrogant.

SEVENTEEN

It had been a long time since the family had the traditional Sunday dinners Hugh and Rose remembered from their childhoods, although Celia did come over once or twice a week on an ordinary evening to have dinner with Rose and Ben and Ginger. Hugh was there often too, and Joan, but both Joan and Hugh usually left soon after they had eaten, Hugh taking the opportunity to walk Celia home and thus hasten her departure. He had grown to dread Celia's appearances. If her life was as full as she claimed it was, he often thought, then her sole purpose in coming over was to make his miserable.

Now that Celia knew she had been right about Hugh's sexual preference she was, in her later years, determined to change it. No matter that this was a ridiculous concept, in Hugh's opinion. She was undeterred, and a nag. Her gentleman friend had a nephew who was an aversion therapist. This was the new technique, for the "mentally ill," or "pathological" men who were attracted to members of their own sex. Celia, and most of the rest of society, was convinced that what Hugh had was a sickness, and that he had a choice to get well.

"My friend's nephew is named Dr. Norton Kidd," Celia announced, when she first brought it up. "He is considered very good. I don't know the details of this therapy, they're much too embarrassing for me, but he will make you dislike the life you're leading, Hugh, and then you can be normal."

"Uncle Hugh is normal," Ginger said.

"Help Joan clear the table, Ginger," Rose said.

With the girls out of earshot, Celia went on. "What you're doing, Hugh, is disgusting and you know it."

"Now, Celia," Ben said. "Hugh is a grown man, and we shouldn't be discussing his private life."

"Indeed? It's hardly private. Just look at him. Wouldn't you like to be straight, Hugh? I'm sure your sister Rose would like that."

"Would you like that, Rose?" Hugh asked, more to needle his stepmother than to get an answer.

"I don't know…I…" She *would* like it. Well, he should have known. Everybody would like it, except Ginger, who didn't know any better yet. "Hugh, there are so many amazing things being developed these days in the field of health," Rose murmured, embarrassed.

"My health is just fine, thank you," Hugh said.

"It is not," Celia said. "You cannot possibly be happy living the life you do. Wouldn't you like to have a nice wife before it's too late?"

"A *wife*?" Hugh cried.

"Do you remember Mr. Bennett, who lived downstairs in my building with his sister?" Celia said. "Well, he went to a psychiatrist for many years, unbeknownst to me, and he just got engaged to a lovely woman. I can tell you now that I always had my doubts about his masculinity. But not anymore. He's beaten his curse. We're lucky to be living in modern times."

"Excuse me," Ben said, putting down his empty coffee cup. "I must watch the evening news." He went into the living room, where they had their television set, a big console model, which had somehow become the heart of the room.

"You've made Ben uncomfortable," Rose said mildly.

"Oh, that's ridiculous," Celia said. "Just let me give you this doctor's number, Hugh." She put a little card next to his dessert plate. Pointedly, he did not touch it.

Now, every time he walked Celia home, Hugh braced himself for the onslaught of her effort to win. She always had another success story to tell him about, and he was sure they were apocryphal. Granted, she was going out with the uncle of this aversion therapist, but her examples were endless: The miserable man who had been contemplating suicide, now the happy husband of a widow who had two daughters. The school teacher who had been about to lose his job. The married bisexual man whose marriage had been saved, whose children were no longer disgraced. The manly leading man in a Broadway show, whose career had been in jeopardy because of his scandalous private life.

"Oh, introduce me to him," Hugh said.

"He's normal now," Celia snapped. "He wouldn't want you."

Hugh wondered if she were getting senile. Old people, it was said, became repetitious, forgetful. They would bring up a subject over and over, like a cat chasing a ball of string. When he looked back it was clear that Celia had never liked him, never, from as far back in his childhood as he could remember. Now she wanted to obliterate him and what he was, and turn him into someone she would no longer be ashamed of. Would he like that, he wondered, to be able to fit in, to make his family so relieved? Was he ashamed of himself? After he dropped her off he would ask himself these questions, and sometimes, to quiet the voice in his head, he would go downtown to a bar.

With his friends in the bar Hugh always felt comforted, but lately the questions had not gone away. He knew how many of his gay friends would have preferred not to be what they were. It was just too difficult. Fairyland was their fantasy world. He was lucky that his family, except for Celia, accepted him as he was. Many of his friends' families did not, and certainly the world did not, except for the small corner of it they had made their safe haven.

He supposed, if he really had to dig into the most vulnerable part of himself, that he was still unhappy being what he was. They called it self-loathing. Was he self-loathing? Was he guilty? How could he not be, when he still had to hide? Was it this guilt that had made it impossible all these years for him to find a lasting relationship with a man, when it was a man he wanted to have?

He could not imagine wanting to have sex with a woman instead of a man. But if he did, if such a thing could be trained into you by an aversion therapist, would he be more manly as well? Not the sissy they were all used to? Would his mannerisms change, his voice drop? What about all those women's clothes? He supposed he could give them to his new girlfriend. The thought made him laugh.

But as soon as he started thinking this way about changing, Hugh realized he thought it might be possible.

"Rose," he asked her one day, "tell me the truth. Do you want me to try this crazy thing?"

"Oh, Hugh, I just don't want you to be alone."

"But I'm not alone. I have my family."

"Have you…forgive me for asking…ever been in love?"

"Of course."

"But it didn't last?"

"Sometimes it was unrequited. A few times it was mutual, for a while. But that's me, who I am, not what I am."

"I have a hard time believing that," Rose said.

"You're such a kind and loving person. You're not so old, you're still in your forties. I know you've told me that in the gay world that's old, but it's not in the straight world. A man your age could easily find a nice wife."

"Who likes antiques."

"But all women like antiques," Rose said. "You could marry a decorator, you could go into business together."

"I meant I'm the antique," Hugh said.

"Oh, Hugh."

So it was that one afternoon after work he found himself sitting in the waiting room of Dr. Norton Kidd, on the upper West Side, staring at a tank full of tropical fish and some photographs of exotic places, taken by this same Dr. Kidd, on his travels, according to the signature on the photos. I guess I'm going to finance another trip for the good doctor, Hugh thought, and sighed.

There were two doors in front of him because the office was shared by two doctors. A man came out of one of the offices, a patient apparently, looking upset and unwell. He gave Hugh a hostile glance that said *temptress*, and headed for the street. Hugh sighed again. One day that will be me, he thought. After a short while Dr. Kidd poked his head out of the same doorway, very much resembling, with his eyeglasses and pointy nose, a cuckoo in a cuckoo clock, and beckoned Hugh in.

"Mr. Smith," he said. "Please sit down."

There was a large desk, with a chair behind it and a chair in front of it, and on the other side of the room there was an apparatus next to an armchair which faced a movie screen. Behind the chair was a slide projector. The apparatus looked harmless enough at the moment, but there were wires attached to it that caused Hugh some concern.

"I'll explain all that in a moment," the doctor said.

He nodded at Hugh and began to write. "Now, how long have you been a homosexual?"

"I don't know," Hugh said. "Always, I suppose."

"And your first experience?"

"What?"

"When was it, did you like it, who initiated it, and so forth. I want to know your story."

Hugh shrugged. "I was in love several times before I had an 'experience,' as you call it. I was not in love with him, but it was very exciting. The seduction, if you will, was mutual, I guess."

"So, when you were in love, you wanted a man who didn't want you?"

"They were straight."

"Aha." More writing. "And now you are here because you want to be straight too."

"I could try."

The doctor narrowed his eyes and peered at him. "Are you wearing *makeup?*"

"Just a little powder," Hugh said lightly. "I wanted to look my best. I didn't think you would be able to tell."

"You are a difficult case, but I've had worse."

"Oh?"

"You don't have to be effeminate. That's an affectation. I'm sure you didn't flounce around as a child."

"Maybe I did."

"Tell me, Mr. Smith, what is your principal reason for wanting to be cured?"

"I don't know."

"But you do want to be normal?"

"Yes, I do. Yes."

"You want to shift your erotic impulses away from men and toward women."

"But how would that be possible?" Hugh said.

"First you have to stop desiring men."

And then I'll be nothing, Hugh thought. He could

not imagine wanting to have sex with a woman. In all the talk of marriage at home he had never actually thought he would have sex with his poor deluded wife. "What's your magic potion?"

"Come with me." The doctor led him over to the armchair next to the apparatus. "Sit down, please."

Hugh sat.

"Now, this projector will show you homoerotic pictures: naked men, men having sex together, and so forth. This wire will be placed around your penis. When you become aroused by the pictures of men you will receive an electric shock."

"Where?" Hugh cried.

"On your genitals, but it's a very low level. Don't be alarmed. You will learn that this arousal is inappropriate. You will associate it with pain."

"What if I'm a masochist?" Hugh said.

"Are you? Do you like pain?"

"No. Actually, I hate it."

"Good. I can also expose you to a very bad odor upon arousal, if you'd prefer that. Ammonia, quite unpleasant. But I think for you, since you are not attracted to pain, the electric shock will do well."

This man is crazy, Hugh thought.

"You will discover when we are working together," the doctor went on, "that the hardest part of the therapy is emotional. You will have to struggle to rid yourself of your inappropriate desires, and you may be depressed and guilty over your conflicts, but that's all to the good. I'm going to turn you into a real man. Now, go into the dressing room over there and put on a gown."

"A gown?"

"A hospital gown. Take off your clothes. We can start today with the erotic pictures, so I can measure your degree of arousal, and then the next time we can start the shocks. Eventually you will find that you are less and less aroused, and then, finally, aversion, and success."

"How do you know the pictures will have any affect on me at all?" Hugh said. "With you standing there, and a wire on me, I don't think so."

"You haven't seen much pornography, have you?" Dr. Kidd said with a little smile.

"No, not really."

"I have never seen them fail." The smile was bigger, almost impish. "They are very erotic photographs."

"And almost worth staying for," Hugh said. "But I have to go now."

He headed for the door.

"Wait! Why are you leaving? Come back!"

"I'm not the sick one here," Hugh said.

He burst out of the office, slammed the door behind him, and stood for a moment in the waiting room—free, shaking, his heart pounding. Now that his consternation had dissipated he felt the anger flooding him, making him weak. How could anyone hate himself that much, to subject himself to such a thing? Did Celia know what they were going to do to him? She had said she didn't, but he wouldn't be surprised if she was simply too genteel—or too manipulative—to talk about it. How much she must hate him!

While Hugh stood there trying to regain his composure, another man came out of the other doctor's office, apparently having finished his latest session. He looked miserable, of course. He also looked like a large and sexy teddy bear.

"Give it up," Hugh told him. "These doctors are insane. It will never work. You're a good-looking man. You'll find somebody. You don't need a wife."

They headed for the elevator together.

"I *have* a wife," the man said.

"No…" Hugh put his fingers over his mouth in surprise. "They made you get married."

They entered the safety of the elevator, down and on their way to freedom. They were alone there for a few moments, in the silence of the confessional.

"Nobody made me," the man said. "I loved her."

"Oh, how sad," Hugh said. "Were you very young?"

He nodded.

"Children?"

He shook his head. He still looked a little in shock, and who could blame him after what he'd just been through upstairs behind that door.

"That's a blessing," Hugh said, "although you may not think so now. I'm warning you, that place up there is like the Spanish Inquisition. You'll confess, finally, but you'll never get the true religion. Trust me, dearie, you'll feel a lot better having a heart-to-heart with me than letting that charlatan put a hot wire around your dick."

The man stifled a smile.

"I'm Hugh," Hugh said, holding out his hand.

"I'm Teddy." How appropriate, Hugh thought. He could see a glimpse of reddish brown chest hair in the V of Teddy's partly open shirt and he wanted to rub his cheek on it. They shook hands, like two straight men. A line ran through Hugh's head of his favorite song from his favorite show: "Some Enchanted Evening" from *South Pacific*. "*Some enchanted evening, you will see a stranger...across a crowded room, and somehow you'll know...*" It's happening again, he thought. And for him too, I can tell.

They reached the street.

"Well," Hugh said briskly, before Teddy could escape, "you look like you need a drink. I certainly do. There's a lovely bar on the corner. I noticed it when I came in. Come along."

The teddy bear allowed himself to be led by this handsome, effeminate man with the long hair and well-cut clothes. "I can't go home just yet," he murmured to himself and his conscience.

"Of course you can't."

The bar on the corner was dark and seedy, but the red leatherette booth was comfortable and their martinis were icy cold. "I went to aversion therapy because I let myself be talked into feeling guilty," Hugh told him. "But I realized instantly that hating myself is not the answer to anything. This is a cruel world. If I'm not on my side, who will be?"

"I just feel sorry for my wife."

"You should. You should divorce her and set her free."

Teddy sipped his martini gratefully and his big shoulders began to relax. "I'm beginning to feel this therapy isn't working for me."

"Then you should quit. Spend your money on something worthwhile. Buy her a fur. Be *friends* with her."

"You *like* women, don't you," he said. He sounded surprised.

"Of course. I have wonderful sisters."

"Cheers." They lifted their glasses, and their eyes met.

After the bar they went to an equally seedy hotel for an hour, since both of them lived with other people. The sex was hot, and they took each other's phone numbers at work. It turned out Teddy was an engineer. Hugh didn't have the faintest idea what that was, but he intended to find out. I'm in love, he thought. He walked all the way home, miles, through the gathering twilight and then the exciting, light-sparkled dark. Take hold of yourself, he thought. You don't know if the man will call. After all, he's terribly conflicted. But who wasn't? If he doesn't call me, then I'll call him, Hugh thought. I'm a modern woman.

EIGHTEEN

Rose felt that time had a surreptitious life of its own, sliding away just when you thought everything was fine, so that the past seemed so far in the distance it was almost unimaginable—and then slow like a heavy, organic thing in the course of one day, so every hour seemed endless. They did not reminisce in her family, so if it hadn't been for Ginger's fascination with their family history Rose often felt it would have melted and disappeared. What did they do then? What did they think about that, Ginger wanted to know. How could they do that? How could they let that happen? And then? And then?

What could she say about Ginger? That Ginger, her youngest, the baby born to her late in life, was unexpectedly her greatest joy. Not that she didn't love all three of her daughters, but Peggy had always known what she wanted, and had left her so early to be a grown-up herself that Rose wondered if she had even touched her; while Joan, untouched too, had never seemed happy and refused to discuss it. Ginger, the most complicated of her children, was in a way the simplest. There did not seem to be any guile or selfishness in her, and she was full of curiosity.

With Peggy, Rose had to be careful. Grandma must not try to take over the rearing of the grandchildren, even with a suggestion. Peggy had her Dr. Spock book. She also had a kind of rivalry with her mother, perhaps because she was still so young that she felt threatened by any show of authority in Rose, and she wanted to do everything herself. The few times Rose went to visit Peggy and Ed in the suburbs she felt like a guest, and what was worse, she knew that Peggy would be glad when she left. It was as if her presence stopped the flow of their lives.

Joan was no better. Her life was downtown and secret. Rose couldn't criticize too much, she couldn't pry too aggressively, she couldn't try to change her. She was afraid to antagonize Joan for fear she would move out. She didn't want Joan to live on her own...*alone* was not the right word, because Rose was sure Joan wasn't alone. Years ago Rose had asked Peggy if she was a virgin, expecting her to say yes and believing her when she did. It had not been a question so much as a warning. But she never asked Joan if she was saving herself for the right man, the one who would marry her, because not only would the answer probably be no, but Joan would be glad to tell her the truth. Rose could only hope that Joan's wild ways, which she could merely guess at, were a phase.

But Ginger...Rose imagined being friends with Ginger forever. Peggy would continue to be distant and content in her own world, much as Maude had been when Rose was young; and the future of restless Joan was still a mystery. But Rose could see herself with Ginger as an equal someday: two women, two soul mates, each of them sharing information. The thought consoled her more than she wanted to admit.

One summer Rose and Ben had sent Ginger to camp, just so she could have the experience before it was too late to interest her, and Rose had missed her dreadfully. The camp, in Massachusetts, on a lake, was quarantined that summer because of the annual polio epidemic, and there were no visitor's weekends. Ginger didn't mind, but Rose did.

Ginger was too young and carefree to really understand about polio, but polio had been one of Rose's fears for years. In the worst year of the recent epidemics there were almost fifty-eight thousand cases. It seemed to strike young people particularly, and children. Little children screaming in splints, crying in casts, filled the hospitals. Doctors tried to force paralyzed limbs that were in spasms back to straightness, immobilizing them, operating. Of course, those limbs were still useless afterward, the muscles dead, although there were metal braces, and crutches, for the victims who weren't in wheelchairs or on stretchers for the rest of their lives.

The iron lung, a huge, barrel-shaped piece of equipment into which the patient disappeared except for her head, with a mirror like a car's rearview mirror for communication—a behemoth that breathed for a paralyzed respiratory system—was a frightening sight. Most people got out after the first phase of the disease, but some never did, and those were the ones with their pictures in the newspapers.

It was thought polio was caused by a virus, and people were advised to avoid crowds, swimming pools, and public events, all summer. There were always quarantines. There was no prevention and no cure.

Their late President Franklin Delano Roosevelt had been a polio victim as a young man, and people knew more about it now. But in photos he had never been seen struggling on his crutches, and seldom in his wheelchair; he was usually shown sitting in a dignified manner behind his desk. People had been afraid of giving handicapped people positions of authority. They donated to the March of Dimes, for the cute little poster child. Somehow it wasn't quite the same as a world leader with a disability, even though he had started the March of Dimes himself.

Sister Kenny, the aggressive, abrasive Australian

bush nurse, working in Minneapolis, was campaigning
tirelessly to take polio patients out of casts and relax
their muscles with hot packs instead. She said she
could make a paralyzed person walk again, and sometimes she proved it. But it was essential to begin her
treatment immediately after the onset of the disease,
and a lot of doctors didn't believe in it. Some of the
doctors hated her and said she was a fake. But there
were results, and Rose had heard about them. She
hoped she would never have to deal with any of this in
her own family firsthand.

When Ginger came back from camp after that one
summer, laden with trophies and medals for everything from best athlete to best camper, she said she
never wanted to go back again. "Why not?" Rose
asked.

"Because people haze each other. In my bunk everyone picked on one girl, all summer. You had to, or you
would be the one who got picked on. They did that in
every bunk. I can't go to a place where you can only
have friends if you're mean to someone."

"Then you never have to go again," Ben said, before
Rose even had a chance to answer, although of course
she would have said the same thing.

With no camp, and crowds forbidden, Ginger spent
her subsequent summers reading books she took out of
the library, and seeing her friends; until now, at fifteen,
with working papers, she got a volunteer job helping
in the foundling hospital uptown. Rose went by one
day, hoping to get a glimpse of her, pretending she had
an errand in the area, and there was Ginger in her pink
uniform outside in the sun with another nurse and a
row of patients in wheelchairs. But what patients! Rose
was aghast. Ten-year-old twin girls with tiny heads,
hardly able to hold them up, something Rose had only
seen as a child in ads for sideshow freaks. She remembered now they had called them Pinheads. The past

seemed very cruel. Ginger appeared matter-of-fact, not upset. Rose waved, and Ginger waved back.

"I didn't know you had patients like that," Rose said when Ginger came home for dinner.

"They're foundlings," Ginger said. "People give them away. The cute ones get adopted. I take care of the ones who don't."

"In my day you never saw people like that," Rose said mildly. She did not add unless it was in the circus.

"Because their families hid them. It was disgusting. I read about it. In your day they hid everything that was different. Did you know that crippled people were locked up? And people with cerebral palsy? If their families didn't want to take care of them, or couldn't, they were sent to institutions. They were like prisons. Nobody was taught anything. They didn't have love."

Rose felt a rush of pride for her fierce daughter. "That's so sad," she said. "I didn't know anything about it. I remember people with TB being sent away to get fresh air, but…"

"They locked up retarded people too," Ginger said. "I bet you knew only one person in your entire town who was slow, and he wasn't all that slow either, just enough to be the local character."

"Well, yes, I do remember that," Rose said.

"They still put people away because they aren't like everybody else," Ginger said. "Kids with Down's syndrome—do you know what that is? It's what everybody calls a mongoloid. Or a mongolian idiot! Don't you think that's cruel? There are a lot of them, but you don't see them walking around with their families. They sit in institutions and get worse. Nobody tries to make them function; all people care about even today is that everybody has to be perfect and fit in."

"How do you know all these things at your age?"

"I read. I ask questions. I listen. When I grow up I'm going to be a doctor."

But you're a girl, Rose thought. "What kind?" she asked brightly, as if such a thing was not out of reach.

"I don't know yet. But I want to find out why some people are born the way they are, and maybe fix it."

"Research?"

"Maybe. Do you know about the two medical researchers who just deciphered the structure of DNA? That's the molecule that carries the genetic code, which tells you what you're going to be. Who knows what wonderful discoveries that will lead to!"

"I can't imagine," Rose said.

"Well, Mom, this is the thing: Will you and Dad send me to medical school?"

"Yes, if you want," Rose said. "If you still feel that way when the time comes."

"Why wouldn't I?"

"Oh, I don't know. You might fall in love and get married."

"I might do both," Ginger said.

What had she done to have a daughter like this, Rose wondered. There were no doctors in their family, no one for Ginger to emulate, and except for her Aunt Harriette, who was hardly what you would call successful, no career women either. Where had she come from?

Where had any of them come from, really, so different from each other, each so totally her own person almost from the day she was born? It must be that genetic thing Ginger was talking about. "Whatever you want to do with your life, I'll be there to help you," Rose said.

"Thanks, Mom."

And thank you for letting me, Rose thought. My baby, my favorite, the only one of my children who still needs me. But of course she couldn't say that.

NINETEEN

It was hot that summer of 1954, as it was every summer in New York, and Ben and Rose discussed, as they did ever summer, whether or not they should rent a house in the country or at the beach, where it would be cool. As always, there were reasons why they couldn't budge. Inertia was one. Their little garden in back of their town house, with the awning and Rose's lovingly tended flowers, was pleasant. Ben had finally even gone so far as to have air conditioners installed in the bedroom windows. They rattled and made noise, but they made the nights cool enough for sleep. In the summer you could get theater tickets, and you could get into the best restaurants. Tourists flocked to New York in the summer, Ben said, so there must be something good about it. And of course, there was still the matter of the children.

Joan had a job now, as a waitress in a coffeehouse, where she also was an occasional part of the entertainment. Rose and Ben, although they felt it keenly, did not berate her that her so-called career was a waste of an education. After all, there was not much in the way of employment for a girl, no matter how well educated, since offices expected girls to get married and quit, and the good jobs were for the young men. Joan had made it clear that if her parents went away for the summer, or even the small part of it that encompassed Ben's vacation, that she would not accompany them. "I'll stay here with friends," she said stonily. What friends? Rose wondered. The ones you won't bring home?

Despite Joan's occasional antagonism toward her parents, Rose knew she was ambivalent about her life and still dependent on her and Ben. Girls Joan's age, twenty-three, either got married or stayed with their parents until they did, because it wouldn't be for long. Girls who came from places outside of New York were the ones with their own apartments, with room-mates—and if alone, then with cockroaches and five flights of stairs to climb. A girl with a nice town house to live in and all her bills paid would have no reason to leave and seek independence unless her parents made her life miserable. Families stayed together.

And then there was the matter of Ginger's beloved summer job. "Next year," Rose said to Ben, "we can decide earlier to rent a house, and then Ginger can do some volunteer work there, wherever it is. It'll be near a town, and towns have hospitals."

"Perhaps near Bristol," Ben suggested. "It would be nice for you to spend more time with Maude and Daisy."

At least they didn't have to worry about Peggy. She lived in the suburbs; she and her family didn't have to go anywhere because they were already there. And on the long July Fourth weekend they all went to visit her, the city relatives, so glad to be where there was grass and trees, so glad to see the sweet grandchildren, so glad to leave when it was over. They were adults going back to their own caves.

That summer Celia went on a cruise with some people she had met. It was amazing how Celia always seemed to be meeting people; she started up conversations wherever she went. She brought the brochure of her cruise when she came for dinner, color photographs depicting healthy-looking gray-haired couples toasting each other with champagne or playing shuffleboard. Celia didn't look anything like the people in the pictures; for one thing she was still a blonde. "Marilyn Monroe," Hugh called her, jokingly, and Celia laughed and accepted the compliment even though she was about forty pounds thinner and forty years older than the cinema sex symbol. Ginger affectionately called her "tiny little Grandma," and Rose remembered when she had thought Celia was tall.

Nobody ever mentioned the fact that Hugh's experiment with aversion therapy had been such a failure. Even Celia had the good grace to let it drop. He was looking happier these days anyway. When he went out in the evenings, jauntily dressed, freshly shaved and fragrant with cologne, he seemed like a man in love. Nobody ever mentioned that either, although they all noticed.

As for Hugh, he was indeed in love, with Teddy, the man he had met in the therapist's office. And on one of those lovely summer evenings when he went out all dressed up, he sat with Teddy in an outdoor café they had grown fond of and they toasted Teddy's recent decision to give up aversion therapy himself, to give up thought of any kind of therapy, to be what he was. After this landmark in his life Teddy had discussed it with his wife, and she agreed that the best thing for her to do would be to get a divorce while she was still young, so she could marry someone else and have children. Not that she didn't love him, she told Teddy, but more like a brother. So the next time that he and Hugh made a toast at their favorite outdoor café they were celebrating his entire new life.

"I am not a woman who wants what she can't have," his wife had told him.

"Ah, how much she could teach me," Hugh sighed.

"But you can have me," Teddy said to Hugh, leaning forward over the small café table, earnest and shy. "Could I?"

"Yes."

They would continue to have separate living arrangements, of course. Both of them were wary of scandal. Hugh knew male couples who had been together for years and kept their own apartments. He also knew some who lived together. He didn't disagree openly with what Teddy wanted, but in the back of his mind was the hope that someday it would be different for them. Who would know? People from work didn't go to Teddy's apartment for dinner, to see whom he lived with, to peer into his closets. If he had to entertain for business he could do it at a restaurant, with a woman friend posing as his date. Gay men did that all the time. The worst thing that could happen would be that people would try to fix Teddy up when he became an eligible bachelor, and Hugh knew he himself would be irritated and jealous, even though there was no reason to be.

I should count my blessings, Hugh thought. I should even thank Celia. Everything in life is a chain of events, some so bizarre it is hard to believe, but all fated. Hugh believed in fate. In the old days he had postulated that fate was arbitrary and cruel, but now he felt it was more benevolent. Or perhaps it was a balance. He had been content, but now he deserved, at last, to be happy. He wished he could share the good news with his family. Maybe one day he would. He would invite Teddy home for dinner, the first time he had ever brought home a guest. Would that be possible? How would he introduce him? A friend, my life's companion, the man I love? Or just invite him. Hugh suspected that Teddy would have more difficulty with the concept than he did, although that, too, would change. He was buoyant with optimism.

This was turning out to be a good summer for Ginger, too. She was sixteen and she felt on the cusp of womanhood. Inspecting herself in the mirror, she liked what she saw for the first time in years. As her mother had promised when she had complained about inheriting her grandfather William's long, aquiline nose, she had grown into it. Ballet lessons had given her curvaceous, pretty legs. She had a good smile. She had a nice body, not voluptuous like her sister Peggy's, but slim and shapely nonetheless. Her blond sisters were the all-American ideal if you believed what you saw in the magazines and the movies, but Ginger thought she herself was rather more interesting.

She and her girlfriends talked about boys and sex, and giggled and wondered and yearned. On some Saturday nights she had dates, although they were only boys she knew from school and she thought of them more as friends. They were too shy to be forward with her, mainly because she was intelligent and independent and that put them off. She preferred it that way. The man she would fall in love with was a fantasy so far, but she was excited at the thought that there was a whole world of young men out there, that she would eventually know a lot of them, probably in college, and go out with them, have fun with them, and then, at last, fall in love forever.

People talked about love all the time, and although Ginger had never let go of her ambition to do some good in the world, she also was sure that she could combine it with love. What she really wanted to do, she thought, was marry a doctor. Then they could practice together, perhaps do research together, and discover something that would make them famous. Why not?

One August night when her escort for the evening brought her to her door in time for her curfew and kissed her chastely on her closed lips, Ginger looked up at the moon and felt chilled. She said good night and ran into the house. The house seemed cold too, and when she went into her bedroom she made sure her air conditioner was off. She pulled her quilt up to her chin and wondered if she was getting sick. Usually so full of energy, she had been feeling tired and draggy the last few days. Sleep cures most things, she thought, and I could certainly use some. She slept.

But the next day she had a sore throat, and a violent headache that aspirin didn't seem to help, and she felt feverish. She called work and said she wouldn't be coming in, and hung around the house.

"Are you all right?" her mother asked when Ginger went upstairs to her room right after dinner. "I'll call the doctor."

"It's just a summer cold. I'll be fine."

"Take some aspirin before you go to bed."

"I just did."

That night she couldn't sleep, even though she was exhausted, and the next day when her mother made her stay in bed and brought her tea she acquiesced gratefully to being a patient. Rose also called the family doctor, who prescribed an antibiotic over the phone, one of the new wonder drugs that were given for everything these days and were guaranteed to cut a cold in half. But Ginger stayed the same for two more days, and by the third night, antibiotics or not, she knew she was really sick. She was throwing up, her headache was the worst she'd ever had in her life, her sore throat was worse, her back and neck felt stiff, and she had sharp, agonizing cramping pains in her legs. No matter what position she tried to put herself into, they wouldn't get any better. Sometimes the cramping was so bad she couldn't breathe. It was stupid to be so stubborn—tomorrow morning she would have her mother call the doctor to come over and save her.

But at midnight, watching the hands of the clock creep slowly, knowing everyone else was asleep, Ginger suddenly knew what was wrong with her. This was not a bad cold, or even a virus or the flu. She hadn't had the thought before because she wasn't a child anymore, and this was supposed to be a children's disease. Even her mother, who had hovered over her every summer of her childhood, kissing her on the forehead but actually testing her for fever, had not thought of the dreaded word this time.

She had polio.

Her first reaction was an instant of numbed disbelief; then the horror washed over her. There was an epidemic this summer, of course, as there was every summer, and the number of the newly afflicted was announced on the radio every day. Polio was the most terrifying thing in the world, but when you were young you lived your life and didn't think you'd get anything like that. She didn't know anyone personally who had polio. Strangers, of course, she'd seen them going by in their wheelchairs and braces, but luckily none of her friends. Now she wondered how she had been singled out. Had she given it to the children at the foundling hospital—one more stroke of bad luck for patients who'd had so much already—or had one of them infected her? What about that boy who had kissed her? No one even knew how you got infected. It was in the air.

The pain was so excruciating she thought of calling her parents to take her to the hospital, and then she dimly remembered the movie she'd seen as a kid about Sister Kenny. Immobilization was bad. People with polio held themselves tightly because of the pain, afraid to move and exacerbate it, and then the muscles went into spasm. If I just keep walking, Ginger thought, I won't get paralyzed. She got out of bed.

She walked all night, holding on to the walls, to furniture, fighting the pain that was like knives being driven into her leg muscles. As long as I'm upright, as long as I'm putting weight on them and moving, she told herself, then I can still walk, and as long as I can still walk I'm okay. But it was more than her own medical theory that propelled her. It was the fear of giving up, of letting the paralysis win. Maybe this is idiotic, she told herself once, at about three in the morning. They tell you to rest. You're not supposed to do anything. But if I stop, then I can't control my life anymore.

At six in the morning her legs gave way and she fell on the bed, and screamed for her mother.

Attendants took Ginger to the hospital in an ambulance, on a litter, to a scene of bedlam. It was a special isolation hospital for polio patients, not near where she lived. Behind a sign saying "Contagion, No Admittance," there were so many beds and cribs filled with sick children that there were even beds in the hall. The little kids were crying and wailing from pain and fright. The nurse at the desk let her parents stay to give information.

A doctor gave her a spinal tap under a local anesthetic, and then he came back and said she did indeed have polio. Rose's face was white and drained, and Ben looked grim, almost angry, although Ginger knew that look was fear.

"I walked all night," Ginger said to a nurse hurrying by. "Did I make it worse?"

"What is she saying?" Ben asked.

"You shouldn't have," the nurse said. "Lie still," and she was gone.

"Why did you do that?" Rose murmured. "Why?"

"What did she do?" Ben asked.

What kind of a doctor will I ever be? Ginger thought. I'm so stupid.

She was lying on her back, and now from the pull of her twisted muscles her legs were doubled up above her like a trussed chicken. She rolled onto her side because the sheet hurt them and because they looked so ridiculous. Everything hurt; she could tell she had a fever even before a nurse affirmed it. A medical assistant came by to see if she could breathe, holding a scalpel, and Ginger knew if she hadn't been able to he would have cut her throat open in an emergency tracheotomy. "Not bulbar," he said reassuringly to her parents, and then he, too, was gone.

There were three kinds of polio, she knew. Bulbar, which affected the respiratory system and could kill you; paralytic, which would ruin the rest of your life; and nonparalytic, from which you would recover. She prayed for the nonparalytic kind, but she was so sick she had her doubts that her prayers would be answered.

She was there and she wasn't there. Part of her was watching whatever she could see from her fetal position, stunned by all the activity, relieved that someone was going to do something for her. Her parents answered questions for someone with a clipboard, and after a while a man came by and wheeled her into a room and put her into a hospital bed, and a nurse gave her Empirin, which miraculously made the headache go away. Her parents, banished now, had disappeared. She was alone.

Not exactly alone. In the other bed there was a girl about her age, who was sobbing. "I can't move my arms," the girl kept saying. "How will I do anything anymore?"

Ginger surreptitiously moved her own arms and hands, relieved and a little guilty that she had been saved from that too. But what were they going to do about her legs? She was too miserable and frightened to think of anything comforting to say, and turned her face to the wall.

She lay in her hospital bed for three days with a fever, sometimes sleeping. Her parents were not allowed to see her because she was contagious, and she was too weak to protest that she had been living with them all this time and they hadn't gotten it from her. Hospitals turned you into a vegetable, made you dependent.

People in authority brought medicine, food, bedpans, dressed and undressed you, washed you, told you what to do. On top of all that she couldn't move her legs, so she couldn't get out of bed and she was in their power. Ginger could not remember ever being so depressed, and she wondered if it was a symptom of the illness or the actual helplessness that made her feel that her life was over.

As soon as the fever was gone a therapist, in that same pink uniform Ginger had worn such a short time ago at the other hospital where she worked—where she had been the healthy one taking care of other people—came into her room wheeling a big canister with steam coming out of it. She took hot packs out of it with tongs, and arranged them around Ginger's legs. The hot packs had the smell of wet wool, which they were, wool that had been soaked in boiling water and wrung out. Under that steamy moist wool there was finally the blessed relief of pain so she could relax again for the first time in what seemed like forever.

They brought the hot packs almost continuously for the next few days, and finally her legs straightened out, although she still couldn't move them. Then they took her on a stretcher into a room where there was a huge tank with a whirlpool in it. They lowered her into the warm swirling water and it felt wonderful. She began to understand that although she couldn't move her legs she would still have all her feeling. That was what polio did; it was not like a spinal cord injury, it was its own thing, destroying nerve cells near the spinal cord but not the spinal cord itself.

Ginger had a wheelchair now, and a nurse put it near the window so she could wave at her parents down there in the street. "Why can't they come up?" she demanded.

"They could carry the disease out to someone else," the nurse said.

"So could you."

A doctor came to examine her, accompanied by a different nurse. "Her legs are completely in flail," he said. What a strange word. Flailing? Flopping?

"What does that mean?" Ginger asked, fixing him with a fierce look so he would answer her. She had already discovered that many medical people talked above her and around her as if she wasn't there or couldn't hear or understand.

"No muscle activity," he said. The nurse was writing it down on Ginger's chart.

Like cooked spaghetti, Ginger thought. The feeling of unreality that had touched her when she first realized she had polio came back.

"We're going to send you home and start you on physical therapy," he said, finally looking into her face, as if she were more than just damaged legs.

"And?"

"And what?"

"Will it work?"

"We'll do the best we can."

The best we can, she thought.

The girl in the next bed had gone home, her arms no better, and had been replaced by a very ill younger girl who didn't move at all. The curtains around her bed had been pulled, and then to Ginger's surprise two people who seemed to be the girl's parents arrived, their faces covered with surgical masks. They went behind the curtains and she could hear the mother sobbing. Then they left, and a few minutes later the orderly who had brought Ginger into her room took the girl away, the sheet over her face, and Ginger realized she had died.

She had never seen anyone die before, and she hadn't seen it this time either. It had simply happened. The girl was there and then she disappeared. My life is not over, Ginger told herself then. No matter what happens, I will fight.

At last she saw her own parents again, in the lobby of the hospital when she was released to their care. She had a wheelchair, her father had brought the family car, and an orderly showed him how to fold the wheelchair so he could put it into the seat beside Ginger. How will I be able to do that myself? she wondered nervously. I'm not strong enough. If physical therapy didn't fix her legs, would it make her arms so powerful that they could do everything else? Fold and unfold wheelchairs, pull herself up to go to the toilet, to bathe? Walk with crutches? But therapy *would* fix her legs. She had to believe that.

When they got to the house Uncle Hugh and Joan were standing on the sidewalk watching the car drive up. Then Ginger saw that her parents had installed a wooden ramp for her leading down to the entrance of Uncle Hugh's room. "You two can switch rooms just for now," her mother said. "The stairs. . . ."

"Uncle Hugh…?"

"I don't mind," he said. "I've already moved some of my things."

"How do you feel, anyway?" Joan said. "I missed you."

"I missed you too. You have no idea how much." Her sister would never know that she had completely forgotten about her, about everyone but her parents, reduced to infancy. Ginger wondered if the polio had temporarily affected her brain. "How is Peggy?"

"She's fine," Rose said, "and she said she's really sorry she can't come to see you, but she's afraid because of the children. I told her we'd call her tonight if you felt up to it."

"Are people going to be afraid of me now?"

"Well, but no one knows anything about polio," Rose said, looking stricken. "It's so contagious."

"But I'm not contagious anymore."

"I know, dear. It's all right."

"Better safe than sorry," her father said. "But we know better, don't we." He put his arm around Joan.

They all think she's brave to come near me, Ginger thought, and felt a lump in her throat. How long am I going to be a pariah? First lethal, then helpless. Her father put her into the wheelchair and Rose pushed it down the ramp into Ginger's new room. Her books were there, and there were fresh flowers in a vase on the dresser. She forced a smile.

"When do you think the visiting nurses will have me walking again?" she asked.

"We aren't going to get you home therapy," Rose said. "You need more. Your father and I have made arrangements for you to go to Warm Springs. We were lucky to get you in. It's the best rehabilitation center in the country." Of course everyone had heard of Warm Springs, Georgia. It was the place President Roosevelt had founded. "You'll go at the end of the week."

"For how long?"

"You'll be there for from six months to a year, but you won't miss any school because they have a high school there," her mother said brightly.

A year? I'm only sixteen, too young to go so far away from home, Ginger thought in dismay. But then she realized she had no choice. She wasn't old enough to leave her family, now when she needed them more than ever before, but she wasn't old enough for her life to be over either. At Warm Springs she would get the best care. They would help her. "Thanks for the loan of your room, Uncle Hugh," Ginger said brightly. "But don't worry, I won't be using it when I get back, you'll see."

Her mother turned away, but not before Ginger noticed that her eyes were full of tears.

TWENTY

The rehabilitation center at Warm Springs was unlike anything Ginger had anticipated. Deep blue skies, dark green Georgia pines, red clay roads, purple wisteria; and, although its hundreds of wooded acres housed every kind of modern medical facility, it had the feel and atmosphere of a college campus.

Like a campus it was laid out in a rectangle of low, white stone buildings. There was a dining room, a recreation room, a theater where movies were shown free three times a week, a school, a large heated pool and dressing rooms, a brace shop where appliances were made for the disabled (which everybody was), a library, a children's ward, and even an apartment where a housewife could practice home management skills. Everything was nicely decorated.

Ginger's room was in a dormitory with other teenage patients. Outside, on the campus, there were "push boys," friendly and flirtatious, teenagers like her, who lived in town and had been hired to be always available to push wheelchairs wherever the patients wanted to go. There was a daily schedule of work: exercises with a therapist in the famous warm water of the pool or in the deep, claustrophobic Hubbard Tank, which she was not afraid of anymore, manipulation on a treatment table, land exercises on equipment to learn how to walk with braces and even climb stairs, and often there were patients watching and cheering the others on. Rehabilitation here was almost like a team sport. And there were parties, concerts, nice dinners, cute boys, romances, sex, and gossip.

But we are all damaged, she thought, *that's why we're here.* And despite the cheerfulness and laughter, she could never get that out of her mind. She knew the name of every muscle in her body now, the ones that would never work anymore and the ones that might take over for them. In the mornings when Ginger woke up there was always just one moment when she forgot she could not get up and walk, when the warm summer sun in her eyes reminded her only that there was a new day with things to be done. And then it was real again.

When she learned how to get out of bed and put herself into her wheelchair without assistance it was a triumph. Then she learned how to get by herself from the wheelchair into a regular chair, and into a car. They told her she would go to the theater, but she wondered who would take her. Nobody would want to date her now.

It was fall. Ginger looked at the pine trees outside her dormitory window and thought about New York. There was a tree outside her bedroom window in their town house, and she had always liked watching the seasons change in miniature, just for her. The leaves didn't turn here. She looked at her legs, already smaller, thin and dangling in her new metal braces, and at her arms and shoulders, by now stronger and more developed, larger, and remembered when she had thought she had the body of a ballerina. All that was over too. When she had arrived she had been impatient to get well and leave. Now she knew she would eventually leave but she would never be the way she'd thought she would be. She was afraid to go home.

Outside on that busy campus there were so many

wheelchairs they might have been an army. There were kids much worse off than she was, some in full body braces, some with utensils attached to their arms because they couldn't use their hands, and even ones almost like her, but who couldn't sit without discomfort because their gluteus muscles were gone. But despite all this tragedy, everywhere there were smiles, friendliness, joking, the sense of community. If people broke down and wept, and how could they not, you never saw it. Each one, in his or her way, had managed to make time stop. They all knew they were never going to be in a place like this again, where everyone was alike. Here, no matter how badly off, everyone was the norm. Nobody stared or turned away. Nobody talked over your head as if just because you were lower you were also deaf. Everyone understood.

Outside I'll be a freak, Ginger thought. We will all be.

She called her parents every few days and pretended to be happy. In a way, though, she *was* happy, because every little thing she learned to do on her own was a triumph, because every moment was filled with either useful activity or social life, and because she had made so many friends. But even these friends would be taken away from her when she left, she knew that. Scattered all over the United States they would go back to the real world and try to fit in. Somehow it didn't seem fair that each one of them would be alone. How could anyone, Ginger wondered, even her devoted parents, or sympathetic Grandma, or her worldly unconventional uncle, or her sisters whom she'd known all her life, ever know what it was really like for her? She very much doubted that any of the boys who had admired her in high school would want to ask her out now.

She was young, and healthy in every way except one. Such a big way....

But there was a boy here she liked. He had been at

Warm Springs longer than she had, and he was in a wheelchair, too, with paralyzed legs. As soon as Ginger met him she realized that he understood everything. He was her age, sixteen, but somehow, perhaps because of what he had been through, or because of his nature, he seemed older. He was the first boy her age Ginger had found interesting.

She had met him when they sat next to each other at the movies. The movie was *Gone With the Wind*, which they had all been too young to see the first time, and she thought it was painfully romantic. "Scarlett was such a fool," she told him when it was over, "and yet you have to admire her spirit." That broke the ice, they started to talk, and then they went to have coffee together.

His name was Christopher Riley, and he was from Boston. He was an Irish Catholic boy named after a saint, but one look at him and Ginger knew right away he was a rogue. He had greenish eyes and curly sandy-colored hair, sensuous lips, and a turned-up nose with a dusting of freckles on it. Standing up, he would have been tall. The minute she saw him come into the theater she was oddly attracted to his strong forearms and his long, graceful fingers, the way he wheeled himself around so expertly, as if it were only a game. At the coffee shop when he needed to cross his legs he plucked a piece of his trouser leg between his thumb and forefinger and flipped the leg over the other one with a casual nonchalance she admired. She knew his leg muscles were more atrophied than hers were in order for him to be able to do that so easily, but she also knew that hers would be that way too eventually. She supposed she would also be casual, but it seemed hard to imagine. She thought he was very brave.

"Try this," he said, putting a piece of coffee cake into her mouth. Then he smiled, and she smiled back. There was something extremely sensual about his feeding her, and they both felt it.

"So what are you going to do when you get out of here?" he asked.

"Finish high school. Go on to medical school if they'll let me, and become a doctor."

"No! So am I!"

"You're going to be a doctor too?" Ginger exclaimed.

"I'll probably do research," Christopher said. "You can sit down a lot in research, and also I want to solve medical mysteries and save an inordinate amount of people. That's all, just a minor little ambition."

"That's just what I want to do."

During that first long evening they made lists of things they had in common, things they liked and disliked, things they felt, and they told each other secrets. Ginger told him how she had walked all night when she knew she had polio, and how that had probably made her case worse than it would have been, and Christopher understood and said that even though it had been a dumb thing to do it represented survival and he was surprised he hadn't done the same thing himself.

"It was the last time I walked," Ginger said.

"Then that night was worth it."

They looked at each other. She wondered what it would be like to kiss him, and felt a little shiver of excitement. "They say I might be able to be on crutches sometimes," Ginger said. "But I'll always have the chair."

"Me too."

"Everyone wants to be on crutches. It's like you've advanced into the real world. Just to walk...! But you know, I find a wheelchair a lot more efficient."

"So do I. Still, you should try both."

"Oh, I will," Ginger said. "And if I have crutches I'll put ribbons on them."

"Good for you."

"It won't change what they are. But I'll do it anyway."

"I bet you will."

"Would you ask me out if you saw that? Colored ribbons? My bravery sign? Telling everyone who's sorry for me to go to hell?"

"I'd ask you out anyway."

I think I love him, Ginger thought.

"There's a lot of sex going on here, I guess you've heard," he said with a mischievous grin.

"Oh, I've heard."

"In the bushes. The third bush on the left after you leave the dining hall is a popular place."

"A girlfriend of mine told me she and a boy stopped the elevator between floors and did something or other," Ginger said. "I can't imagine they had much time."

"They had time," he said. "Everybody thought the elevator was out of order."

"You knew about it?"

"It wasn't the first occasion."

She had also heard, since there was an abundance of gossip here, mostly sexual, that people used Saran Wrap to make condoms, but of course she didn't mention it. She had only the vaguest idea of how you would keep such a contraption on. At home every unmarried girl was a virgin or pretended to be, and a pregnancy without a husband to make you respectable was every girl's worst fear. "This place certainly doesn't sound like home," Ginger said.

"Not the home I know."

They looked at each other.

"No rules," he said.

"Hooray for no rules," she said lightly. "Sometimes I think I'm dreaming."

A few months ago she wouldn't have believed she could be talking about sex like this with a boy, particularly one she had just met; but somehow here, and now, with this boy, it seemed right, safe, accepted. Like every girl she knew, Ginger believed in love at first sight. She had been fantasizing about the unknown lover for years, but she thought how amazing it was that just when she thought her romantic life was over before it had begun, she should have met this devastatingly attractive boy, here of all places.

Their hands inched together along the tabletop and then their fingers touched. I really do love him, she thought. He's gorgeous, he's perceptive, he's easy to talk to, he likes what I like, he wants to be a doctor too, and he'll always understand about being different.

"Do you know why they let us do what we want?" he said.

"Why?"

"They want us to feel normal. It's their way of getting us back into the mainstream. But being here is really a kind of vacation, Ginger. You know that, don't you?"

"Yes."

His smile faded. "What we all know is that when we get out of here and go home we're going to be freaks."

There, he had said it. *Freaks:* what Ginger had always thought, had always known. The world she had left behind for this brief time was too conformist; everyone had to be complete. "I won't leave," she said. "I'll stay here forever, I'll work here. I'll learn physical therapy."

"We're sixteen. We have to go home."

His hand, when he took hers, was strong and comforting, as she had known it would be. For the first time since all of this had happened to her, Ginger began to cry. The few people in the coffee shop ignored her and let her have her moment. She was shaking with sobs, and Christopher put his arm around her.

"I wish you lived on my street," she said. "I wish we went to school together. I wish you were my best friend."

"I could still be your best friend," Christopher Riley said.

"It's so unfair. Just this, just us, just everything."

When her grief subsided he pulled a handful of tissues out of his pocket and dabbed gently at her tears. "Will you be my girlfriend?"

"Where? In what stupid, perfect world?"

"Well, we're here. Could we start with here?"

"Yes," Ginger said.

They wheeled out of the coffee shop side by side, as if they were taking a walk—by themselves, without calling the push boys to help them—and they went to a secluded place they both knew about and he kissed her under the stars. The breeze rustled the pine trees and carried the scent to her with the sound. She had never been kissed like that; she felt it running through her body like electricity. His lips were full and soft and firm, and not wet like the boys she had known, even when he opened his mouth. He must have been practicing kissing for years, Ginger thought, and then she stopped thinking.

Their chairs impeded them and it was awkward, but they were able to hug and to feel one another. When he put his hands under her blouse Ginger did not stop him. When he touched her nipples she felt it clear down between her legs and could hardly catch her breath. When he tugged at the elastic of her panties she helped him. His fingers were caressing her then, inside and out, and she pressed against his hand, feeling waves of pleasure that were a revelation. She was an innocent girl of her time, despite everything, despite what her mother thought, and she had never masturbated. It was what the husband was supposed to do to you. To do it to yourself was embarrassing. She did not want Christopher Riley ever to stop.

He unzipped his pants with his other hand and took out his long, hard penis, white in the moonlight, and put her hand on it. Just holding it was enough; he was a boy, after all, and he ejaculated right away. He had more tissues for that. In a little while they did it all over again, and that time he showed her how to rub.

She couldn't believe she was doing something like this. For years, it seemed, she had been warned about getting "carried away," and she had thought it was parental propaganda. But all she wanted was to be with him, to be with him forever. "Carried away" was sex and it was love.

After that night they met as often as possible, and everyone was aware they were a couple. Since Ginger was determined that carried away would not be allowed to be the same as "going all the way," they did everything with their lips and hands. He taught her things she had never read about, and she told him to do the things she had discovered she liked. Despite the virtual absence of rules, you couldn't bring a person of the opposite sex into your bedroom, so everything she did with Christopher Riley happened out of doors, even when it got too cold. Once they tried the stop-the-elevator trick, just to see how it would be, but it made her nervous. They were Romeo and Juliet, they were fated for tragedy, and they were insatiable.

It comforted Ginger to remember that her sister Peggy had been only seventeen when she got married, a year older than she was. But Ed had been older, a veteran, a man. Chris was a high school kid, and a long way from making any real money or living on his own. Ginger didn't know what kind of promises you could make or extract, and Chris got upset when she tried to talk about the future. They would call each other, of course, even write, and because Boston wasn't so far from New York they hoped to visit. But in the back of her mind Ginger suspected that things would get in the way of a happy ending, that life itself would be on their fragile romance like a pack of wild dogs and tear it to pieces.

"We should apply to the same college," she told him.

"Yes. We'll go together."

"And then the same medical school."

"Yes."

And what were the chances of their both getting in? Easier for him, he was a male, but she was a female and medical schools accepted one girl for every ten boys. She would have to go to college and probably medical school near home, so she could live with her family, where she knew they would fix everything she had to use so it would be accessible for the handicapped. And she needed a school with elevators, and wide doors, and no steep curbs, as did he. Maybe by the time they were actually going to medical school things would have changed; they could get an apartment together with everything the right height, and safety bars, and get engaged…. Even if they couldn't afford to get married for a long time they could break the rules because they were already "different" to begin with.

How crazy; she had only recently learned how to give herself a bath, and already she was planning on living with a man. First things first. It was easier not to think about it.

"Have you made nice friends?" her mother kept asking her during their phone calls.

"Yes," Ginger said. And finally, "I'm going with a boy."

"A patient?"

"Same as I am."

"I'm glad you're having a social life, dear. But be

sure it doesn't get in the way of your studies. When you come home I want you to be able to graduate with your old friends.''

It was clear that no one would take her love affair seriously. But it didn't matter. Ginger took it seriously. Chris had put her ruptured world together again, and sometimes, despite her misgivings, she thought that she would make it work, that she wasn't going to lose him, that somehow, sometime, somewhere, they would have a life with one another. You couldn't want something that desperately and not have a chance.

TWENTY-ONE

Seven months after she went away to Warm Springs, Ginger came home. There was nothing more they could do for her. It was deep winter in New York, with a cutting wind, and snow. The city streets were icy and the whole family wondered how and even if Ginger would be able to navigate herself. Ben wheeled her down the ramp into her room, Hugh's room, now hers for good because it was on the ground floor. Safety bars had been installed in her bathroom. There was a low rack in the closet so she could reach her clothes. Her crutches were propped against the bedroom wall. Ginger could walk with them, but at a painstaking, crablike crawl, and she was more comfortable with her wheelchair. Rose and Ben had already investigated getting a motorized wheelchair for her, and one was on order, the best, the newest technology.

They were doing whatever they could, but of course there were some things all the good will in the world could not accomplish. Rose knew this was a fact because of all the things that had happened to her in her life, but she pretended it was not so, that everything you did mattered. It made no sense, but she was a mother.

Everyone came to visit Ginger when she came back—as if they were coming to look at a new baby, which in a way she was, or as if they were coming to pay a condolence call, which in a way they were.

Maude came down from Bristol, as did Daisy, and even Harriette from Washington, D.C. They had no idea how to deal with what had happened. Daisy brought her a lacy bed jacket, as if she were sick in bed.

Celia popped in every day now, but she was more cheerful and realistic. She brought presents too, but Celia liked to give gifts, so it was not all that significant. One of Celia's hobbies was shopping, but then she got tired of what she had bought and gave it away to the grandchildren. She presented Ginger with a tiny diamond and ruby ring she had found at an antique shop. "For luck," she said slyly. "To bring you a boyfriend."

"I have one," Ginger replied as slyly, and put the ring on the third finger of her left hand.

Ginger had her own phone in her room, the phone that had been Hugh's, and the very first thing she had done when she came home was call Boston to speak to Christopher. He had been released too, she said, and she had promised to let him know how she was. Rose left her to her privacy.

Ginger called him every night, and he called her too, but not as often. Girls didn't telephone boys; they played hard to get, they waited, but Ginger would have none of that. She kept saying that she and Christopher Riley were different from other people, and although Rose suspected that was what everyone in love thought, she pleasantly agreed. The conversation she would have normally had with her daughter, her objection that this boy was a Roman Catholic and would want Ginger to convert, or at the least bring up their children in his faith, was not one Rose was prepared to have at this time. The fact that Ginger needed a husband who was able-bodied and could take care of her was another conversation Rose put off. She felt Ginger's crush was a Band-Aid on a larger wound, and whatever it was, if it helped for now then that was fine.

Because at least Ginger had a crush, Rose thought, something to make her feel like other girls her age. Only one of her friends had come by since she had been home, her best friend, Nancy, but she would see the rest of them when she went back to high school next week, and Rose thought hopefully that as soon as they saw Ginger was the same girl they had all liked so much before she went away, her friends would rally round and things would be as they had been before. They were teenagers, they were self-conscious, they didn't know how to handle things. Ginger's condition scared them. But when Ginger and Nancy went into her room and shut the door, Rose soon could hear music and giggles and shrieks emanating and knew everything would be all right.

Yet, every day it seemed there was something to remind you that everything was different whether you liked it or not. The people at the hospital where Ginger used to do her volunteer work had sent her flowers, but then when she called to thank them they told her she couldn't have her job back. It would be too difficult, they said, she couldn't wheel the children, she couldn't carry them, or dress them.... She could read to them, she said, and hug them, and play board games with the ones who were capable of it. They answered that they would see.

As for her high school friends, they continued to be remarkably absent, except for the faithful Nancy. "It's all right," Ginger said, when Rose seemed concerned. "Everybody needs only one best friend. The rest are a waste of time."

She had gotten very good marks at the high school in Warm Springs, and had already decided that she would go to NYU. That is, she added, if Chris wanted to go with her. There were some problems there too. He told her his parents wanted him close to home. There were many colleges and universities for him to choose from in his area, and he wasn't ruling them out. Ginger was surprised; Rose was not.

"But he promised," she wailed to Rose. "We discussed it. What will I do?"

Forget him and find somebody else, was the answer Rose would ordinarily have given to a daughter of hers, but she couldn't get the words out. Who would Ginger find? He would have to be very special, very kind, very loving, and *how* would she find him? Would she have to spend her life alone? The thought was unbearable, but it had often entered Rose's mind lately. Her daughter was only sixteen, and already Rose was worrying about how she needed a perceptive man who would appreciate her. Of course she had wanted that for her other daughters: Peggy, who had lucked out so early, and Joan, whose days and nights were a disquieting mystery; but Rose had never worried about Peggy and Joan the way she now did about Ginger. There were things she simply could not do to make her youngest daughter's emotional life easier, and the thought broke Rose's heart.

She remembered the fortune-teller she had gone to with Celia as a lark, so many years ago, when she was young. The woman had told her she would be rich and have a surprising life, and when she had married Ben everyone thought the prediction had come true. But money was not riches, and surprises were not necessarily good. She promised me an extraordinary life, Rose realized. I didn't know what that meant, but I do now. If I can help my daughter fulfill her dreams, then that is what she meant. Ginger will be a doctor. Ginger will be independent. I will do whatever I can to help her, and when she has her dream then I will know what my life was about.

Hugh found himself a little short of closet space upstairs in Ginger's old room. After all, she'd had only

dresses, while he had suits *and* dresses. The rest of fitting in was not so hard. Luckily she'd had white
painted walls instead of girlish flowered wallpaper—
an eccentric insistence of hers as a child when her
mother asked her how she would like her room to be
decorated—so there was little he had to do. He had
kept his sleigh bed, of course, and his favorite pieces,
but the antique shop had benefited from quite a few of
them because of this new limited space. Teddy had
benefited too, in his bachelor apartment, with a pair of
masculine leather chairs, and a mirror-framed Vene-
tian mirror that Hugh had to talk him into accepting
because Teddy thought it looked too gay.

What kind of mongrel apartment would we two
have if we lived together, Hugh wondered. He also
wondered, at this moment in time, having turned fifty,
if he shouldn't get an apartment of his own. He could
rent something within walking distance of Teddy's,
and entertain him in his own home at last, as often as
he liked, in whatever way he liked. He could dress as
Camille in dishabille if he wanted, and when Teddy
found it claustrophobic he could go back to his safe
bachelor lair.

After all this time Teddy still could not come to grips
with his feelings about Hugh in drag. Sometimes he
liked it and found it seductive, sometimes it made him
uncomfortable. On Halloween Hugh had gone out as
Camille with his own friends. Afterward he had met
Teddy in an obscure coffee shop far on the West Side,
because Teddy didn't want him to feel rejected. Poor
Teddy, Hugh thought. It was one thing for him to accept that he fell in love with a gay man, but that the
man was a drag queen was quite another. Still, you
love whom you love, and you take everything that
comes in the package. You worked out your problems
in a relationship by facing them. It was not normal,

Hugh thought, for a grown man to continue living with his birth family.

Family... The things we chose when we were young and thought were heartwarming and wonderful often lose their luster, Hugh thought sadly. I imagined I would be happy forever with my sister Rose, and with her children, and now I think the ultimate paradise would be to share an apartment with Teddy and have a dog. He wondered when society would change enough for him to have his wish. The two of them would be so old, he mused grumpily, that no one would care that they were living together because two old codgers like that needed to lean on each other.

He started to look at apartments. There were a few he actually liked: one with a terrace overlooking the East River, another with a little garden. But when the real estate agent pressed him for a commitment Hugh delayed, and finally demurred. He wanted to leave his family, as if the new apartment would be a kind of halfway house, and yet a part of him didn't want to leave, and he wasn't sure why.

One evening when he came home Ginger was waiting for him in the living room. "Uncle Hugh," she said, "would you take me up to my old room?"

"Of course." He lifted her from her wheelchair with comparative ease and carried her up the stairs. People were always surprised that someone as effeminate as he was should be so strong, but then, Ginger was rather light. When they got upstairs he set her on the bed.

"Ahh," she sighed, looking around. "It's different, isn't it."

"Yes, of course."

"I had this silly idea that I wanted to say good-bye to my old room," Ginger said. "At first I was afraid I'd get upset. And now there's no old room to say good-bye to."

"Ginger, you can come up here any time you want."

"Thank you. But you know what I mean."

"None of us want to leave anything," Hugh said. "Our family probably more than most."

"Not Peggy."

"No, there's always the misfit who has a happy life." They looked at each other and laughed.

"What will become of you, Uncle Hugh?" Ginger asked.

"Me? What do you mean?"

"I just always wondered if you...how can I say it? If there was ever a significant man in your life."

"Me?"

"You're talking to Ginger, not Mom. Everyone falls in love sometime, don't they? I did. I am. Why not you?"

So someone had finally asked. Hugh felt a lump in his throat. God bless you, Ginger, the somnambulist, my soul mate. "Yes," he said. "I am in love. There's a man I've been seeing for five years."

"Then where is he?"

"We're secret," Hugh said. "He's a very straight kind of man, with a straight job. We can't have people talking."

"What's his name?"

Hugh hesitated for only an instant. "Teddy," he said then.

"Where did you meet him?"

"You won't believe this, dearie," Hugh said, smiling and warming to the topic. "We met at aversion therapy."

"No!" Ginger shrieked and fell back on the bed. "I remember when I was a little kid and they kept sending me out of the room so I wouldn't know, but I knew anyway. Oh, if Grandma knew she'd have a fit. She's the matchmaker!"

The matchmaker. He hadn't thought of it like that,

but in a way it was true. They both laughed until they had tears in their eyes. "We won't tell her, though," Hugh said.

"Of course not." Ginger thought for a moment. "I'd like to meet him. Could I?"

"You want to meet Teddy?"

"Why not? You could take me out to lunch."

"All right," Hugh said. "I guess he has to meet someone in the family sometime."

"I'm glad we had this little visit," Ginger said.

He took her downstairs then and put her in her wheelchair, and walked over to the antique store to call Teddy. He had gotten into the habit of calling Teddy from there, not because someone in the household would listen in, but it made them both feel safer. Teddy agreed to lunch, and they made the plans; he sounded amused, but also almost eager. I should have done this a long time ago, Hugh thought.

Walking home to the town house, he thought again about why he was so ambivalent about leaving the bosom of his family. They were necessary to each other. Most of all now, Ginger needed him. And he needed her—for the moment—not that things wouldn't change later on in a better world, if he lived long enough to see it, but for now, they were both outcasts. They had one powerful thing, however, and Hugh saw it now clearly as the miraculous force it was; they had love.

Peggy had made the effort to come into New York to visit Ginger several times, once with the children and the other times alone. She had an excellent house-keeper now, Mrs. McCoo, who cleaned up and also took care of Peter and Marianne when Peggy and Ed went out. It still felt strange to give orders to a woman who was older than she was; things should have been the other way around. Mrs. McCoo was an English war bride who had married a virtual stranger. Her husband had never managed to make ends meet, so now she worked in other people's houses. Peggy shared her with another woman on the block, who had recommended her.

On the days when Peggy came into the city to see Ginger, Ed met her later and they went out the way they always had. If the family was disappointed that they didn't stay for dinner, no one made an issue of it, and if they were surprised at being deserted there was no sign either. Peggy and Ed were country mice enjoying their night in the city. Of course they always went back to Larchmont to sleep.

"You could bring the children and stay over," Rose sometimes offered gently. "I would be glad to babysit." But she knew Peggy didn't want to stay that long; her own little world was so tight.

"Mom, they're so much trouble for me I wouldn't wish that on you," Peggy would answer gaily, rolling her eyes. She liked to pretend her children were annoying, because her friends did that with theirs, but the truth was she didn't mind at all. What would she do if she didn't have her children?

All their little lives she had worried about polio—the plague—watching them, feeling their foreheads for temperature, keeping them away from public places and even other children when the summer epidemics struck. At night she prayed for their safety, and in the morning she always thanked God when she saw they were still well. And now here was her sister Ginger, a polio victim. It was ironic, strange, and frightening.

Every time Peggy saw Ginger now she felt a little ill, and she didn't know why. It was more than sympathy or anger, she was sure. She was constantly reminded that it could have happened to one of her own children. In a way, Ginger's fate was a reproach. It was almost as if Ginger was a sacrifice. There was a limit on the bad things that could happen in one family, or in one life, Peggy believed, and the disaster had happened to Ginger instead of her own Peter or Marianne. She had no idea why, and she was too superstitious to mention this to anyone, even Ed. Sometimes, when she looked at Ginger imprisoned in her wheelchair or struggling to walk on her crutches, Peggy felt guilt and fear. The fact that Ginger was so cheerful, happy, and normal, made it worse.

Aside from pretending things were as they had always been, which was, of course, ridiculous, Peggy knew there was nothing, *nothing* she could do. Did the sleepwalker walk in her dreams? Peggy brought Ginger magazines and home-baked cookies, as if she were still in the hospital. Then Ginger surprised her by prattling on about her boyfriend in Boston, and things that she was doing at school, and Peggy knew she herself would never understand what it was like. If it had happened to one of her children she knew she would never have been able to deal with it. She didn't know how Rose handled it.

Joan was staying at home more these days. Her affair with Henry Collins was long over, and so were her affairs with Frank Abruzzi and Steven Cohen, neither of whom she had ever mentioned or brought home to meet her family. Her parents wouldn't have liked them anyway—scruffy beatniks, no money, into the arts. She needed to keep her two worlds separate, for everyone's sake.

Her heart had been dented but it had never been broken. She was twenty-four, and people wondered why she wasn't married yet. She wasn't sure herself. She thought it was because she wanted to be free. This was a concept that had rarely occurred to a girl her age in her time, since all of them believed that marriage was the happy ending. So happy, in fact, and such an ending, that there was very little thought about what would happen afterward. Joan had thought about her aversion to legal commitment, and her conclusion was that she would be obliterated as an individual.

These were things men called their wives: the little woman, my ball and chain, my better half. She thought the latter was condescending, that no man would actually believe it. It was bad enough that her parents still had to support her, or at least keep such a nice roof over her head, but what would be insupportable would be having to ask a man for money. Peggy, she knew, had an allowance from Ed. An allowance! Like a child! Peggy felt their marriage was a partnership and was proud of it; she took care of the home front and Ed went out to the wars. The war had changed, it was advertising now, not guns and bombs, but their position was essentially the same.

Everyone in the family had been affected by what had happened to Ginger, and Joan had too. She was beginning to realize for the first time how much they all really cared about and needed one another. Her parents had never been strict, they had been tactful and accepting. The three sisters were very different, but still, they had a bond. It was a shame, Joan began to think, that she and Peggy had grown so far apart.

She should go to visit Peggy in the suburbs, invite herself for a weekend. How dreary could it be? She wanted to get to know her little nephew, and her baby niece. How could you object to nature, to fragrant grass and trees, or to clean, white, fluffy snow? She and Peggy could have the kind of heart-to-heart talks they had never had but that Joan saw female friends doing on television. They would sit in the kitchen and have coffee. The idea became so appealing she called Peggy on the phone.

"Peggy, I've been thinking. I'd love to come to visit

you for a weekend sometime soon. Or during the week, and stay over."

"You would?" Of course what Peggy was really saying was *why?*

"Mending fences," Joan said.

"Mending what?"

"You know. Doing sister stuff."

"Great," Peggy said. She actually seemed to mean it. "This weekend we have to go to a dinner party, but you could come the one after that. Bring warm clothes and waterproof shoes. We'll take a long walk. Gee, I can't think of a lot of things to amuse you. I hope you aren't bored."

"I won't be bored," Joan said.

She went up to Larchmont on the train, and Peggy met her at the station. They hadn't been alone together for a very long time, and the two of them were self-conscious for the first few hours, but then they both warmed up. Peggy stopped being such a good hostess and Joan stopped being the polite guest. They started to laugh together. The kids seemed glad to be able to spend a weekend with their Aunt Joan, because for the first time Peggy had prepared them with a glowing report that made Joan seem worldly and interesting.

"Could you show me how to write a poem?" Peter asked.

"Sure."

"Here's *Aunt Joan*," Peggy said to baby Marianne, in that enthusiastic voice people put on for small children to make them think it's a good thing.

When Ed came home for dinner he made martinis. Joan got high and began to think that her sister and brother-in-law were absolutely lovely people, that they were lucky to be so attracted to each other after all these years, and that the kids were as cute as could be.

After that she came to visit them again from time to time, bringing house gifts even though it wasn't necessary. "Take Aunt Joan to her room, Peter," Peggy would say, as if it were really hers.

Who would have thought that prickly Joan could have changed? Part of the time she felt as if she were watching her step, not to fall, wondering who this cordial person was she had become, or at least was pretending she had become. There was still something unreal about the bond she was forging with Peggy, but Joan wanted to try. Maybe Peggy wasn't all that interesting, maybe they were too different, with different values and goals, maybe she herself in many ways wasn't even worthy enough to be a part of their world, but Joan wanted herself and Peggy to be again the way they had been when they were very young, before people became judgmental, when they had simply accepted each other, when love had been a given and not something that had to be earned.

It was April, 1955. And then the bombshell struck, the news that changed everything. "The vaccine works," a little-known doctor named Jonas Salk announced, and became famous overnight. There had been a year of clinical trials on humans, and now the polio vaccine he had discovered would be given to people. In the beginning, while they were making more, the inoculations would be restricted to children and pregnant women, because the research had shown those were the ones most likely to contract polio. Later on, everyone would be able to have them. Of course, until the vaccination program was up and running on a massive national scale there would still be cases, but everything had changed now, it would be a new world. The most terrifying plague of the first half of the twentieth century had been conquered.

But for Ginger, and Christopher, and their friends, who had once been statistics and now had become a part of history, it was too late.

TWENTY-TWO

Her junior year in high school hadn't been hard, but when the summer came Ginger was glad to be alone again. Not that she hadn't been alone at school. But this way she could go to the public library and take out books, she could read, she could hide. She read a book every day, novels and nonfiction, but more often she devoured anything about medicine. No reason, she thought, why she shouldn't get a head start on her life.

She had tried the motorized wheelchair, but found it too clunky and unwieldy with its big battery; it could hardly fit into a crowded elevator, she couldn't gauge the speed, it didn't fold into a car. Her parents said they would wait until there were better ones, and replaced it with a conventional wheelchair so she could be in control. But she still had to fight her feeling of not being able to take charge of her existence. Curbs still made her stomach lurch because she kept thinking she would tip over and fall out, break her skull, or lie helplessly on the ground until the cops came. This was not a silly fear, it was a distinct possibility. Usually her mother or father, or Uncle Hugh, insisted on going with her to the library, to help with the curbs, to push her when she got tired, to protect her. Her father had driven her to high school every day too, and it emphasized her differentness. The other kids went to school by themselves, walking or taking public transportation. Everyone her age wanted to look alike, dress alike, do the same things. Every little difference counted, and it was cruel.

Christopher had a summer job, working in his father's office, sitting down behind a desk in his wheelchair, fitting in, liking it, pleased with himself. They still talked on the phone several times a week. Well, twice a week, tops. It hurt her not to speak to him more often because she had so many things to say to him, and because she was keeping a kind of record. She would wait until Thursday, and if he hadn't called, she would call him. Once, suffering, sweating, and sleepless, Ginger didn't call him for an entire week, but then, finally, on Monday he called her.

"Where have you been?" he asked, as if she had neglected him, as if her life were interesting and she had better things to do than keep in touch with him. She had felt relieved, but also disappointed. She had hoped their relationship was better than that; that they didn't have to play games.

But of course she was the one playing games; he had no idea. He was living his life, he didn't count days the way she did. He called her when he thought of her. She thought about him all the time.

She remembered their months at Warm Springs, and their kisses, and the sex; she relived the night he had asked her if she would be his girlfriend, and she missed him terribly. "Do your parents mind that you make long-distance calls?" she asked him.

"No. Why?"

"I just thought they might. Mine don't."

"Mine don't either," Chris said. "But you're the only person I call who lives out of town."

Oh, how she glowed when he said that. She was still special to him. But then Ginger wondered, as she had to, whether Chris had so many friends, and even girlfriends now, that he didn't need the past. She was afraid to ask him.

At the end of that summer, when Ginger was about to go back to school and was busy with the purchase of school clothes, Aunt Harriette surprised everyone in the family by getting married. Celia told them, delighted that she could stop worrying about her renegade daughter at last. Imagine that, Ginger thought; Aunt Harriette is ancient, why, she must be over forty. Who would think she would fall in love and get married at her age? Not to mention her reputation. Her new husband, Julius Wanderer, was a well-to-do shoe manufacturer, quite a bit older than she was, with two grown children, and he was divorced. Had Harriette broken up this marriage? Who would ever know; she wasn't telling.

What she did reveal to them was that Julius was Jewish, and that although he didn't mind that she didn't convert to his religion, out of respect she was learning to make gefilte fish and other specialties so that she could do his holidays for him. Their family found the situation exotic.

"Harriette, you cooking anything, imagine!" Rose laughed on the phone. "And gefilte fish!"

"It's quenelle of pike," Harriette told her. "You made that once, remember?"

The happy couple had gotten married privately in Washington, the ceremony conducted by a judge Harriette knew. She had registered her dishes and silver pattern, just like a young bride, and they would live in Boston because that was where Julius was from. She said she hoped everyone would come to visit her. Ginger knew who would.

"Mom, we all have to go to Boston," Ginger insisted. "Just for a weekend. She has a house, she told us. I can stay on the ground floor."

"And see Christopher Riley," Rose said, smiling.

"Well, of course."

When her mother agreed, Ginger was overjoyed. She

called Chris and told him. They hadn't seen each other
for almost seven months. Seven, she thought, was her
number. Seven months in Warm Springs, seven
months parted from the boy she loved....

"Great," he said. "You can come over for dinner and
meet my family."

Family, that was good, they were friends. But Ginger
couldn't help wondering where and if she and Chris
would be able to hold each other and touch and kiss
with all this family around. "I miss Warm Springs,"
she said. "Don't you?" She hoped he would get it.

"Some things," he said, in the mischievous tone she
remembered with love and lust, and she knew he did.

The four of them, Rose and Ben and Ginger and
Hugh, went to Boston together on the train. Peggy and
Ed, with their children, had decided to defer their visit
until a time when there wouldn't be so many people
for Harriette to deal with. Joan didn't go to Boston either, because she had to work at the coffeehouse on
weekends. That was when it was crowded, and she
was allowed to read her poetry.

"How pretty!" Rose exclaimed when they got there.
"In some ways it reminds me of Bristol."

Aunt Harriette and her new husband lived in a suburb called Brookline, in a two-story house with white
columns in front of it and a gray roof. They had large
trees, and a flower garden. There was a little brass or-
nament attached to the door frame, which Harriette
told them was called a mezuzah, and that it was a part
of her husband's religion, something a good Jew put
on his door frame for luck.

"How charming," Rose said.

Like the religious Catholics hang crosses on the
walls of their houses, Ginger thought, and wondered if
Chris's family had crucifixes around. He had never
acted as if his parents were particularly pious. She realized that she knew so much about him and yet she

didn't know anything about where he came from. The two of them had not discussed their families except in passing; they had talked about themselves, the most interesting subjects in the world.

Julius was an almost elderly, massive, handsome man with a large head and thick gray hair. Aunt Harriette seemed to have become more Jewish than he was. It was Friday night, and he took the family to a seafood restaurant that was a favorite of his, and on the way she told them that she would have been perfectly happy to make a traditional Sabbath meal but that he didn't want her to. "I had that with my first wife," he said. "I don't need that. She was the one who cared."

She'd better not turn into his first wife, Ginger thought. As exotic and strange as the family found Julius Wanderer, so did he find Harriette Smith. It was their difference that seemed to have attracted them to each other. Although Ginger had not had much life experience, she had never met two people so unlike, and she could see they flourished on it. She hoped Aunt Harriette would stay her crazy, nervous self and let Julius keep rescuing her.

Ginger had telephoned Chris the moment she had arrived, and they had made plans to have dinner at his house on Saturday. He had extended the invitation to her parents too, but they had promised to let Julius and Harriette take them to their country club, so Uncle Hugh volunteered to drop her off at the Rileys', in one of the Wanderers' two cars, and join the others later. Ginger put him on the phone with Chris to get the directions.

She hated that people always had to take her places, as if she were still a child. But she could hardly sleep the night before for excitement that she was going to see him at last. How would they have to behave in front of his parents? Would they kiss hello? Shake hands? She supposed formality was the best course to take until his parents decided they liked her. She had no idea how much Chris had told them about her, if anything.

It seemed as if everyone she knew lived in the suburbs of Boston, although there was a large central city. Christopher Riley's family lived in a suburb called Newton. They had a nice white-painted house like Aunt Harriette's, and grass and trees. Chris opened the front door himself, sitting in his wheelchair—the same beautiful muscular arms, the same adorable face. Ginger was so in love that her breath caught in her throat at the sight of him. Nothing had changed, not the way he looked, or the way she felt.

"I'm the uncle and I'm late to dinner," Uncle Hugh said, and left.

"Oh, Chris," Ginger said. "Oh, Chris…" She looked into his eyes and thought she was going to die right there.

"Hey," he said. "You tied ribbons on your wheelchair."

"The way I said I was gong to do with my crutches," she murmured, telling herself not to feel hurt. She had expected a more romantic greeting. Look at *me*, she thought, you're not like the others, who only see the equipment. Do I look pretty, sexy? Are you glad to see me? Then his mother appeared behind him, a slender sandy-haired woman, wearing a green dress and an apron. She had Chris's turned-up nose and sensuous lips, or rather, Ginger supposed, he had hers.

"Mom, this is my friend Ginger Carson, from Warm Springs," Christopher said.

"Come right in, dear. How nice of you to visit us when I know you have your family. Chris has spoken about you often."

What am I to think? Ginger thought in despair. Nice of me to visit? But at least he did talk about me, he mentioned my name. "Thank you," she said. "It was good of you to invite me."

His father, dark-haired, and from whom Chris got his height, rose from his seat in front of the television set to greet her. "How about a Coke?"

"Thank you."

His father gave them Cokes and went back to his TV, while his mother went back to making the dinner, leaving Ginger and Chris alone. He immediately took her on a guided tour of the ground floor. The furniture was modern, there were watercolors on the walls, and no crucifixes. "My room," he said finally, leading the way in there.

He shut the door, and then he leaned over and kissed her. Ginger felt it just as if it had been the first time. She kissed him back, and held on to him, but then he moved away.

"My parents," he whispered. "We can't get excited."

Ginger looked around his room. He had posters of sports figures and racing cars, and on the bookcase there were some tennis trophies he had won before all this happened to him. "The emotional life goes on," she said.

"What?"

"Your room. The things we like. Our dreams."

"Oh, yes."

He knew her, they were in tandem again. "Where's your sister?" Ginger asked. He had a younger sister who was twelve.

"She'll be thundering down any minute."

Ginger looked at his bed, a single bed, like hers, the first time she had ever seen any bed he lay on at night. She imagined lying on it with him. There was a night table next to the bed, and on the table a black telephone. That was where he took her calls. She found it all overwhelmingly intimate.

"I missed you so much," she said.

"I'm glad you could come tonight."

"Me too."

There was a framed photograph on the night table, of four people, two boys and two girls. They were all smiling. One of them was Chris. He was sitting down and the other three were standing up, leaning over him to get into the shot. The picture had apparently been taken at a party. Their eyes were orange from the flash-bulb. Next to it was a more formal framed photo of a girl alone, the same girl as one of those in the group picture. She was pretty, with short brown hair, and now you could see her eyes were dark.

"Who is that?" Ginger asked.

"Oh, my friend Laura."

"You have her picture?"

"Why not?"

"I don't know." You don't have mine, Ginger thought. She felt something cold crawling up her arms and waited for it to overtake her heart. "Is she an old friend?"

"We go to school together."

Then why do you need her picture by your bed when you see her every day, Ginger wanted to say. But she didn't.

"I guess I'm jealous," she said lightly, and smiled.

He didn't smile back. "You shouldn't be jealous," he said. "I live here, you live in New York. I have people here, and a life. You have one too, don't you?"

"I tell you everything I do."

"You do?"

"Yes."

He shrugged. "You're the best friend I ever had, Ginger," he said. "Nothing will change our friend-ship."

The cold creature had touched her heart now. She didn't know what had happened to love, but all she knew was that she had become his friend. His best friend, but only that. "Is Laura your girlfriend now?" she asked, and immediately wished she hadn't.

"For now." He sounded embarrassed.

"Are you going to go to college with *her*?"

"No. I don't know. Why are you asking me these things?"

"Because I guess you're not going to college with me."

"My parents want me to go to B.U. I probably will. I told you I was thinking about it." He looked distressed, as if he had been unjustly accused of some sin he knew nothing about.

"She can walk, can't she," Ginger said bitterly. Her words sat there for a moment, a hated presence, showing who she was and who he was, and how the world was. He looked even more distressed, as if he would like to depart, but of course he couldn't; it was his house, and where would he go?

"Do you think that's why I *like* her?" Chris said.

"I don't know why you like her."

There was a rapping on the door. "Dinner is ready," his mother's cheerful voice called out.

"I'm sorry, Chris," Ginger whispered. "I didn't mean to start a fight."

"Oh, that wasn't a fight," he said. He put his arm around her and squeezed her shoulder, and then he kissed her cheek. "Come on, let's go."

Ginger could hardly eat a bite of the meal his mother had obviously prepared with care, a special dinner— roast beef and Yorkshire pudding and home-baked chocolate layer cake—and she knew she was being impolite. His parents asked her harmless personal questions, about school and home and her family and her interests, and she answered them, trying not to cry. Chris's little sister, who looked just like him, seemed bewildered. Children always picked up on tension. Chris didn't say much either. I should never have come, Ginger thought. But it's good to have reality. We are still best friends. We are. And people change from friends to lovers after time, it's the best way, friends first. We did that once before, the night we met, and we can do it again. We have years. We're both young.

"Hey, Dad," Chris said, "do you have film in the camera?"

"Yes."

"Then would you take a picture of Ginger and me? Neither of us has one."

Why are you doing this, Ginger thought, but the coldness in her heart began to thaw. His father got the camera. Chris, who was sitting next to Ginger at the table, put his arm around her and smiled. He was so sweet, she thought. He had to have some love for her to want to pacify her this way....

"I'll mail it to you," Chris said to her.

"Will you frame yours?" she asked lightly.

"Of course."

"Then so will I."

After the family and their guest had finished dinner and sat in the living room for a while making more small talk until there was literally nothing left to say—almost to the point where Ginger thought someone should be humming—Uncle Hugh appeared to take her home. She had never had dinner with a boy's family before, and this occasion didn't bode well for what she hoped would be others to come with other boys. But she still loved Christopher Riley. Nothing could change that. Maybe she would never have to have dinner with other boys' parents; who would ask her anyway? And she could always say no.

At the front door she shook hands with his parents and thanked them, and then Christopher kissed her. It was a quick kiss so his parents wouldn't think it was anything but good night, but he put his tongue into her mouth. He was being seductive, he felt safe because she was leaving, he wanted her to keep on wanting him. She understood all this, because she had always understood him, but she didn't understand that it was manipulative.

"Call me tomorrow," he whispered to her. "Okay?" Of course she would.

TWENTY-THREE

Lately, like touching her tongue to an aching tooth, Joan had been seriously thinking about her life. It was 1956. Time was marching on. She was growing more and more aware that she needed to pull herself together and get a normal job, or even to do the previously unthinkable: find a man she could bear to marry and start a family of her own. She was twenty-five already, and if not now then when? She was accustomed to being the black sheep, the aimless one, but it was becoming ever more obvious that her two sisters, as focused survivors, made her look even worse.

Ginger, a senior in high school, had been accepted at NYU, and would be taking premed, which surprised only the people who didn't know her. She would continue to live at home. Cellular biology fascinated her, and she had said she was not going to her senior prom, even though her best friend, Nancy, and her date had offered to take her along with them. Ginger said she didn't care about proms and dating, that she was devoting herself totally to the life of the mind.

Joan couldn't imagine how that could be true. Ginger loved the new sexy singer Elvis Presley, she played his records all the time, and how could a girl like that not want to do the things girls her age did—have fun? But Joan understood that having no escort and being unable to dance would be enough of a deterrent to someone with an even more robust will than Ginger.

Apparently talking to her friend Christopher on the phone once a week was all the social life she needed, but Ginger was pushing ahead with her life as best she could, and she was ambitious.

Compared to her, that compassionate and stubborn creature, Joan with all her physical faculties intact felt frivolous and useless.

Peggy too, with whom Joan had become much closer now that she went to Larchmont to visit from time to time, continued to make Joan feel guilty by being such a good wife and mother. Her days were full with things that Joan knew would have driven her crazy. But Peggy was happy, and her sole complaint was never getting enough sleep. It was only Joan who slept until noon, who still took three Dexamyls a day to stay awake, when one would have been enough to make a normal person climb the walls, who had no ambition. Her parents didn't nag or push her, but she knew they would have preferred her to be a better person.

"Joan, I need to talk to you," Ginger said finally, in a voice that did not bode well.

"What about?"

"I think you should go to a doctor."

"Why?"

"You sleep way too much, you drink coffee and Cokes all day, and they don't help. You only have to sit down in a chair and you fall asleep. I've noticed. My friend Nancy's cousin is an endocrinologist. You should have him look at your thyroid."

"I did that once. I blew into a bag and he said I was fine."

"That was a long time ago and that method is outdated. They have a blood test for it now. It's more accurate."

"And besides, I'm not fat," Joan said. She avoided going to doctors if she could; they seemed a waste of time for a young, healthy person.

"A person doesn't always have to be fat," Ginger said. "Just take his number. Trust me."

"Oh, all right," Joan said. She didn't feel guilty about the Dexamyl tablets, which no one in the family knew about anyway, but still it would be nice to find something that worked better.

Ginger's friend Nancy's cousin the endocrinologist was a dark, youngish man named Dr. Stanhope. He was wearing a wedding ring, but Joan didn't think he was cute enough to flirt with in any case. She told him her problem and it didn't seem to surprise him. He drew blood rather painfully from the vein in the crook of her arm. On her next appointment when she came for the results he was almost laughing.

"You have one of the lowest thyroid functions I've ever seen," he said. "On a scale of zero to six, you're a one. If you were one point lower you would be a cretin."

"So that's why the Dexamyl doesn't work."

"You're addicted to it, like most people who come to me with low thyroid," he said calmly. "I want you to get off it and then I'll give you Cytomel, which is a synthetic thyroid."

She had seen people suffering from trying to get off drugs, and she wasn't eager to go through anything like it. "What will getting off Dexamyl be like?" she asked nervously.

"It will take a weekend, and it's the nicest detox I know of. You'll just be tired and you'll sleep."

"Okay."

"Where did you get that scar on your forehead?" he asked. She hadn't noticed that her hair had gotten pushed back. Automatically she moved her bangs over it again.

"It's a radium burn."

"A *what?*"

"I was born with a blood blister, and the doctor put

radium on it, and the radium slipped and I got burned."

"Radium," he said. "Very nice. He should have left the 'blood blister,' as they called it, alone. They go away eventually. Meanwhile, the radiation probably is what knocked out your thyroid function. I can't believe they did that to you."

"It was the new wonder drug, my mother said."

"Overkill. Hiroshima. Maniacs. But don't worry. You'll be all right. You have a few small nodes on your thyroid gland, but the action of the Cytomel will keep them from turning into anything we don't like. When you take a synthetic thyroid your own thyroid gland just goes to sleep. It's the same with most medications. The body needs just so much, no matter what the source is, and then it says okay, I don't have to bother."

"A *cretin*?" Joan said. "You think I'm almost a cretin?" They looked at each other and smiled.

Dr. Stanhope hadn't lied. Dozing all weekend, Joan had never felt so calm. She had expected to be depressed, but instead she was happy. Her family was used to her peculiar sleep habits and didn't say anything. She realized that it had never occurred to her parents, or anyone else but Ginger, that her behavior all these years had a medical basis. They had thought it was a sign of deficient character.

How many people, Joan wondered, get blamed for things that have absolutely nothing to do with their minds or will?

On Monday she started her new medication, and in a few days she felt like everyone else. Then she told her mother about her visit to the doctor and what had happened, although she omitted the cause, since Rose had always felt guilty enough about the radium incident. "So you see," Joan said, "I wasn't lazy and undisciplined after all."

"Oh, I'm so sorry," Rose said, her hand at her throat,

where her own thyroid gland was, feeling her daughter's pain in her own cells without even being aware of it. "We didn't know anything in those days. Remember, I did take you to a doctor. I wish we had found out sooner."

"Well, I'll be fine now," Joan said.

It was to Ginger, of course, that Joan told the whole story. "My first case," Ginger said happily.

"When you're famous we'll tell people."

Finding an answer and getting rid of some of her guilt made Joan even more determined to do something about herself before the noble feeling went away. After some thought she quit her gig at the coffeehouse and got a normal daytime job at a bookstore in Greenwich Village called Toward the Light. She liked being surrounded by books; there was a richness to it, all the bright covers, the stories wrapped within, like being in a candy shop. As a bonus, a lot of Beats hung around the bookstore, so it didn't seem strange to her to be there. She sold, kept inventory, met the public in a different way than she had as a waitress, and was able to purchase books at a discount. In her free time, she read. Her salary was as meager as it had been before, but at least she felt a little more conventional. Her parents seemed pleased.

On a nice weekend in summer she went to visit Peggy and Ed and the kids, her suitcase full of children's books. Peter, who was almost eight, could of course read by himself, and Marianne at three, liked to be read to.

Peggy picked her up at the station as usual, in her big, wood-sided station wagon, and rapturously pointed out all the new luxuriant growth as they drove by everyone's yards. Mrs. McCoo had fixed a pile of tuna fish sandwiches for anyone who wanted them, the crusts cut off, the bread cut on the diagonal, because that was the only way the kids would eat them and she prepared the adults' food the same way as she did the children's. She had her straw hat on, standing there in the kitchen, and she left for the weekend as soon as Peggy walked in. The house was quiet. Peter was at day camp, his first year there, and Ed was out playing golf, his new passion. Peter would be back at half past three, and then later Ed would be home in time to make his excellent martinis and put steaks on the backyard grill while the three grown-ups got a buzz on.

Joan put her things in her room, sniffed the cut flowers Peggy had put in a vase on the dresser for her, braided her long hair, and changed into shorts so she and Peggy could coat themselves with iodine and baby oil and sit in the sun. They brought their lunch out to the lawn on paper plates. Letting herself be drawn into the household, settling down, Joan felt the familiar combination of boredom and envy, security and discomfort that she always felt when she visited her married sister. She had recently read the Kinsey Report on women, and she wondered how many times a week Peggy and Ed had sex.

She and Peggy lay out on the lawn in long white metal chairs with green cushions. "How's your love life?" Peggy asked. "Tell an old married lady what's going on in the city."

By now they had become so comfortable together that Joan could even discuss her downtown escapades, telling her older sister the things no one else in the family knew. Peggy seemed to enjoy her stories; living vicariously, Joan supposed. She wondered when she would get comfortable enough to ask Peggy about Ed. It was silly of her, she supposed, but she followed what she thought of as the marriage taboo. When you're single you can tell everything; when you're married it's sacred, grown-up, private, like your parents.

"Well," Joan said. "I met a really sexy man at the

bookstore last week, and he took me out for cannabis and cannoli, but…''

"But what?"

"I don't know. I think I'm actually beginning to look for a man with substance. You know, a real job, a normal life."

"You?"

"Yes, me."

"Well, I'd gladly introduce you to one," Peggy said, "but everyone here is married."

"I know. You don't have to."

Joan settled Marianne on her lap and began to put the child's hair into braids like her own. But Marianne's silky blond baby hair was so soft that the braids never kept long, and the barrettes Joan put at the ends slid right out. Peggy wouldn't let her use rubber bands; she said they tore the hair.

"Did you know," Joan said, "that a child's head at two years old is almost the size it will be as an adult? That's why they look so top heavy."

"Where did you hear that?"

"Ginger."

There was a silence. "Poor Ginger," Peggy said then. "Do you think she'll ever have children?"

Joan didn't answer. You might also ask if *I* will, she thought. We are each handicapped in our own way. But yes, poor Ginger. Joan put her nose into her niece's neck and breathed in her little girl smell. "Look at those cute pigtails!" she said. "Just like mine."

Marianne flashed her a smile of absolute pleasure. Sometimes Joan thought it was those open instants of emotion that made it all worthwhile to have kids. When you made them happy you *really* made them happy, not like grown-ups. It took so little to make kids feel good, just as it was too easy to make them cry, to give them bad memories. Did they forgive you? Did they forget? Maybe it was that ugly adult power that had always made her afraid to have a child of her own, for fear of ruining its life, bad black sheep Joan.

Joan put her head back and watched the huge, fluffy clouds moving across the cobalt blue sky. A speck of a plane flew by deceptively slowly, its buzzing far away. Peggy, Joan knew, worried about those things too, but she accepted them as a part of human existence, not a big issue, something she dealt with as best she could. She had her books on how to raise a child, and took them seriously, like homework.

How could two sisters be so different? Maternal instinct was in your genes, but apparently Peggy had inherited the genes for both of them. Or maybe the difference was that Peggy had a good husband.

"Do you know what I'm dreaming of?" Peggy said. "Eskimo Pies. Remember we used to eat them when we were kids?"

"Of course, and there were no sticks, so they always melted in your fingers before you were finished."

"I want pie," Marianne said.

"It's not pie, it's ice cream, honey," Peggy said.

"I want ice cream."

"Not right now, and dear, Mommy's talking."

"What made you think of Eskimo Pies?" Joan asked.

"I don't know."

"I used to love them."

"Mommy, I want ice cream," Marianne said, in her piercing little voice. "Mommy..." She pronounced it Momm-*ee*.

"Not right now, dear," Peggy said. "We just had lunch, and soon we'll have dinner."

"Momm-*ee*. I want ice cream."

"There isn't any," Peggy said. "If we ask him nicely later, maybe Daddy will get some for dessert."

"I want ice cream *now*, Momm-*ee*." Marianne jumped off Joan's lap and planted herself in front of her mother.

"When they're three they repeat," Peggy said. "They think they'll wear you down." She sighed. "And they often do. I don't care what they say about the 'terrible twos,' three is the worst age. When it's over nothing will ever be as bad as that. No, Marianne. There isn't any. We are an ice creamless house."

How tiny Marianne's feet were in her white sandals, how shrill her voice. I want a kid, I want one not, Joan thought.

"Momm-*ee!*" Marianne demanded. "Momm- *ee!* I want to get ice cream."

"No."

"Momm-*ee* . . ." Her voice rose to a piercing wail.

Why don't you make her stop, Joan thought. You're her mother, the boss, she worships you; make her shut up. Suddenly she had to get away.

"How would it be if I go pick up some at the store?" Joan said pleasantly, good Aunt Joan. "We can have it later. Ed won't have to bother." She stood. "Can I take the car?"

"Sure. The keys are on my dresser. You really don't mind?"

"Least I can do," she said, and smiled.

Joan went upstairs in the cool house and slipped on a pair of shoes, and put her wallet into the pocket of her shorts. I have very little tolerance for brats, she thought. I probably shouldn't be a mother. She went into Peggy's bedroom to get the keys to the station wagon. There was the king-size bed where her sister spent every night with the attractive and sexy man she loved, who comforted her, who probably held her in his sleep. Maybe the best reason to get married, Joan thought, was to have someone to hold you. She tossed the car keys up and down in her hand, thinking how many evenings Peggy had gone to get Ed at the station, confident he would be there, happy to see him, bearing him home. Maybe I could just get married and not have kids....

Was she jealous of Peggy having Ed? No, not Ed himself, but only what he represented. He was everything you could want in a man. All those good qualities were there clear as life, and there had to be more than one of him in the world, but she had never even looked for it. Why not? Did she think she didn't deserve it?

She went out into the warm sun. The station wagon was in the driveway. Joan got in, started the motor, slipped it into gear, released the brake, and backed up—fast, efficiently, as she did everything these days, the new Joan, normal like everyone else, for one moment the pretend housewife, the gatherer, with perfect children at home. As the car moved backward she felt and heard the softest thump on her rear bumper, as if she had hit something, and a tiny squeal, like an animal.

What was that? She stopped the car and got out.

Then she heard Peggy screaming, and saw her running up the driveway. In back of the station wagon, lying on the gravel where it had been hurled, was the little body of Marianne, her soft blond pigtails covered with the blood that was running out of her mouth. She had obviously run in back of the car, and because she was so small Joan could not possibly have seen her.

Joan felt as if someone had poured a bucket of ice water on her shocked skin. Every nerve ending leaped to attention. Her heart was pounding, into her mouth. And out of her heart came her own scream, as loud as Peggy's: terrified, grief-stricken, desperate.

The only one who was absolutely silent and still was Marianne.

TWENTY-FOUR

Marianne Glover, age three, of Larchmont, New York, died in the ambulance on the way to the local hospital, of internal injuries suffered when she had been struck by a station wagon that belonged to her mother, which was being driven by her Aunt Joan. That was not what the obituary said; it simply said auto accident. It also did not say that this was the incident that was going to threaten to tear an entire family apart.

The doctor gave Peggy a sedative, and she spent the days between the death and the funeral in such a haze of grief and medication that Ed had to help her dress and undress, put her into the shower, and comb her hair. Ed was accustomed to being a stoic; he was a World War II veteran, he had his ideas of what a man should be and he followed them. But although he was in deep mourning too, Peggy was oblivious to it. She only came alive when she was with her son, holding and stroking him in a hypnotized way that seemed to calm her. She even smiled at him. But her remaining child was the only person she smiled at.

Peter didn't want to go back to day camp after Marianne was killed, and Peggy and Ed didn't force him. He had gone off happily for a day of fun and swimming, and returned to find his little sister had vanished. When he asked to sleep in his parents' bed they let him. He wanted to be able to watch over them, so they could watch over him. As for Peggy, she welcomed his strong little body next to hers; it helped her sleep.

She also liked that he slept between her and Ed. She didn't want her husband to touch her, this man she loved so much and was so attracted to, because she didn't want to remember that she was a woman. She was anguish, sorrow, pain, a knotted clump of woe, but not a body. The body was irrelevant. She could not bear to remember what Marianne had looked like after the accident, but her mind wouldn't leave it. She tried to tuck Marianne's soul into her own but it fled, like a ray of light. Somewhere outside her view it was laughing at her.

How could she ever have been angry at her child, how could she ever have thought her child was less than perfect? Peggy was being punished, she knew. She should never have let Marianne out of her sight. A child that age was too fast, and too determined, and had no idea that things were dangerous, even when you had told her a hundred times.

And what of Joan, who deserved the real blame? Before Peggy got into the ambulance to be with Marianne she had asked Joan the murderess to stay behind so she would be there to greet Peter when he came home from day camp. After the initial screaming neither of the two sisters was really hysterical. They were partly in shock and partly trying to do normal things to survive. Before the ambulance came Peggy had called Ed at the golf club and told him to meet her at the hospital. By the time he arrived, Marianne, of course, was already dead. It was only later that Peggy realized she herself was dead too. And yes, what of Joan?

At the funeral Joan hung back, trying to become invisible. She wore a black veil so no one could see her face. It was only at Rose's insistence that Joan was willing to sit with the family at all. She wanted to sit far back, alone, the penitent, but her mother wouldn't let her. Not that she had been forgiven, or even understood, but making herself into a pariah in front of everyone would only have made things worse, the family felt. They had discussed it at great length, with and without her. At the graveside Joan stood with Rose and Ben, Hugh and Ginger, but not of them. She was so alone she might have been a stranger who had wandered into the cemetery by accident. Peggy couldn't even look at her.

"I'm so sorry," Joan kept saying, "I'm so sorry." She had tried to hug Peggy, but Peggy had recoiled, and after that Joan hadn't tried to touch her again. "I would do anything to make it not have happened," Joan said. What could Peggy reply? Not have been born?

"Joan was always the bad one," Peggy had told Ed after the funeral. "She pretended she'd changed, but she hadn't changed. She was always trouble."

Ed gave her an odd look, and then Peggy realized that Joan was near enough to have heard. If Peggy hadn't been filled with sedatives she would have been embarrassed. You didn't want people to hear you say terrible things about them, even when the things were true. She hoped Joan wouldn't come closer and start saying again how sorry she was, and Joan didn't. She quietly left the room. Afterward Peggy avoided her.

On one level, where sanity dwelt, Peggy knew that it had been an accident. Joan could not have seen someone as small as Marianne behind the long car. But logic didn't matter. Whatever resentment Peggy had felt all these years with her awkward and unpleasant sister, whatever rifts they'd had, came back full blown. The undeniable fact that she missed their period of friendship, which had been recent and short but had made her feel happy, now made her feel worse. Their good relationship was something else Joan had taken away.

Peggy was perceptive enough to know that Ed was

the only person she could trust with her true feelings about her sister Joan. Their mother would make excuses. The others would try to defend her, to make peace. They couldn't understand what it had been like to live your entire life with a person who had rubbed you the wrong way.

Peggy had stopped going to New York to visit because she didn't want to go anywhere, and more than anything she didn't want to set her eyes on Joan. So on a brisk fall afternoon when the leaves were turning, Celia arrived in Larchmont, chirpy, with too much luggage, and put herself into the guest room where the last person whose head had been on the pillow had been Joan. Grandma had taken a taxi from the station because Ed was at work in the city, and Peggy didn't drive anymore. She couldn't bear to look at the murder car. Even after Ed replaced it with a zippy Thunderbird convertible, because he couldn't bear to look at the station wagon either, Peggy wouldn't drive. She was afraid to. Mrs. McCoo did all the driving now, for the grocery shopping, and Peter's social life, and Ed carpooled from the railroad station with some men he knew. Everyone of their friends knew that Peggy was depressed, and they were willing to help as long as they had to.

"You've gotten very thin," Grandma said.

Peggy shrugged. Thinness was a reward that meant nothing to her now.

Celia pulled an afghan out of a large duffel bag. "Look what I've taken up now," she said. "I'm an old lady tending to my knitting."

"Hardly," Peggy said.

"Well, you're speaking. I was told you refused to speak."

"Who told you?"

"Never mind."

"I suppose they think I'm crazy," Peggy said.

"Nobody does."

Celia put down her knitting, went briskly into the kitchen, and found the bar. Peggy trailed after her because being with someone was less painful than being alone. The part of the day she hated most was when she was all alone in the house. That was when she took Miltown, and cried anyway. She watched Celia mixing drinks.

"What's that?"

"A delicious whiskey sour. I've switched from Manhattans. And one for you."

Peggy took it gratefully. It always amused her to see Grandma having her evening cocktail; she sometimes had two, and she always got a little tipsy. Now, though, Peggy thought about death; about how old Grandma was, although not so much older than her mother, and how some day, without any warning, Grandma would be gone. Like Marianne. Like everyone.

"Ed makes martinis," Peggy murmured. She didn't know what she was saying; she had no conversation anymore.

"A man's drink, in my opinion," Celia said. "A whiskey sour is a woman's drink. Of course, many people would disagree with me."

The nice thing about Grandma, Peggy realized, was that whatever you said, no matter how trivial or what a non sequitur, she would pick it up and go with it. That was probably the secret of her success with strangers, and of her vast social life. Or perhaps she was just stupid. Lately a part of Peggy's mind, the section that wasn't completely fogged, had opened in a new way, sharp and raw, so that she saw the worst in everybody. Sometimes she thought it was perception, sometimes just misery.

She sipped her whiskey sour. It was quite sweet.

"Very few people understand what it's like to lose a

child," Grandma said. Peggy's eyes immediately filled with tears and she felt a lump in her throat. "You can cry," Grandma said. "Let me tell you a story."

I don't want to hear a story, Peggy thought, but she said nothing.

"I was your grandfather's second wife, and he was my second husband," Celia said. "But you knew that."

"Yes." Years ago, who cared anymore? She had known Grandma all her life, and her mother had known her almost all her life. Celia had brought the children up, all of them.

"I came into the marriage with a little boy of my own," Celia said. Had Peggy known that? She couldn't remember. Surely someone would have mentioned it, but she couldn't recall. Maybe it had been a secret. Suddenly, to her surprise, her grandmother's eyes were full of tears, too.

"His name was Alfred," Grandma said. "He would be the same age as your Uncle Hugh. He died many, many years ago, of blood poisoning, after being scratched by a thorn in the garden. They didn't have antibiotics in those days. You were cut, you might die. An accident. Like being hit by a car. When I was growing up there were no cars. So then you could be killed by a runaway horse and carriage, or a bolt of lightning. You could die of a disease. A lot of people died, a lot of children. It didn't make it any easier."

"I lost so many babies," Peggy murmured. "But Marianne was the one I *knew*."

"As I knew Alfred," Celia said.

The two women sat there looking at each other. "I grieved like an animal," Celia went on. "I made his room a shrine. Oh yes, I know what grief is. I understand what you're going through."

"But what will I do?" Peggy cried. "I can't stand it, it's too much."

"You must have another baby," Celia said.

Peggy turned her face away. "No," she said. "No more. I can't go through that again."

"And what if something happens to Peter?"

"Grandma! How can you say that?" Peggy looked back at her, appalled. She wanted to run out of the room, but lately she was so tired she could hardly move.

"I say things as they are," Celia said. "Sometimes people don't like it, but too bad. My other children were a comfort to me, and so will yours be."

Peggy shook her head. "My little girl just died and you're telling me to replace her."

"No. Nothing will ever replace the one you've lost."

"I can't. It's too soon."

"As soon as possible is my advice."

I don't even make love with my husband anymore, Peggy thought, so where is this baby going to come from? That woman is heartless.

Go home, Peggy thought. Leave us alone. But of course she couldn't say it, so instead she said, "I'm really tired, I'm going to take a nap now," and went upstairs to her room and locked the door behind her.

Celia stayed for a week. She had brought a huge jigsaw puzzle of Davy Crockett, which she persuaded Peter to put together with her; she chattered when Ed was silent; and of course, being Celia, who always tried to have her way, she mentioned having another baby to Peggy again several times, and whenever she did Peggy always felt such a pain in her heart it was as if hands were wringing it out like a plump sponge. She could picture the drops of blood leaving her heart, see it empty and pale, and wondered how she was still alive.

She supposed she was making Marianne's room into a shrine the way Grandma had said she'd done with her own dead little boy, Alfred. Marianne's crib had been replaced by her first grown-up bed only a month before she died, and all her stuffed animals were on it, neatly piled up on the pillow, just as they had been that last day. Her dresses were hanging in the closet. Her tiny toothbrush was still in the bathroom, in the cup shaped like an elephant's head. The sight of it made everyone miserable, but they were afraid to touch it, for Peggy's sake, and for their own. The brightly painted step stool was there too, which Marianne had used to reach the sink.

If she tried, Peggy could pretend that Marianne was just out playing, that soon she would be back, accompanied by the vigilant Mrs. McCoo, or perhaps Ed, that it was time to bake her daughter's favorite Toll House cookies. No one ever mentioned getting rid of Marianne's things because it was much too early, and as for Peggy, she supposed they could stay there forever. She had no idea of the proper protocol; how could she?

She realized that except for Celia, none of them had mentioned Marianne's name for a long time. It was too distressing. But that only made them all more conscious of her loss, so her loss itself became a presence. When Celia finally left to go back to the city Peggy and Ed were glad. She had brought too much energy with her, and it was the wrong kind. What the right kind would be they had no idea.

Although she still couldn't bear to let him touch her, Peggy had no idea how she could have survived all this without Ed. Since she was a woman without a body, he had become her soul mate. When she told him secrets, he understood. The one secret he could not understand was why she refused to let him come within her circle of grief, to heal her and himself. But he only questioned her with his eyes. He knew her well enough not to ask for anything yet, only to give her what she asked for.

A few days after Grandma left, Rose arrived. It was as if they were a group of diplomats, taking turns. Rose went right into Marianne's room and burst into tears. "Oh, sweet baby," she murmured in a choking voice. Then she came out and embraced her daughter. "And you sweet baby, too," Rose said. Her mother had not been so physically affectionate since Peggy was a little girl. Peggy hadn't let her.

She remembered when she had thought her mother was a pest, a nag. Would Marianne have thought the same way about *her* when she became an adolescent? It would have been worth it, Peggy thought, even if she had hated me. She let Rose hug her and felt vaguely embarrassed, and hoped her mother didn't sense her stiffen. The only person Peggy didn't mind putting his arms around her was Peter.

"Ginger sends love," Rose said. They sat in the living room, waiting for Ed to come home from work, for Mrs. McCoo to fetch Peter from school, for the shapes of all these people to push away the spectral shape of Marianne. "She's really enjoying college. She's made friends. I was so worried about her, but I think it's going to be all right."

"Who wouldn't like Ginger?" Peggy said. She was drinking vodka. They always had vodka in the house now because Ed had recently replaced the gin in his famous martinis with vodka and she liked it better. But before he came home to fix them Peggy started on the vodka by herself, over ice. Nothing to make her drunk or mix badly with the Miltowns, but just a little to keep her heart from hurting.

"Peggy dear," Rose said, "we need to talk about Joan."

"No!"

"Joan loves you, Peggy. She's devastated. I think if she could give her own life to bring Marianne back, she would."

"Why doesn't she?" Peggy murmured. Her mother pretended not to hear her.

"You can't hate her forever. She's your sister."

"What has that to do with it?"

"When you were little girls, Joan worshipped you," Rose said.

Peggy didn't answer.

"She still does, Peggy. She thinks you have the answer to life. Joan doesn't. She's just a lost soul. More lost now that you won't find it in your heart to let her try to be friends again."

"My heart is busy," Peggy said.

"It was an accident, darling. It could have happened to anyone."

"I know," Peggy said.

"Then why won't you forgive her?"

Peggy thought for a moment, and took a sip of her vodka. "I can't," she said.

"Why not?"

"I don't know."

"You need someone to be angry at."

"That's normal, isn't it?"

"You could be angry at God."

"God?" Peggy said ironically. "Do you think God cares?"

Rose's look was faraway. "I thought that way when I was a little girl and lost my mother," she said.

Deaths remind people of other deaths, Peggy thought. She sighed. Don't tell me about your mother, she silently warned Rose. Don't tell me about your grief and loss. I want mine. You keep yours. I don't want to share. Rose looked down at her hands, knotted together in her lap, and subsided. Good, Peggy thought. At least Rose was soft; she was not like Grandma. For an instant Peggy wondered if Rose had loved or resented Celia when she was a motherless little girl learning to live with the replacement, and then she stopped thinking about it because thinking was still too much trouble.

Who would come to visit next? she asked herself, as if it were a game. Aunt Maude from Bristol? Uncle Hugh? Ginger in her wheelchair? Joan herself, evil incarnate? When Joan broke Marianne she broke a lot of other people too, Peggy thought.

I wish I didn't hate her, but I don't know how to stop.

TWENTY-FIVE

Hugh sometimes thought his life experience was very limited, although from the outside it might have seemed bizarre. But it was only the ball gowns that were bizarre, the wigs and boa and size-twelve evening slippers, the makeup. He was in other ways a simple man; he looked at his family and saw the messages of the world. Ginger being paralyzed had made him want to stay home where he felt needed; Peggy losing Marianne made him want to spread his wings. How ephemeral our existence was, he realized. One moment a person was here, warm and breathing, and the next moment vanished. You are not getting any younger, dearie, he told himself, and he knew he was right.

And Teddy was not getting any younger either.

Ginger had accompanied Hugh and Teddy to lunch in a Village café, and she had been so accepting and curious that Teddy had loved her immediately, as Hugh had known he would. She was the daughter Teddy had never had. After that the three of them went to lunch nearly every week, if Ginger had time between her classes. They were an odd-looking trio: the vivid girl in her wheelchair, the beautifully groomed and effeminate middle-aged man in his elegant suit, with just a touch of powder on his face, and the burly, reddish-haired teddy bear with a lusty laugh like a hug. But the places they frequented had plenty of unusual-looking people, and no one ever stared. In fact, they were so jolly together that they became a kind of welcome fixture.

The death of little Marianne and Peggy's lasting grief could not entirely freeze their joy in the moments they spent together. If anything, Ginger and Teddy joined Hugh in his realization that happiness should not be deferred. Ginger invited Teddy to come to the family for dinner, Hugh seconded the motion, and Teddy, shyly and nervously, agreed.

"Who will you say I am?" he asked.

"My life's companion," Hugh said.

Ginger applauded and Teddy blushed.

So Hugh slipped Teddy into the life of his family like a letter under the door. At dinner Ben and Teddy talked about the construction and repair of buildings, something Teddy knew about well and Ben was interested in, having been in charge of the problems with his town house for many years, and Hugh thought with pride how masculine this discussion was. Rose was sweet, as was her nature. Ginger, of course, was Ginger. And poor Joan, so tightly held together she seemed pathetic and about to fly apart, let it all flow by her, the drama of someone else's life that could never touch or compete with her own.

Hugh and Ginger were the only ones who hadn't yet been to Larchmont to visit Peggy. Now that Teddy had been accepted into the family with no hysteria or repugnance, Hugh decided to take him with them. On a crisp fall Saturday, when most people were either at football games or watching them on television, the three of them borrowed Ben's car and went to pay a condolence call that was also an introduction. We'll shock her out of her stupor, Hugh thought, but he didn't really mean it.

Ed opened the door. Hugh was stunned at how much older he looked. His blond hair was streaked with gray, and even his face was gray, and seemed elongated somehow, pulled down by the weight of his sorrow. So it was possible to turn gray overnight; Hugh had wondered about that. He'd heard of the phenomenon, but never seen it. And Ed was so young!

Behind Ed was little Peter, a stalwart boy turned clingy. Peter had seen Ginger only once since she had come home confined to her wheelchair, and although what had happened to her had been explained to him, he peered at her as if trying to decide if her condition was really permanent. The two of them were at eye level. She knew, of course, what he was thinking. Ginger knew what everyone thought about her; her radar was much too strong.

"Hey, big Petey-boy," Ginger said. "Remember your Aunt Ginger?"

He nodded.

"I've got a great machine here. Want a ride? I can do wheelies."

Peter ran behind Ed and hid.

"I lied, anyway," Ginger said to the rest of them, feigning cheer. She headed into the living room at full speed.

"This is my friend Teddy Benedict," Hugh said.

"Ed Glover. How do you do?" The two men shook hands. "I'll see if Peggy is up," Ed said. "She's taking a nap. Please come in, make yourselves comfortable. There's beer in the refrigerator and I have the game on if anyone is interested."

"Yes, I would take a look," Teddy said. He went into the family room, where the TV was, as Ed, followed by Peter, disappeared up the stairs.

"My man," Hugh said to Teddy, and flounced. "I love that he likes football."

"You love everything about me," Teddy said sweetly. He had changed a lot, Hugh thought, since he had been accepted into the family.

"Isn't this a beautiful neighborhood?" Hugh said.

"Teddy, what you and I should do is buy a little house in the suburbs and live the natural life. We could both commute with the husbands."

"Well, that's butch," Teddy said.

"But it's not so crazy," Hugh said. "I know two gay couples who have bought houses outside the city, in a quiet place, not a family suburb but something really isolated and lovely. They go up on weekends, and during the week they live in their separate apartments like we do."

"No, I'm a city person," Teddy said. "And so are you."

"Well, then," Hugh said tentatively, bringing up the subject again, not that it ever did any good, but he had been thinking about it a lot lately. "Maybe finally after all this time we should look for an apartment."

"You should," Ginger said.

"Ginger dear, you have no idea what the world is like," Teddy said.

"Oh, yes, I do. Who would know that you lived together? The people you care about know already, and it would be easy to keep the people at your office in the dark. People don't know what they don't want to know."

"She's right," Hugh said. "We could live in the Village. In an apartment house with all different kinds of people in it. Families, gay people, straight people, old people, young people. We'd just be part of the microcosm."

"And if you have an elevator I'll visit you," Ginger said.

"Of course we'll have an elevator," Hugh said. "I can't go up stairs in heels."

Teddy chuckled. We are making progress, Hugh thought. Some months ago Teddy would have responded that was exactly why he couldn't live with me. Now at least he knows when it's a joke.

They all looked up to see Peggy coming into the room. Hugh was startled at how drawn she looked. Peggy had always been so voluptuous and creamy, and now she looked ill. Her eyes had a foggy look, as if clouds were blowing across them, or something the rest of them could not see. "Hi," she said. "Hi, Ginger."

"Hi," Ginger said. She wheeled over and put her arm around Peggy's waist for a moment and rested her head on her sister's hip.

"This is my friend Teddy Benedict," Hugh said.

"Hello."

"I was so sorry to hear about your daughter," Teddy said. "Hugh told me."

"Thank you."

Hugh waited for her to suggest they move into the living room so they could talk, but she didn't. Peggy was so obviously damaged that he, who was never at a loss for words, didn't know what to say. They all sat there in the family room pretending to be interested in the game, except for Teddy, who really was, and then Ed came in with a pitcher of martinis. He handed a martini to Peggy, and her eyes when she looked up at him were clear for the first time.

"Where's Peter?" she asked.

"Up in his room."

"How are Mom and Dad?" she asked, turning to Hugh.

"Fine."

"Mom came by recently," she said.

"I know."

Peggy sipped her drink. "Doesn't anyone want anything?"

"I'll have a beer," Teddy said. "I'll get it."

"I'll have a lovely martini then," Hugh said. "I'm not driving."

They sat there playing cocktail hour in the suburbs,

drinking and smoking, but intimidated into muteness by Peggy's powerful and awkward grief. Hugh told himself that they were family and therefore Peggy didn't have to try. The game went on in the background; Ed and Teddy were too polite to watch but unable to offer a different diversion. Hugh had always found the sounds of football reassuring because it was something Teddy liked, and boring because he didn't, but now he found it all bizarre. Rose and Celia had reported to him how badly Peggy was still doing, but he had not been prepared for her silence. They had said they'd had talks. He wondered if he should not have brought Teddy, since Teddy was a stranger to her, but then he realized it didn't matter; she hardly realized Teddy was there.

In his fantasies before this visit Hugh had planned to redo Peggy's wardrobe, perk her up, tell her about the new makeup. But you couldn't do a beauty makeover on a zombie. He was reminded of his poor old friend Zazu, who owned the antique shop, who had sold it to the current owners and then gone into a decline and eventually died some years ago; and what he remembered was that Zazu had become so forgetful and then finally so silent that most of his friends, those who hadn't already died, had drifted away. Poor Zazu, paint collecting in his wrinkles, food stains on his dressing gown, sat there like Miss Havisham, stroking his moth-eaten little Yorkshire terrier, who was ancient too.

Peggy was clean enough, and she didn't have a senile lap dog, but she might have been a hundred and ten years old. Hugh had the strong feeling that she never went anywhere, did nothing, and that her mind was stilled by the cacophony of her disjointed and shrieking memories.

"Peggy!" Hugh said. "What are you thinking? Right now?"

"Not much."

"That's not true."

"Maybe not," she said, and gave him the saddest smile imaginable.

"What can we do to help?" he asked, and waited for her to tell him something, anything, so he could feel of use.

"But it's very simple," she said, finally.

"Then I'll do it. What?"

"Make it all not have happened," Peggy said. "That's the only thing I want. Can you do that, Uncle Hugh?"

Hugh sighed and shook his head.

They didn't stay for dinner, and Peggy and Ed seemed relieved. Teddy said he didn't want to drive back to the city in the dark because he didn't know the way—a pathetic lie that they accepted with grace.

"I don't know the way into my next day," Peggy said. "Thank you for coming. And you too, Teddy." Peter had come down from his room, finally, at the prospect of food, and she was encircling him with her arms.

In the car they were quiet for a while, somber and re-membering the visit, hurting for the miserable family they had left behind. "God!" Ginger said finally. "She kept looking at me in such a weird way."

"That's your imagination," Hugh said. "She was looking at everyone like that."

"No."

"Hugh," Teddy said, "not to change the subject, but I have an idea."

"About dinner?"

"No, I thought we'd eat in the city, but this is about next week."

"And what is it, my life's companion?" Hugh said.

"Why don't you call your realtor and you and I can look for an apartment."

Hugh's heart leaped. "For us? For you and me?"

Teddy nodded. "I don't want to waste my life anymore."

Hugh beamed and kissed him on the cheek. Ginger didn't mind the display of affection. She was beaming too.

"Oh, I am so excited," Hugh said. "The man has a way with words, does he not, Ginger? I never want to waste another moment either." The bridge approached them, the strings of glittering lights like a necklace, the city skyline like a glorious toy.

Although the three happy people in the car did not know it, Peggy had indeed been looking at Ginger in a peculiar way. What Peggy had been thinking was how all those years she had been afraid her two children would get polio, and how horrible it would be if one of them were to be paralyzed and had to spend life in a wheelchair. She had thought Ginger was the sacrifice, to keep Marianne safe. And now Peggy realized how glad and grateful she would have been to have Marianne alive and in that wheelchair; crippled, struggling, making do, but *alive*. Just alive…

Ginger was so strong, and so cheerful, and so full of life. To have Marianne back, Peggy would have had her change places with Ginger in an instant.

TWENTY-SIX

Joan reran what had happened that afternoon in the driveway as if it had been a movie, over and over every day; but to save herself from her desperate guilt and grief, in order to stay sane, she spooled it backward until it had not happened and Marianne was alive. Marianne had not run in back of the car; she had stayed on the lawn. Joan had not backed up the station wagon. No one had wanted ice cream. Joan was not a monster, and the peaceful calm of their sisterly afternoon was untouched.

But of course, that was only her wish, and before she squeezed her eyelids tightly shut to try to block out the picture that remained on her brain, she saw again the image of little blond pigtails covered with blood. Everyone hated her, she was sure of that, but no one hated her more than herself.

Every day she went to work, relieved to be out of the house and among strangers, and at night when she returned home she imagined all of them looking at her with revulsion. The truth (when she told it repeatedly to herself, also to stay sane), was that Rose looked sad, which was natural; that her father looked inscrutable, because he was sad; Celia, when she came to visit, made small talk as always and had no opinion; Ginger was busy with her own life; and Uncle Hugh, who at first had seemed bewildered, now looked happy because he was moving in with his boyfriend.

Joan had never seen Peggy again after the funeral, and she knew why. Peggy could not stand the sight of her. She wondered if they would ever speak to each other again, much less with love. What Peggy did, Ed did, and so he was gone forever too. Joan realized she missed him.

Was it only months that had passed, or was it years? She had no sense of time anymore. The others went to visit Peggy and came back without a word of encouragement. A large moving van arrived and took all Uncle Hugh's furniture and many boxes of clothing out of the house, while he supervised, and then he was gone. Their town house, where the girls had grown up, seemed emptier now. Except for Ginger, who was a part of the eccentric triumvirate that included her, Uncle Hugh, and his lover, Teddy, the others made only one pilgrimage to his new home in a tall Greenwich Village apartment building, for a lavish family dinner party, because Hugh had been so eager for them to see it. The event was a housewarming of sorts, although his friends from his real life were not there, and the family brought presents. Even Joan went to that. Peggy and Ed, of course, did not.

Joan thought she shouldn't look askance at Ginger for hanging around with Uncle Hugh and his boyfriend; at least she had somebody, everyone had somebody, except for herself. It was not that she couldn't find a pal or a lover, there were plenty of those from the past and others unknown waiting for her in the future, but she felt too horrible about herself to try to be friendly. Slowly, she distanced herself from everyone she knew. She didn't want to tell anyone what had happened that day in Larchmont, but there was nothing else on her mind. Her new routine was work and home.

But she didn't feel as if the place she lived was her home anymore. There were too many memories, too much guilt. What Joan really wanted, since she couldn't wipe out the past, was to obliterate herself. Had she been a suicidal person she would have tried overdosing on pills or cutting her wrists, but that had never been her nature. Her self-destructive impulses were more sociable. She wanted to vanish. She realized she had to go.

Go where? Anywhere that no one in the family could find her. Away so that Peggy and Ed would forget her. Away from the sight of all those disappointed familial faces and their noble hypocrisy. She was a pariah and she had to flee.

She went down to the Lower East Side and rented a railroad flat for forty dollars a month in a tenement filled with noisy families who didn't speak English. It had the usual bathtub in the kitchen and toilet in the hall, but at least the toilet was her own. She bought a cheap single bed and had it delivered, and some sheets and blankets from a pushcart in the street. They were secondhand, but clean and soft. The apartment suited her, although during those few days of transition she was still living with her family, preparing to vanish. The apartment was like a cell and she the penitent. There was a small hole in the wall that someone had dug with a knife, and Joan imagined him as another prisoner, planning his escape.

She quit her job. She took what little money she had saved out of the bank, and packed her things in two suitcases. She could not bear to leave New York, to go too far away from the family she loved, so she would lie to them. She would hide in plain sight and they would never know. It was possible to disappear into a city as complex and various as New York and never be seen again. Joan knew that; she had seen it happen before.

"I'm going away to live in California," she told her parents.

"But why?" Rose asked.

"Maybe you can stand the sight of my face, but I can't," Joan said. "My plane leaves tonight. I'll let you know where I am when I get there. Meanwhile you can write to me at this post office box number in New York, which belongs to a friend who will forward my mail."

"But why can't *I* forward your mail?" Rose asked.

"I need to cut contact for a while," Joan said.

"Please don't go, Joan," Rose said. "Things will work out. Just give it some more time."

"I have no more time," Joan said. "Kiss me good-bye, Mom."

Her parents looked stricken. "What will you do for money?" Ben asked.

"I'll get a job."

"They won't pay you enough to live decently," he said. "I want you to live decently."

Joan shrugged.

"I'll send you money," Ben said. He put his hand into his pocket and pulled out his wallet and emptied it. "Here's what I have right now, two hundred dollars because I went to the bank today, and next week I'll send you more."

"I can live on two hundred dollars for a month," Joan said.

"No, you can't."

"Oh, Joan…," her mother said, and embraced her. "I won't try to stop you. I know how much you've been suffering. Maybe a new place, new scenery, a new life, will make you feel better. And then you'll come back, won't you? When you're happy again?"

"If I'm happy again," Joan said. What was one more little lie? She knew she would never be happy and she would never be back.

She didn't say good-bye to Ginger because Ginger liked to ask too many questions. She was gone before Ginger came home from school. The next to last thing

Joan saw from the window of her taxi was her mother's tearful face, and the last thing was the house she had been born in and loved. Standing there on the sidewalk to see her off, her parents had been holding hands. She had seldom seen that. Joan realized that even though they were not physically demonstrative, at least not in front of the children, her parents really needed each other and had a rich affection. They would comfort each other when she was gone. She watched them grow smaller. She had the cab go uptown until they disappeared from her view, and it from theirs, and then she had it turn and take her downtown to her new life.

She was miserable and homesick in her secret apartment, but she was safe. No one could hate her anymore. The first thing she did was cut off her hair. That long, silky, blond hair that had been her eccentric trademark became an Audrey Hepburn pixie cut like everybody else's. She was a girl of the fifties now, and she could fit in. She got a job as a waitress in a tacky restaurant where no one she knew would ever think to go. As a last touch she changed her name. Joan Coleman, instead of Carson. She didn't want to change her first name because she was afraid she wouldn't answer. She took her new identity from the telephone book, where there were a lot of women with her adopted name. In any case, she didn't have to worry about her family looking her up in the phone book because she didn't have a phone. Let them look for her in California.

As the months went on she began to like the colorful street life of her neighborhood, which at first had only seemed sleazy. She was not overly friendly, but people knew her; the woman who sold her things from what had become her favorite pushcart, the man who sold her pickles and lox. Bit by bit Joan furnished her apartment with household goods that had belonged to other people. The objects cried out to her, with the voices of the people who had lived with them before, and drowned out the voices in her mind from her own past.

Christmas week was so difficult that she called her parents from the phone that belonged to another waitress in the restaurant where she worked. Her mother had sent her a Christmas present, to the post office box: a silver compact from Georg Jensen that Joan had long wanted. When they heard each other's voices Joan and her mother both wept.

"Thank you for my gift," Joan said.

"Where are you?" Rose cried.

"I'm living in Sausalito," Joan lied. "In Marin County, near San Francisco. It's very pretty. I'm working in a bookstore again."

"Oh, Joan, please come to visit us for Christmas. We'll send you the ticket. Everyone is coming from Bristol to New York this year, and we're having a big dinner at our house."

"How is Peggy?" Joan asked, by way of response.

There was a moment of silence. "Well, the holidays have been hard for her," Rose said. "But they're difficult for everyone. Joan, can't I at least have your phone number and address?"

"I'm moving soon," Joan said. "How's Ginger? How's Uncle Hugh?"

"They're all fine. Are you well? Do you have friends?"

"Of course," Joan said. "I have to go now. Give my love to Dad."

"I'll put him on. Wait."

"Joan…" When she heard her father's voice Joan started to cry again. "Come home," he said. "We miss you."

"I can't," Joan said. "Merry Christmas. Say Merry Christmas to Mom," and she hung up.

Christmas Eve was unbearable, so although she was

not religious, Joan went to church. She hoped Hugh and Teddy would not decide to go to the same one. She sat far in the back and listened to the music and looked at the colorful stained glass windows, and prayed for Peggy to forgive her, to find some happiness again, to have another baby. When the service was finished she walked for a while and then took a subway uptown to the Village. It was after midnight, and the streets were empty. She walked to the house on West 10th Street where her family lived, and stood across the street in the shadows, looking up at their lighted windows.

In their living room she could see the ceiling-high tree, glorious with ornaments, with presents piled beneath it. Apparently no one was asleep yet. Aunt Maude would be there, and Uncle Walter, and Aunt Daisy and her husband, and all the cousins, and Celia, and maybe even Aunt Harriette and Julius. Uncle Hugh and Teddy, probably, come home to the family. She wondered if Peggy and Ed were there, with Peter, now that she was gone from their sight. She knew the family had been having wine and eggnog, and thin cookies shaped like stars and crescents, and that tomorrow they would be having a big holiday meal. Joan's mouth watered, imagining it, and she realized she had forgotten to eat.

Don't think you're the Little Match Girl, Joan told herself. This was your own choice. She didn't deserve to eat, she didn't deserve multiple presents, she didn't deserve the arms of her family around her. If she wasn't careful, someone would look out of the window and see her loitering there.

She left and went back downtown to her self-imposed jail. For once, finally, after all the terrible things that had happened, she realized she was in control. It gave her some kind of comfort to think that, even though she wasn't quite sure why.

TWENTY-SEVEN

Everyone was leaving, Ginger thought. She had not minded losing Peggy to marriage and motherhood and the suburbs, because that was natural, and she was happy for Uncle Hugh, who had found Teddy and an apartment to share with him. But Joan's defection frightened her. If Joan had simply moved out to be on her own, even if she had gone to another city, that would have been natural too. She would have kept up, they would have followed her career, or whatever. But Joan in hiding, incommunicado, made a terrible loss in the house.

Their mother tried to be brave, but Ginger knew she was devastated. No one could have stopped this chain of events, it was Marianne's death that had started it; but even knowing this, the feeling of being completely powerless frightened Rose. I guess I'm all my mother has now, Ginger thought, and she wondered if she would ever have a life of her own.

She was still hopelessly in love with Christopher Riley. He was happy at B.U., he told her on the phone, he was liking cellular biology as much as she was, and still dreaming of becoming a doctor, as she was; and he had a new girlfriend. He had been reluctant to tell her about the existence of the girlfriend because he knew these things hurt her even though she had no right to be hurt. The two of them knew each other so well after all this time that it was as if they had known each other all their lives, and it was impossible to keep a secret for long. It hadn't taken much for Ginger to pry the information out of him. She teased him then, of course, and Chris was uncomfortable, because he knew Ginger was making a joke of it for all the wrong reasons.

The new girlfriend was not in a wheelchair. It was sad how men could always find someone, Ginger thought, while women had to be perfect. If she could have been able to walk she would no doubt have focused on her other imperfections, but being the way she was, her legs became everything. Why couldn't Chris love her? They had a world of things in common, they always had. Her brain told her that even though you had everything in common with someone else it didn't mean he would love you. The deeper, unreasonable, primitive part of her remembered the way they had been together in Warm Springs, and the seductive way he had put his tongue into her mouth when he kissed her good-bye at his parents' house, and the beast won. Eventually, Ginger knew, Chris would get tired of all those other girls and realize she was the one he needed to spend the rest of his life with.

She had friends now at college, some of whom were commuters, like herself, and some of whom lived in the dorms. She longed for that dorm life, and envied them in a way, and she knew many of the other commuters did too. They were all aware that it was different being a commuter than living in the dorms because they were not thrown into the intimate social life of communal living; but nevertheless it was easier for the other commuters than it was for her because they could go anywhere.

By now some of Ginger's new friends invited her to come along with them when they did things in groups, but she still didn't have a boyfriend. She didn't go on study dates, she didn't get taken to the movies or out alone for a beer. If she had gone to the movies with a date, in any case she would have had to sit separately; most movie theaters didn't even have a place for people like her. She couldn't go on buses and subways. Ginger knew by now that things weren't going to change; everyone thought of her as the freak Chris had warned her she would be. You couldn't not notice her. She couldn't just fit in.

Once, when she had been at a Saturday night party with a group of boys and girls drinking, one of the boys had gotten so drunk he had grabbed the back of her wheelchair and started wheeling her around too fast, spinning her, whooping, as if she were a toy, someone who didn't exist. If she had been capable of violence Ginger would have smashed his face. As it was, their friends made him stop. She held back her angry tears, but she was shaking.

"He's plastered," someone said.

"It was just in fun," someone else said.

I will not be the cripple who is a good sport, Ginger thought; I am not Quasimodo. "It wasn't fun for *me*," she said.

The next day he apologized and asked her out for coffee to make amends. His name was Jerry. The two of them sat at a small table in a Village coffeehouse, and everything he said Ginger found superficial and boring. He told her about other occasions when he had gotten drunk, and he seemed proud of it. He told her, with delight, about a party where all the boys threw up. She wondered if Jerry had tormented her because he secretly liked her, as if he were a ten-year-old. She couldn't imagine liking him.

"My sister used to work here," Ginger told him.

"As what?"

"A waitress, and she sometimes read poetry."

"Why would your sister be a waitress?" he asked. "Your father's a lawyer, you live in that big house."

"Don't be a snob," Ginger said. She had no desire to

explain or make excuses for Joan. Chris would have understood.

How much she missed Chris when she was out with someone she didn't like. How much she missed Joan all the time, when she had hardly even noticed her when she was there.

My first college date, she thought. He didn't ask her out again.

"Why don't you invite some friends over?" Rose suggested.

"Oh, I have too much work." She was getting all A's, partly because she was smart and partly because she studied so much.

"You know, Ginger, your college years are very special, not only because you're learning things that will help you in your life, but because all those intelligent young people, the same age, are gathered together in the same place. If you were friendlier . . ."

"Friendlier? How do you know I'm not friendly?"

Rose ignored that. "I'm sure in your classes you must meet a lot of men."

"You call them *men?*"

"Isn't that what you call them—college men?"

"Ha," Ginger said.

"You know, I was thinking, you should have a group of friends over once a week. Boys, men, whatever you call them. And girls. You could have a salon."

"That's from your day, Mom."

Rose smiled wistfully. "I see you as the center of attention. These things can be done, Ginger. An eccentricity doesn't have to be a liability, it can become an asset. People have become leaders who stand up less often than you do."

"My wheelchair is an eccentricity?"

"Uncle Hugh would call it a fashion accessory," Rose said. They both smiled.

"I wish Chris lived in New York," Ginger said.

"But he has his own life now, dear."

"I'll never find anyone else who's right for me."

"That's what you say now. It isn't true, believe me."

"It is."

"Let me tell you something," Rose said. "This is an old story from long ago, so everyone forgot it, but it isn't a secret. When I was your age I was engaged to a boy from Bristol, whom I'd known all my life."

"Before Dad?"

"Well, I'd met your father too, but I wasn't interested. I was interested in the boy named Tom."

How curious, Ginger thought. Her mother so much in love with someone else, not her father, that she intended to marry him? Well, of course she must have dated other guys, but engaged? "But you didn't marry him."

"He died of the flu during the war. The epidemic in World War I."

"Oh…" She tried to picture her mother being her age. She'd seen the family photos and heard the anecdotes, but this was something she could not have imagined. "I'm sorry," Ginger said. "Were you devastated?"

"I was. And I was in mourning for years. Your father came around to court me, but I still wasn't interested. Then we began to depend on each other. The way you depend on Christopher."

"Everything in common, you mean."

"Yes, eventually I discovered that. But when I knew Tom I was sure that he was the one I had everything in common with."

"But you didn't?"

"For then I did. But later not. Ginger, there will be someone else for you. I promise you. You're going to change. This boy you love so much is going to change too, or maybe he won't, but I guarantee you there is no one road for anybody. You must force yourself to have new friends."

So Mom was in love with someone else. And now she seemed so happy with Dad. Ginger sighed. Those old people were another species entirely; you thought you knew them and then they surprised you. She wanted to think of her parents as secure and devoted, but not as sexual beings, courting, mourning, moving on. It was normal of her to feel that way. And how could she have a "salon" anyway? Who would come?

"If I have a party," Ginger said, "would you let us have champagne?"

Rose hesitated for only a moment. "I could put it in the punch, how's that?"

"Everyone will love it. They're used to drinking punch with things in it, believe me." They would come if there was booze, she knew. Alcohol was always a draw. And the ones who got drunk would never be asked back.

She invited twenty people to come over the following Sunday afternoon. To her surprise, they all came. Rose had supplied various kinds of sandwiches, and there was the promised punch with champagne in it. Ginger eschewed her Elvis records for Ella Fitzgerald and Louis Armstrong, because they were more sophisticated, and because people wouldn't be impelled to dance. Rose and Ben went out, leaving Ginger with her guests, since having one's parents around, while it would ensure decorum, would ruin everything.

She was in her own house, and it was not like other parties she'd been to; it was better. Something about the decor of an elegant home and the food and alcohol nicely presented, the soft jazz background, and herself as hostess, in charge, made everyone behave differently toward her. They were actually enjoying themselves, Ginger realized. She was so busy supervising that she didn't have time to worry about being a wall-

flower. She had to talk to everyone, and to make sure
they talked to each other. And because she was not
nervous she was able to be herself. The guests stayed
until Rose and Ben came home at suppertime, and
even then they wandered away rather reluctantly, to
their homework and austere little dorm rooms, or to
their crowded apartments with their families who
couldn't afford to send them to a dorm, much less supply them with these festive things as hers could.

"I think it was a success," Ginger said.

"Then you must do it again next Sunday," Rose said.
"Make it a tradition."

"Mom, I can't throw you out every Sunday. It isn't
fair."

"We went to the Metropolitan Museum," Ben said.
"We saw the Impressionists. I was thinking how New
Yorkers use so little of this city that tourists enjoy. We
put everything off. I rather like being a Sunday tourist."

"I'm making a list of things to do, places to go," Rose
said. "I have you to thank, for shaking us up."

"They won't want to come again next week," Ginger
said. "Don't get too excited."

For the second "salon" she invited some of the people from the first one and several new faces. To her surprise, they all showed up, again. Ginger realized it
wasn't just the idea of a free party, although that certainly was a draw, but because they'd had a good time
and they liked her. They thought she was worldly, cul-
tivated, glamorous. Amazingly, no one crashed. They
seemed too intimidated. Her guests stayed as late as
they had the week before, and when they left a few of
them said, "I hope you invite me to the next one."

So she had to have another "salon" the next week;
what else could she do? There was now a core group of
friends she liked to be with, and then there were addi-
tions. The number of guests rose from twenty to thirty.

They filled her family's living room; Ben had to set out bridge chairs. After the third Sunday a good-looking boy she had sometimes talked to in her chemistry class, who she didn't think cared at all about her, came up to her after class and said, actually sounding hurt, "Why didn't you invite me? You invited some of my friends. I heard your parties are great and I really want to come."

"I have to keep the number down," Ginger said. "I can't have more than thirty-five. But you can come next week."

Who would have dreamed that people would be inviting themselves to her little social events?

During reading period and midterm exams she called the parties off, and everyone studied. But afterward she started them again. She was beginning to be concerned about how much money her parents were spending to make her popular, but they insisted they didn't mind. After all, Rose said, it was only sandwiches, and the amount of champagne in fruit punch was inconsequential. Still, Ginger saw the empty bottles waiting outside for the garbage collector and wondered if people would have liked her if she were poor.

If I *were* poor, she told herself, I would serve bread and cheese and Chianti, and they would still show up. It's the idea they like. They have someplace to go every Sunday afternoon when they're depressed from their Saturday night hangovers, and they feel chosen. She was a hostess, she was popular, she had a social life now, albeit on her own territory—wheeling around on her chair as if she were the virgin queen on her throne and her family's living room her little kingdom. If I asked boring people, she told herself, no one would come after a while.

But of course, Ginger realized, she would never know. Boys still didn't try to date her in a romantic way. They weren't quite sure what to do with her.

They should ask Christopher, Ginger thought. He would tell them. Chris Riley was still her ideal man, and no matter what her mother did to open the world to her, nothing had happened to make her feel any other way.

TWENTY-EIGHT

For Peggy, phase two after the shock and grief was a kind of estranged numbness. She was behaving more normally now, but she wondered if other people were aware that she was really not with them when they acted as if they thought she was. After it was clear that Joan had left town for what would be a long time, Peggy and Ed had gone into New York to have Christmas Eve and Christmas Day with her parents and the out-of-town family, and to bring Peter to see his young cousins; and Peggy felt as if she were sleepwalking through the whole thing. The only reason she had agreed to make the effort to go was that it was less painful than having Christmas in her own home without Marianne.

When the twenty-four-hour command performance was over and she could return home, she was worn out and relieved, as if she had survived a marathon. Everyone had tried so hard to be nice, and cheerful, and she saw and listened to them as if they were at a distance. She spent the rest of the holiday period in Larchmont, and on New Year's Eve she and Ed went to bed at ten o'clock.

Before all this happened they would have gone to bed at ten to have sex, after sharing a bottle of pre-midnight champagne, but that night they only slept, far apart in the large bed. Their mutual exhaustion was a sort of avoidance. She knew she was not being fair to him, but every time he touched her, even brushed against her, something inside her screamed. He was too good. You could not fault goodness, and yet his very decency filled Peggy with despair.

Hate, along with anger, were her constant companions. It was not enough simply to blame Joan, even though it had been an accident; Peggy still hated her all the time. None of this was rational, she believed, but it was the way things were. The passage of months, winter into spring, changed nothing. Only Peter seemed to have recovered. He slept in his own bed again, and he played with his friends instead of clinging to his mother. Peggy thought his timely recovery was partly due to the resilience of children and the survival instinct, and also because Peter sensed that she was so odd.

It was summer then, the first anniversary of Marianne's death. "We should go on a trip," Ed suggested. "You and me and Peter, or just the two of us."

"Why would I do that?" Peggy said. She needed to go to the cemetery and lay flowers on the little grave. She didn't want to be somewhere else trying to have fun.

"This is such a hard time," Ed said. "Maybe if we go to another place it will help you to…"

"Help me forget?"

"No…"

"You want me to forget her, don't you," Peggy said.

"No. I won't, and you won't. Never. We're different people now. Reality won't ever be that carefree again. But it's time for us to get on with our lives."

"I thought I was living my life," Peggy said, although she knew that was not what he meant.

That afternoon, after she and Ed had come back from the cemetery, the house empty, Peter safely at day camp, Ed took her in his arms. Peggy knew that men, more than women, used sex as a way of surviving death. They needed the closeness. Lose a baby, make a baby, even if it was symbolic because you were using birth control. Sex was oblivion. She gently moved away from him. There was no way she could respond, and she wondered if he would care if she did or not, if all he wanted was comfort and not her pleasure.

Who were those people so long ago, young Peggy and young Ed, who couldn't keep their hands off each other?

They were silent at dinner and she was sure he was hurt, perhaps even angry. Nobody knew this because nobody asked, but she hadn't let him make love to her for a year. Other husbands would be cheating already. Maybe he was. There were plenty of pretty, young, innocent secretaries in the city who could easily have a crush on the sophisticated, interesting executive. The stress of the past twelve months had taken its toll on Ed, but he was still an attractive man. Thirty-three wasn't old, it was prime. Some girl would find his look of tragedy appealing, even sexy. She would want to save him. From what? His harridan wife, his dead baby? His celibacy?

As soon as dinner was over Peter went outside to play with his friends. "Go with him, watch them," Peggy said to Ed, as always. Peter didn't like being hovered over, but Ed invariably managed to make it all right by playing baseball with the little boys, coaching them, or turning whatever they were doing into a game where he was valuable as an adult.

A woman could not ask for a better husband, Peggy thought. Why can't I force myself to have sex with him? It would be so easy. He wouldn't be angry if I didn't do anything. He knows how I feel. He just wants to be with me. But I can't do it tonight, not tonight. Not after Marianne… Later. Another time.

When would the other time be? Peggy didn't know. One evening at the end of summer the phone rang, and

when she picked it up the other person was silent for
longer than was natural, and then she heard a click.
Was it a wrong number or did he have someone, some
silly girl who called and then hung up? Was it his sum-
mertime romance? She looked at Ed, but he didn't
seem different, not nervous. Peggy looked away. Even
if he was in mourning, how long could a healthy man
go without sexual release? Did he masturbate in the
shower? Did he do that to be faithful to her?

She held out her drink for him to refresh. They drank
before dinner, with dinner, and after dinner these days.
They didn't get drunk, or slur their words, or make a
scene, they never argued, but the vodka was a part of
their routine. Drinking, Peggy thought, is supposed to
make people more receptive. Can I make myself more
receptive? Can I at least try?

In the beginning she had not wanted him to touch
her because she wanted to disappear. Then it was because he was so nice and she was so filled with fury
that it took all her energy away. Now Peggy did not
have any idea why it was. She had gotten too used to
his not touching her. Was this the way it happened in
other people's marriages? She couldn't ask her friends.
Except for their family tragedy, she and Ed were considered perfect people. She couldn't betray him by revealing they were not.

When Peter had been put to bed and she and Ed
went into their bedroom, Peggy couldn't get the
thought of that caller out of her mind. There comes a
time when you must fight for what is yours or lose it,
she told herself. If it wasn't his girlfriend it was, at
least, a warning.

She undressed in front of him instead of in the bathroom with the door locked as she had taken to doing
since she started keeping him away. She knew she still
looked good, although she had been too thin for a
while now, since she had gone into mourning and

stopped eating. But she would always have big breasts.
Ed had liked them. He was looking at them now. She
was wearing a black bra, and she stood there looking
into his eyes as she started to take it off. Ed strode over
and unhooked it, and then he put his arms around her
and buried his lips in the place where her shoulder met
her neck, and he gave a choked little cry.

He carried her to their bed. Scarlett O'Hara and
Rhett Butler, Peggy thought, with humor and irony,
not lust, and she realized she was trying to think of
other things than what Ed was doing to her, that she
was again trying to get away from her body. She must
not, she told herself, she must concentrate. She stroked
him and made appreciative soft noises. She helped him
take off her underpants, and helped him get on top of
her, although he knew very well how to do it himself.
He was kissing her, and Peggy thought how odd it was
that she had never before noticed how much saliva
kissing generated, and how it wasn't pleasant at all.

When Ed tried to enter her it felt to her as if he were
striking a wall. There seemed literally no place for him
to go. She knew it felt that way to him, too. Could the
vaginal muscles be that strong, to close up, to keep
away an erect and passionate man? He was hurting
her, but she would have tried to tolerate it if that would
have let him get in. The citadel, Peggy thought. The
army with the battering ram at the gates of the citadel,
and the citadel will not surrender.

It had not hurt nearly that much when she had lost
her virginity to Ed, many years ago. The alarming
thing was that not only was her husband hurting her
on this night when she had meant well, but that short
of tearing her to pieces, and perhaps not even then, he
could not go where she would not let him. No, where
her body would not let him. She would have. She
prayed silently to herself to relax, to help, or at least not

to hinder. But the body had its own strength, and its own message.

Or perhaps it was the mind. The body and the mind were one, and she was the creature who lived within that body and dwelt side by side with that mind, and they ruled. Peggy no longer had any idea why her own mind had turned against her in this way. She felt helpless and frightened. She wondered if what had happened would become chronic.

Ed rolled off her and sighed. He didn't put his arms around her but he held her hand. "I don't want to hurt you," he said. "I'd better not try anymore tonight."

Or ever, she thought. She breathed deeply and moved closer to him. They lay that way for a while, side by side, their bodies touching because she felt safe now.

"Peggy, you can't live with hate," Ed said, finally.

"Hate? What do you mean? I love you!" she said.

"It's not me you hate."

"No, it's you I love," she said.

"I'm talking about Joan."

Peggy felt the blood rising into her face as if her head were going to explode. She had not realized she was that angry. Her rage could kill her. No, Joan would kill her, through her rage. "Don't mention her name in this room," she said.

"Just think about it," Ed said. "Please? Don't let her destroy us. I love you, Peggy." His tone though, she thought, was not so much loving as ominous.

TWENTY-NINE

It was fall now, no longer hot, and the air on the Lower East Side was not so stultifying, the smells a little lighter, the street activity even happy. The children were in school. The anniversary of Marianne's death had come and gone. Joan was still working in the obscure, greasy restaurant, still living in the same dismal apartment, and her father was still sending her money, thinking she was in California. Her mother sent notes with the money: sad little flags to make her notice the family she had left behind.

Ginger was Perle Mesta, the "hostess with the mostes'," Rose wrote. Hugh was happy in his relationship with his "roommate," Teddy, and had enrolled in a cooking class, laughing because he now considered himself a gourmet and the first thing they were taught to make in class was a hamburger. Maude and Daisy were both grandmothers again, which was so convenient because the children would grow up close. Perhaps Joan would like to send the proud parents a nice card?

Peggy and Ed were not mentioned.

Joan saw the man on a fine autumn night when he came into her restaurant to eat dinner, alone. She was surprised to see anyone so tall and young and handsome there, when their main clientele were old, overweight, argumentative, and poor. He had fair hair and looked like Ed had when he was first dating Peggy.

Joan had a crush on the stranger from the first moment she laid eyes on him. Luckily, she was his waitress.

"Here by accident, I guess," she said, handing him the menu that was so food-encrusted it made you not want to order anything.

He smiled. He had perfect white teeth and blue eyes. She wondered if he were Ed's younger brother, brought here by some nightmare of fate, but then she remembered that Ed's brothers were much older and had never given any indication of wanting to leave Iowa. "What do you recommend?" he asked her.

"Me," Joan wanted to say. He was the first man she had noticed in over a year who made her think flirting was worth the trouble. "The chicken is edible," she said. "On the days they clean it."

"You talked me out of that," the man said. "I'll have the pot roast."

"You want the steak," she said. She took the menu out of his hand. "Trust me."

She returned with ice water. "You're funny," he said. "What's your name?"

"Joan. What's yours?"

"Trevor. Well, Joan, with the steak I'd like a baked potato instead of the French fries."

"It's steamed," she said. "They bake them in the morning and then wrap them in foil and steam them all day long until they fall apart. You want the spinach. I'll have the cook make it up fresh for you."

"Is it house policy or is it you?" he asked. "To be a stand-up comedy waitress?"

"It's me," Joan said. "You're a gorgeous-looking man and I wouldn't want to be responsible for your ill health. Besides, I want you to come back."

He was smiling at her while he ate and she brought food to other tables and removed dirty dishes, and once in a while she smiled at him. She could tell he liked her. She felt a little tweak in the area of her heart and wondered if it was Ed she'd had a secret longing for all these years without knowing it, or whether she liked this Trevor anyway and looking like Ed just made it easier.

"So," she said when she brought his coffee, "do you live around here or are you lost?"

"I just moved in," he said. "In fact, I live next door."

"But you speak English."

He laughed. "I'm a struggling actor and the price is right. Do you live around here?"

"Yes."

"And are you an actress?"

"No, I'm a waitress."

"That's it? No ambition?"

"None."

"But you're so pretty," he said.

Joan shrugged. "Thanks."

When he had finished his meal he put money on the check, and when Joan tried to take it away he put his hand on hers. "Where does a stand-up comedy waitress with no ambition go when she gets off work?" he asked.

"Walking," she said.

"Really? Not drinking, not dancing, not bowling?"

"If you want to bowl you go to Little Italy and play bocce," she said. "At least, the guys do."

"Would you like to play bocce with me later?"

In Little Italy? She had never ventured up there for fear someone she knew might see her, but she was tempted. If caught, she could always pretend she was here visiting from California; the family would not expect her to come to see them, at least not at first. "It will be too late," Joan said.

"Then how about a walk? You can show me the neighborhood."

"I get off at eleven," Joan said. She thought how odd it was that men never asked if you had a boyfriend.

They just assumed you were free. And there is no one freer than I am, she thought. "I'll meet you in front of here."

He was waiting, and they walked down to the East River, to the piers, and sat on a damp bulkhead and talked about their lives. She avoided telling him anything real. She said she came from Sausalito, which was a place she knew a little about since she was pretending to her parents that she was living there. He was from Pennsylvania. He asked her why she had come to New York if she had no ambition, since New York City was the place where young people came to have exciting lives and seek their fortune. She replied that an exciting life without the fortune was enough for her. He did not seem to notice that the life she had apparently chosen for herself was dead end.

He told her how much he wanted to be a successful actor, how he was going to acting classes, and to auditions, and how he had just signed with a small, independent agent. His dream was to go to Hollywood. He was studying theater, and the stage was what everyone aspired to, but he coveted a career in the movies. He talked about himself nonstop, and Joan remembered that most men were perfectly happy talking about every detail of their lives and their day and thought you were a good conversationalist if you just listened. His last name was Winslow. Hers, Joan told him easily, was Coleman. She'd had her new name long enough to be used to it. He asked her if she was related to some Colemans he knew in Philadelphia and she said no. After that he continued to talk about himself.

When dawn came up Trevor Winslow walked her to her apartment house. He lived just down the street, it happened. He invited her to go to a free play with him in a church basement on her day off, and she accepted with pleasure. He kissed her good night, which sent her off into an instant lustful fantasy, and he waited until he saw that she had entered her building safely before he walked away; on top of everything else he was a gentleman.

After they went to the play in the church basement, an amateurish and unintelligible effort that was as bad as Joan had expected it would be, she and Trevor went for a drink and dissected it. "There are so many people here who want to act," he said bitterly. "And most of them are hopeless. I just need my chance."

"Of course you do."

"I've started studying fencing," Trevor said.

"For what?"

"So I can do Shakespeare. Every actor needs to cut his teeth on Shakespeare. And I'm taking diction lessons too, so I can be in classical plays and have an English accent."

"When do you have time to work?" Joan asked.

"It's a lot of work."

"No, you know, earn money to pay for all of that."

He looked embarrassed. "My father sends me money."

"How generous of him."

"It's mainly because he doesn't want me to come back."

"You're kidding."

"No. I don't get along with him, or with my stepmother."

"Where's your mother?"

"Remarried. I hardly ever see her. Her husband is a jerk."

"How sad," Joan said, thinking how alone he was. Except for Aunt Harriette's husband, she didn't know anyone who was divorced. People just put up with each other, unless they were socialites or movie stars, who got divorced all the time.

"And you?" he said. "What is your family like?"

She felt a chill. They are wonderful, she thought, and I miss them, and two of them hate me. "Oh, just a family," Joan said, in a tone that told him not to ask more.

On their next date Trevor invited her to come to his apartment for dinner, and suggested she chip in for the food and help him cook. Joan didn't mind. There was no way she could have entertained properly in her horrible apartment. She and Trevor shopped for food together, and he bought a bottle of scotch and paid for that himself because he was the man.

His apartment was not much better than hers, except that he had apparently painted it, and hung up some theatrical posters. Because it was his and not hers, Joan found it cozy. They cooked and laughed and ate, and cleaned up together, and then they listened to his favorite Frank Sinatra album, *Only the Lonely*, which was very melancholy. They sat on the studio couch, which was also the bed, of course, and they sipped more scotch, and they necked.

How sexy he is, Joan thought. How gorgeous. When he started trying to go further she let him. In order not to disturb the spontaneity of their encounter, should there be one, she had put in her diaphragm before she left home.

"Are you...prepared?" he asked. "Do you want me to..."

"I can't have children," Joan said. She didn't know where that lie had come from; it had just popped out of her mouth. She had no idea if she could have children or not, but most people could. What she had really meant, she supposed, was that she didn't deserve children.

There was a tall mirror on the wall opposite the bed, without a frame, propped on the floor, and when they were naked Trevor had her sit on the floor in front of it with her legs apart, with himself behind her holding her breasts, and he told her to gaze at the picture they made together. It seemed to make him excited. "Isn't that beautiful?" he said.

Joan had the feeling he was talking about himself. After all, he was an actor. "Yes," she said.

He looks like young Ed and I look like Peggy when she was happy, she thought. We are Ed and Peggy. If Trevor Winslow and I had a baby and it was a girl it would look just like Marianne.

She thought about that later when she lay pressed against him in his narrow bed, sleepless. She knew it was leading to a crazy idea, and she didn't know where it had come from. She wasn't even that drunk. But she couldn't get it out of her head. And then in the night, smelling the warm beachy scent of him, listening to him breathe, so alive, so filled with energy, Joan began to see the random illumination as an actual plan.

I could have a baby with Trevor, Joan thought, and then I could give it to Peggy, and then she would forgive me. I could actually replace Marianne. I wouldn't tell her it was my baby, I'd just see that she got it, and then she would have a normal life again, and once she was back in the world of new motherhood she would be able to see everything much more clearly. How it wasn't really my fault, and how I'm not a terrible person. I could do all that if I really thought it out.

She could get pregnant and disappear again. Trevor wouldn't know she was pregnant and wouldn't care that she moved on. If he got his dream he would go to Hollywood, and the last thing on his mind would be to invite her to come with him. She could not imagine falling in love with him; he was just another of those wrong guys she always met and became attached to. Why, Joan wondered, had she not thought of this insane, wonderful, perfect idea before? A baby would solve everything for Peggy and Ed. That is, if the baby was a girl.

THIRTY

In their brief affair that fall and winter of 1957 and 1958, Trevor was as mesmerized by Joan as a self-involved person like him could be, and she was aware of his melting weakness and it made her more passionate. He was fascinated by the combination of her passion and the obvious fact that she was also detached. He couldn't find her a threat because she made no demands. Girls always wanted you to say you were in love with them before they would go all the way, and they always professed love for you, but Joan couldn't be bothered. Yet she was a nice girl, not in any way a slut, and she was faithful to him as best he could tell. This endearing combination of independence and willingness had never happened to him before. In addition, she was pretty and funny, and he was flattered that she liked him. They saw each other as often as they could.

As for Joan, she was much more emotionally involved with him than he would have dreamed. If their affair had not been hopeless, something she wanted only in order to conceive a child, she would have loved him less. She was not ready for love, had not been before the tragedy in the driveway, and certainly not afterward. She looked at Trevor and thought of Ed, she imagined herself sometimes as Peggy, and she knew this charade was doomed. She would get pregnant and slip away, and she could not keep the child. She was a vessel, a convenience, a benefactor for Peggy and Ed, and she knew she would have to remember that.

When she missed her period for an entire month she went to her gynecologist. "You're pregnant," he said. He waited to see her reaction because she had told him she was single.

"Good," Joan said. "My fiancé will be delighted. Now my parents can't delay the wedding anymore."

"Then congratulations," the doctor said, looking considerably relieved. He was a middle-aged man with eyeglasses and iron-gray hair, he had a wife and three children of his own. He did not do illegal abortions, and he did not enjoy sending girls to homes for unmarried mothers because they were always so ashamed and unhappy. A single woman did not keep her baby, even if she could afford to do so. The stigma was too great. He was willing to dispense birth control and fatherly advice, and a girl could pretend to be a virgin forever. But conceiving a baby was the sure sign a girl had been fooling around, and her life, of course, would be henceforth ruined, in one way or another. That was just the way things were.

That night Joan was very kind to Trevor. They cooked dinner together, and when she looked at him her eyes were sad. "I love you," she allowed herself to say. She didn't know if it was true.

He looked at her, seeming stunned. Then he smiled. "I love you too," he said.

"You don't have to say that."

"I know."

The smell of the cooking, even though it was a stew they both liked very much, was making her nauseated. She knew the morning sickness was not far behind. And her breasts seemed to have ballooned overnight; she wondered if Trevor noticed. When he touched them they felt sore. "I'm going to have to go away for a while," Joan said casually. "My grandfather in Califor-

nia is very sick. Probably dying. After all, he's ancient.
I need to see him and help my mother."

"How long do you think you'll be gone?"

"I don't know."

"Well, give me your number," Trevor said. "I might
have to go to California myself. My agent is setting up
some auditions."

"But I'll be in Northern California," Joan said.

"So? We can have a sexy weekend together."

She smiled. "That sounds irresistible."

The next day she went out looking for apartments in
Brooklyn. She knew nothing about Brooklyn, except
that it was another place you could hide in plain sight;
across the bridge, near, yet as far away as Nebraska if
you didn't know anyone. She needed a building with
less stairs to climb than the tenement she was living in
now, because it would be hard when she was large. To
her delight the rents were cheaper than in Manhattan,
so she was able to get a pleasant, large studio with a
view of trees, a few blocks from the park, on the parlor
floor of a brownstone building that had once been a
private school. In a way it reminded her of home, and
Joan felt a flash of homesickness.

She bought a wedding band in the five and ten, and
when she filled out the forms for the lease she wrote
that she was Mrs. Coleman, a divorcée.

Poor Trevor, she thought, when she had the moving
van come for her few things while he was at acting
class. Not that he would know she had moved out; the
two of them always went to his apartment, not hers.
She tacked a note on his door. "Grandpa is worse. I'll
call you when I get to California. Love, always, Joan."

Working in a restaurant again was out of the question now because every food smell made her need to
throw up. After looking for a while, Joan found a job as
a salesgirl in a men's clothing store, selling shirts and
ties—things the men didn't have to try on—in the front

room. She supposed when her pregnancy started to show too much she would get fired. Her father was still sending her money, and she knew she could live on that when she had to. She still had to go to Manhattan to her post office box, but Trevor didn't know about it and never went there, so the chances of his running into her were remote. Knowing she was still so close and yet so distant from everyone she knew gave her a feeling of danger and even power.

She made a few friends in the store, and customers sometimes asked her out, but she usually said no. In any case, she never went out with them more than once or twice, and only for a free meal because she was lonely. "My divorce isn't final," she would protest if any of the men she had rejected got persistent. They thought that was an additional attraction, but Joan said, according to her mood that day, that it was too complicated because she and her husband might get together again, or, conversely, that her husband was jealous and having her followed. Eventually, though, she started to look pregnant, and the invitations ceased. She was rather relieved.

She could live in her pregnancy now, following the rhythms of her body, imagining the life growing inside her, feeling it quicken. She bought little maternity outfits with smock tops and holes cut out in the front of the skirts for the burgeoning baby. These ensembles always featured "interest" near the face: a collar or a bow, to detract from what was below. Her social life now consisted of going for her checkups.

She had found a different doctor after she moved to Brooklyn, Dr. Veeder, a soft-spoken and motherly woman obstetrician who believed the revised version of Joan's situation, which for the doctor's benefit was that her husband was dead, tragically killed in an auto accident after drinking too much at a bachelor party, right after she had found out she was pregnant. It was best, Joan had decided, to get rid of the fictitious husband, so there would be no one legally responsible for this baby but herself. "What a terrible thing alcohol is," Joan declared. "I never touch it. I could not have lived with him the way he was. I knew his problem would destroy our marriage someday, but I never knew how quickly."

Joan liked the idea of a woman doctor; she seemed more sympathetic somehow. During these months of waiting Joan had begun to formulate her plan of how to give her baby to Peggy. It had to be a girl! Joan prayed every night for this baby to be a girl, even though she knew nothing would change if it were a boy. Dr. Veeder, moved by the sad plight of the young, widowed mother, had already agreed to find her a private adoption agency. A small one, Joan stipulated, where in this case the mother could have control over who got the child. What she did not add was that it had to be a place where they would believe the next story, where someone would follow the script she had prepared.

Twisting and turning, changing colors like a chameleon, Joan went through her days; growing bigger, feeling the baby kick now, watching the little lumps its active limbs made on the surface of her belly that was tight as a drum. It was the first time in so very long that she had actually felt happy.

Whoever she said she was, she believed it for that moment. She saw herself as the fiancée planning a shotgun wedding, the deserted wife, the abandoned widow. Joan had hardly ever lied in her life, but now she found the interesting thing about making up these stories about herself was that it was so easy to think they were true. Was this what habitual liars did? Was this why they were so good at it? She had been someone other than herself for quite a while now, and it gave her a rich store of memories that had never happened. The further she could get away from bad Joan the killer, the better she liked it.

She thought about Trevor from time to time. She missed him. He was another doomed part of her past that she had to put away, and she knew that, but it didn't make her want him less. Maybe some day, when all of this was over, when her family was reunited again and Trevor was, perhaps, a movie star, she would look him up. He would remember her because you always remembered the one who disappeared.

A month before the baby was due, Joan went to the private adoption agency Dr. Veeder had arranged for her. It occupied all of a small brownstone house very much like the one she was renting her own apartment in. Unmarried pregnant girls were living there, hiding, but Joan's case was different. She was only coming for a meeting. She sat down in the tidy office, across the desk from a thin woman her own mother's age, named Mrs. Key, who had pale eyes and a surprisingly masculine voice, and was actually wearing a hair net, and began to tell her tale.

"My older sister, Peggy's, little girl died some time ago," Joan said. "She never got over it. She can't have another baby. I know if Peggy knew that I was letting her have my own child she would refuse to take it. She could never understand a sister with so much love, who could make such a sacrifice. But Peggy would be an excellent mother. I've seen that already. She has an older child, a boy, who would welcome a new sibling. And she has a wonderful husband, and a home in the suburbs. I want my baby to have all the advantages I can't give it. I want my baby to stay within my family. I will tell you how to approach my sister and what to do. You'll have to do exactly as I say. I have to be kept completely out of it. Peggy will be reluctant at first because she's still grieving. But in the end, everyone will be better off the way I have decided this matter should be resolved."

"Are you sure you want to do this in secrecy?" Mrs. Key asked.

"Positive. I want the records sealed as usual."

"Are you sure you can't keep the baby? It's all you have left of your late husband."

"No," Joan said. "I won't let him ruin this child's life from beyond the grave." That was a little dramatic, but she could see it got results. The woman looked moved.

"Don't you think your husband's parents…?"

"They're the ones who ruined *his* life," Joan said.

"Ah…" She thought for a moment. "Will you ever tell your sister the baby is yours?"

"I don't know. Maybe later. We'll see. I want Peggy to think of the child as her own before I do anything like that."

"This is a very unusual case," Mrs. Key said. "Not giving the baby into the care of a relative, but the fact that you're making it a kind of anonymous gift. You must love your sister very much. And your child."

"Of course I do. And I am going to pay my own medical bills," Joan said. It would empty her entire savings account to do so, but having Peggy and Ed pay the expenses for a pregnant woman did not fit the scenario she had invented.

Mrs. Key looked surprised, but nodded agreement. It was now clear that Joan could have anything she wanted.

Thanksgiving was coming, but Joan hardly minded that she was alone, that she was unemployed, that she didn't have friends. She felt almost too big to move. The baby would be her Thanksgiving present. And then, if everything went perfectly, Peggy would have her new baby for Christmas. Joan felt surprisingly serene now that everything was going as she had hoped.

She woke up one morning in agony, gasping. In her

world of plans and fantasies, she had been completely unprepared for the reality of labor pains; she felt as if she were being cut by a knife. Why would anyone want to have children? What could she have been thinking of? But in the hospital Dr. Veeder promptly put her to sleep, and when she woke in her hospital room the nurse put a daughter into her arms.

Joan looked down at the pointy comb of white-blonde hair, the little face like a crumpled flower, and felt tears running out of her eyes. This was Marianne, exactly as she had looked when she was an infant. She had done it! She had recreated Marianne. She could hardly believe the miracle of it. Surely she wasn't such a bad person after all to have been so rewarded. *My baby*, Joan thought, feeling the pull of love and dragging herself out of its orbit, distancing herself.

Now let the drama begin.

THIRTY-ONE

Peggy had survived Thanksgiving, another long day at her parents' house pretending to be normal, and now there was Christmas looming ahead. She thought how cruel it was that the autumn months were so filled with holidays that broke your heart. There was Halloween, with the little kids in their costumes, asking for candy, and the picture in her mind and in her photo album of Marianne, dressed as a ballerina princess. There was cheerful Thanksgiving, when Marianne and Peter had brought home from school their drawings of Pilgrims and turkeys. Before she died, Marianne had made her first-ever painting of a turkey that looked like what it was supposed to be. When you had children, every holiday involved seasonal decorations, and crafts—therefore souvenirs, memories.

And almost directly after Thanksgiving had passed there was the planning and purchase of presents, the baking and stockpiling of cookies, which would be devoured, and fruitcakes, which would be ignored, and the children's letters to Santa. And eventually there would be the adventure to buy the tree. Peggy knew you couldn't avoid the holiday excitement even when you derided it as being too commercial; it was in the streets, the newspapers, the store windows, it was part of the culture.

Ed had tried a few more times to have sex with her, and then he had stopped. (She did not think of it as making love; it hurt too much.) She knew they were consciously avoiding arguments. She tried to be kind to him, to look and even act in love when she was in a safe and neutral place, with the result that the two of them were like a very old, long-married couple, the kind who surprise you by a lingering stroke, a pat. Peggy had never wondered if Ed still loved her, but now she thought about it. She knew she loved him, but so much about her love had changed. It was pushed aside into the pit of her sorrow.

One day a week before Christmas, there was a phone call. At first Peggy thought it was a man, but the caller introduced herself as Amanda Key, a name that meant nothing to Peggy. "I am a good friend of Dr. Suddrann," Amanda Key said.

"Who?"

"Sam Suddrann. The doctor who was in the emergency room the day your daughter died."

Peggy felt a wave of nausea and fear. She didn't want to remember any more about that day, and had in fact even forgotten the name of the attending doctor, if she had actually known it in that time of blind hysteria. "What do you want?" she said.

"Dr. Suddrann was so moved by your tragedy," the woman on the phone said. "It was such an unusual thing, and your daughter was an angel. He told me he couldn't get it out of his mind. Now, you may think this is strange, but I am the director of the Parkway Adoption Agency in Brooklyn, and we have a baby girl here who is the image of your daughter. Her parents were killed in an auto crash, and there are no relatives. The baby was with their neighbor at the time, and thus was spared. What an accident of fate takes away, an accident of fate returns, it seems to me. Perhaps that is too mystical, but in my business one sometimes becomes a philosopher. I don't know if you have thought of adoption, but I wonder if you would let me send you a photograph of the baby. She's only a few weeks old."

"My child was three," Peggy said coldly. "You have no idea what she looked like as an infant. Is this a crank call?"

"No, no. Dr. Suddrann suggested I telephone you. He thought you and your husband would be perfect parents for this little girl."

"I don't want a baby," Peggy said. "Leave us alone."

She hung up, and a moment after she did she was a bit sorry. She had actually no idea if she wanted another baby or not. Celia's words came back to her, and she knew Grandma would be delighted. No, she didn't want a baby, but who wouldn't be curious? She was not curious enough, however, to call the woman back. The whole concept was too morbid.

When Peggy told Ed about the strange phone call that night, he looked inscrutable. She had no idea what he was thinking, and despite their closeness from so many years she didn't want to ask. Either yes or no would be unacceptable to her. The intrusive offer had set her mind going in all sorts of directions: fantasy, reality, practicality, madness. Why would she want to adopt some other people's child? And yet, the image of a new baby girl arriving in the house from almost nowhere, without thought or planning, an unprotected creature who needed her, had an unexpected emotional pull.

A few days later the envelope arrived in the mail. When Peggy saw the return address she didn't know whether she wanted to tear the envelope open or toss it away. She hesitated for a moment and then opened it. Inside, folded into a letter, there was a photograph of a baby girl, and when she saw it she felt as if that child's soul was flowing directly into hers through the child's eyes, a child she had known all its life, and her hand began to shake so badly she almost dropped the picture. It was Marianne.

"Dear Mrs. Glover," the letter read. "I feel you and your husband should look at this picture. This orphaned child is meant for you. She will bring a new life to all of you, and you to her. Think about it, and please call me. I would like to make an appointment for you to see her in person. Sincerely, Amanda Key."

In that instant Peggy's day was over. She could not think of shopping for Christmas gifts or of wrapping the ones she had, she could hardly greet Peter and his friends when they came rushing through the house shepherded by the indispensable Mrs. McCoo, she was even afraid to answer the phone. She took the photograph of the infant girl into her bedroom and sat on her boudoir chair, holding it in her hands as if the picture were the baby itself.

There you are, Peggy said silently to the infant. How are you? Do you know me? It's nice to see you again. I missed you so much.

She knew she had to be deranged.

That night she showed the picture to Ed, and when he had seen it he looked up at her with a glance so startled and tragic that Peggy took him into her arms without even thinking about it. "Could we bear to do it?" she said.

"It's not Marianne," he said. "Babies change."

"But by then we would love her," Peggy said. She even surprised herself.

"Another child in this house would be a good thing," Ed said slowly. "Peter shouldn't be alone. Unless…you want to have one of your own?"

"Why?" Peggy said, "when this one is already here."

"We could look at her," he said. "We can always say no."

"Maybe this is happening too fast," she said.

"If we don't take her someone else will. If you really want her you shouldn't take the chance of losing her."

"You sound as if you're talking about a house," Peggy said, and to her surprise she gave a little laugh, the first one she'd heard coming out of her mouth in so long she almost couldn't remember.

They slept on it, albeit sleeplessly, and the next day at breakfast she and Ed decided she would call to make an appointment. It wouldn't do any harm just to look....

Neither Peggy nor Ed had been in Brooklyn before, and driving there they got lost, but mainly because they were both so nervous. The bony and odd-voiced Mrs. Key in her old-fashioned hair net looked like someone out of a movie, but the adoption agency seemed a pleasant, reputable place. The two of them sat in armchairs in her office while a young woman brought the baby in. The infant girl looked just like her picture, except that she seemed restless and cranky, as if they had woken her up.

Peggy felt a tightness in her chest. She reached out and took the baby—who relaxed into her arms, as if she belonged there. Her hand closed over Peggy's finger and she gurgled. Peggy looked into her blue eyes and remembered the shape of those eyes very well. She brushed her lips across the soft thatch of white-blond hair and sniffed. "She smells like Marianne," Peggy said.

"All babies smell alike," Ed said.

"No. Take her. Touch her. Look."

He picked up the baby gingerly, as if he were afraid. But Peggy could see from the way he gazed at her that he was as moved as she was.

She was Marianne and not Marianne, the past and the future. This baby was meant to be in my life, Peggy knew, and she wondered why she had never before thought of having one.

"I can hurry the paperwork so you can have her for Christmas," Mrs. Key said.

"Could we discuss this outside?" Ed asked.

"I'll go out and leave you alone," Mrs. Key said. "Call when you want me." She and the young woman and the baby were gone in an instant, and Peggy felt loss.

"What kind of careless people would leave such a young baby and go out in a car?" she said. "Their only baby? Who would do that?"

"Maybe they had to be somewhere, for a short time," Ed said. "They left her with the neighbor they trusted. They didn't know they would be killed."

"She's all alone. I want her," Peggy said.

"Then so do I."

"It's a miracle. Isn't it? A miracle."

"I suppose so," Ed said. "It's strange, all right. What are the chances of this happening, just out of the blue; this coincidence, this gift?"

"Don't question a miracle," Peggy said. "I want to name her Marguerite."

He looked distressed for a moment. "Isn't that a little too much like Marianne?" he asked gently.

"No. We can call her Markie for short."

"All right."

"So it's settled?" she said. "We'll take her?"

"Yes. I know this is the right thing to do."

"Of course it is." She strode to the door and opened it. "Mrs. Key?" The woman was there so quickly you might have thought she had been outside in the hall listening, but even if she was, what difference did it make? "We want this baby," Peggy said.

The baby was theirs in time for Christmas, as promised. Before she arrived it seemed every moment of Peggy's life was taken up with related activity. Marianne's room had to be redecorated in order not to be obsessive, but then the new room looked very much like the old one had years ago. All Marianne's toddler things were removed to the attic and placed in a trunk. Peggy and Ed had discussed how they would treat the new baby, and they both agreed immediately that Markie would not have to live in Marianne's shadow. She had a right to grow up to be her own person, and if being brought up by the same parents, in the same home, with the same older brother, and the same caretaker, made her somewhat like Marianne, so be it.

Marianne at three years old, Peggy was beginning to realize, had shown characteristics that would have changed with time and socialization. Other aspects of her personality had been destined from birth. Peggy didn't know how Marianne would have turned out, and she had no more idea how Marguerite would. Look at her own two sisters! She and Ginger and Joan were each so different, and always had been. This was the first time Peggy had been able to think about Joan in a normal way, and she wondered if having a new baby might someday mellow her.

The whole family—except Joan, of course—came to the Glover household in Larchmont to celebrate Christmas and the arrival of Markie. If it was nearly impossible to handle a Christmas dinner and a tiny baby, Peggy didn't notice it. Everyone pitched in to help. Rose was in ecstasy over her new grandchild. Celia looked smug, as if the entire idea had been hers all along, and only Peggy's stubbornness had made her take so long. Ben remarked that Markie looked just like Peggy had when she was that age. Ed took movies of each one of them holding the baby. Hugh brought piles of boxes of beautifully wrapped baby clothes, and Teddy brought a red rocking horse. Ginger brought cloth baby books. Aunt Harriette, her beaming husband by her side, brought an expensive white crocheted afghan for the carriage.

Aunt Maude was there with her Bristol family, except for the children who were living out of town with their own adult lives, and so was Aunt Daisy. If it hadn't been for the arrival of Markie after such tragedy and loss, Peggy's two older aunts would have spent this Christmas out of town too, and Harriette would have been on a cruise, but the occasion was special. Everyone had heard the story and everyone needed to look, as much as to wish the new parents well.

"How do you like our baby?" Peter asked them all, as if Markie was his. His parents weren't crazy anymore, he could see that, and he was relieved.

With so much excitement and happiness in the house, it was even more obvious that Joan was missing. Joan had called her parents that morning, Rose whispered to Maude, although Peggy overheard. Joan was still in California and wanted to know if everyone was well. Of course Rose had told her the good news about the baby. Joan had seemed pleased.

Joan's absence, Peggy thought, is better than that ghostly presence I was used to. Her absence seems merely neutral today. Joan isn't here. That's an improvement, because usually she is too much here. Today I feel calm. Poor Joan, I wonder if she has people who care about her to spend Christmas with.

When the dinner was over, and all the presents unwrapped, the people who were staying in New York hotels headed there, the rest of them off to Rose's to beat the traffic, Peggy, Ed, Peter and Markie were alone. It was the peaceful family she remembered: four people, the four corners of her universe.

"To bed," she told her son, and he was so tired he obeyed.

Markie was asleep in her own room, a night light next to the crib. The door was open to keep her safe. Peggy and Ed slid under the sheets in their own bed, and put their arms around each other—naturally, affectionately, without hesitation, a happily married couple after a long day. Peggy felt as if cool rain was sliding down her dehydrated body when he touched her. They both smiled.

"Let's shut the door for just a minute," she murmured. She knew if the baby cried they would hear her.

Ed shut their bedroom door, and they moved into one another's arms again. It was not as if she could pretend nothing terrible had happened to them after all, but that she knew now they had another chance.

When Ed began to make love to her Peggy wondered what would happen this time, but she wasn't afraid. She knew her body wouldn't betray her. Her body knew she was safe too, like Marguerite, like all of them, normal people, simply living their lives. It was the only thing she had always wanted.

THIRTY-TWO

It had been a long time since Rose had dropped in every day to visit her friend Elsie Wilder next door, or Elsie had come over unexpectedly to say hello. "Just passing by. Why weren't you in the park today?" They were still dear friends, but life's responsibilities had intervened, and now they made appointments to see each other when they could. Rose had imagined their children would grow up to be lifelong allies, but they hadn't. Their children had chosen their own playmates and confidantes, partly because of the age difference, and partly because they were their own people. Her daughters did not marry Elsie's sons, in fact they never even dated. Rose knew that back home in Bristol, a much smaller place, at a different time of the century, young people often fell in love with neighbors, as she had so long ago. But New York was an indifferent and electric city, and there was more to do.

It was her own daughters whom she had chosen to be her best friends. Rose wondered if she had made a mistake.

Ginger had graduated from college and was going on to medical school, again at nearby NYU, as she had long planned. She would not give her Sunday salons anymore; there would be too much schoolwork to do. Ginger seemed so much more confident now, a woman both in body and in mind. Although she still lived at home, Rose hardly ever saw her. She had friends, work, and purpose. That was what a parent wanted for a child, and the only thing missing was a husband and children, but Rose knew that for a person of Ginger's totally focused disposition, even if she were not physically handicapped, it was probably too soon. Of course, there was still that boy in Boston. When would she get over him? But Rose couldn't try to reason with her yet again. Ginger knew quite well how her mother felt, and to pursue it further would be useless nagging.

Peggy had settled in with her new baby, Markie, and every time Rose called her or saw her she seemed to have recovered more of her happiness and former spirit. It was eerie how much Markie resembled Marianne. And in a way, even after all the dramatic and tragic events, little had changed: Peggy, Ed, Markie, and Peter were as strong and self-sufficient and isolated a family unit as they had been when Marianne was there. Rose knew they didn't need her. She loved Peggy more than Peggy loved her; she was aware of that, and although it hurt, she knew the abyss of difference between the love for a mother and the love for a child.

Joan was still missing.

Ben had started to send money to Joan far less frequently than he had in the beginning. He was pained at the lack of response. In a way, he had begun to feel that if Joan wasn't asking for money and was not communicating with them, then she must be all right. But whether there was a check or not, Rose still wrote to Joan at her post office box every week, even when there was no news. She kept thinking that perhaps this epistolary onslaught of love and memories would make Joan feel ready to come back, if only for a visit. She tried to keep the letters cheerful.

Hugh and Teddy had bought a dog, Rose wrote, and the poor thing had become the child they'd never have. Or perhaps not the poor thing, perhaps the lucky thing.

She was a little golden spaniel with a white muzzle, and Hugh had named her Blanche, after Blanche du Bois in *A Streetcar Named Desire.* Rose did not imagine there was a dog on this earth who was more doted upon. The dog dish: silver, and an antique! The dog bed: a wine-colored velvet pillow with gold tassels, but it was never used because Blanche slept in the bed with them. (Although she didn't write this to Joan, Rose could never quite get used to the fact that Hugh and Teddy slept in the same bed, even though she knew they were lovers. Somehow the bed made it all too obvious, and on that one occasion when the family had gone to their housewarming she had been rather embarrassed.) She and Ben didn't go to visit Hugh and Teddy, but they were always happy to have them come to the town house for dinner, which they often did, and sometimes they brought Blanche, and Rose always had new toys for her.

"Your granddog," Hugh called her.

Markie is six months old, Rose wrote to Joan's post office box, and Peggy gave a birthday party for her. Thought you'd enjoy seeing this photo of the occasion, darling, and you might notice how much Markie looks like both Peggy and you when you were little. I wish you'd just send Peggy a card. She has changed. She's happy now. You must stop punishing yourself, Joan. California is so far away.

Another dog letter! Grandma's sick old Spunky passed away. He was almost eighteen. Where does the time go? Grandma says she won't buy another dog, she wants to travel. My goodness, she has more energy than any of us. She says she'd go to California and look you up, but no one knows where you're living. Why don't you tell us, Joan?

No matter how many times Rose wrote to Joan, no matter how optimistic and nonincriminating those letters were, Joan never wrote back. Hugh and Ginger wrote to her sometimes too, but she never answered them either.

Although Rose and Elsie never just popped into one another's houses anymore, they still called each other frequently, relieved themselves of whatever emotional baggage was ruining their week, and then they sometimes made a date. How odd it was, Rose thought, to telephone someone who lived just next door. Yet, the mystery of New York was that you could live in your neighborhood for years and not run into someone on the street, not see her in the grocery store. You were more apt to run into her in a favorite restaurant, each of you dining with other people, and even that did not happen very often. Sometimes she looked up at the lighted window in Elsie's bedroom and wondered if she were at home at all. And then sometimes Rose had the eerie feeling that Elsie never left her house. Somehow she was afraid to ask.

"When can we have lunch?" Rose asked, on the phone. "You and I haven't had one of our silly lunches together in such a long time."

"I don't go out to those long lunches with friends anymore," Elsie said.

"No?"

"It ruins my day. But come over. We can have a drink. You're right, it's been ages."

"When should I come?"

"Thursday?"

"That would be fine." She remembered when Elsie would have said, "Come now." But that was a long time ago, and everyone was so busy. What exactly they were so busy with, she had no idea. Running a household, even when your children were gone, doing some volunteer work, going to charity luncheons, shopping, having your hats made, getting your hair and nails done, chatting on the phone, keeping up, pleasing your husband, attending to your social calendar, worrying about your children—was that the career that kept their days so occupied? You could spend an entire afternoon lining the kitchen drawers. You read: women's magazines and popular novels. Rose and Elsie had had household help for years, so they didn't clean, and they cooked only on special occasions and on the nights that the girl was off if their husbands were reluctant to go out. Their days were not stressful, but they were full.

Rose had never doubted her life and those of her friends, and she didn't intend to do so now, but it occurred to her that she was always running just to stay in the same place. Perhaps she would talk to Elsie about it and they could figure it all out.

She got dressed up to go next door to Elsie's for drinks, since it felt like an occasion. An Irish maid in a little black uniform with a white ruffled apron opened the front door. This was new. A fire was neatly laid in the fireplace, but not lit because it was still summer. The drapes were drawn against the late afternoon heat, and an air conditioner hummed. There was the usual huge arrangement of fresh seasonal flowers on the piano in the living room, perfuming the air. Elsie's tall, narrow, tranquil house smelled familiarly of flowers and smoke. She was a chain smoker and had been since before they had met.

"Rose!" she cried, emerging from the gloom, wearing a cocktail dress and her good jewelry. "Come in." She kissed Rose lightly on the cheek, brushed it, rather, since she was wearing lipstick. She looked very thin.

Elsie led the way to the living room sofa, where a silver tray had been set up bearing a frosty shaker of martinis and two glasses, a jar of honey and a pitcher of water. There was a tiny bowl of peanuts next to the cocktail napkins, and a large ashtray, already partly full of lipstick-ended butts. "Oh, Siobhan, please," Elsie said, waving at the ashtray, and the maid whisked the butts and ashes away in a silver container with a lid.

"You are so elegant," Rose said admiringly.

"But it's my avocation," Elsie said smiling.

Rose held up her martini in a toast. "Cheers."

"Health," Elsie said.

"That too." Rose sipped at her drink. It was perfectly made, but even after all these years she had never acquired a taste for alcohol and one was all she could stand.

"And how is your family, Rose?"

"Well. And yours?"

"Fine. Any news from Joan?"

"Of course not."

"She'll be back," Elsie said. "Trust me."

"Let's talk about something more amusing," Rose said.

"Or less amusing." Elsie doubled over in a paroxysm of coughing. "Excuse me." She measured out a teaspoonful of honey and swallowed it, and washed it down with a half glass of the water.

"What's wrong?" Rose asked, concerned.

"Oh, my doctor said to take this. I have some lung problem. He says it might be from smoking so much. The honey makes it feel better."

Rose nodded. Elsie's voice was husky, almost hoarse, but it had been for years. She was much thinner than usual, but she had always been careful of her weight. Years ago her husband, the businessman who looked, as Elsie put it, like a monkey, had been discovered keeping a young woman in an apartment uptown on Park Avenue, and although he and Elsie never got divorced, after that they seemed to have a marriage of convenience. The clothes and jewelry, the beautiful house, the social engagements that they attended as a respectable married couple, were Elsie's rewards. And of course, there were their children. Elsie had always made fun of her husband behind his back, and Rose had never been really sure that she had loved him, but she knew Elsie was devastated by his infidelity.

"We're not so young anymore, are we, Rose?" Elsie said. "I don't tell anyone, but I'm almost sixty."

"Fifty-nine and a half," Rose said. "The same as I am. You and I both know that."

"So given the alternative it's not so depressing."

"Not so depressing at all."

Elsie lit another cigarette and refreshed her martini. "You don't smoke much, do you, Rose?" she said. "I always remember that."

"Some," Rose said. Elsie had always put her own pack of cigarettes on the dining table next to the food, and smoked all through the meal, but Rose preferred to smoke only afterward. It was partly the way she had come of age, when smoking for women was rebellious and not feminine, and then, eventually, desirable.

"Just as well," Elsie said. "Do you know what they call cigarettes? Coffin nails. Not that it's ever stopped me any."

"I know."

"No one has any idea *really* if these things are bad for you," Elsie said. She looked down at the glowing tip of the cigarette in her hand. "If someone told you that if you gave up all the things that you liked—cigarettes, alcohol, the fun they represented—and you would live an extra ten years, or you could just live your life the way you want and then drop dead, what would you do?" Before Rose had a chance to answer, she went on. "I wouldn't stop," Elsie said.

"I might," Rose said.

"Besides, who knows if it would be ten; maybe you could be buying only one more year. What good would that be?"

"A year?" Rose thought about it. A year didn't seem

so much in a long life. "Well, maybe for just a year longer on this earth I wouldn't reform my ways."

"Then again, though, if you didn't drop dead—if you had a long, terrible illness...or even a short terrible one...?"

"Elsie, why are you talking about this?"

"I don't know," Elsie said quickly. Her voice was strained. "Have you seen any good movies lately?"

She's dying, Rose thought. She herself knew very little about medicine, and cancer was a secret, the word no one dared to say, but she was an intelligent woman and she could see that Elsie was not only unwell but afraid. "Elsie," Rose said, "you can tell me anything. You know that, don't you?"

"Of course."

"Tell me what the doctor said. I care about you. I want to help."

Elsie gave a little smile. "Help? I have a little lung problem. I will probably outlive everyone, including my husband's latest girlfriend. Rose, do have another martini. I don't like to drink alone."

Rose let her friend pour some more into her glass, and pretended to sip. "Have you told Lionel?"

"Heavens no, he'd be too thrilled. Maybe the doctor told him. Certainly the doctor didn't tell *me.* My dear doctor suggested I take a trip. Europe, he said, somewhere glamorous. I suppose that was his way of suggesting that I do all the things I've always wanted to do before I can't."

"Then it is serious? Elsie, don't play games with me."

"But they play them with me, don't they? I suppose I'll find out when the time comes. In the meantime, everyone wants me to be happy, so I'll oblige them."

"Oh, Elsie," Rose said. She got up impetuously and put her arms around her old friend. Although she knew Elsie was thin, she was so unexpectedly bony to the touch that Rose was startled. Get well, she wanted to say. Get well backwards, as she had said to her childhood friend, the first Elsie, in their secret code, so long ago as she was dying of diabetes. I can't bear to lose you too, she thought. And yet, even as she thought it, Rose knew life had brought her so many losses that she was already becoming inured to this one; even as she hugged her friend, she was beginning to say goodbye.

"I'm so frightened," Elsie murmured. "And then, sometimes I'm not. I believe everything will be all right, that I'll get well. And then, usually at night, I can't sleep and I think how they know something I don't know…. Or maybe they don't know either. Whoever wrote that ignorance is bliss? You'd have to be terribly ignorant."

Rose knew there was nothing she could do. Well, she could see her more often, try to cheer her up if that were possible. Elsie drew away from her embrace. "Do you ever wonder," Elsie said, "what you would do if they told you it was your last night on earth? Would you have an amazing meal, make love, call everyone and tell them what you think of them? Or would you just sit in your house, curl up in a miserable little ball of fear, and tremble? I don't know what I would do, and so I vacillate. Right now I'm curled up in that little ball."

"Make Lionel take you to Europe," Rose said. "He will. Have a good time. And then if what you're afraid of never happens, having had a wonderful time will be the best revenge of all."

"You agree with my doctor."

"Yes."

"Maybe I will," Elsie said.

When Rose walked the few yards home night was moving in, the long, lingering, pale end of a summer day. There were so many secrets, she thought, behind the facades of each of these houses. So many betrayals, so many wasted lives. Compromises and regrets. She felt very sad. She and Elsie Wilder had known each other for almost thirty-five years, and yet, in a way, they were like trains rushing by on parallel tracks. She suddenly missed Joan so much she almost doubled over with the pain of it.

But no matter how upset she was, whenever she opened her front door she felt flooded with safety. *My home.* Sometimes, Rose thought, if I don't look too hard I can pretend nothing has changed. She went into the living room.

And there, sitting in a chair, her newly short blond hair gleaming in the last gold rays of the setting sun, was Joan.

"Hi, Mom," Joan said.

Rose almost sobbed for joy. "Joan!"

"I thought I'd come back," Joan said. "Is that okay?"

THIRTY-THREE

When the family noticed how reluctant Joan was to talk about her time in California, they did not persist. Although she seemed more womanly somehow, a little more filled out, she also appeared damaged. They all assumed that her voluntary exile had been as difficult for her as it had been for them, if not more so. Joan seemed to be a convalescent, soaking in the nourishing atmosphere of home. But after she had been there two days she started looking for a job.

This time she wanted to work in publishing, even though that was the glamour career that every girl who was a college graduate coveted and very few attained. But she was also more practical than she had been before she left; she took a crash course in typing and shorthand at Katherine Gibbs, she told the employment agency about her (partly fictitious, but how would anyone know that?) expertise in running a bookstore, and before long she was working as a secretary to an editor at the large commercial publishing firm Webster and Dally and bringing home manuscripts every night to read.

Joan had not yet seen Peggy face-to-face, although Rose had told Peggy she was back. The two had not even spoken. Rose knew they were both afraid, and she waited for the right moment to push them, because by now she was used to waiting.

All Rose wanted was to help repair the hurt and

make things the way they were so long ago. She wanted to restore the relationship between Joan and Peggy, and she wanted Joan to stay. Joan was twenty-eight, she had lived alone in another state, she was obviously used to being independent, but Rose hoped she would like being back with her family so much that she wouldn't decide to get her own apartment as so many unmarried girls were doing lately.

Hugh had come over to see Joan as soon as he heard she was back, bringing Teddy and Blanche. Celia had come too, of course. Ben, while he was relieved to have his middle daughter back, was also wary that she might bolt again if she felt threatened. Ginger, who was impatient, had suggested calling Peggy the very first night, but Joan had put her hand firmly on the phone and fixed her with such a dark look that Ginger had giggled nervously and said, "All right, all right," and Ben had been so unsettled by this seething emotion that he had left the room.

Joan was sweet and pleasant to all of them, less moody, nicer than she had been before. But she was clearly treading through this portion of her life with extreme caution, and they were obviously meant to respect that.

What they didn't know, of course, was that Joan was so desperate to speak to Peggy, and so afraid that Peggy would hang up on her, that she rehearsed their first conversation over and over whenever she had a chance. She wanted to be Peggy's sister again, and even more, she wanted to see "their" child. As much as Joan knew Markie was Peggy's and Ed's now, she also knew Markie was hers. She would push her motherly feelings away, she would remind herself that she had never been or wanted to be parent material, she was aware that the birth mother should never know the adoptive mother, and yet she was yearning to see Markie, and each stage of Markie's development that she missed filled her with frustration. She just wanted to look at her, that was all.

How many evenings she had been poised to dial Peggy's number, and then had drawn back, wary. "Why don't you call Peggy, darling?" her mother ventured, from time to time.

"Why doesn't she call me?"

"You were this way when you were little girls," her mother said. "If you had a fight neither of you would give in."

"This was hardly a fight, Mom."

"I think you should invite her to come over Sunday for dinner."

"Me?"

"Should I?"

"She won't come," Joan said. "By fall Peggy has her life scheduled right through Christmas."

"Oh, you'd be surprised. Peggy is so proud of her new baby she'll want you to meet her. May I invite Peggy and Ed? Will that be all right?"

"That's fine," Joan said, pretending she was not terrified.

She knew Rose called Peggy often, and every time Joan noticed that Rose was talking to Peggy she was tempted to lift the receiver and listen in. She supposed they discussed her. She wanted to know and she didn't. When Peggy came with Markie and Joan wanted to touch or embrace the baby, would Peggy pull her away? Joan thought her fantasies were far more punishing than the eventual truth would be, and her dream was far too rewarding. Her dream was forgiveness and even thanks. And that last, she knew, she would never have.

"They're coming Sunday," Rose said. She was beaming and triumphant. "We'll have dinner at two o'clock, a nice family dinner, as if it were a holiday. I'm going to bake a cake; I haven't done that in a long time.

A Martha Washington cake—you know, with the sugary marshmallow icing you girls used to love and the walnuts and cherries in the icing inside the layers. Wait till Peggy sees your new haircut, Joan, I bet she'll want one just like it."

I'll take that bet, Joan thought. We never wanted the same things.

On the Sunday they were to come, Joan watched the street from her bedroom window, her heart pounding. The Glovers drove up in a car she didn't recognize: light blue, four doors, with fins and a hard white top. This must be the new car her mother had told her about, since Peggy had started driving again. Joan watched them park and get out and go up the stairs to the house. Peter had grown a lot, he was almost gangly. Peggy was carrying Markie. Markie was wearing a round wool hat with a narrow brim, that matched her coat, but Joan could see that the baby's white-blond hair had turned gold now, as had happened with Marianne, and herself and Peggy, when they got older. The little head bobbed up and down, and turned to look at the sights.

I can't believe I made that baby, Joan thought, with a rush of love. I made a miracle. Peggy doesn't know what I know. I am a good person. A noble person. All debts are over now, on both sides.

She took a deep breath, unclenched her fingers, and went slowly downstairs.

The instant that passed when they first looked at each other seemed much longer. Peggy had taken off Markie's coat and hat, and was holding her in her arms. Ed stood behind them, in a sort of gesture of solidarity, as if he were their protector. From the background noises Joan could tell that Peter had gone to the kitchen with Ginger, to help get sodas. Rose and Ben were in the corner, in the shadows, trying not to be there, afraid to leave.

"Hi, Peggy," Joan said.

"Hi." There was the briefest pause. "Well, this is Marguerite," Peggy said. "Markie to all who know and love her."

But Marguerite to me, Joan thought, feeling stabbed. Did she mean it that way, or is it just Peggy being flip? "Well, hello," Joan said. She advanced a few steps until they were all face-to-face. "What a beautiful baby you are," she said. "I'm your Aunt Joan."

Markie beamed at her. "She's a flirt," Ed said.

"Hi, Ed," Joan said. "It's good to see you again."

"You, too."

"And you, Peggy," Joan said. "And . . . Marguerite."

"Markie," Peggy said. She smiled.

Without thinking, because if she had paused to think she wouldn't have done it, Joan, fighting back the lump in her throat, put her arms around Peggy and the baby. But Peggy did not recoil. When Joan looked at her she had tears in her eyes, too. "I missed you," Joan said. Her voice sounded strange, strangled.

"Well, we're here," Peggy said. She bit her lip. There was another pause. She can't say she missed me too, because she didn't, Joan thought. But I wish she'd just lie and say it.

"Do you want to hold her?" Peggy asked.

"Oh, yes!" What a gesture of trust and forgiveness that was. Joan was overwhelmed. She felt again like the warmly accepted sister she had been during that brief period before everything fell apart, and she swore to herself that she would watch herself every moment to make sure she never did harm again. She held out her arms and Peggy placed Markie in them. Joan waited for the baby to stiffen and draw away, but she didn't. Instead she peered into Joan's eyes curiously, and Joan realized that because of the strong family resemblance this new adult seemed familiar.

This is my baby, Joan thought. How odd. I made

these cells. Look how contented Peggy and Ed are. This one infant saved a whole family. I never dreamed everything would work so well. She kissed Markie's silky cheek. Then Markie turned back to look at her mother, and strained to get away, and Joan handed her over. "She looks just like Marianne," Joan said.

"Yes, but she looks like us, too," Peggy said. "There's a lot of Ed in her, don't you think?"

"Yes," Joan said. Not Ed; Trevor, she thought. Viewed at a certain angle the baby looked so much like her father that Joan missed him again. If I had Trevor with me we'd all be couples, she thought; I'd be like the rest of the world.

"Why doesn't everybody sit down?" Rose offered brightly. "We're going to have dinner in an hour."

They sat, and Ginger and Peter came in with the cans of soda and a bucket of ice, Ben opened wine. Uncle Hugh burst in with Teddy and their dog, followed by Grandma, and Ben mixed martinis. Grandma had her one whiskey sour. Peter had greeted Joan calmly, with a sweet boyish smile, as if they hadn't been away from each other for years, and for that she was grateful too. They all made small talk, the way they used to in the old days.

This is the nature of family, Joan thought: When things go badly it's a nightmare, and when they go well it's nothing special. She couldn't take her eyes off Markie, but she didn't want to take her away or keep her. Just being accepted again, finally, made her feel exhausted. With everyone talking gaily about nothing—the nothing that was the stuff of family, without which there was a cosmic emptiness, with which there was coziness and boredom—Joan realized she would never fit in completely anywhere, but it didn't matter. She fit in well enough.

THIRTY-FOUR

The sixties, the decade that would overturn almost everything people believed in, that would replace complacency with chaos, came in quietly at first. There was an undeclared war in Vietnam, but many people did not even know if this faraway place was spelled as one word or two. As for the war itself, two cultures that could not, and would not, ever understand each other, were about to tear each other apart for no purpose that anyone could fathom, except for the incendiary word *Communism*. America had a new young president, the charismatic John F. Kennedy, the first Catholic in the White House, with a beautiful, fashionable, young wife and two adorable children, and America was besotted with Camelot. People chuckled that it was nice to know someone was having sex in the White House again.

"Ask not what your country can do for you," this president said, "but what you can do for your country." To the silent generation brought up under Granddaddy Eisenhower, who were now coming of age, the notion of activism, of being able to make a difference, was appealing and empowering. People joined the Peace Corps, they traveled the world.

Empowering too was the birth control pill, which in 1960 was approved by the FDA. Although there were frightening warnings attached to this new miracle—

seizures, embolisms, heart attacks, and strokes, especially for smokers—the Pill was in the culture to stay.

There was also an IUD available, for women who were afraid to take the pill. This early intrauterine device, called the Grafenberg Ring, was a coiled wire ring, a kind of cross between a wedding ring and a Slinky. The history of this birth control discovery was interesting: Desert nomads would place a smooth stone in the uterus of their female camels to make sure they would not conceive on a long trip; something was in there already, fooling nature, so an egg would not fertilize. This premise led to the discovery of the IUD for people.

The babies who had been born in such large numbers after World War II were teenagers now, a generation that was becoming a power group by virtue of its size and, more importantly, its disposable income. People still married and fled to the suburbs and their dream of permanent safety, as they had in the fifties, but it would not be long before others wanted to try something new before they settled down. Reliable birth control was about to open up a whole new world. Joan, relieved to see the end of clumsy diaphragms and messy jelly, or the Pill that required remembering, got an IUD.

Joan and Ginger each moved into their own apartment. No one was surprised by Joan's decision, since a girl her age, nearly thirty, did not live at home with her parents, and Joan had always been independent anyway. There were so many apartments available in New York that people didn't bother to paint; they moved instead.

Joan had found a one-bedroom apartment in a new building on the upper East Side, where on nice days she could enjoy a long, healthy walk to work. She was an assistant editor already, and seemed, for the moment at least, to have found her metier. Rose thought

Joan might become a career woman, although that was not what she would have fantasized for her daughter because she felt it carried too much personal unhappiness. Joan was still so attractive; she looked in a way like a pale rose, and she had one boyfriend after another, each of whom lasted several months, and none of whom became permanent.

Ginger's defection from the family town house had caused her parents more concern than Joan's had, although they knew she too had an understandable reason to want to go out on her own. She wanted to be like other people, even if other people had no one to take care of them. It was not as if, Rose was forced to reassure a few of her conservative friends, Ginger wanted her apartment as a place to do something rash and sexual with men. All she did was go to classes and study. Her own apartment was a gesture, a symbol, and she needed it.

Ginger was stunned by the enormity of material she would have to learn at med school. It was not possible for anyone. The medical text book was two thousand pages long, so was the surgery textbook. No one could memorize it all, or even retain large chunks for the short time until they got dizzy; yet, miraculously, many of the students passed their exams anyway. This was only the beginning. For the next two years she would be working in a hospital, learning by treating real patients, albeit in an underling way and with supervision, trying not to be too ignorant, trying not to hurt them by stupidity, by hubris, by mistakes.

She was always aware that in her class of a hundred students there were only ten women, and that everything was more difficult for women than for men. Medicine was macho, it was still a man's world. Your immediate thought of a doctor was as "he." It was made clear to her that she was lucky to be in medical school at all. A woman physician could become a gynecologist or a pediatrician or a psychiatrist, or go into research. Ginger had always wanted to do research anyway, so that was agreeable to her. She wondered now if she wanted a life devoted to painstaking experiments because she had the temperament to sit in a lab all day, or if it was because she thought she couldn't do anything more mobile. It encouraged her that Christopher was planning to go into research too, although he intended to stay in Boston.

Her small apartment, where she lived alone, refusing the idea of a roommate, was in Murray Hill, a nice neighborhood, but on a not particularly nice street. Other med students lived in the neighborhood too. Her building had an elevator, was near to her medical school and the hospital where she hoped to do her internship and residency after she graduated, and her parents had hired someone to install the safety bars she needed for mobility. She would have preferred a wider door and a lower sink, and a higher toilet, but this was a rented apartment, not a house she had built, so it would have to do.

Rose insisted Ginger use the family's cleaning woman, Mavis, once a week, and since Ginger had hardly any time to see her family for dinner, even just to eat, leave, and take a package, Rose always sent over cooked food with her. Ginger knew Mavis was a kind of spy. She was perfectly aware that the cleaning woman reported to her mother that there was no sign of any man in Ginger's apartment—no visiting, no entertaining, no flowers, no scotch whiskey—but that she seemed happy enough, or at least she never said anything.

Why would she tell the cleaning woman about her private life, even though it was still a life of the mind? What a fantasy her mother lived in! Ginger had very little time to think at all, but Christopher Riley leaped uninvited into her thoughts anyway. Wistfully, feeling empty, she imagined his activities in Boston—what was he doing at that exact moment?— and every time she talked to him on the phone just the sound of his voice made her compare him to all the other men she had ever met, and those men seemed like strangers. Sometimes she wondered if after graduation she should move to Boston to be close to him, and do her internship and residency there. Would it be that much harder to do things in a different city than New York? She didn't think so. She could take driving lessons, get a car that was specially equipped with hand controls for the handicapped, as he had just done. What he could do, she could do.

She didn't know if she would ever get over him; she didn't know if she wanted to. He was her hope, her fantasy, her love. If she forgot him she would have to find someone else, and how did she know if that would be possible? Nobody even asked her out. Her unrequited feelings for Chris made her fears about her emotional future recede, and then she could turn back to her work, to which she desperately needed to give her entire attention. She told herself that, for now at least, she had worked out a perfect compromise.

Hugh's antique shop was very successful, and Teddy too had made a lot of money and saved it, so now, perhaps inspired by all the family moving, they gave up their high-rise apartment for a picturesque little mews house on a winding old street in the Village. It had four floors, so they could pretend that each of them lived alone on two of them. However, they bought the house in both their names, and each left his half to the other in his will. We are married now, they told each other, only half in jest, and their joint real estate was there to prove it. Of course, the concept of a marriage between two men was unbelievably bizarre, so they told no one, although Hugh let it slip to the family because he was, despite what the world thought of him, so proud that he had Teddy in his life.

"Too bad you're not actually married," Ben said. "You'd save a fortune in inheritance taxes." Hugh shrieked.

Celia was seventy-five this year, and still spry, still blond, still acid-tongued. Rose gave her a birthday party and everyone came: Maude and Daisy and the other Bristol relatives, the cousins, the husbands, wives and babies; Harriette and her husband, Joan, Ginger, Peggy and Ed and their two children; and Hugh and Teddy, who disappeared right after Celia cut the cake. And then they as quickly reappeared, driving up in a hansom cab Hugh had specially arranged, and took her off for a ride through the city and Central Park.

It was a magical night, crisp and moonlit, and Celia said the experience reminded her of when she was young. Hugh knew Celia didn't like him and never would, but so what, it was her seventy-fifth birthday, and he was happy with life. He hadn't planned the carriage ride to win her over; it was too late for that and they were all too old. Still, she seemed charmed, and talked about her surprise for weeks.

Peggy had a surprise of her own, although, superstitiously, she did not tell her parents until she began to show. She was pregnant again. It had been an accident in a way, but she and Ed were thrilled. She had come from a family of three children, and it was natural to her. All the things she had thought were over for her—only two years ago but now it seemed so much longer—were not over at all. Whether the new arrival was a boy or a girl, Markie would blend into her adoptive family even more when safely bookended by siblings.

When Joan found out Peggy was pregnant she was almost disappointed. Peggy can have children so why shouldn't she have them, she told herself. Still, she felt as if her gift, her sacrifice, her gesture toward expiation, had somehow been minimized. Of course, she acted very pleased.

Rose's old friend Elsie died of lung cancer in the beginning of the new decade, four years before the Surgeon General would announce that cigarettes caused the disease. When he did, of course no one would pay attention and would keep on smoking, even starting if they didn't smoke already. After Elsie's death Rose was one of the few people who stopped smoking altogether before the connection was made official, partly at Ginger's insistence, since Ginger already felt tobacco was dangerous, and partly because quitting was a bargain with God not to let any more bad things happen to her or her family.

When Elsie died Joan went with her parents and Ginger to pay a condolence call at the Wilder house. At one point in the evening Joan went into the bedroom, looking for the bathroom, and the grieving widower, Lionel, followed her.

"I feel so guilty," he said thickly, tears in his eyes. "All the time my wife was dying I was having an affair."

Well, we all knew that, Joan thought, but said nothing and nodded sympathetically although she was in no way sorry for him. He was fat, old, and simian, and nonetheless he had managed to make a woman miserable, perhaps two if you counted his girlfriend as well as his wife. She wondered if he was drunk. Then he reached out and tried to draw her to him. She realized he intended to kiss her, perhaps do something worse. She pulled away in disgust and ran from the room. She felt she was right to be cynical about men.

She did not tell Rose what had happened. Why bring up anything that could cause her mother to think there was something about her that would have incited the fool? When she lived her own life, a single woman was always suspect. Rose was a little perplexed that Joan left the Wilder house so soon after they had arrived, but she knew Joan was busy. It was nice that she had gone at all.

So, in their way, this family at the beginning of the new decade understood each other and they did not, they kept their secrets and revealed them, they, like their country, enjoyed a year or two of peace. They would need it.

THIRTY-FIVE

In 1961 Peggy had her baby, a girl, a welcome companion for Marguerite. Peggy was a conventional housewife with an unconventional penchant for French names, so she named the new baby Angelique. Ed rather liked it. They would call her Angel. The new baby girl had brown hair and a strong nose; she looked like Rose and Ginger, not like Markie, Peter, Peggy, and Ed. In fact, everyone thought (and said, but not within Peggy's hearing) that if you had to pick which one of Peggy and Ed's children was adopted you would choose Angel in a flash.

When Angel was older and didn't have to be attended to every two hours, the two sisters would share the same room, Peggy announced. She said she wanted them to be close. What was also unsaid was that she wanted her daughters to be unlike her and her sister Joan.

As if a room made the magic, Ginger thought ironically. She was taking psychology this year as one of her elective courses, and was fascinated by the factors that made people what they were: Genes and upbringing. Environment changed things, but genes won. Somehow she was not sure she agreed with that, but how would she know? Her mother said she did not have the faintest idea why all her children had turned out to be so different, but that she found the variety refreshing.

In 1962 Ginger entered her third year at medical

school, and became a rotating gofer in the hospital. She drew blood, attached IVs, did spinal taps, questioned and wrote up patients for admissions, kept the records on their charts, fetched and carried, and as soon as she got off, before she collapsed into sleep, she went to the library to read about the meaning of the symptoms she had just recorded because she was sure to be quizzed on them the next morning at rounds.

She, like other medical students looking at symptoms, couldn't help thinking of the most esoteric causes instead of the most obvious; partly, she supposed, because they all wanted to be heroes. It was an old hospital joke that if a group of doctors heard hoofbeats, all of them would think: "Horses," except for the medical student, who would exclaim: "Zebras!" So the least likely affliction was called a zebra.

Everyone started out with the best intentions and boundless enthusiasm, but after working one-hundred-hour weeks, with thirty-hour shifts, surrounded by pain and suffering and death, existing on junk food, being treated as the lowest of the low (which she knew she was), a confused and frightened tourist, trying to hide her ignorance, Ginger realized she had to guard herself from changing into someone she didn't recognize and maybe wouldn't like. Someone heartless, inured to it all, like doctors she had seen? Someone hysterical, who collapsed into tears, which was totally unacceptable? And always, always, she was so tired, so sleep-deprived.

Attaching an IV was the hardest task for all of the new med students. Invading the body and causing pain, finding a vein even when the veins were good, was anxiety-provoking and you often missed. The saying was: "See one, do one, teach one," but Ginger secretly rephrased it as: "See one, miss ten, teach one." She finally learned, but she knew she was not as good at it as the nurses, and that she would always hate doing it.

She also learned to stitch a wound, and she was good at that, at least. Because of her wheelchair she could not work in the operating room, since she was the wrong height, and since surgery involved long hours of standing, even though the medical student never did anything more difficult than holding a retractor (not that this was easy) or snipping the ends of a knot. But you needed to pass surgery to become a doctor, so in a moment of humanity the authorities bent the rules for her and let her observe from above, through a window. It was the only time they ever made anything easy for her.

So long ago, it seemed now, when her class had arrived at medical school, a professor had told them: "Look at the person to the right of you and the person to the left of you. Next year one of them will be gone." In Ginger's case, both of them were gone; one flunked out, the other burned out. She knew she had to try harder than anyone else because she was a woman and handicapped; that these factors would be against her despite the permission to watch operations from afar.

One doctor hated her, but then, he hated and intimidated everyone indiscriminately. His name was Dr. Sweet, and behind his back the students called him "Dr. Sweat." One time, during surgery, the intern who was assisting was so wet with nervous perspiration that his eyeglasses fell off into the sterile operating field. Dr. Sweat picked them up and threw them on the floor, and then furiously ground them under his heel. Ginger was shaking. What will he do to me? she wondered. Tip me out of my chair and tell me to crawl home and stay there? She thought med school was probably like the army; harassment was the name of the game.

There was a real world outside of medical school,

but she and the other students had little time to notice it. The popular dances were the Twist, the Watusi, the Mashed Potato, and the Loco-Motion. There was still enough innocence in the country for a song called "Happy Birthday, Sweet Sixteen" to be in the top ten. That summer Ginger got a job as an assistant in a lab. So did Chris, but still in Boston, of course. In August Marilyn Monroe committed suicide, with rumors of foul play, and Uncle Hugh was devastated. Marilyn had apparently been having affairs with both Kennedys: the President and the Attorney General.

Beautiful actresses who wore tight glittery dresses and had affairs with famous men were so removed from Ginger's life that they might as well have existed only on the screen. She hardly ever went to movies, and if she did, she fell asleep in them, and the only television show she watched, and not often, was *Dr. Kildare*. Rivalry among the students, and desperate, blatant ambition were rampant. On New Year's Eve she went to a party, without a date, where some of the male med students claimed to have put human breast milk into the eggnog; but despite occasional moments of goofiness and fun, everyone Ginger knew was afraid of doing something wrong. They often did, they were publicly humiliated for it, and yet they still fantasized about finding a cure for cancer or making a ton of money.

Some of the boys she knew at medical school were getting married. People were getting married young anyway, and this way the wives, who usually had no career ambitions of their own, could work to pay the husband's tuition bills, and of course do the laundry, the cooking, and clean the apartment. It was worthy, and expected, for a woman to help her man achieve his dream, the dream that would provide for both of them: the practice, the money, the lovely house, the cars, the kids; and then she could retire and become Peggy. The few female medical students Ginger knew were getting married too, usually to other med students who understood them, who didn't think they were too smart to be feminine; and their parents helped them out with living expenses.

Seeing all this, the pairing off, Ginger felt alone and different, socially naive and inept, too young for grown-up life because no one wanted her, and at the same time getting older every minute until it seemed grown-up life might pass her by.

The idea of transferring to Boston to be near Chris for her internship and residency began to seem more and more realistic, even achievable—her first chance. Her parents, when she broached the subject, were anxious about it, but they said, finally, that it wouldn't hurt for her to take a trip to Boston and look, even though it was a little premature. Maybe she would change her mind, they said, but they didn't want her to think she had missed something.

By now, Ginger's parents knew that when she set her mind to something there was very little they could do to talk her out of it. All these years they had willingly paid for her expensive education and what it cost to get by decently on her own. It was their investment in her survival. Rose and Ben prided themselves on being kind, modern parents, and besides, they knew Ginger had little chance of achieving a conventional destiny, and they admired her courage and her wish to help people. They would not be around forever, and it was important that she should become equipped to take care of herself.

So, on a sunny September weekend, Ginger went to Boston with Hugh and Teddy, in the station wagon they had bought for the weekends they sometimes spent at country inns. "Maybe I should stay a bachelor too," Ginger joked. "All that money just for me and my good times."

"You know I'm not a bachelor," Hugh said. "I'm a married woman."

"Well, of course," Ginger said. "I keep forgetting."

"And so will you be too," Teddy said to her. "You'll see. You'll find a man worthy of you."

"I just want Chris."

"Still? Ah, well. Then perhaps it's destined," Hugh said.

Of course Christopher knew they were coming, and he had volunteered to help her sightsee and look at hospitals, residential neighborhoods, all of it, in his new car. How independent we both are, Ginger thought hopefully. We're not freaks, the way we thought we would be when we were kids. We're part of the community. We will do great things. With a good night's sleep behind her, her love for him fired her with courage and dreams. Driving past Cambridge, on the way into the city where she would meet him soon, Ginger noticed the sculls on the Charles River, the Harvard boys in them, paddling hard, skimming gracefully over the water, and she felt her heart leap with such crazy optimism that she thought: I could do that! I have so much upper body strength.... Never mind that girls couldn't, that she would not have time anyway. In this new future life she envisioned for herself she could do anything.

She, Hugh, and Teddy were staying at the calm and elegant Ritz. Across the street was the Common, with the lake, and the swan boats, about to be put away for winter. It had been a long trip and she was tired. The three of them unpacked and ordered a late lunch from room service. Her room was next to theirs, with a view of the trees and gardens. As soon as she checked in she had called Chris, and he said he would come by to meet her at five o'clock, they could have a drink in the bar and talk, then tomorrow morning they could devote to seeing whatever she wanted.

Ginger took a bath and put on makeup, the first time she had worn makeup in so long she almost couldn't remember. Although she and Chris had been overworked and exhausted, they had managed to telephone and commiserate with each other nearly every week, like soul mates, and on holidays they even sent photographs, like family watching each other grow up and mature, but they hadn't actually laid eyes on each other in seven years. It was hard to believe, and she would be ashamed to tell anyone. She thought that anyone else would consider her persistent infatuation with him deranged. Yet, they spoke to each other more often and at greater length than she spoke to any other friend, and they had become a fixture in each other's lives. It was Victorian, anachronistic, romantic. She knew he dated, although not much, and he probably thought she did too, on the same level. But none of his interludes were ever serious—who has time? he said—and he always came back to her. "No one else understands me like you do," he would say. "You're a part of me. We'll see each other soon. We'll work something out."

Well, now she was working something out. She wondered why she hadn't done it before. But she had been too young, too immature and afraid to uproot her life, and so had he. His parents weren't as sophisticated as hers. Unlike hers, it was clear that his called the shots because they controlled the money and he was in a wheelchair. Christopher had finally gotten his own apartment too, just last year, but he'd told her it had been hard to convince his parents, and the only reason they'd given in was that he needed to be nearer med school because of the long hours and they were afraid he would fall asleep at the wheel.

It was not considered odd for a young man with paralyzed legs to live at home, although in Ginger's opinion it was as crippling as their polio. In many ways

Chris was not like other people his age, and she thought that their friendship and exchange of ideas had probably saved him from being, in some way, destroyed. He needs me just as much as I need him, Ginger thought; perhaps even more. I would never admit it to him or to anyone else, but if you had to decide, I'm the strong one. It didn't make her love him less; in a way it enhanced her tenderness for him.

She was sitting in her wheelchair next to a small table in the dark, cool bar when Chris rolled in. "I can't believe it's you!" he exclaimed.

"I can't believe it's you, either."

They hugged, and then he kissed her on the lips and Ginger felt the electricity go through her whole body. He was larger somehow, more mature, more muscled, more a grown man, and although she had memorized his latest photograph with the passion of a grieving wife, he did look different. But his eyes and smile were the same. "How pretty you look, Ginger," he said.

"Thank you." She couldn't stop smiling, nor could he; they were glowing there in that artificial twilight and he took her hand and wound his fingers around hers. I could stay here like this forever, she thought, but she knew there was more.

"What are we drinking?" Chris asked.

"I haven't ordered yet."

"How about champagne?"

"Champagne?"

"Why not?" he said happily. "We have lots of things to celebrate."

Their waiter brought a bottle of Veuve Cliquot and opened it. "To us," Ginger said, holding up her glass.

He touched hers with his. "To us, forever."

"I'm so glad to see you," she said.

"And I to see you. You're staying at a very fancy hotel," he added.

"Did you have a problem parking?" she asked, to deflect the inference that she was richer than he was.

"Actually, a friend dropped me off."

"Good, then we can get drunk. We never did, do you realize? We never had a drink together."

"We were too young. It was illegal."

"And now we're too busy."

They beamed at each other again and sipped their champagne. "So you're going to try for B.U. Hospital," Chris said.

"Yes, and Peter Bent Brigham. Of course I'd have to see them. But I would take your advice, I trust you. I'd go where you go."

"Then when we graduate we can become a research team and get the Nobel Prize. Remember all our plans?"

"Of course I remember," Ginger said. But I'd rather not, she thought. It seemed I was the one making the plans and you were the one getting out of them. "I think I'm going to like Boston," she said. "It's beautiful."

"Wait for the beautiful treacherous snow."

"You're still alive and well."

"Always," he said. He looked her over carefully, nodding as if assessing her. "I can't believe we haven't actually seen each other in such a long time. How can we have done that? People should live in the same city with their best friend."

"I know."

"So you came here with the uncle?" They always referred to Hugh as "the" uncle because of the way he had first introduced himself. It still made them laugh.

"Yes. 'The' uncle and the uncle's roommate."

"What a family you have."

"I love them."

"So do I, and I don't even know them."

Something about the champagne and being in his

presence at last made Ginger feel all the barriers she had put up the past three years to survive in medical school start melting away. She was down to the core of her real self, and she was safe. "Chris, you are the most special person," she said. "You have no idea how wonderful you are."

"That's what I like to hear." He was playing with her fingers. "I want us both to have happy lives, Ginger. You know that, don't you?"

"Well, I guess so. We'll do our best."

"If you decide to come here for your internship and residency I'll help you in any way I can. It's hard to start in a new place."

"I'm not afraid."

"You won't have to be."

I was right to make this decision, she thought. She felt peaceful and happy. "Can we start at nine o'clock tomorrow morning?"

"No problem."

"I'm sorry you're not free to have dinner with us tonight," she said, although they had already discussed that. Now that she was face-to-face with him she felt even more strongly than ever that she didn't want to let him out of her sight. Oh, I could so easily get obsessed with love and ruin my whole career, she thought, and sighed.

"What is that big sigh?"

"Nothing. I'm unwinding."

He sighed too. Then he let go of her hand. "I do have another piece of news," he said. "I thought I'd save it until you got here so I could tell you in person."

"I'm here, so tell me."

"It's a big piece of news."

"What?"

"I just got engaged."

Ginger started to tremble and couldn't stop. "What do you mean?"

"Engaged to be married," Christopher said.

"I know what engaged means."

"She's someone I've known for quite a while, and then it turned into something more. I mean, one day we just looked at each other and then we started dating. I proposed on the second date."

Am I to be spared nothing? Ginger thought.

"She's quite wonderful, you'll like her," Chris went on. "Her name is Susan. People call her Sue Sue. She's a happy person, always up. That's good for me because I tend to be moody and get discouraged."

"I know what you're like," Ginger snapped. Her eyes were filling with tears. Chris was engaged to be married. Her life with him, which hadn't really started, was over. "Do you love her?" she asked.

"Yes, I do."

If I hold on to this chair as hard as I can and take deep breaths maybe I can stop shaking, she thought. She knew no medical intervention for a broken heart, so perhaps she should just think of her condition as shock.

"You look terrible," he said.

"I do?"

"You look like I did something unforgivable to you. I mean, you knew we were always best friends, the best in the world, and you'll always be important in my life, but . . ."

"No, I . . . ," Ginger stammered. "What does she do?"

"She's a travel agent. Well, an assistant. She'll work while I finish getting my MD, and then . . ."

"Of course she will," Ginger said. "She'll put you through school. Then she'll quit and have kids."

He nodded. "Unfortunately my parents don't have as much money as yours."

"Is this about *money*?" Ginger said. For an instant she hated him.

"No, I'm sorry. I didn't mean that to sound like a criticism, but it's a fact."

"I thought I knew you," Ginger said.

"You do. Please wish me well."

"I wish you well."

They looked into each other's eyes, a long, angry, guilty, complicitous look. She knew what he was thinking: *Ginger, did I ever propose to you? Did we ever discuss marriage? No.* Unfortunately he also knew what she was thinking, even though there was no basis for it: *You lied.*

"We're getting married the day before Thanksgiving," he said. "I've already arranged to get the day off. Will you come to the wedding? Her mother is sending you an invitation."

She didn't answer. She didn't know what to say and she was afraid if she tried to speak she would burst into tears.

"It's a very small wedding," he went on. "I don't have that many friends. You're very special to me, Ginger. It would mean a great deal if you came. If you were a guy I'd make you be my best man."

"Well, I'm not a guy."

"I've noticed that."

"I have to leave," Ginger said.

"Well, wait a minute. Sue Sue is coming to get me. I wanted the two of you to meet."

I would never go to your wedding, Ginger thought. Never, never, Sue Sue. It would kill me. "All right," she said pleasantly. "Just for a bit."

He doesn't want a partner, she thought. He wants a civilian, he wants a little wife.

"I know you so well," Chris said. "I know what you're thinking all the time."

"No, you don't."

"I'm happy to say you're more confident than you used to be."

"In what way?"

"You didn't ask me if she could walk."

"Can she?"

"Yes," he said. "Yes, she's a totally ambulatory person."

"I don't *care*," Ginger said.

I know more about love now, she thought. It could be about money and normal working legs and a sunny disposition, or it could be about honesty and sex and closeness, or it could be none of those things. Love makes no sense at all. And that's all I know about it.

She couldn't think of anything to say to him, but that was all right because he was talking a blue streak about medical school to cover up the awkward silence. Then Susan arrived, tall and slim and sexy with wild reddish curls and green eyes and definitely walking, no, striding, and gave Chris a kiss and Ginger a firm handshake, and said she was double-parked and thank goodness for the handicapped sticker, and then when Chris had paid the check she took hold of the handles on his wheelchair and wheeled him away with the determination of a dominatrix. "Come to the wedding!" she cried cheerfully. "We'll see you there!"

"I'll pick you up here in the lobby at nine sharp tomorrow morning," Chris called.

"Good-bye," Ginger murmured, but he had no idea what she meant.

That night there was room service again because Ginger couldn't stop sobbing and Hugh and Teddy couldn't comfort her. There was another bottle of champagne, which she was grateful for, and then she threw up. The next morning at seven she insisted they leave and drive home. She didn't even leave a note or a message for Christopher. The concierge would tell him they had checked out. She was reminded of a novel she had read some years ago called *Marjorie Morningstar*, about a girl who was in love with a man who was not what he pretended to be, who followed that man to Paris and realized he didn't love her. So Marjorie Morningstar had left Paris immediately without even seeing it. At the time Ginger had thought she was a fool. I would at least have waited to see Paris, she had thought those years ago, as long as I was already there. City of Lights.

But Boston was not Paris. Marjorie had been too devastated to see Paris, and Ginger, equally devastated, had no reason anymore to be curious about Boston. No, she was going to become a doctor in New York. Boston was not Paris and Christopher Riley was not Noel Airman, but driving home Ginger knew one thing: She had more in common with Marjorie Morningstar, a fictional heroine she had giggled at, than she would ever have believed possible.

THIRTY-SIX

The strangeness, as Celia thought of the events that were happening to her, started slowly. She would telephone her friend Violet, or her friend Dorothy, and they would sound surprised, abrupt. "Yes?" they'd ask, not unpleasantly, but as if they had no time for her.

"Well I thought I'd call you," Celia would say, puzzled at the response she was getting from such dear old friends.

"But we talked twice this morning and you just called me five minutes ago," they would answer. "Didn't we speak?"

"Oh, well...," Celia would answer, flustered. "Did we?"

"Am I forgetful or are you?"

"Who knows, at our age," Celia would laugh, and then cover for herself. "I actually dialed the wrong number."

It frightened her that she could forget something like that. She had been talking to her friends for years and years. In fact, she remembered very well when the telephone had been invented and nobody wanted one. Why, they asked, amused, would we need such a thing? We send notes, we pay calls. We run down the street to see our friends if anything seems urgent. If we had telephones, they would just be another difficult modern thing to get used to. Of course, now Celia didn't know how she had ever existed without one.

So as not to embarrass herself and annoy her friends, now she copied each friend's name from her address book when she made the first call in the morning, in her neat little penmanship, the kind you didn't see anymore, and as soon as she had gotten through with the call she checked it off. Then if later, five minutes later or an hour or so, she thought of telephoning that person, she would look at her list to see if she already had. She kept the lists for several days so she wouldn't turn into a pest. After the first few days she realized she had to put the date on top of the page too, and she kept her calendar open on her desk with each day checked off. She knew what day it was because she had the *New York Times* delivered and it told you on top.

The grocery had become part of the strangeness too, although it didn't really bother her. Unless she brought a shopping list she always ended up duplicating things she had bought only yesterday. Well, then I'll have a backup supply, Celia told herself. It wasn't a tragedy.

She remembered certain things so well: The sound of a hammer hitting steel in the clear morning air when she had first come to New York and everything was in the process of being built. The excitement that sound created in her spirit. The motes of dust that flew around her head when she was at the blackboard in the First Grade. She must have been writing her alphabet, or perhaps her sums, but naturally she couldn't re- member that.

Her mind was awash with memories; she would wake up in the morning and lie in bed and just let them arrive. Alfred, of course, dearest Alfred, her little boy, and the smell of warm sand when they went to the beach. What itchy woolen bathing suits they wore then, on those hot days! It was a wonder a person didn't drown in them. And Celia remembered those lemon cookies she used to make, and still could, which everyone loved. Yes, she had given lemon cookies to every child who came into the bake shop, including the ones who later became her stepchildren.

She remembered bits and pieces of her life in Bristol, so long ago. How easy Daisy was, growing up, and how much trouble Harriette gave her later. But was that in Bristol? Yes, Celia thought it was. She remembered Rose, as a flapper, in her short dress, which, when you thought about it, wasn't so short after all, and the beaded Indian headband Rose wore around her forehead. These pictures and memories floated in and out of her mind, usually giving her pleasure. There were other memories of incidents in her long life, not so friendly, but Celia chose to push them away.

She could not remember the names of her great-grandchildren, but there were so many, how could anyone be expected to?

Sometimes, for a few years now, Celia would walk into a room in her apartment and did not have the faintest idea why she was there. She knew she'd come after something, but what? Her mind was a total blank. She would retrace her steps, but to no avail, and then, perhaps an hour later, it would come back to her. But these days, since the strange things had started happening, it never came back. All her life she had heard that old people were forgetful. She was seventy-eight, which was far older an age than she had ever expected to live to see, but she didn't want anyone to know she wasn't just as she always had been. She didn't want anyone to feel sorry for her or think she could not cope.

Then one morning something really disturbing happened. She sat on the toilet to urinate and realized when it was too late that she had forgotten to pull her underpants down. They were soaked and Celia was horrified. She pulled them off and threw them into the washing machine. She was certainly compos mentis enough, she told herself, to know how a washing machine worked. She remembered how glad she'd been to get one, when they first came out, even though they were so clumsy with the big wringer. Of course now she had the newest model. She had always been proud to be modern. And today she was wetting herself, like a baby. She swore to herself she would never let it happen again.

It did happen again, and the worst part was she remembered it was not the first time. Celia stopped wearing underpants. She could pee through the opening in her girdle, no one would know. That was probably why it was there in the first place.

Her dog, Spunky, was dead, long dead, but sometimes she thought she saw him, running to her, his ball in his mouth, ready to play. Why had she decided not to get another dog, when she had loved that one so much? She remembered now, finally; it was because she had wanted to be free. And she had been free, hadn't she, and had adventures? Sometimes Celia had to look through her photo album just to be sure things had really happened to her. Her trips, for example, which she knew she had enjoyed, although she did not have the faintest idea of the identity of those people in the pictures with her, who seemed from their happy expressions to like being in her company.

"Don't get old," she admonished Ginger, "it's no fun," and Ginger had laughed. Of course, that was before the really strange things started happening.

One day Celia found herself on the streets of New York, carrying a bag of groceries, and had absolutely no idea where she lived. It was like a bad dream, and at first she thought it was. But she didn't wake up, and after wandering around for quite a while she realized she was truly lost. Where had she come from? Where was she going? Suddenly, she was very frightened. There was a policeman on the corner, and Celia knew

who she was in case he asked, but he wouldn't know
how to help her. She had no address on her person,
only her name on her medical card in case she had to
be taken to the hospital. She didn't want to go to a hospital, she wanted to go home. She knew why lost children wept and screamed when they found themselves
deserted. But for whom should she weep and scream?

Now she was terrified. Walking, walking, looking
for something she might recognize, she found herself
on a tree-lined street of brownstone houses. She knew
one. She had been there before, several times. She went
up the stairs and rang the bell.

"Celia!" Rose said with pleasure and surprise, opening the door. "Come in."

"Oh…," Celia said softly, and it was all she could do
not to fling her arms around this reassuring and familiar figure.

"Come on," Rose said, taking her groceries. "Would
you like some coffee?"

Celia looked at her watch. It was still morning.
"Yes," she said, "that would be nice. I was just in the
neighborhood and I thought I'd say hello."

"The neighborhood?" Rose said. "But you've been
to Gristedes, that's really far away."

"I took a cab," Celia lied.

"You don't need an excuse to visit us," Rose said.
She was peering at Celia as if she knew there was
something wrong. "Your face, your blouse, you're
soaked," she said.

"It's not raining."

"I know. You must have been running."

"I'd like to sit down."

When she had sat in the drawing room and had coffee, and reassured herself twice that Rose had put the
milk she had bought into the refrigerator, Celia began
to wonder if she should tell. I was lost, she could say, I
forgot where I've lived for years. She waited for the

memory of her home to come back. My own house, she begged her mind. Tell me where it is.

"Celia, you look so distraught," Rose said.

"I do?"

"Yes." Rose waited expectantly. "I hope it isn't bad news."

You have no idea how bad, Celia thought. She didn't answer. They'll make me go to a doctor, she thought, and he'll tell me I'm going senile. They'll get me a paid keeper, or worse, put me away. I'd rather be dead.

Rose looked at her watch. "I don't want to rush you," she said, "but I have an appointment at ten-thirty. I'm having some hats made. Would you like to come?"

"If you're taking a taxi you could drop me off at home," Celia said, feeling crafty. "I'm a little tired."

"Of course," Rose said. "Are you sure you're feeling well? I won't go if you're sick."

"I'm fine."

"All right then."

When the taxi stopped at Celia's house she knew she was safe. It was familiar…why, she had lived there for ages! And it was so close. What a bizarre and terrible experience this morning had been. She hoped it would never happen again.

"What are you doing this evening?" Rose asked, by way of farewell.

This evening? Celia did not have the faintest idea. "Perhaps have a friend in for dinner," she lied. "I bought all this food."

"Call me later," Rose said.

"I will."

Celia forgot to call, of course, so Rose, the caretaker, called her. "How was your dinner party?" Rose asked.

Dinner party? Celia knew she had not been out to dinner. "The usual," she lied, sounding cheerful.

"You're amazing," Rose said. "You have more energy than any of us."

Celia chuckled. When they had said good night and hung up she went into her bathroom and looked into the mirror. Yes, she was an old woman now, her skin hung in folds, her eyes were very small, her roots were pure white. But she still had her spirit, her strength. That was all she had left. This terrible thing that was happening would stay her secret for as long as she could keep it. She couldn't tell Rose she was losing her mind to cobwebs. She couldn't tell any of them. They all had such a high opinion of her.

THIRTY-SEVEN

By 1963 the safe world Peggy, and everyone else, had known was beginning to be turned upside down again. The war in Vietnam escalated, the Bay of Pigs invasion was a fiasco, and the Cold War escalated too. In the South there were peace marches, Freedom Riders, and murders. Martin Luther King spoke eloquently of the legitimate claims the Negroes (who were not yet called Blacks) were now demanding of their society; because of the color of their skin people were killed and gassed and attacked by dogs and fire hoses while trying to gain ordinary rights like voting and decent schooling. And then, in November of 1963, President Kennedy was assassinated by a mild-looking man named Lee Harvey Oswald. No one who was alive that day would ever forget where they were when they heard the news. Peggy was folding the laundry.

Now that things had returned to normal in her household, she was a full-time housewife again. Mrs. McCoo, who had been so devoted when Marianne died, was back to working her second job and making Peggy share her. Angel was two-and-a-half, and Markie nearly five. Only Peter, already his mother's height at fourteen, was relatively independent, although he was still in many ways a child who needed supervision, and of course he had to be driven places. Having two little girls not yet school age was harder than Peggy had expected. Keeping up the house was a lot of work too. She seemed to do laundry forever, vacuuming was endless, cleaning up after people more so, but she prided herself on her cleanliness and skills. She went to the PTA, she attempted to read a good current novel every month, she tried out different recipes at dinner, she even made her own bread. Her children had lovely clothes, lots of instructive toys, and were relatively well behaved.

She and Ed watched the films of the assassination and the funeral on television. The riderless horse seemed to symbolize their country at this moment, the small fatherless boy saluting the coffin made her eyes fill with tears. Ed didn't like Lyndon Johnson, so Peggy didn't either, although she had little interest in politics. But the phrases "conspiracy theory" and "grassy knoll" were a part of everyone's vocabulary now.

But there was something else that had crept into people's vocabulary this year that, to Peggy, seemed equally ominous. It was "the Feminine Mystique." The Betty Friedan bestseller posited that housewives were overeducated for their chores and frustrated in their lives, that women were victims of the media and the men who ran it, that the ways in which a woman was supposed to be "feminine" were simply ploys to enslave her. Peggy would have laughed at all of it, so ridiculous it seemed, but there was a minor revolution going on in her neighborhood. Her friends were declaring to each other that they were unhappy, unfulfilled, frustrated, even angry, and now they had discovered the reason why. They didn't want to be housewives. They were not married to the house. The house's wife? They had discussed philosophy at college and now they were scraping baby shit out of diapers. Yet, what else could they do? Work and take care of their family? Were there enough hours in the day?

Peggy remembered an ad she had seen from Ed's agency one Mother's Day, for frilly nightgowns and

negligees. It read: "Show Mom she's a woman too." At
the time it had meant nothing; it was cute. But, was she
not a woman? Peggy thought now, in alarm. Just
"good old Mom"? Taking care of her home and loved
ones, doing it well, was what made one a woman, or at
least she had always believed that. And mothers had
power. She'd never been an educated woman, even
though it was her own fault. God knows, her parents
had tried hard enough, but all she had wanted was Ed.
She had hated working. She had never wanted anything to do with a career, and actually, she felt sorry for
Joan, who had an expense account now in her publishing job and was allowed to take authors to lunch. Joan
was a misfit, and who knew if she would ever find a
husband? She had a sex life, that Peggy knew, but what
good was it if the men always left? Sometimes, Joan
threw them out. But what difference did it make; she
ended up alone.

Secretly, with annoyance and contempt, Peggy
thought of her sister Joan as a slut. She herself had slept
with Ed before they were married, against the stan-
dards of society, but they had been engaged and then
they did get married and she had never been touched
by another man, not before him and not afterward. If
she hadn't met Ed, Peggy was certain she would never
have acted like Joan. She would have married someone
else, married young, and she would have been a virgin
until they declared their future.

Despite their mutual pretense, she and Joan were
still not close. They were just too different, in too many
ways, and always had been. Peggy was disturbed and
threatened by the things people were saying now
about the lives women were forced to lead—or had
chosen! she thought angrily, no one *made* us do it—and
Joan was delighted by the growing dissatisfaction and
felt vindicated. Peggy hated how smug Joan seemed
these days.

Sometimes Joan came for a weekend, inviting herself most times, and brought manuscripts to read, and gossip about literary people Peggy didn't know and didn't care about. Actually, she brought Peggy most of the novels Peggy read, because Joan could get all the publishers' books free. Ed would leave the two sisters alone, pretending to be gracious about "the girls' time together" but in truth delighted that he could watch sports on television or play golf or tennis with the men. Peggy showed off her home, her garden, her acre, her children. She wondered if Joan's apartment was clean; she doubted it. But at least Joan's fascination with Peggy's two little girls never wavered. Joan could just sit and watch them playing. Sometimes the two children hugged, like a picture from a greeting card. It was a sight to make a mother's heart proud, but apparently it inspired their aunt, too.

"Ah," Joan sighed once, "they're me and Ginger, aren't they? Just closer in age."

"You mean, Ginger and me," Peggy said.

"Oh, never mind the grammar."

"I'm talking about the likeness. Markie is a total duplicate of me."

"And me," Joan said, oddly. "But it doesn't matter."

"No, it doesn't."

It was obvious what was the matter with Joan, poor childless thing. "You should have a baby of your own before it's too late," Peggy said to her.

Joan just shrugged and changed the subject. Her face snapped shut, like a door. "I guess you heard, Grandma's getting forgetful," she said. "Mom told me."

"Yes," Peggy said, "she mentioned something like that."

"It's pretty serious. Twice Grandma went out and forgot where she lived. She came over to Mom and Dad's house. Apparently she recognized it. The second time Mom made her confess. Mom made her go to the doctor; she practically had to drag her. The doctor said she'd had a few tiny strokes. He said it's more common than you'd think. No one knew about the strokes at the time, not even Grandma. It's as if one day she was fine, feisty and independent as ever, and now all of a sudden she's scared.''

"She's seventy-eight, after all," Peggy said.

"That's pretty old."

"Well, if she's wandering around she can't live alone anymore," Peggy said. "They'll have to get her a companion."

"Poor Grandma."

"Yes, poor old Grandma."

They thought about this for a while in silence. "Do you think she could live with Mom and Dad?" Peggy asked.

"She'd give *them* a stroke. They're too old already, and you can't go back in life. What's done is done."

"What does that mean?"

"It's just…some people should move on. Mom and Grandma were always nice to each other, but they were never that close. Not enough to live together. Celia isn't Rose's real mother."

"But Celia brought her up."

"It's not the same," Joan said. Her voice sounded distant and Peggy supposed Joan knew things she didn't know, but she didn't care enough to ask her. It was ancient history by now.

"Then, maybe she could go back to live with Daisy in Bristol," Peggy said.

"No, she'd hate that. Grandma is a dyed-in-the-wool New Yorker."

"Not if she doesn't know where she is."

"Peggy, that's mean."

"No, it's realistic."

"Anyway, Grandma insists she's not that bad yet," Joan said.

"I suppose she could live with Harriette," Peggy said. "Grandma and Harriette have been getting along a lot better since Harriette married Julius."

"That's because they don't see each other," Joan said.

"It's terrible to get old," Peggy said. She was thirty-six, not young, but too far away from Celia's predicament to take it personally. "I guess I'll be an old widow myself some day," she said, and she felt as if she were talking about someone else. "But I don't want to think about it. I'm lucky I have three children. At least one of them will take care of me if I don't nag them too much while they're young."

"I wouldn't count on it," Joan said.

Peggy glared at her. "Joan, you're really mean. You're meaner than I am."

"Just realistic," Joan said flatly, her tone imitating Peggy's.

"At least I know you and I won't live together."

"Don't count on that either," Joan said, and laughed in a strange and phony way. What a weird one she was, Peggy thought.

Sometimes, when she had time to dwell on things other than her immediate family, Peggy wondered about Joan. There was a subtext under Joan's banter that remained a mystery. Love and resentment; she could feel the two forces pulling them both. Some sisters were so estranged they never saw each other. Joan had gone away but she had come back. Obviously that was her own choice. The two of them were united by blood and nearly a lifetime of experience, but they were both aware that if they weren't sisters they wouldn't be able to bear spending these weekends in one another's company. It was strange to look at someone you'd known almost all your life, who looked just like you, and whose thoughts and motivations and wishes were so different from yours that they were obscure.

If Joan was the liberated woman of the future, Peggy didn't like it. The best thing about Joan was that she so obviously loved Markie. She loved Angel too, but Markie was her favorite. Sometimes, when Joan thought Peggy wasn't looking, she just stared at Markie, as if the two of them were alone in another world.

But the motivation for that too, while it should have been normal, was obscure, and Peggy wouldn't have known how to begin to analyze why she wasn't simply pleased. Instead of being flattered, something about Joan's fascination with Markie made Peggy uncomfortable, although she had no idea why. It wasn't as if Joan was going to influence her. Peggy was much too strong to allow anything like that to happen to her daughter. Joan can look down on my life all she wants to, Peggy thought, but a part of her wants it too, I'll bet, and that's her problem. She chose her way.

THIRTY-EIGHT

The thalidomide babies were in the newspapers. The drug, which had been prescribed in England and Europe during the late fifties and early sixties for sleepless, nervous, nauseated pregnant women, had been rejected for approval by the FDA, and therefore kept out of America, by the resolute efforts of one stubborn woman doctor, Dr. Frances Kelsey. Now here were photographs of the children who had been born to these women: with flippers instead of limbs, arms and legs sometimes deformed, sometimes altogether missing; the fetuses' little peripheral stubs stunted in the womb. Still too young to comprehend what had happened to them, the thalidomide babies were laughing and happy, crawling like seals, rolling like balls, always moving, in the way little children do. The older ones were being fitted with prostheses.

Some of them were blind, some were deaf, some had cleft palates; all had malformations of some kind. As ever, in the rush to make everyone healthy and comfortable, the people who discovered new panaceas also made various mistakes, quite often, in fact. The curing business was still primitive, although doctors who looked back at the limited knowledge of the past thought the present was full of wonders.

Ginger had thought she knew a lot about the sick. She had been around patients ever since she was a teenager volunteering with handicapped foundlings, and then in Warm Springs when she was a patient herself, and later in medical school when she worked at the hospital. She was an intern now, people called her "Doctor." She had a stethoscope and a white coat. She was still sleep-deprived, working every day and every third night, looking at every kind of human misery. Gunshot wounds, stabbings, cancer, the people for whom surgery worked, quite simply, and those for whom it did not, no matter how complicated. People who would die without regaining consciousness and the ones who knew they were dying; and the ones who would have pieces of them removed over and over in order to try to live. Chemotherapy so strong it burned the skin and made the flesh turn black. She saw physical pain and emotional pain, bravery, terror, and resignation. She said good-bye to the patients who walked out of the hospital cured and she said good-bye to the patients who did not. She tended to deranged people and drug addicts and killers and attempted suicides. She caught babies when they were born and loved them all, even when their mothers didn't.

And finally it seemed as if everything she had seen throughout her hospital years was falling into place. She wondered why she had not understood life before. The Ginger who had felt sorry for herself because she was in a wheelchair seemed immature. It was not an easy situation, but it was, by and large, manageable. She had seen so many sick people, so much death and suffering, that she had begun to think she was actually lucky. She was intelligent and productive and immersed in work, she saw her future as something both predictable and a glowing surprise. Paralyzed legs were a minor disability. Chris had known that for far longer than she had.

She had not gone to his wedding, even the thought was too painful, but she had sent a gift: a silver picture frame, in which, she supposed, he would put a photograph of himself and his wife, or perhaps their children when they had them. A picture frame was both personal and impersonal. He might remember that they had sent each other photographs through the years, and had framed them. But a picture frame was actually nothing; without a person inside it was merely a staring eye.

There was no picture in the frame she sent him for his wedding present because what she was saying was: "From now on your life is up to you." As hers was up to her. The thank-you note, from both of them, was in Sue Sue's handwriting. Of course. It hurt for only a little while.

To her amazement Chris still called her from time to time, just to say hello. She had been his best friend, but now Ginger knew his wife would have to be his best friend or the marriage would not work. Ginger had been about to tell him that, but then he had stopped calling. He had probably figured it out for himself, or perhaps Sue Sue was jealous. Ginger didn't call him anymore, although she sent Christmas cards, and so did he. When she got the second card, the second Christmas, she realized how long it had been since they had communicated, and after a brief pang of sadness she went back to start her day.

That Christmas was sad for another reason: Grandma. She could not come to family functions anymore because she didn't know where she was, she was in diapers as a precaution, although "precaution" was a family euphemism for necessity, and she often had to be fed. Sometimes she got angry for no reason, her mind like a spinning top. No one took her to have her hair colored, and it was white and sparse. Her dresses always had food spots on them. Celia had loved clothes, but now she didn't care. She had been vain and cheerful, and now she had lost her dignity along with the memory of all the things she had been so interested in. No wonder she was angry—poor Grandma—although Ginger knew the anger was also part of the disease.

Grandma had had a companion for a while now, a woman who spent her time taking care of such people and living with them, but it was clear that sooner or later Celia would need either full-time nurses, which would be prohibitively expensive, or have to go to a home. Grandma had faded so quickly! Rose looked at suitable places near New York City, and Aunt Daisy, who seemed even more distraught than Ginger would have thought she would be, wanted Celia to come back to Bristol, to an old folks' home there. Bristol was where she would be buried, next to Grandpa. Right now, Ginger thought, she's only buried alive.

Ginger went to visit Celia before Aunt Daisy and the soon-to-be-discharged companion took her back to Bristol. Her things had been packed, some to go with her, some to go into storage, others to be given away. It was as if she were already dead. She couldn't take a lot of things with her to the home; she would have a roommate and there simply wasn't enough space. Ginger was glad Celia didn't know what was happening. Somehow Celia had gotten it into her mind that she was going on a vacation trip, and she seemed pleased. Over and over she asked where she was going, and when they told her, over and over, she nodded.

"Little Ginger," she said, peering, recognizing her. They were eye level, both in their wheelchairs. Ginger could see from her expression that Grandma thought she was still a child.

"Tiny little Grandma," Ginger said, and choked back the lump in her throat.

"Did you sleepwalk again?" Celia asked.

"Sleepwalk?"

"Oh, yes. You like to wander away. You give your parents so much trouble."

"Not anymore," Ginger said.

"You'd better not." Celia looked stern.

"I won't."

"I don't have much truck for children who disobey their parents," Celia said. "Lock you in your room is what you deserve. I told your mother, but she cried when you cried. Did you know that? She let you out."

Ginger recalled those nights when she was a prisoner and her skin began to crawl. "That was a long time ago," she said.

"Was it? I don't remember. Don't let Hugh come to visit me on my vacation. I have no use for him. Never did."

"All right," Ginger said.

"Something wrong with that boy," Celia said. "Always has been. I can't stand him."

"Look at the beautiful apple I have for you, Grandma," Ginger said brightly, picking it up from the plate on the table beside Grandma's chair. "Would you like me to cut it up?" Celia nodded, distracted.

She always was kind of mean, Ginger thought, and felt better. She, being a grandchild, had seen a more good-hearted Grandma than perhaps her mother and Uncle Hugh had, but she knew the other part of Celia had always been there, not even really disguised. Now she felt some relief. She knew the meanness would stay till the very end, and thus she would be able to see Grandma as a person; she would feel sorry for her, of course, but would not feel compelled to idolize her just because she was sick and pathetic. In a way, it would make it easier to see her go.

For the first time Ginger wondered if this was a natural reaction. Is it perception, or self-preservation, she wondered now. Have I changed without noticing it and is this the way I've gotten to be because I see so much illness and suffering all the time? No, she thought, I haven't changed that much. I'm not like a lot of other doctors I've seen. I still have feelings, I care. The doctors who don't are cut off from their patients, and from other people, because they worked and studied so hard they never had a chance to develop social skills. They're immature, and they may stay that way. They think they're God. I know I'm nothing like that. I'm lucky just to be human. They would be lucky too.

THIRTY-NINE

Disco Joan, swooping through the perilous 1960s, was out nearly every night, part of the youthquake by sheer chance. Here in the decade that was just finding its raucous voice, when no one over thirty was to be trusted according to the baby boomers, when youth was idolized and age considered to have nothing to do with wisdom, Joan was in her mid thirties, passing; and still wild, still hungry, still unsure. During the week she went to work like a normal person, even if she'd had four hours' sleep, toned herself down a bit although she was still in the vanguard of fashion, and kept her own counsel. She was, after all, an editor, and some people looked up to her. In these current, surprising times, she was taking pills again.

It took her an hour to get ready in the morning, and longer at night, but the ritual was part of the fun. She wore false eyelashes that looked like furry black caterpillars, which she glued on above thick black eyeliner; she wore pale pancake makeup and white lipstick; her hair was teased high. At night she added a voluminous hairpiece that rivaled the best Uncle Hugh had worn to his drag balls. Her little dresses were copies of Courreges, sleeveless, A-line, miniskirted; worn with short white boots, or sexy thigh-high boots, and the pantyhose (sometimes flesh-colored, sometimes made of fishnet) that had come into fashion by necessity because of the tiny skirts. When pantyhose first appeared

Joan didn't know whether to wear her underpants underneath or on top, and by the time she figured it out, like many others she had decided to wear none at all.

Her nephew Peter turned eighteen. The Korean "police action" had not affected the immediate family because no one was the right age, but the war in Vietnam was what they all feared now. When, after a time of great anxiety, the annoying asthma he'd had since childhood got him a medical deferment, they were all deeply relieved. Peter confided to Joan afterward that if he had been classified 1A he would have left the country to live in Canada; he was against the war. Joan knew she was the one to be trusted with such a secret because she was considered the rebel, the iconoclast. She would understand. Markie and Angel thought she was glamorous and Peter thought she was hip. Peggy and Ed talked about her behind her back. She supposed, and hoped, her own mother still defended her.

In the terrible spring of 1968 Martin Luther King and Bobby Kennedy were assassinated. Watching these two deaths, so close to each other, on television, Joan was, for the first time, ashamed to be an American. What must people in Europe think of such barbarians? The death of King sparked major riots in more than fifty U.S. cities, but not New York, where the liberal Republican mayor, John Lindsay, managed to keep the peace.

Between the two murders Andy Warhol was shot, but not killed, by a crazed feminist, founder of the Society to Cut Up Men. *The times they are a changin'.* Bulletproof glass was put up at the stock exchange, and people were afraid to ride the filthy, dangerous subways. Two of the top songs were the double entendred "Yummy, Yummy, Yummy (I've got love in my tummy)" and the acid high song "MacArthur Park."

Hair was the hit show now, and Joan had seen it twice, owned the album, and knew all the songs. It was a longtime convention that actors in Broadway plays who needed to do something as innocuous as zip up their trousers tactfully turned their backs to the audience first, for there must never be any inference of what was inside that fly, but in the memorable last moments of *Hair* actors and actresses stood singing onstage stark naked, facing the audience, proud.

How extraordinary this new era is, Joan thought, part of it and yet standing aside to watch. It was the Age of Aquarius. *Love your brother.* Unless you were a cop, smashing and teargasing college kids who were demonstrating against the war. Or a kid, burning down your draft board. Or a white person trying to preserve the status quo in the South. *Love one another right now.* Which everyone who could get away with it did, and there was a marked surge of reported cases of venereal disease. If you got gonorrhea you were given penicillin and it went away. It was embarrassing but not a disgrace in Joan's world.

Her IUD began to make her bleed. The lymph nodes in her groin swelled and hurt, and once a ribbon of blood ran inopportunely down the inside of her thigh while she was in a restaurant on a date. Her doctor took the IUD out then, under general anesthesia in the hospital, discovering it had eaten its way into the lining of her uterus, and gave her birth control pills. Now, with her big and tender breasts, she looked the way she had during her early pregnancy, but, as he assured her, she could make love without fear.

Make love? Joan was beginning to wonder what love had to do with any of this.

Love meant a lot of things, and people talked about love all the time. Threesomes and bisexuality had become interesting variations on dating for quite a few people, although homosexuality—considered a psychological illness and/or a disobedient optional lifestyle—was still something to be hidden from employer and family, even in a place like New York. One night Joan was taken to a straight orgy by a randy date. She refused to participate, but she was fascinated to be an onlooker. She knew some of the men there—they were men she had known from parties and would never have gone out with, so she certainly wasn't going to have sex with them now—and she wondered if they had given the orgy so they could get laid by girls they otherwise wouldn't have had any luck with.

The ebullient, "mop top" Beatles were still the favorite musical group, and by now, looking back, their original shocking haircuts seemed clean cut and tame. Everyone, men and women, had long hair, and if you were confused as to which one was the male, then the more fool you, old fogy. Man, and a dog, had orbited the earth, the first moon walk would be coming soon, and the big-eyed model Jean Shrimpton appeared on the cover of a fashion magazine in a space helmet to celebrate the successful travels of astronauts. Another model, Twiggy, twig thin, concave, androgynous, insisting she ate candy bars, turned a generation of young women who idolized her look and did not have her genetic construction into anorexics, bulimics, takers of diet pills that were only speed in an acceptably named form.

Anorexia nervosa was a disease that was rampant but was still unknown, undiscussed. If you didn't die of starvation you might die of an overdose of drugs, and who would know the difference? You could not be too thin. Drugs made it easy. And as Joan, along with everyone else, had discovered, they also made you able to stay up all night. Except for her hormonally induced big breasts, Joan was thin, but she was not anorexic, and speed was her drug of choice. It made her able to juggle her two worlds. As always, her family disapproved and worried about the "normal" part of her life—an unmarried career girl with no lasting relationship, who wore too much makeup and knew the clubs—suspected a tiny bit of the part that would have shocked them speechless, and had no idea of the extent of it.

Recreational drugs, Joan knew, made you happy, even though they occasionally made you paranoid or permanently deranged. There was pot, and hash, and now there were Tuinals, Valiums, Percocets, Placidils, methadrine, cocaine, mescaline, poppers for sex, and for mind expansion the beloved LSD. *Turn on and drop out.* Or just turn on and fake your life. And there were still the old faithfuls: Although cigarette advertising was now forbidden on television, cigarettes and alcohol continued to be major sources of pleasure to millions.

That year Celia died, trapped in the forgetfulness and confusion of her ripped brain synapses, slipping away in her sleep after a bout of pneumonia in the retirement home. It's time, Joan thought; if Grandma knew what the world has become it would have killed her anyway.

Joan was ambivalent about it herself. She had grown up with a certain morality even though she had always broken the rules, and by separating herself as an observer while participating at the same time, she was able to adapt. If only I'd chosen a different life, she sometimes thought, with a moment of odd longing, but knew that was stupid. She had chosen this one.

Joan's favorite discotheque was Arthur, named after George Harrison's haircut. With the velvet rope outside to keep out the crowd, and only the famous, beautiful, or lucky people let past it, Arthur was the chicest club in New York. It had two little rooms and a band, and was filled with celebrities and stars and intellectuals mingling with hookers and hustlers and the occasional unknown young couple from Queens who were pretty to look at. She was known at Arthur and was allowed in whenever she came. She always brought a friend or two, or a date, and then when Arthur closed for the night she went on to an after-hours club, not always with the friend she had arrived with, but a different one, and stayed until morning.

The after-hours clubs were constantly being closed down by the police, so when you got there they had often vanished, although there would be someone to tell you where a new one was. On the night before Thanksgiving, Joan was at an after-hours club in a dingy little building somewhere on the West Side (she was too stoned and high to be sure where she was) with a gay man she would probably leave later, or he might leave her, if either of them met someone appealing, or just got tired enough to go home.

In this club, as in all of the very late ones she frequented, there was one room for heterosexual couples, which was fairly empty and fairly staid, another room for lesbians, where Joan never went, and a third room for homosexual men, which was the room she liked. Joan always went to the room for the gay men because it was crowded and lively and she had a lot of acquaintances there. She would go to the bar and drink vodka and tonic, smoke, and talk to strangers. Sometimes there were celebrities at the bar, famous men she would never have had the courage to speak to under other circumstances, but who were perfectly charming to her here.

She wasn't planning to stay long because she had to go to her parents the next day for Thanksgiving dinner, which Rose liked to have early in the afternoon, but as the night wore on Joan decided it didn't matter if she stayed up late. It was at that moment when she looked across the room and saw what she realized, after a couple of minutes of staring at this oddly familiar person, was Uncle Hugh in drag.

At first she was disbelieving, then bewildered, and

then horrified. He was not a pretty sight. She knew about Uncle Hugh, she had figured it out years ago, but she had never seen him this way and certainly not at this age—he was sixty-three, why was he still doing it? He looked like an overdone old matron who had once been very attractive. He wasn't the oldest drag queen in the room, although close to it, but he was the only one who was her uncle. Joan's first reaction was to turn away and pretend she hadn't seen him, and hope he hadn't seen her.

And where was Teddy? Was Uncle Hugh *cruising*? Were all men pigs? Was she right to think there was no such thing as lasting commitment? Did they too have separate lives? Did Teddy *agree*? She was standing there with her mouth open and her eyes probably bugging out when Uncle Hugh turned and saw her. Even under the heavy makeup she could see he was taken aback. He had never been judgmental about her, how could he be, but seeing her here in this place made the secret part of her life all too real. Not that there was anything wrong with her being here. You saw everyone at the clubs. It was just that she and Hugh were family.

Of course he came over. "Camille," he said, holding out his hand. "And you must be Joan."

"What are you doing here?" she hissed. She had meant to be kinder, but it came out all wrong.

"But what are *you* doing here?" he said, kindly. He did not seem surprised anymore.

"It's my first time," Joan said.

"Of course. It's new, I've been told."

"Where's Teddy?" She knew she sounded like a disappointed child. She had believed in the solidity of Hugh and Teddy and now she didn't know what to think.

"Home. He's never felt really comfortable with this aspect of me. Or at least that's what he says, although I wonder if he isn't secretly charmed, poor thing. He's so confused. Aren't we all? So I hardly ever do it anymore; just in bits and pieces, in the privacy of our residence. And for special occasions, like this one. Tonight was one of my girlfriends' birthday party, so a group of us finished off here for a nightcap. Would you like to meet my friends?"

Joan shrugged. He must mean the linebacker in sequins over there, she thought, with Porky Pig in the mantilla. Birthday girl. No wonder Teddy isn't thrilled.

"No? Well, maybe later," Uncle Hugh/Camille said. "Joan dear, I didn't think anything could shock you."

"I'm not shocked."

"Oh, yes, you are."

"I just…I thought…I was afraid you were stepping out on your loved one."

"And if I were?"

"It's not my business."

"Oh, Joan," Uncle Hugh said, smiling, "do you seriously think a woman my age can find new love so easily?"

"I was thinking more about sex, to tell you the truth," Joan said.

"Dearie, I'd have to pay for sex."

"Do you?"

"No. But it's very rude of you to ask."

"I guess I've seen too much," Joan said. "I'm feeling burned out."

"Then maybe you should figure out what you really want in life."

"Maybe," Joan said. She was suddenly filled with a grief so heavy and explicit it was as if she had plunged down a well. It's the vodka, she thought, but she knew it wasn't. She was so devastated by the pain and blackness of her loneliness that she couldn't even sigh; she was surprised she was breathing.

"What is it you do want?" Uncle Hugh said.

I want Markie, Joan thought. I want Peggy to respect me and thank me for what I sacrificed to make her happy. I don't want to be here, an outcast, with Camille and the rest of the outcasts. I'm tired. I want a normal life.

"Well," Uncle Hugh said when she didn't answer, "I'm sure you'll figure it out in due time."

"Oh, God," Joan said. She put her arms around him. He was wearing fake breasts and a corset and felt like a hard-bodied female mannequin. She was afraid she was going to cry. "I'm leaving now," she said. "Tell your friend Happy Birthday."

"Do you want me to put you in a cab?"

"Oh no, no," she said. "I'll see you tomorrow at the house for Thanksgiving." And then she fled.

FORTY

Rose and Ben had a good group for Thanksgiving that year, even though Maude and Walter had not come because they were celebrating with their children and grandchildren in Bristol. I have such a mob, Maude had exclaimed, and of course there was the problem of Walter's arthritis, but they promised to come for Christmas. Daisy wasn't so well either, but she had insisted on coming to New York to prove she wasn't dead yet. Daisy had discovered a lump in her left breast while taking a bath. You just didn't think about cancer, you didn't look for it, and you didn't talk about it, until it came along and stunned you. During the biopsy surgery the doctor had found the lump was malignant and had removed the breast. When she woke up in the recovery room and put her hand where her breast used to be her whole life was changed.

They didn't give her chemotherapy, and there was no such thing as reconstruction, so she went home to her family, put a prosthesis into her bra, and waited. She'd had a radical mastectomy, which took away not only the breast but the muscle in front of her armpit and the lymph nodes in her chest. "So my armpit is a little higher on this side," she said, smiling bravely. Joan and Peggy wished she wouldn't talk about it; it gave them the creeps. It could happen to any of them. Ginger, of course, wanted to know everything. Cancer was mysterious, personal and fearful, but there was something about facing danger that made Aunt Daisy want to share. She took the women aside, she confided in them, she seemed so desperately gay that somehow it made it worse. "I'm all stitched up like Frankenstein's monster," Aunt Daisy said, "but I'm alive."

There was only a fifty percent survival rate for breast cancer. Aunt Daisy smiled and drank champagne with Uncle Hugh and Teddy, and they made her laugh.

Life is so short and so filled with terrible things, and I'm so glad to be here with my family, Joan thought. When her eyes met Hugh's across the room she knew everything that had happened last night would be a secret from the people who would never understand. For her, it was over. She had not taken any pills today, and in a few weeks when she had the courage, she would give the rest of them away to someone who wanted them.

The children were watching television. Markie had recently turned ten, and for her birthday Joan had sent her a cute little disco dress with a silver skirt, but of course Peggy hadn't let her wear it. She was dressed like a boarding school girl. If I had any say about this, and I soon will, Joan thought, I wouldn't keep putting her in front of the TV set; I'd give her something good to read. You hardly ever saw children read anymore, it was sad. It was Peter, of all people, who had surprised everyone by his interest in books; he had been getting good grades at Columbia and he said he wanted to become a writer.

"He got his talent from his father," Peggy said, looking fondly at Ed, "not from me, that's for sure."

Nobody denied it, although Joan, who rather enjoyed that everyone accepted Peggy's modest statement, didn't think writing advertising slogans was exactly Henry James. She looked at Markie longingly. She could come into New York to visit me and I'd take her to the theater, she thought. I'd take her to museums. She has such a limited little world.

The room was softly lit, the turkey smelled appetizing, or perhaps it was the stuffing. Joan hadn't cooked in years. When was the last time? That farewell dinner she made for Trevor? Of course Peggy was discussing recipes with Rose, and telling her cute things the kids had said and done, pulling out her credentials. Joan went to get another drink. Look at Peggy, she thought, how smug she is. Smug and yet threatened. The modern world is coming, Peggy, and you have no idea how close it is. You think I'm nothing; you think I've wasted my life. Even with my interesting job, you and Mom—yes! Mom—look down on me; it's always Peggy the good one, Peggy the real woman, Peggy who's making everyone proud. Here's poor Joan, the misfit forever, who couldn't even bring a date to Thanksgiving dinner.

The world is going to fall apart, Peggy, Joan thought, and you will be left wondering what happened. Look around you, look at everything, and realize you can never know how a story will end. You never understood me.

She felt the truth trying to burst out of her skin, a kind of birth, the start of the new life for all of them. What could ever have made her think that once you had a baby you could get over it and forget about it? Peggy wasn't the only one who had lost a child. Let me tell you about my gift, Peggy, Joan thought. You never thanked me for anything, in all our lives, but now you will.

"Joan," Teddy said gallantly, pulling out her chair for her. She was seated next to Aunt Harriette's husband, Julius, with Aunt Harriette on his other side. Teddy was next to her, and then Uncle Hugh, as if they were a couple. Rose did not believe in man woman, man woman, at table, or in separating couples; in her opinion people liked to sit with the person they had come with. I wonder if I'll ever bring anyone, Joan thought.

She smiled lovingly at Markie, seated across from her, next to Peggy, with Angel sitting next to Ed. Markie had known she was adopted since she was tiny, so that fact, at least, would not be a shock. The sight of little children next to their parents, all dressed up, hair neatly combed, trying to behave themselves, made Joan dissolve into sentimentality. We won't tell Markie who I am, Joan thought. It would upset her, and she wouldn't understand. I know Peggy will agree.

Daisy was next to Rose, beside her husband and son and daughter-in-law, with their children lined up, and Ginger was next to Ben, with Peter on her other side— the young people, Joan thought. I'm not with the young people, I'm not with the parents, I'm still just Joan alone. Suddenly her seating place at the long table depressed her. She tried not to think about it. Was this what it was like to come off speed, to be tearful with love one minute and miserably sorry for yourself the next? She was glad there was wine, and drank hers right away.

Harriette had just had a face-lift. People talked about those things these days. Julius had said he didn't understand why Harriette wanted to go through so much pain, but Harriette had insisted. Now she seemed too young to be Rose's sister. *"L'chaim,"* Aunt Harriette said to Julius, raising her glass, beaming; the gracious matron now, no longer a pariah at her family's holiday table, no longer trailing, like sultry smoke, questions about whom she had left behind.

"L'chaim," Julius said. He cocked an eyebrow at Joan and looked proud at how his wife had taken on his culture, and he and Joan then raised their glasses too. She was ready for her second already, and he poured it for her.

"Would you say grace, please, Ben?" Rose asked. Except for Christmas they were not a very religious family, but Thanksgiving with its opulent bounty was one of the occasions when they would have felt guilty not to have given proper thanks.

Everyone bowed their heads. "Thank you, Lord, for this good food and for the joy of having so many of our family with us to share it," Ben said. *"Amen,"* they all murmured.

"And I would like to say something," Peter added. They all looked at him expectantly, with some curiosity. He raised his glass. "To peace," he said. "To the end of this unjust and terrible war."

Peggy and Ed looked alarmed for an instant, as if their political son had brought something unnatural to the dinner table. Then they smiled in a frozen way and raised their glasses too. After all, they had worried about Peter being drafted, and they had rejoiced when he was saved. They certainly didn't want their son to be killed or maimed or taken prisoner, but on the other hand, this was the first war in their lifetime that people objected to out loud, the young people demonstrating in the street discomforted them, and it didn't seem quite right to discuss this at Thanksgiving. When Peter had joined the student protesters at Columbia in the spring and closed the school down, they had thought of making him leave. Joan thought Peggy and Ed were lucky Peter hadn't said, "To withdrawing the troops," but they probably knew that.

"Hear, hear," Joan said to be obnoxious, and Peter smiled at her.

Peggy and Ed, she thought: Mr. and Mrs. Follow the Leader, Mr. and Mrs. Status Quo, Mr. and Mrs. Hold on to the Fifties. She had never been particularly interested in Peter because he was a young boy, but now, especially since he had told her he had been planning to skip the country, she had begun to like him a lot.

They ate and chattered. More wine was opened. When the selection of pies appeared after everyone was already stuffed, they all oohed as if they were surprised, but of course there were no surprises at Thanksgiving, at least not in the food department. When everyone finally left the table Joan sidled up to Peggy.

"Come up to my old room with me, will you?" she whispered.

"Why?"

"I want to tell you a secret."

"Oh?" They went up the stairs. "You're getting engaged," Peggy said.

"No, no. Come on."

Joan's old room was a mess, of course, because there were guests staying there. But the flowered wallpaper, faded now so the petals were white and only the vines held their color, was from their childhood. Peggy sat on the bed.

"I've kept this secret from you for over ten years," Joan began. "But now I have to tell you." Peggy looked at her curiously. She didn't seem concerned; Joan had always kept a lot of things private. "It's about Marianne," Joan said.

"I don't want to talk about Marianne," Peggy said. "It's Thanksgiving. What's the matter with you?"

"And Markie," Joan said.

"Markie *what*?"

It was like the moment you had finally jumped off the diving board into a frigid lake, there was no going back even though you knew the cold would swallow you. "After Marianne…died," Joan said, "I thought you would never forgive me. I thought you would never be able to get out from under your grief and have a life. I loved you, Peggy, and I wanted us to be sisters again. And then, finally, I figured out how to make it all better."

"What are you talking about?"

"Do you remember Amanda Key?" Joan said.

"Who?" Then Peggy's face got pale.

"A very bony woman," Joan said. "With a deep voice like a man, and an old-fashioned hair net that made you want to laugh. Or at least it did me."

"*You?* How would *you* know her? Where is she? Has she come to make trouble?"

"Don't be silly," Joan said. She sat next to Peggy on the bed and took her hand. It was a completely unnatural gesture because they had never been either loving or demonstrative toward each other. Peggy was taken aback by this sign of reassurance, and turned a look on Joan that was so bewildered and full of anxiety that for an instant Joan thought she might be wiser to back off. But she couldn't; not now, she had already gone too far. She was under the water and swimming for the surface.

"I knew her ten years ago, at the Parkway Adoption Agency."

Peggy pulled her hand away. "I don't understand."

"Markie's parents weren't killed in a car accident," Joan said. "I made that up so you wouldn't know. I gave you the best thing I had, Peggy. I did it to save our relationship, and maybe your life. I gave you Markie." Peggy was just gaping at her. Obviously Peggy didn't get it. "Markie's mother was me," Joan said.

"You?" Peggy's bewilderment turned to disgust. She looked at Joan as if she were contaminated. "How could you be her mother?"

"Just look at her. She looks exactly like me. Don't you remember when I disappeared? I became pregnant, I had a baby, I gave her to you. I set up the whole thing. I had that woman call you."

"Dr. Suddrann...," Peggy murmured stupidly. "He said..."

"I'm sure there was no Dr. Suddrann in the emergency room when Marianne died, Peggy. I made him up. I wasn't even there. You had me wait for Peter and you were so upset you couldn't even remember anyone's name."

Peggy sat there stunned. Then she gave a feral sound, part gasp, part growl, from the primitive core of her being. She jumped up and moved away from her sister. "You were pregnant and you didn't know what to do with the baby so you gave her to me?" Peggy said. "And now you want credit for it? If I believed you, and I don't know if I do…"

"You believe me," Joan said calmly. "The records are sealed but we can always take a blood test."

"A blood test only proves who the parent isn't!"

"I feel quite safe."

"Why are you telling me this, Joan?"

"Because I want to share my daughter."

"Share her? You aren't even her mother. I was the one who brought her up. I nursed her through her fevers, I worried about her, I dried her tears, I taught her, I put her drawings on the refrigerator door, I went to her school plays. You're just a slut who got pregnant without being married."

"So were you, bitch, as I remember," Joan snapped. "I was at your shotgun wedding." This wasn't turning out the way Joan had planned.

"I hate you!" Peggy screamed. "I always hated you. You ruined everything you touched. You killed my daughter and now you want to take my other daughter away."

"No, I don't." She truly hadn't expected Peggy to be so upset. She supposed now she should have, but it had not occurred to her. She tried to turn it around and make it get better again. "I didn't get pregnant accidentally," Joan said. "I did it on purpose, to make a baby for you."

"Then you're even crazier than I thought," Peggy said.

"We were all crazy. It was a terrible time."

"Does Mom know this?" Peggy asked.

"No."

"You didn't tell anybody?"

"Who could I tell?"

"Who's the father?"

"Nobody you know."

"I guess he didn't want any part of you."

"I never told him. He was just the seed."

"What kind of a woman are you?" Peggy asked, in that same tone of disgust that tore at Joan's heart and made her want to hit back.

"A good woman," Joan said.

"Ha."

"I thought you'd thank me," Joan said. She hadn't expected her voice to come out sounding so lost, like a little girl's. She realized she had always wanted Peggy to love her, and Peggy never had, and never would. Even their warm suburban weekends had been a sham; both of them pretending, trying, holding on to the family bond they had made and wishing the weekend were over so they could be alone.

"I'll thank you if you never tell her."

"I won't. That's up to you, when she's a lot older, if you think it's right."

"And I'll thank you if you go away again," Peggy said.

"You can't make me go anywhere."

"Really? Perhaps not. But you'll never see Markie."

"Really? How is that going to happen? Are you going to cut yourself off from the family?"

"Joan, what do you want?"

"I just want you to like me," Joan said. She wanted to say "love," but she knew that was impossible. Maybe "like" was too much to ask too.

"Like implies respect," Peggy said.

"I take it back. I don't like or respect you either."

"Fine."

They stood there staring at each other. This was the way they used to fight when they were little girls. Nothing had changed. And everything had changed. Because now, whether they detested one another or not they were bonded, because of Markie, and Peggy was in control.

Peggy went downstairs then and Joan followed her. She stood silently while Peggy swept up her children and husband and said a hasty good-bye. Joan wondered if it was possible to be both numb and in pain, because she was both. When Ed and Peter and Markie and Angel kissed Aunt Joan good-bye, Peggy's face had turned to stone.

I wish I hadn't told her, Joan thought. But it was too late.

FORTY-ONE

Rose was used to Peggy's early departures from family events, but the grim look on Peggy's face when she left disturbed her. Probably, Rose surmised, it had something to do with Peggy's conversation upstairs with Joan. *Again*, Rose thought, disappointed. I just want everyone to be happy, but those two girls are so difficult.

The morning after Thanksgiving Peggy called her with her voice shaking. "Oh, Mom, my God, the most terrible thing happened last night. Ed and I couldn't sleep at all. I don't know what to do."

"What is it?" Rose asked, alarmed.

"Joan told me..." She started crying and Rose had to wait for her to calm down before she could continue. "She told me that she's Markie's real mother."

"Joan? But how could that be?"

Peggy told her everything that had happened. By the time she was done she was no longer weeping; she was angry. At first Rose had thought this new development was entirely too strange to be believed, but when Peggy had finished the extraordinary tale, all Rose could think was how little Peggy understood her sister. Joan was impetuous, and reckless, and rash, but what she had done for Peggy, Rose thought, was almost noble. It was a Joan thing to do. She knew exactly how Joan's mind had worked. There was no subterfuge there; Joan had told Peggy the truth. Joan had wanted to replace Marianne. "Peggy," Rose said gently, "why are you so angry at her?"

"Why?"

"Yes, why?"

"Mom, are you taking her side?"

"There is no side to take, Peggy dear. You have Markie. If you were two different sisters, with a better relationship, you would think what Joan did was heroic."

"Heroic? Ed said it made him sick."

"Then Ed has a problem, dear, and I don't know what it is. I think bearing a baby for someone else is a very beautiful and kind thing. Only our eccentric Joan would think of it. You shouldn't be angry at her, you should find it in your heart to be thankful. Markie turned your life around. Angel wouldn't be here if it weren't for Markie. You'd still be in your house drinking yourself to death, and your husband would probably be regretting he married you."

"Mom!"

"Well, it's true, Peggy dear," Rose said. She sighed. She wanted to hold Joan in her arms, and bristly Peggy, and all of them; she wanted to make Peggy and Joan kiss and make up, the way she'd tried to have them do when they were children; but they had hated the gesture even then. "What are you going to do now?" Rose asked.

"Try to go on with my normal life. Pretend I don't know what I know. Attempt not to see my sister Joan's face every time I look at my older daughter."

"But they always looked alike," Rose said mildly. "It's the family resemblance."

"What scares me the most, Mom, is that Joan is going to want to butt in and tell me how to raise my child."

"Did she say she would?"

"We didn't discuss it."

"Why don't you just wait then?"

"And?"

"And then you'll see. In Joan's mind, Peggy, she gave you a gift. She isn't going to try to spoil it."

"When we were kids, Mom, do you remember how Joan would give me a birthday present and then she'd always want to play with it? She'd say: 'I gave you just what I wanted for myself.' I don't think she's changed."

Rose tried not to laugh. "It's not the same thing. Joan isn't very maternal."

"Like to bet?"

"I'd win the bet. If she wanted a husband and child she would have gone ahead and made it happen. A pretty girl like Joan didn't have to be alone. That was her choice. I don't understand it, and neither do you, but that's the way it is."

"Are you going to tell Dad?" Peggy asked.

Rose thought about it for a moment. Poor Ben, who had so looked forward to enjoying his older years without turmoil. Life had made him tired. He did not deserve to have to make decisions of morality and loyalty at his age. "I don't know," she said. "In some ways, even though he's accepted Hugh, Ben is still old-fashioned. This might be too much for him. I think he would be shocked. As long as you're not telling people…"

"Do you actually keep secrets from your husband?"

This time Rose did laugh. "I don't know a marriage that has survived without them."

"I don't know a marriage that has survived *with* them," Peggy said.

"That's your generation. 'Togetherness.' It's not mine. We preserve each other's peace."

"You're right," Peggy said carefully. "We won't tell Dad. He might agree with you that my sister is a heroine. I certainly don't want to have to deal with that."

Oh, Peggy, Rose thought, there has always been something missing in you, and I wonder if it isn't compassion.

Telling Hugh was another matter than telling Ben. Of course Rose told Hugh the whole story, swearing him to secrecy. Nothing ever shocked her brother.

"What an amazing thing," Hugh said. "Poor Joan. No wonder she's been so unhappy these past years. There was Peggy, with the life everyone approved of, raising Joan's own child while Joan had to look on like an outsider. What must that have been like? I have always been convinced that a part of Joan wanted a husband and children of her own but she just didn't know how to go about it."

"Do you really?" Rose said. "I didn't think that."

"Well, I did," Hugh said. "She's so popular, but after a while something about her just scares men off. Trust me, dearie. I wasn't always old; I've had experience with those brutes."

"You don't know if they left her," Rose said. "Maybe Joan broke up with *them*."

"No," Hugh said. "You know how Joan will say something she doesn't really mean, that makes other people angry? She can't help it. Do you remember how when she was in school her teachers used to say she was her own worst enemy?"

"Yes," Rose agreed. "Poor Joan. Perhaps she scares sincere men off eventually; that might be it."

"So what will Peggy do?" Hugh asked.

"Nothing. And we will do nothing. It's the way both Peggy and Joan want it. Everyone will go on with their lives."

They looked at each other and sighed.

"We must not tell anyone," Hugh said. But of course Hugh did not include Teddy with "anyone," since the two of them had no secrets from each other, or at least very few, and he knew Rose knew that.

So Hugh told Teddy. For reasons neither of them expected, it made them both sad.

"I wish someone would give us a child," Teddy said.

"I know," Hugh said. "I'd make an exemplary mother."

And of course Hugh and Teddy told Ginger. It would not be fair, they agreed, to leave her out. They knew the telling would stop there; Ginger had no one to tell.

Ginger was thirty years old now, a doctor, working in a lab as she had always wanted to, one of the many researchers who were looking for a cure for cancer. She had another, better apartment now, although as always she spent very little time there. She had friends, as she always had, but usually she sublimated herself in work. She knew she must be the world's oldest virgin.

Sometimes Teddy and Hugh teased her about it, since they all saw how outside, in the world, things were changing, and even she was aware of it. People took drugs, they were euphoric, they slept with each other for no reason other than that they could. Suddenly, it seemed, in the last part of this decade, social life was a grab bag of amorous possibilities, and everyone was invited to share. Anyone could sleep with anyone, and could have as much sex as they felt like having. Ginger was a workaholic perhaps, but she was not a hermit. She had been to parties, and she knew that, if she wanted to, even she could have sex, if she were willing to have it with a man who didn't love her or even much care about her, who would think fucking her was odd and interesting, an adventure, an evening's interlude. *I fucked the cripple,* she imagined them saying afterward; it wasn't bad, but she wanted me to go down on her.

The longer she waited the more afraid she was, but she knew she couldn't wait forever, whatever it took.

Veterans were coming back from Vietnam now in wheelchairs, like herself, young men, even younger than she was, heroes, bitter. Everyone knew someone who'd been paralyzed from polio, that vanished disease, and many of them had made lives for themselves, as Christopher had. But it seemed to Ginger she belonged on the fringe of the maimed and the bitter, with the people who had been deprived of something important for no reason, with no reward. She wanted to meet a veteran in a wheelchair; she thought he might understand her. On the other hand, she might be just the person he wanted to avoid.

It was when she heard about what Joan had done that all these thoughts came marching relentlessly into Ginger's mind until she couldn't hold them off any longer. It seemed to her that Joan could do anything, and she herself could do nothing. Joan's casual sexuality—whether it brought Joan happiness or not—made Ginger think about sex. It was ironic, Ginger thought, that a situation that was really about a mother and a child, about a gesture, about salvation, only made her think about getting laid. It made her more aware than ever that she was being deprived of sensuality. If everything made her think about sex these days she had good reason, but what Joan had done was the catalyst.

That Christmas Peggy and Ed and the children did not come to the family for Christmas Eve or Christmas dinner. Everyone knew why. Peggy was avoiding Joan. Instead of gathering at Rose's house as they had planned, the Glover family went skiing. Since none of them could ski they were all going to learn. Of course it was a slap in the face to Joan, and it made the usual fes-

tivities somewhat strained, but the people who knew
the sisters' secret said nothing, and those who didn't
know didn't even notice there was a problem. Joan had
never gone to Larchmont to visit Peggy again after her
revelation, and Ginger knew she had been looking forward to seeing Markie at Christmas. Joan left the family dinner early, whether because she was upset or because she had a date Ginger didn't know. But she
herself left soon afterward because there was a party to
which she had been invited, and seeing Joan, miserable
or not, made her conscious all over again that she had
only half a life.

So, over the Christmas holidays, Ginger lost her virginity at last. The man was a doctor she had known for
a while, who was quite a ladies' man. It didn't hurt as
much as she had expected. Nor was it as much fun as
she had hoped, but she had always heard experience
would improve things. Meanwhile, marijuana certainly did. Aphrodisiac drugs, everyone said, made it
all much better. In anticipation of her new adventures
she went to her gynecologist and started on the Pill.

The man who relieved her of her virtue never called
her after that one night, but then she found someone
else, and then eventually someone else. It was easy after all. In six months Ginger had five lovers, if you
could call them that since they never lasted, and she
felt like a part of the world. She was not sure by now
that she wanted to be, but here she was: a girl whose
values had been forged in the repressive fifties and
who had been set free.

There were the men who ran away in a hostile panic
as soon as it was over, and the ones who were friendly
and kind. None of them were leisurely lovers and they
didn't even seem experienced. Perhaps no one had told
them they had to be good at it, or maybe they were
afraid they wouldn't be; most were obviously more interested in penetration than in getting there, and the

sooner the better. Her fevered days with Christopher at Warm Springs had been, she knew, the result of sublimation, of fear of "going all the way," and what they did with each other was so all-encompassing, so passionate, because it was all they were willing to do. Exciting foreplay, Ginger was beginning to think, was just what you performed when you couldn't have anything more. And if it were up to the man, foreplay would be what the woman did to him, not vice versa. Or maybe that was only how men treated her.

She would have liked to ask Joan about her own experiences, but they were not intimate enough with each other. She certainly couldn't ask Peggy; it would be too specific—is Ed good? Ginger was too shy to confess her feeling of vague disappointment to her friends, and besides, she knew people pretended it was all wonderful. Maybe, for them, it was. For her, the knowledge of having had sex was the wonderful thing, and if she didn't have her memories of Warm Springs, she would have thought this was all there was.

When Ginger told Hugh and Teddy she wasn't a virgin anymore they congratulated her, in the same tone they had used when teasing her. None of this was to be taken seriously. Sex was recreation; better to have it than do without. For young unmarried women like Ginger and Joan the onus of having a sex life was long gone. But it was still considered wrong for two men to be lovers. It was easier in the world for Teddy than for himself, Hugh thought, because Teddy appeared straight, and thus it was possible (and often necessary) for him to pass. As for himself, he had always been so effeminate and flamboyant, even before he knew he was gay, that none of this was an issue he had any control over. People would like him or they wouldn't. Hugh didn't want to get bashed on the head in the street for who he was, he didn't want to be arrested for what he was doing, but he couldn't hide or pretend he was what he was not. He was used to the insults. He had heard them all his life.

There was a revolution sweeping through society, and Ginger was only one of the people who were beneficiaries of it. Everyone wanted their rights. I have been waiting all my life to be respected, Hugh thought, and if I were much younger I would be an activist too. But who would join me? Who would be so brave?

It was June now, the beginning of summer. Rose had reported to him that whenever Joan asked Peggy if she could come to visit her Peggy said no, and Joan had given up and seemed depressed. Rose, hurting for her middle daughter, had told Joan she knew Joan was Markie's mother, and that she was proud of her, and after that Joan seemed closer to Rose if to no one else. How cruel Peggy is being, Hugh thought.

But Peggy was getting her comeuppance. Peter was turning into quite the hippie. He was wearing strange ethnic clothes, his hair was long, he had a beard, and he was planning to go to the big outdoor music festival to be held at Woodstock in August and sleep in a grassy field. And, most outrageous of all, Peter saw Joan on his own. He liked her; he thought she was modern and understanding, all the things his parents were not. So Joan would end up being friends with Peter instead of Markie, Hugh thought, and it served Peggy right. When Markie was older she could make her own decisions too, if Peggy hadn't poisoned her mind.

One hot night that June, at one o'clock in the morning, Hugh and Teddy were awakened by the noise of a crowd. They looked out of the window. There were droves of people running, on the sidewalk and in the street as well, shouting, excited, going to see something. It didn't take long before Hugh and Teddy, their curiosity piqued, got dressed and went outside to see what was happening. It seemed everyone was rushing to the famous gay bar, the Stonewall, where, Hugh discovered from some people on the street, the most extraordinary event had transpired. The police had raided the club, as usual, but this time the normally meek patrons, led, amazingly, by the more outrageous drag queens, had rebelled. There was a riot going on.

The police had never expected this, nor had anyone else. As soon as the cops started to punch, the drag queens pulled off their wigs and fought back. Following their lead, the gay demonstrators, shouting "Gay power!" were throwing rocks, bricks, bottles, coins, and blows. Windows were shattered, a parking meter was uprooted and used as a weapon, there were bonfires in the street, fires were set in trash cans, and the inmates of the nearby Women's House of Detention were throwing lighted pieces of toilet paper out of their cells. The mood was both dangerous and festive. When the Tactical Police Force, which had quelled many student riots, arrived on the scene in their helmets and bulletproof vests, the drag queens sang and danced and blew kisses to the crowd, while photographers and newspaper reporters recorded it all. Hugh's heart was thumping and there were tears of joy in his eyes. My people, he thought.

"What are they doing?" Teddy murmured, embarrassed and nervous.

"Changing the world," Hugh said.

Perhaps he was being premature, he mused, but when Hugh saw his own look of pride reflected on the faces of the younger gays, he knew he was still young at heart and that what he had always wanted, to be accepted and let alone, was finally in sight. It was here right now, tonight, and it would be a lesson. Nelly queens, he thought in wonder—like me—who would think it?

Now, Hugh thought, I want to live forever, just to see what will come.

FORTY-TWO

On a fall day in 1970 Joan read in the newspapers that her former lover, Trevor Winslow, the man who had fathered her child, was starring in an off Broadway production of *Henry V*. And to think she had not taken him seriously years ago when he'd said he wanted to do Shakespeare. She had still thought about him from time to time over the years, remembering him sometimes just as a means to an end, a tool, and sometimes as someone much more romantic, even dramatic. In these dramatic moments she felt Trevor was the Progenitor, in the larger sense, as if he were a part of history and of miracles. She didn't know if he would remember her or recognize her, but she decided to buy a ticket to the play and afterward to go backstage and look him up.

After that first hurtful Christmas Peggy had begun coming back to the family for holiday celebrations, and although occasionally Joan glanced at her and caught Peggy watching with suspicion, she was able to be friends with Markie again. Not that an old aunt, nearly forty, was so interesting to children who preferred to play with their visiting cousins. Sometimes Joan felt a real wrench, even when she was with Markie, because she had no idea what she could do to change anything, to become closer to her, if indeed she really had the patience to.

Once, this past summer, Peggy had finally allowed

Joan to come to Larchmont—for the day with their parents, to attend Peggy and Ed's Fourth of July picnic. Lost in the midst of the patriotic festivities, Joan was aware of all the things her sister did so well that she could not do: give enormous parties for family and friends, entertain children, plan fun. If it had not been clear before, it finally became irrevocably clear to her that Markie already had a complete life, there with Peggy and Ed and her siblings, with her friends and her school, and that nothing Joan the interloper said or did would change that; it was too late.

She wished Peggy would understand this, but she was tired of trying to appease people and she didn't bring it up. Later, Joan told Rose.

How odd, Joan thought, that the person she was closest to these days was her mother. The two of them had never been at war, but lately it was as if they had declared a relaxing and lovely truce. Rose understood what Joan had done for Peggy. Rose loved her. And Joan, who had not really thought about it before, realized that she loved her mother much more than she had known.

She was trying to take control of her life now, since she had realized she would have control of no one else's. It was very important that she see Trevor again, if only to attain closure. And, she had to admit, she was curious about him. When she remembered him she was still physically attracted to him. She wondered how much he had changed.

She wore a stylish new midi skirt to the play, and took a taxi instead of the subway. It was a tiny theater, so from her second-row seat she was almost on top of him. He looked twelve years older, of course, but once she had gotten used to the difference she decided he was more handsome than ever. She wondered if he was married. He was even good in the lead, and she was impressed. If he had been bad she would have been embarrassed to seek him out backstage, no matter what their history was.

There was a couple in his dressing room congratulating him, while she hung back, but then they left, and Joan was alone with Trevor. "Do you remember me?" she asked, at the same moment he was exclaiming, "Joan!"

"Well, I guess you do remember me," Joan said.

"Joan Coleman," Trevor said. He kissed her lightly on the lips. "What a delightful surprise." The electricity, she realized, was still there, at least for her.

"You were excellent," Joan said. "I mean that."

"Still studying all these years. Out on the Coast. I've been living in Hollywood, you know. Or maybe you don't know. You didn't call, and you disappeared, but even after I moved West I kept hoping you'd get in touch again."

She was surprised and flattered. "I didn't know where," Joan said.

"All struggling actors are in the phone book."

"Ah, silly me."

"You and I had a nice little thing going, didn't we?" he said.

A nice little thing? Yes, she supposed one could call it that. How amazed he would be to find out he had a twelve-year-old daughter, but of course she would never tell him. "My name isn't Coleman anymore, it's Carson," Joan said.

"You got married."

"No. When you met me I had changed my name because I was hiding from my family. We'd had a sort of contretemps. But everything's okay now."

"I got married," Trevor said. "Then I got divorced."

"Yes, well, that seems to be the trend."

"She didn't want to be married to an actor. A star would have pleased her, though."

Joan smiled. "Are you going to buy me a drink?"

"I'd love to."

She waited while he took off his makeup and changed, noticing that he seemed a bit uncomfortable at the instant intimacy. He was probably still disgruntled because she had left him in such an odd way. Why would he be upset? Lots of men had left her without so much as a warm good-bye, and she was sure women had done the same to him. Trevor had liked her, she realized. Maybe he had even loved her. They had said, that one time, that they did.

"How's your grandfather?" he asked.

"My grandfather?"

"Wasn't he dying?"

"Yes. He died."

He took her to a small Irish bar in the neighborhood. It was dark and smelled damply of beer. She was drinking white wine now instead of vodka, and Trevor suggested getting a bottle because the house wine by the glass, he said, was like battery acid. There were people in other booths whom he knew and he waved at them, and they waved back cheerfully, making "join us" motions, but he shook his head.

"I've got a sublet here in New York for the run of the play," he said, "but I'm still keeping my little apartment in Hollywood. I want to continue to do television." He told her the shows he'd been on, and she admitted she hardly ever watched TV.

"I'm an editor now," she said. "At night I have to read manuscripts." And in the old days I went out all the time, she thought, but I won't tell him that.

"Good for you," Trevor said. "I knew someday you'd have an interesting career."

"Did you? I didn't."

"Why did you leave me that way?" he asked. "Did you get bored?"

"We always remember the ones who disappear,"

Joan said. It seemed a long time ago when she had thought that.

"You're too hard on yourself."

"No, I'm not. It happens to be an observation."

"So if you aren't married, do you have a serious boy-friend?"

"No."

"I don't have anyone now either."

"We were too young," Joan said by way of an expla-nation. "It was bad timing."

"How about some dinner? Are you hungry?"

She shook her head. She knew she couldn't chew or swallow anything and realized she was nervous. He was making her nervous because she was still attracted to him and she still liked him. She hadn't liked him enough the first time, but now, Joan thought, she could *make* herself like him, even fall in love with him. If he cared about her, too... She had wanted closure, well, this would be a different kind of closure.

"You have no idea how glad I am to see you again," Trevor said.

When they had finished the bottle of wine they walked for a while and he put her into a cab. He had told her he lived in the neighborhood, but he didn't ask her if she wanted to come up to his apartment. Joan was rather glad. She was afraid to sleep with him. He took her phone number and asked her if she would have dinner with him on Monday night when the the-ater was dark, and she said yes.

Her mind was already whirling. I want a date, she thought. I want a relationship. I'm exhausted from be-ing alone. And at least I know him already. The Pro-genitor. I could have another baby with Trevor. What is it about him that makes me want to get pregnant again with him? I never wanted to be pregnant again, it was never an issue or even a thought. Maybe it's his looks. I know our children would be beautiful. It's not his character; I don't even know if he would be a decent father. But I'm probably too old to have another baby anyway.

She couldn't stop thinking about him and wondered if he was thinking about her. After he called to tell her where to meet him he got off the phone right away. The idea of the two of them having a date was so strange. Maybe not to him, but certainly to her.

If Trevor still likes me and I still like him, Joan thought, maybe this will be our second chance. What a stupid time to want to settle down, when everyone around me is splitting up, or cheating, or mate-swapping. But I'm so sick of that life; I've done it forever, it seems. Maybe I could even marry him. Wouldn't that shock everybody: Joan becoming normal!

On Monday night he took her to dinner at a little French restaurant not far from her apartment, a fact Joan was very conscious of, and again she couldn't eat a thing. He seemed concerned by that, and she thought either he had changed and matured by being married and having to deal with a woman, or that losing her had made her seem more valuable. He seemed genuinely interested in her life and told her about his, and after the meal he paid the check and didn't ask her to share.

"I'll walk you home," he said.

She asked him to come up for a drink. At last he actually seemed as nervous as she was, and Joan liked him for that. But once he was in her apartment, the moment he touched her, it seemed natural to resume what they had done years ago. They had been a good sexual match, and they still were.

"What does this mean?" he asked. That was the line the woman usually spoke, Joan thought.

"It means what you want it to," she said.

"Could we try our romance again?"

"Who's going to disappear this time?" Joan said. "You, to Hollywood?"

"Would you come with me? I know you care about your job...."

Did you never hear about a bicoastal relationship, she thought. "Let's see how it goes," she said, reaching for him.

They were inseparable after that. It was not so hard to force herself to fall in love. Just one little jump over the hurdle of her fear and she landed safely. She could love him. It was all right. The first time, years ago, she had forced herself not to fall in love, but there had been a reason for it. This time there was a reason to allow herself to be weak.

At her invitation Trevor gave up his apartment and moved in with her, contributing to the rent. "I'm not rich, but my father doesn't have to send me money anymore," he said. "That's a relief."

Joan was aware that at this point in his life he was unlikely to make much money, unless he became unexpectedly successful, but it was clear he got along, and she could help. The moment she had thought of giving up her career she had realized how much it meant to her to be independent. She didn't intend to give up working. And she *liked* her job. When she informed him of her decision he was more amenable than she had expected him to be; he actually was pleased. She told him she could never have married an old-fashioned man who wanted a conventional wife, and without blinking he began to talk about marriage.

"I remember you told me you couldn't have children," Trevor said. "I don't mind."

"Did I say that?" Joan asked. "Well, it turns out I can."

He didn't press for details and she supposed he thought she'd once had an abortion, if he thought anything at all. "I'm not poor, but I'm afraid I can never afford to have a baby," Trevor said. "I would want our child to have advantages."

Our child does, Joan thought. "Let's see how it goes," she said again.

She didn't say anything to her family about Trevor, until she brought him to dinner and then, of course, her parents knew. She had never brought a man home before. He charmed Rose and Ben, as Joan had known he would. The next time he came to dinner Hugh and Teddy were there, and Ginger. Trevor took it all in stride. I'll take him, Joan thought.

When his play finished its run, Trevor got a continuing part in a soap opera that was being shot in New York. Joan knew this was a compromise because of her. He had always wanted to become a movie star, or have a continuing role in a television series, but, she thought, the compromise might also be for himself. He was tired of reaching for something that might be impossible, of being rejected, and he had begun to understand that it was the work itself that counted, the ability to act, no matter where the opportunity was. And the money, after all, was quite good.

"Being here in New York will make it easier for you to be in a play," Joan said encouragingly. "You're so versatile."

Throughout her two relationships with this man she now loved there had been so many secrets kept from him that sometimes it made her sad. Marianne's death, her own family problems, and finally the birth of Markie, all secrets. Now, as they talked about marriage, Joan was reminded that he would be recognized as a member of Markie's family, and yet he would never know the truth and neither would anyone else. Their daughter, hers and Trevor's, would be hiding in plain sight.

She felt a reckless yearning sometimes to tell him everything, but she knew she could not. There were children everywhere who did not know the identity of their birth parents, and fathers who had never met their children. Joan had made peace with all the events of her life, except for one, and she had made peace with that one as well as she could. She would never tell Trevor about their child. It was not a betrayal, it was survival; not so much his survival but her own. He didn't have to know.

One day near the holidays, near Markie's birthday, near all the times that had been so important to her, she and Trevor went downtown to City Hall and eloped. Peter and Ginger were their witnesses. Then they went back to their apartment and had a cocktail party for everyone they were fond of. The guests had no idea there had been a marriage until Joan announced it.

"How could you do this to me?" Rose said. "I wanted to be at your wedding." But Joan knew she wasn't really upset. She was just relieved.

"Ginger is next," Ben said.

"Oh, no," Ginger said, and laughed.

Of course Peggy wasn't there. She would have come to a formal wedding, not to a cocktail party whose purpose was undeclared, but Joan wasn't going to change her plans just to lure Peggy. I have my own life now, she thought, and the sooner I get over her the better.

Perhaps because she felt guilty, Peggy sent an extravagant gift.

FORTY-THREE

Markie Glover was sixteen now, and all she wanted was to escape from the suburbs. She had waited for years to be old enough to get her junior driver's license, and now at last she had it, but it was not enough. She yearned to find out about the outside, she dreamed of freedom. She hated Larchmont: leafy streets full of pretty houses with the same nervous people in them having the same tedious lives. She knew that years ago her parents had come to this place thinking it would be such a paradise for their children to grow up in, and that now they were surprised and disappointed that Peter had not turned out to be what they had expected, that Markie was discontented, and that, since Angel wanted to do whatever Markie did, Angel was already restless too.

We did it for you, their parents said, looking at their estranged and confusing children. We would have been so happy to have your life. Their parents' domestic heaven was basically just a small town where there was nothing for a teenager to do. You could go over to a friend's house after school and watch television or fool around, there were the Saturday football games in season, where Markie was a cheerleader, which she liked; or, once you could drive, you could go to Cook's in New Rochelle, a nondescript restaurant with mediocre food that was the only place where kids from all the neighboring towns could meet each other. Al-

though the towns were all similar, the newness of see-
ing unfamiliar kids had somewhat of the romance of
Europe, so there was a sexy, electric atmosphere in
Cook's. People fell in love. Fights broke out.

At sixteen you couldn't legally drive out of the city
or the state, or drive after eight p.m., but you did. The
kids drove around and around through the boring suburban streets, getting high on pot. Everyone smoked
pot, including Markie. It wasn't hard to get.

On rare occasions only, because their small town
was a self-contained world that they hardly ever left, a
group of them would get on the train on Saturday
night and go into Manhattan, with their driver's li-
censes that they had altered to make themselves older,
and go to clubs, where they would listen to music, and
drink sloe gin fizzes or vodka gimlets until they got
drunk and nauseated. Then they would go back to the
suburbs and sneak into their houses and pretend they
were all right and go into their rooms and shut their
doors before their parents started trying to "talk."

The seventies' suburban parents wanted to be
friends and advisors to their teenage children, but all
they saw was the outside of closed doors. They tried to
be hip but they hadn't a clue. Markie thought it was hilarious that her mother thought the booty referred to in
the song "Shake, Shake, Shake Your Booty" was a
shoe. God, she wished her mother wouldn't try to get
into her world; it was a lost cause and embarrassing.
She didn't want to get into her mother's world.

Sometimes Peggy tried to explain to her that she, too,
had thought her mother was old-fashioned, but Markie
secretly thought Grandma was hipper than her mom.
Nothing really bothered Rose. She had such a sweet
nature, and was so accepting. Of course, there were
things you wouldn't tell her, but that was normal. The
one Markie confided in was her Aunt Joan.

Their friendship had started slowly. At first, Markie

had been going into New York more frequently than the other kids, with her friends Bronwyn, Larry, and Michael, her posse, her group—despite Peggy's constant protests that the city was filthy, crime-ridden and dangerous. After all these years Peggy still acted as if the forbidden city, less than an hour away, was at the end of the earth. Peter had lived there ever since college. He had his own apartment, with his latest live-in girlfriend, and was going to film school. Before that he'd gotten a master's degree, and then he had studied writing. The student, the family called him, not exactly thrilled, since he was twenty-five.

Peggy always wanted to know where Markie and her friends had been on these reckless nights, and what they had done. "I dropped by to see Peter," Markie often said, although she hadn't. There was quite an age difference between them and he couldn't be bothered. That's nice, her mother would say. And what else did you do? Markie couldn't pretend she'd been to see Grandma (why would she go to see her grandmother anyway?) because her mother would find out she hadn't, and she wouldn't go to look up Aunt Ginger because not only was Aunt Ginger a serious and dedicated grown-up but also she was usually busy. Apparently there was a theory now that cancer was caused by a virus, and Ginger and the other researchers were excited and working harder than ever.

"Oh, I saw Aunt Joan," Markie said after one trip, although she hadn't done that either. To her surprise, her mother didn't like that idea at all.

"Don't get started with her," her mother said, her lips tight. "She hasn't got our values."

Of course she doesn't, Markie thought; she's interesting and worldly—she's in publishing and her husband is an actor. Her mother's obvious disapproval, which she had noticed before, now made Markie curious to get to know Aunt Joan better. So one day she telephoned Aunt Joan and said she was coming in on Friday night with her best girlfriend, Bronwyn, and asked if they could come by to see her. Aunt Joan immediately invited them to dinner.

"Trevor is in rehearsal for his play," she said. "So you and I and your friend could go to a restaurant together. We'll go to Maxwell's Plum, you'll like it."

Maxwell's Plum was glittering with dozens of colorful Tiffany glass chandeliers, and there were ceramic animal heads hanging on the walls. It was big, noisy, overdone, hip, and funky. The bar was crowded with single people trying to meet each other, and with couples who had already met. "Friday night is the big singles night," Aunt Joan said. "Not that I care anymore."

She was as chic as ever in the black she wore as faithfully as an Italian widow, and Markie thought she shone with her own kind of light next to all the bright psychedelic fashions. They were seated at what Aunt Joan told them was a good table, and while the two girls drank the sloe gin fizzes she had calmly let them order she regaled them with stories about her world, her life, famous people she had spent time with, things in New York they should do. She knew the museums, the galleries, the theater. Bronwyn was speechless, her big eyes open wide. Markie was glad they had come.

When the food arrived, Bronwyn, who weighed barely ninety pounds, hardly touched her green salad with no dressing, which was what she always ordered as her entire dinner, and Aunt Joan understood right away. Most adults didn't really notice, except for Bronwyn's mother, who nagged her all the time to eat, for all the good it did, since her mother was anorexic too.

"When I was a kid," Aunt Joan said seamlessly, "my mother had two friends, two fat sisters, who lived in the neighborhood, and they decided to go on a diet. They didn't eat anything but apple skins and black coffee for an entire year."

"Ugh," Markie said. "What happened to them?"

"They died."

"Died?" Bronwyn said.

"Mmm." Aunt Joan lit a cigarette. The two girls glanced at each other, looked at her, and then pulled out their own. She didn't object. "When you look around," Aunt Joan said, "you'll see that nothing is really new in life. People do the same crazy things. They think they know, but they don't."

She would have been a good mother, Markie thought. What she liked about Aunt Joan was that she was supportive and subtle. You knew she was really looking at you, and that she had an opinion, but she didn't tell you what to do. Nonetheless, you were well aware that she knew better than you, that she'd been around and had learned things, more than she'd told you, even though what she'd told you was enough to impress. She and Trevor had apparently decided not to have children, or perhaps they couldn't, and Markie thought it was a shame.

"I'm glad you came in to town," Aunt Joan said.

"Oh, so are we," the girls said.

"Maybe sometime you'll come in and stay overnight, and we can see a play."

My mother will never let me, Markie thought, but she nodded agreeably because she didn't want to hurt her aunt, who had been so gracious. Markie was mindful that before she got married Aunt Joan had been considered the family slut, which of course made her more interesting and accessible; but now she could understand the real reason why her mother wouldn't want her to hang around with Aunt Joan. It was not about morals. It was about grabbing the world and chewing it up. She could see why Peter had always liked her, and why her mother was afraid of her. Aunt Joan knew how to have fun.

After that Markie began spending more time in the

city with her aunt, without Bronwyn. She came in on a Saturday afternoon, or on a Friday or Saturday evening, although she couldn't stay over. She never told her mother what she did in New York because, although she rather enjoyed annoying her mother, the consequences could only have made her sorry. It was easier to say she'd seen a play with her friends, when the fact was she'd been at the matinee alone with Aunt Joan, or with her at the Museum of Modern Art seeing whatever the latest exhibit was, followed by an ancient movie, and then drinks and conversation about art and about life.

They could even talk about sex. It was good to have an adult to talk to about your doubts and fears, and peer pressure. Markie was still a virgin, although some of her friends were not, and Aunt Joan told her it was sensible to wait until college. Markie couldn't imagine her mother taking such a calm and flexible attitude about the charged issue of her virtue, and chalked up another plus for her aunt.

When Trevor's play closed Markie went out occasionally with both of them. But Aunt Joan seemed to prefer having her to herself—two women of the world, the young one learning, the older one teaching—and Markie was flattered. She'd always been somewhat intrigued by bad Aunt Joan, a background figure in her life, a relative stranger with an air of mystery about her; but now she admired her and felt lucky that the two of them had become such good friends. Aunt Joan has saved me from mediocrity, Markie thought.

Sometimes she thought of telling Angel about these stolen afternoons and evenings and even asking her along, but she didn't. She supposed she was being selfish, but she just couldn't. When you had a slightly younger sister who'd always been in your life, following you everywhere, wanting to be you, no matter how much you loved her sometimes you just wanted to have something special that was only yours.

One time Markie admitted to Aunt Joan how she'd been sneaking around in order to see her. Maybe it was rather tactless, but there wasn't anything she couldn't admit to her aunt. Aunt Joan wasn't shocked; everyone in the family knew that she and Peggy didn't get along. "I was always very secretive too," Aunt Joan told her. "I think in that way you're like me."

"Like you?" Markie said, smiling happily, totally flattered. "I'd love to be like you."

She thought it was odd that Aunt Joan, although she smiled back, suddenly had tears in her eyes. She hadn't thought of her aunt as a very emotional or sentimental person, but you never knew.

FORTY-FOUR

The shade tree in the Carson garden was so big that it had to be trimmed back again so there could be light inside the house. The ivy on the front of the house had long since grown all the way up to the roof, giving the building a classical, English look. Ben had been amused to hear that adult ivy was expensive now, if you wanted to buy it that way because you didn't have the patience to wait for it to grow. People were in a hurry. Little did they know, Rose thought.

Time passed and people were gone, or changed, in the wink of an eye, it seemed. Markie was applying to colleges. Rose had two great-grandnieces in high school in Bristol, descendants of her older sister, Maude. Beautiful Maude, elderly and overweight, had died of a heart attack just two years ago. How sad; dearest Maude, who had been like a mother to her in her early childhood, now vanished. Busy with their own lives, she and Maude hadn't talked to each other as often as they should have, Rose thought, but still, each of them knew the other was there, and just knowing that was always a comfort. Rose felt empty without her.

Heart trouble was the family curse. Their father had died of heart failure, they knew, but no one had ever seemed able or willing to determine why their mother, Adelaide, had died. Now, more than ever, Rose would have liked to have that information, even though it was impossible to find. She wondered if bad hearts ran in the family, although her doctor told her she was in excellent health, particularly for her age. Many people born before and around the turn of the century didn't live long lives, not as long as people born later did. Medical knowledge and good nutrition were changing things. He praised her for her good health, although she didn't know what she had done to deserve it.

After Maude's death poor Walter, feeble and failing, had moved in with one of their children; an aged man living with his old child, a burden, a worry, an expense, but no one wanted to warehouse him away. Another year and he, too, was gone, as if Maude's passing had robbed him of his last bit of will. No one in the family but Ben is older than I am now, Rose told herself in a kind of shock.

The tragedy she'd had the most trouble dealing with was when her younger half sister Daisy had succumbed to the breast cancer that had metastasized to her bones and organs. Radiant Daisy, who caught my bridal bouquet, shrieking, when I left for New York on the train…not a shadow of the future fell across our lives that day, Rose thought. It seemed so long ago now. Daisy's had been a difficult death, and she had been sick for a long time. But the obituary in the newspaper did not have to say "after a long illness" because former First Lady Betty Ford had gone public with her breast cancer in 1974, although Betty Ford had survived. Each of them was a different statistic, one of sorrow, one of hope.

Viruses weren't blamed for cancer anymore. Now Ginger's research into the causes of cancer dealt with damaged genes that went crazy causing certain cells to reproduce too much. Oncogenes, they were called. The tumor suppressor genes didn't work against them. Heredity, Ginger said, and environment, and cell error, were to blame. It was a side effect of evolution, she said; cells replicated and made mistakes. Imagine cells with a life of their own, Rose thought. Why, it's like a science fiction movie.

Four years ago the Supreme Court's decision on Roe v. Wade had made abortion legal for every woman who wanted it. Rose remembered when even birth control information had been forbidden, and Margaret Sanger had gone to jail for trying to give it. And she remembered Maude's illicit abortion during the depression because she couldn't afford to feed another child.... Maude had been lucky she didn't die right then. All those days of desperation, so long ago, and now there was "a woman's right to choose."

Rose had been married for fifty-two years. Sometimes she felt it had been all of her life. People were gone and you carried on. The Thanksgiving table became smaller. The Christmas presents massed under the tree were often mailed now, to relatives scattered everywhere. You got photographs of growing children instead of hugs from them. When she had been young, people had died in droves, it seemed, and now they just moved away.

The world around her had changed so many times, and she had changed with it, and Ben had tried. But Ben, grown frail in ways that had been almost imperceptible to her because she saw him every day, who was eighty-one, had begun finding the world perplexing. He had always tried, but now he was like an elastic band that had stretched and stretched until it could move no more.

You didn't have to adjust to the outside if you didn't want to. There were so many ways to remain the same. Not for her, because she was always interested in the new, but for him. He refused to change their telephones to Touch-Tone service because he was used to a rotary dial, even though it would have been easier for his gnarled fingers, and an answering machine was completely out of the question—too complicated—although Rose would have liked to get messages. Ben was rereading the classics because, he said, the new novels had too much sex in them. So just skip those parts, Rose said, laughing, but he answered that he would have to be *reading* it before he realized what it was.

Rose hummed along cheerfully when the Bee Gees sang "Stayin' Alive" or "Night Fever" on the radio to the disco generation, but Ben made a face and moved the dial to classical music. She remembered when he had liked modern music, but that had been different modern music. He said there was too much bad news in the newspapers, and the crime statistics upset him. Turn to something more cheerful, Rose would tell him. Think about it, she would say; we have all read much worse news through the decades, and we survived. Remember all those wars....

And did we survive! she thought. Two years ago she and Ben had had their fiftieth anniversary party, with all the generations there, perhaps the last time she would see them all together, she had suspected rightly, and Rose felt like the old woman in the shoe. Looking at them all, so dissimilar, gave her even more strongly a sense of history—family history and the history of their times.

Joan liked to say that there was nothing new, that people did the same crazy things in different ways, and Rose tended to agree.

Rose read magazines and she knew what was happening. People her grandchildren's age went to dance at Studio 54 and Xenon, in outfits she considered ridiculous, starting their evenings at an hour when she was glad to be ending hers, and she thought of speakeasies in her own youth. Her daughters' contemporaries—although thank God not her daughters—sometimes went to Plato's Retreat, where there were orgies, and

Rose remembered with a smile when a simple extra-marital affair was considered enough. Hugh marched in gay pride parades commemorating the anniversary of the Stonewall riots, where being a sprightly senior citizen gay activist gave him a kind of status in a young man's game, and Rose remembered when no one in the family knew about him. Teddy, although he was proud of Hugh, stayed at home so that no one would know about *him* even now.

I am lucky to have lived so long, Rose sometimes thought, although she was only seventy-seven and, with her doctor's blessing, had no intention of dying yet.

But Ben did not have her same need to hold on to life. One cold winter afternoon he said he felt a little odd and went upstairs to have a nap. And while Ben was asleep that afternoon he died peacefully; his heart just gave out. When Rose went upstairs and found him gone she was shocked and grief-stricken and in awe of his kindness. He had slipped away after a happy lunch in front of the fire, with his loving wife by his side and a glass of wine in his hand; instead of lingering in ill health and helplessness, instead of turning her into an overworked shadow from taking care of him, and himself into an angry, bewildered shell, like so many other people she'd known. The angels had done him a favor. And he had done her a favor. He had died near the beginning of his decline, just when he had begun to believe he would not mind missing what was to come in the world.

Ben had always been good and chivalrous and courtly, in life as in death. He had been her best friend.

When Rose, after a few moments of getting used to the reality of his passing, remembered for how long Ben had been her best friend, she found herself lying on their bed sobbing. Then she wondered if she were crying for herself too, for her vanished youth, and she pulled herself together.

She was flooded with memories. You kind and gentle man, she thought, softly kissing his dead face. You gentleman. Thank you for all my adventures. Thank you for changing my life. When she had said her private good-bye to Ben she called the doctor, and the funeral parlor, and finally, dreading it, her children. A funeral was only the beginning, not the end. There was much work to do.

People surrounded her, too many people, they pressed into the corners of the house, they messed up her kitchen, they asked where things were. Everyone had an opinion, they wanted to be helpful. Ben, long ago retired from wills and trusts, had nevertheless efficiently arranged to take care of his wife financially for the rest of her life. Rose could do whatever she wanted to now.

Oh, Mom, you're all alone, her children said. We mustn't let Mom be alone. That was the first time Rose realized she was alone, and she wasn't sure she minded. She felt very tired.

But it was not long after the funeral when the others, particularly Peggy and Ed, began trying to plan her life. It was almost as if becoming a septuagenarian woman without a husband had thrust her into the status of being a child. Peggy and Ed, Harriette and Julius, even Ginger, wanted her to sell the house and move into an apartment where there was a doorman and neighbors to be sure she was all right. Only Joan and Trevor demurred. It was Mom's own business, they said, and Rose was grateful for their intelligence.

"How could she possibly sell this house with its beauty and its memories?" Joan said. "Hasn't Mom had enough losses?"

"You were never even here," Peggy said.

"And were you?"

The others would not give up. They warned her about the crime wave in the Village these days. How could she go out alone? I always did, Rose responded tartly. What do you think I did when your father was alive; wait for him to protect me? They warned her about robberies, murder. Drugs were being sold openly; you could go into nearby Washington Square Park in broad daylight and see drug dealers. Rose remembered when she had been a young mother meeting the other young mothers in that same park, pushing her baby carriage, curious, innocent, and uninformed, but perfectly safe. No one in his right mind would bother to try to sell me drugs, she said.

What if you fall in the house? they said. All those stairs…Rose reminded them that the stair lift she'd had put in some years ago for Ben would do nicely for her too, when and if she ever needed it. What if you get sick? they asked. I have Mavis, Rose said. She's not going anywhere. The housekeeper was old too, but not nearly as old as she was, and she was enough. Often Rose sent her home early with some excuse, because secretly she longed to be alone, to be able to eat when she chose, what she chose, or not at all; to read, to choose her own television programs, play her own favorite music, or just to have silence.

But then, of course, she thought of the silent, companionable hours with Ben reading beside her, and she felt a jolt of sadness. She reminded herself to cherish these memories, not let them depress her. His spirit was still with her, and his love. It would take a while to adjust to her new life, Rose knew, and leaving the house she'd lived in ever since she came to New York as a young newlywed was not the way to do it. Losing the house would be a serious bereavement. It was more than her home; it was the repository of all their vanished lives, of the faces of the children who had grown and gone, of so many happy occasions. It was the day she had seen Joan in the living room when she came back. It was the surprises and the reunions and the laughter.

Rose let them nag her about selling the house and paid no attention. If I can't stay in my house I won't live long, she threatened, and they glanced at one another, alarmed, and finally then they backed off, although she knew they were not reassured. Sometimes old age was useful, Rose thought, amused. Peter bought her an answering machine and showed her how to use it, so they wouldn't worry about her and she'd call them back, Peggy said. Rose remembered all the long periods when Peggy hadn't called at all. She knew those faithful phone calls would trickle off soon and she would be left in peace.

She decided to redecorate because some of the fabrics had gotten threadbare. It gave her a project, and the young male decorator she hired on Hugh's recommendation was good company. Hugh helped her too. He loved to fix up houses. How could anyone think I would have nothing to do? Rose wondered. Ginger even had her reading books on tape to give to the blind.

From time to time there was a remark from someone in the family about how prices of real estate had gone up so sharply that this town house that Ben had bought at a bargain so many years ago was now worth millions. But what would I do with millions? Rose said. I'll leave it to all of you. No, they protested, you'll live forever, don't talk about it; but she knew they were thrilled.

Nearly all of her friends in New York were widowed too. So now Rose lived in a world of women, and she liked it. She was the social director, arranging get togethers, outings, nagging them to come with her to the theater or a concert even if they were afraid. She called friends she had lost touch with over the years and renewed their acquaintance. Sometimes they tried new restaurants or went back to old favorites. Oddly, except for their card parties, none of them prepared meals for their friends or entertained at home. It was too much trouble. A plate for one in the kitchen, or in front of the TV, suited a single person who had spent over fifty years taking care of other people. For holidays there was still always family to go to.

This will be the next chapter in my life, Rose thought, and was content. She remembered when Ginger was little and she had thought that of all her daughters Ginger would be the one who would grow up to be her friend and confidante and stay that way forever. It had never occurred to her that Ginger's driving intelligence would be what sent her into her own world and gave her little time to be her mother's companion. Rose knew she had encouraged Ginger's independence and her career to save her life, and now if Ginger was busy and successful it was a reward, not a disappointment. Still, she was a little disappointed. How could you not be?

And yet, her surprise gift was Joan. They talked often on the phone, and when they did, Joan talked about Markie like a proud mother. She thought Rose was the only one who knew. None of the others mentioned it; it was part of their history, not their business really, too charged. It was easier just to try not to think about it.

Joan had changed, she was softer, kinder, happier. It had taken her a long time to grow up. Rose felt that Trevor had been a part of that growth as well, because he made her feel secure.

Sometimes Peter came over to visit, bringing Rose a new gadget or fixing whatever was broken in the house. He had a nice girlfriend, Jamie, who worked for animal rights, apparently, a worthy but not a well-paying vocation, and they had been living together for several years but they hadn't gotten married. When

Rose asked why not he said it was financial, that they weren't on their feet yet. He had a part-time job as an outside reader for Joan's publishing company—a job Joan had gotten him and that Peggy unreasonably resented—but he still wanted to make movies, and he didn't want to tie himself down. "But in two years you'll be thirty!" Rose said, as if that were the end of the world. In her day it had been.

That summer Peter brought her an extravagant—for him—gift: a new air conditioner for the downstairs bedroom in Rose's house, the room that had once been Hugh's and then was Ginger's, and since Rose had been decorating had been made into a den. She thought it was generous but strange. Then he told her why.

"Tell me how this idea sits with you, Grandma," Peter said. "I would like to move in with you. Me and Jamie. We'll pay you rent. You shouldn't be alone and it would be a good arrangement for us. Great house, great neighborhood, and a separate private entrance. That beautiful room shouldn't just be empty. We'll be company for you."

"I don't need company," Rose said. "You're a grown man, you should live on your own." She loved Peter, and she liked Jamie well enough, but she didn't want people around anymore.

"Just for a while?" he pleaded. "Jamie is an excellent vegetarian cook."

"I have a cook."

"We have three cute cats and a brilliant little dog she rescued from the pound. They'll fill the whole house with life."

"And babies."

"No, they're spayed and neutered. Grandma, you have no idea what pets bring to a home."

"I just redecorated," Rose said. "No."

"They'll stay in our room. They're used to it, we live

in a studio. We don't smoke, neither of us drink too much, you won't believe how neat we are…"

"What about your asthma? Aren't you allergic to cats and dogs?"

"I have my inhaler. Love conquers all."

"Peter, why can't you live with your parents?"

"My *parents?*" He sounded horrified. "In the suburbs? Listening to my dad pontificate?"

"They probably wouldn't approve of you living at home with your girlfriend when you're not married to her," Rose said. "I know Peggy and Ed."

He looked at her with that wide-eyed look she remembered from when he was a little boy, when she always gave him what he wanted. "Do you disapprove?" he asked.

Rose thought about it. No, she didn't care. She had adjusted to a lot worse, and Peter and Jamie were old enough to know what they were doing. She shook her head no. In her day an unmarried man lived with his family until he had a family of his own, but that was in her day. The next generation couldn't wait to get away. And now here was her adult grandson wanting to come back. She had never thought this would happen to her. She didn't know whether to feel threatened or flattered.

"Just think about it, Grandma," Peter said. "I know it's a shock; just give it some thought."

"I'll think about it," Rose said. She gave him a strict look. "This is merely a hypothetical question, but how much rent?"

So finally Peter and his girlfriend moved into the downstairs room with the private entrance, but of course they used most of the house. It was not Peter, finally, who changed Rose's mind, but Peggy. Peggy called her and apologized. "I can't imagine why you'd want my son living with you," Peggy said. "What an inconvenience. I told him not to dare ask, but you know how Peter is, he won't listen to me."

So at least it wasn't a plot, Rose thought, relieved. For a while she had wondered if Peggy and Ed had cooked the whole thing up so she wouldn't be alone and they wouldn't have to worry about her anymore. And, in a way, as she thought about it, having young people in the house again might be more pleasant than annoying. As long as they stayed out of her way when she wanted to be alone.

They promised they would.

FORTY-FIVE

At eighteen, it was Markie's opinion that each generation had a duty to be better than the one that had come before. Wasn't that what everyone's parents wanted—normal parents, anyway—to give their children advantages they hadn't enjoyed? When the children refused this gift the parents felt betrayed. Fortunately, it would not be so hard to do better than her mother had, she thought, since Peggy hadn't done much of anything. Except, of course, bring them up, and of that at least her children were aware, if not particularly grateful, since they assumed this was the obligation of decent parents.

Markie knew she'd had a baby sister who died before she herself was born, and that she had been adopted afterward because her parents loved children. When she got old enough to understand these things she had asked how her baby sister had died, and her mother had told her it was an auto accident, that she had been hit by a car. Peggy was so unexpectedly close to tears, even after so long, that Markie hadn't asked much more. You read about these hideous events every day in the newspapers, heard about them on TV. She sensed she had been adopted as a kind of palliative, to ease their grief. As a small child Markie had had a fantasy of a garden of babies, like cabbages, available to be picked—take one home and be happy, go on with your life. Thus Peggy and Ed had found her.

Later on, of course, since the age of reason came soon, Markie had asked about her own parents, the ones who had given her away. Who were they? Hadn't they loved her? Couldn't they take care of her? She knew about the disgrace and difficulty of being an unmarried mother (such horror stories were what people of her mother's generation used to keep their daughters in line) and Markie asked if her birth mother wasn't married.

Peggy said no one knew anything about her parents because the adoption agency wasn't allowed to tell. That led Markie to wonder if there had been something wrong with them. But, because the other fantasy of an adopted child was of the mysterious parents who were preferable to one's own, she sometimes dreamed that her real parents were brilliant, or talented, or royalty, so that she was heiress to something remarkable. Eventually she gave that up. Reason prevailed; her birth parents were probably average people, possibly desperate, unable to keep her because of the circumstances of their lives. Maybe they were very young. Some day, she supposed, she would try to find them. She wondered if she would be disappointed.

This was part of her history, but as Markie grew older she seldom thought about it. Everyone had a story of some kind, even though hers was an enigma. When you thought about these other stories, sometimes the very ordinariness of her adoptive parents seemed a blessing. The long-ago death of her sister was grief enough. She understood that her family was lucky that in her lifetime there had been no major events to make their lives dramatic.

When she had told Aunt Joan her feelings about her annoyingly secretive adoption and her difficult mother and their boring lives, Aunt Joan had laughed. Markie wasn't insulted. Aunt Joan laughed at odd things for no particular reason, and Markie was used to it. "When you look back, years from now," Aunt Joan said, "you'll see that you had a very happy childhood."

Markie had been accepted at three colleges, including Harvard-Radcliffe, which was the one she had chosen to attend. She would be living in a coed dorm at Harvard, a concept that disturbed Peggy and Ed, but didn't bother Markie because she had been used to living with her brother Peter. She would have a suite, with two female roommates, and, of course, her own telephone. She and the roommates had written to each other and she liked them already. One was from Montana and the other was Chinese. She could see that college was going to expand her universe considerably, and as far as she was concerned she would never go back to Larchmont, except as a guest.

Aunt Joan had gone to Radcliffe herself, for a brief ill-fated time long ago, until she flunked out—in the days when the two schools, Harvard and Radcliffe, were separate, one for girls, one for men. "Girls" and "men" were offensive terms, Markie thought, since the girls and men were the same age. Aunt Joan had confessed to Markie that not having finished at Radcliffe was a regret of hers because it was such a good college. "And I suppose your parents were upset," Markie said.

"Oh, everything I did upset them," Aunt Joan had replied lightly. "Maybe you'll go. I'd like you to." For sentimental reasons as much as anything else, Markie applied, and when she got in she was glad.

She had drawn the line, though, at majoring in English and going into publishing. There was a limit to how much you could echo someone else's life, no matter how much you admired that person. Besides, Markie thought, Peter was working for Joan's company, and she knew that even for Aunt Joan, who was successful, publishing paid very little.

It was important to make money, to be independent, to live well. She could see how much prices had gone up in the few years since she'd had an allowance to spend and started to notice these things. Despite her theory of advancement, Markie was already beginning to fear that her generation wasn't going to have the economic rewards for themselves and their children that their parents had given to them and expected them to have forever; everything was just too expensive. She knew that the big house in the suburbs hadn't made her happy, but there was another existence out there somewhere that would, and she wanted to be able to get it for herself. Being told no, or having someone else hand it to her, was not part of her plan. She did not intend to marry until her life was set, although of course her mother believed that marriage was what did that.

Law school was the big thing for women now, and Markie was thinking that after college she might get a law degree; maybe at Harvard Law, which was a prestigious school. If you were a lawyer you could get a respected, even an interesting, job, you could make good money at the right firm, and you would know your legal rights, which would help you protect yourself in the world.

Her parents didn't even pretend anymore that they weren't disappointed in Peter. He still hadn't made the independent film he was dreaming of, and he still wouldn't get a full-time job in publishing because he claimed it would suck all his creativity. Aunt Joan's throwing him novels to read as a freelancer kept him from starving, and Grandma gave him a roof over his head. When he wasn't reading manuscripts he was writing a novel of his own, but after all this time none of them really believed anything would come of it. No one asked him when he would marry his live-in girlfriend, and Peggy and Ed preferred not to mention her, although Markie thought they should be glad he wasn't gay.

Markie supposed Angel would be like her. The family, too, naturally assumed it, because Angel had always copied her older sister. We girls are the strong ones, Markie thought, and she was pleased by that.

So at last she was leaving, to start the rest of her life. Angel was watching her pack, in the room in their parents' house that as children she and Angel had shared, and now was hers alone since Angel had taken over Peter's old room. Both of them were feeling rather sad knowing it would seem strange to be without this person who had been there for their entire lives. It was the end of childhood. "Take this sweater," Markie said. "You always liked it. Otherwise you won't be able to borrow it again until I get back for vacation."

"Thanks." Angel took the sweater and smiled. Then she bit her thumb. Her nails, Markie noted, were looking a mess. "I've decided not to apply to college," Angel said.

It took a moment for this to sink in. Not get a higher education, be a failure? Not you too! *"Why not?"* Markie asked, appalled.

Angel shrugged and looked guilty. "I've been going to a psychiatrist."

Her normal little copycat sister? "For what?" Markie said. "Why would you need a shrink?"

"I needed to know who I was. I love you, but you and I are too alike. I need to be my own person."

Markie looked at her sister, younger but taller than she was, with straight dark hair, not blond like the rest of them, the child she had once overheard someone joke was the adopted one instead of herself. "How long has this been going on?" Markie asked, dismayed.

"The therapist or the problem?"

"Either."

"I've been in therapy for nine months. Twice a week. Didn't you notice I've changed?"

"No, I didn't notice."

"Well, I have," Angel said.

Markie looked at her with new interest. What did I do to her? she thought. Was I too controlling, too much of a role model? It must have been hard on her to be a younger sister, close enough to want to be the same, young enough not to be able to do it right. "Who knows you're in therapy?" she asked.

"Well," Angel said, "Grandma does."

"Grandma?"

"She's paying for it."

Markie sat down on the bed. "Wow," she said, "this is a surprise." They both had their New York connections; she had been seeing Aunt Joan, and Angel had been visiting Peter and Grandma; confessions had been exchanged, and suddenly there was a psychiatrist in the background. Generous Grandma, with her own money now, and her own secrets too. "Do Mom and Dad know?"

"I thought it was a better idea not to tell them. They'd think I was crazy, or that they did something wrong. I couldn't ask them for the money. They'd never understand. Besides, I'm not going to be in therapy forever."

"I hope not," Markie said.

"No, I'm going to go to art school."

"Instead of college?"

"Yes."

It was better than nothing, Markie thought, and a relief that she had a goal after all; but she wondered, for a brief, nervous moment, if Angel was going to become a dilettante like Peter. "I didn't know you wanted to paint."

"Remember I was always scribbling, those little sketches nobody paid attention to?" Angel said. "I really want to be an artist. You can be the successful one, the lawyer with the career. I'll be the artist, and maybe, who knows, I'll make a living at it. I'm not like Peter, if that's what you're thinking. Mom and Dad won't complain for long. They were willing to pay for a dorm, so they can pay for a little apartment for me in New York. I'm going to go to the Art Students' League. I've already been accepted for when I graduate from high school."

It was true she had never paid much attention to Angel's drawings. Not that Angel had hidden them, but there had always been the feeling that they had been a private little hobby and not worth mentioning. I overwhelmed her, Markie thought. She wanted something just for herself and she thought no one would think they were worthwhile. Poor kid. "When are you going to tell Mom and Dad?"

"As soon as you leave in your blaze of glory."

"You're going to tell them about the therapist too?"

"Not unless they give me a hard time."

"Actually, I'm impressed with your initiative," Markie said.

"Wish me luck?"

"Of course I do."

"If you want, I'll give you a painting to take to school and put on your wall," Angel said. "I mean, it's not as good as I'm going to be, but it will be something to remind you of me."

"I'd love that," Markie said.

Angel came back with a picture in her hand. It was a watercolor, and she had put it into a cardboard folder to protect it. When Markie looked she saw that it was a rendition of two girls, one dark, the other fair, sitting close together, the older one reading a book to the younger one. They bore some resemblance to herself and Angel. "Every artist starts doing paintings of things and people they know," Angel said. "Then you get your own style and it can get wild. So think of this as part one."

"It's great," Markie said. "It reminds me of Mary Cassatt."

"Mary Cassatt? I hate her. She's too romantic. I hope you don't think mine looks like that."

"I just meant it's professional," Markie said. "I'll frame it when I get to school. You'll be the first artist in the family."

"Not really," Angel said. "We have Uncle Hugh."

"He's not an artist. He's a decorator and a drag queen." Everybody knew about Hugh's private life; it had gone into the treasure trove of family legend.

"Do you know he designed and made his own costumes? Grandma said he could have been anything he wanted to in the arts. She says he was always very talented. And you, of course, take after Grandpa Ben. If you don't go to Harvard Law School you can get in to Yale. You'd be a legacy."

He wasn't my real grandfather, Markie thought, but it was nice of you to say it. She would have liked to take after somebody, and she knew she did, but who that person was she had no idea. She didn't even have a medical history of her own, and some day she would need one. It was as if she came from nowhere.

Her mother had told her the records of her adoption were sealed, which was always done in New York back in those days. Of course Markie knew there were reasons—people didn't want you to find them—but still that was an insensitive thing to do, she thought. It only made you more curious. It occurred to her once again that someday she might try to find out who her real parents were. There had to be some way, particularly for an attorney.

FORTY-SIX

Hugh did not consider himself old enough to retire; his interest in beautiful things was what kept him young. Many of his clients had become long-standing friends. After fifty years at the same little landmark shop, he was a Greenwich Village fixture. If he had worked at a large company, he thought, the people on top would have thrown him out by now—a man in his seventies—would have thought him redundant. But he dealt with antiquities, thus old was better, and he was his own boss. His sense of humor would not fade, nor would his curiosity and his knowledge. And he liked young people, especially young gay men. Having them around amused him and kept him au courant.

The handsome young gay man who had been helping him in his shop for the past four years was named Bill. In a way he reminded Hugh of himself when he was that age, newly arrived in New York, working for Zazu. But Bill was not a paint queen; he went to the gym and kept his body buffed, he seemed more like a smiling, tawny-haired, Ivy League college boy. He was very popular, and Hugh enjoyed hearing about his exploits and parties and summer weekends on Fire Island with other young male beauties, the New York nights at the newest, and sometimes rather sinister, bars, the discos and drugs, the bathhouses with uncountable and soon forgotten sexual partners—the hedonistic new homosexual freedom taking place in the decade that had gone merrily past.

Ah, Hugh thought, these lovely boys remind me of the frieze of figures around a Grecian urn; something I can look at and fantasize about but never join. Not anymore. The flesh becomes an embarrassment instead of an allure, and the suitors have long since disappeared, but I am content because I still have Teddy.

It had been quite a few years since he and Teddy had had sex with each other, or even thought of one another in that way. They were best friends and life companions, as comfortable and devoted as good brothers; two men who had once been lovers for longer than many of the lovers he knew. Many of their friends had separate rooms now. Hugh and Teddy still slept in the same king-sized bed, and often held each other in their sleep.

Hugh had become convinced that a short attention span in sex was natural for most men. Certainly the homosexual couples he knew who had been together for many decades were more often companions than lovers, as were the heterosexual couples, from what he had gathered. He didn't even like to think of elderly people, of whatever persuasion, having sex, because physical appearance was very important to him. He supposed one could hire a hustler at any age, but why would you want to? Who could believe such paid-for pretense was passion, at least on the part of the young, attractive one? Just close your eyes, dearie, and pretend I'm your granny. One thing Hugh never wanted to do was to be made a fool of.

He and Teddy had cheated, secretly and considerately, in their heyday. That, too, Hugh thought, was a province of men, although what he had read lately was making him realize he was old-fashioned and limited to think it. They had been sure they would never leave each other, and they were still surprised when they hadn't. Love was ambiguous.

Beautiful Bill's mysterious affliction appeared slowly at first. A purple blotch on his neck. Annoying, ugly, but not threatening. More blotches. His dermatologist told him it was a kind of cancer. How could that be? He was twenty-eight years old and in the best of health. Then he got pneumonia. Then something else, and something else, until he was wasting away and dying in front of Hugh's eyes—the young man who had been so full of fun was now unrecognizable and in hideous pain. All Hugh could do was visit him and bring him soup, hold his hand, be appalled at the symptoms, and be grateful Bill's friends had not deserted him.

Some of them were getting sick too.

At first most people did not know about the spreading plague, did not want to know, but in the world where he traveled Hugh was aware. The purple blotches of Kaposi's sarcoma, or sometimes the stab of shingles, followed by toxoplasmosis, or pneumonia, or tuberculosis, or lymph cancer or massive thrush or herpes—in short, any opportunistic infection that could destroy the body and brain—were striking young homosexual men. Handsome young men in the prime of their lives were dying quickly—and yet too slowly when you considered the suffering—of horrific things. In a year or two it finally became recognized as an epidemic. At first the epidemic was called GRID: Gay-Related Immune Deficiency.

Later it would be called AIDS.

Bringing the sensationalism, the otherness, the strangeness, of this mysterious tragedy to the straight world, *People* magazine ran a cover story about a former drag queen named Brandy Alexander who was now a mortally ill patient in a hospital, almost bald, covered with sores inside and outside of his body, a dying man the nurses were afraid to go near to tend because whatever he had they didn't want to get it. The "gay disease" was weird, straight people thought, and although they were sure it had nothing to do with them, it was frightening. To Hugh it was more. Any of these men could have been me, he thought, if I had been born in a different time. I, too, was young and beautiful once, and wild.

The researchers found that exchange of bodily fluids spread the disease, whatever it was. Doctors warned their gay patients against anal sex, some against any sex at all. Gay sex had become lethal. "This is retribution," said some of Hugh's young friends, in terror. "I'm not going to give up my lifestyle," said others of them, defiantly. Everyone Hugh knew had lost friends and people they loved; the outcasts who had formed merry extended families of young men like themselves were now constantly going to funerals. There was fear in the streets of the Village these days, but despite warnings, men still went to bathhouses, still looked for sex in clubs. There was no test yet for a disease people didn't understand, that remained without symptoms for years; and if there was a test, who would want to take it, to find himself condemned to death?

Straight people didn't want to invite gay people to their homes anymore, or touch what they had touched. Some of Hugh's customers looked at him oddly, and avoided coming near him. One, a young wife and mother who had been planning to have him help her decorate her new apartment, stopped coming to the store altogether. Everyone was afraid, except for the people who were in denial. The disease also afflicted heterosexual Haitians, so now everyone was afraid of them too.

AIDS, Hugh thought, was to the twentieth century what syphilis had been to the straight people of his grandfather's and father's generations: lurking and incurable, the wages of sin as death. And then, finally, a cure for syphilis had been found, and it was nearly gone. Now here was another scourge.

Thousands of men were dying and the number was growing. AIDS victims were fired from their jobs and deserted by their loved ones, evicted from their apartments, turned into outcasts. Paranoia was rampant. Hugh, who had marched in gay pride parades and stood so proudly as an onlooker at the Stonewall riot at the end of the sixties, which ushered in the new era of freedom, now joined the Gay Men's Health Crisis, helped organize fund-raisers, tended the sick and dying patients he knew, and finally even went to visit desperate people he had never met before. His life had changed, just when he had thought it would fade away in peace. Unexpectedly, he had a mission.

He was almost eighty now, alert and trim; and the sight of this feisty old man marching on the politicians with a placard in his hand, enthusiastically becoming so much a part of the quest for research aid, made people smile. They considered him a character and they liked him. The press liked him, and took his picture. His family didn't know what to think.

Rose, of course, was proud of him. "A crisis always brings out the best in you," she told him. "Remember how you enlisted in the war when you didn't have to?"

"Bravo, Uncle Hugh!" Joan said, and saved the clippings.

"Uncle Hugh always finds a way to embarrass us," Peggy grumbled.

Ginger told him to be careful around the sick. "The nurses in the hospital won't wipe the blood off the AIDS patients for good reason," she said. "Wear surgical gloves. Wear a mask."

"There is no 'good reason' to be cruel," Hugh said, but he wore the gloves anyway because no one knew for sure how you could become infected. He stopped short at the mask because it was off-putting, and hoped no one would cough on him.

Teddy was nervous to see Hugh playing at nurse. "You'll get it," he said. "No, I won't," Hugh said. He didn't know why he was so sure of it, but he felt that in some way he was meant to be helpful and the same force that had made him compassionate would keep him safe.

He and Teddy knew they were lucky that no one had given either of them AIDS. That my life was spared was a simple case of timing, Hugh thought, and he felt a kind of survivor guilt. Then, to expiate it, he packed up another basket of food and went back to feed the sick, like Little Red Riding Hood going to feed the Big Bad Wolf, except the wolf he visited was too weak to get out of bed.

In 1984, AIDS was discovered to be caused by a virus. It seemed to be knocking out the immune systems of not only gay men and Haitians, but hemophiliacs of whatever sex or age, even children, who had received blood transfusions, and heroin addicts who had shared needles, and babies who had been infected through the placental blood supply from their mothers in the womb. Only a while ago herpes had been the dreaded sexually transmitted straight disease of the decade, but now AIDS was. Men could get it from women. Women could get it from men.

Hugh warned Markie and Angel about the dangers of unprotected sex—not that they hadn't heard it from the media—since he knew they weren't going to hear it from their parents. Markie was a young lawyer now, working in New York, as lovely to look at as her mother and aunt (whichever was which) had been at her age. Angel was a downtown painter, and Hugh knew her life was as free as that implied. Men loved those two young women, and they loved men. Markie and Angel assured him they used condoms, but Hugh wasn't sure. They seemed resentful, annoyed, nervous, at his meddling.

"I always know my dates well before I sleep with them," they said, and he knew that meant nothing. Straight women who did not sleep with heroin addicts or bisexuals still thought they were safe, and straight men thought they lived charmed lives because they were throwers not catchers.

In 1985 there was, finally, a test. Now you could know the truth about what you most feared. The masculine movie star Rock Hudson revealed that he was gay and that he was dying of AIDS, and people began to realize it could happen to anyone. For gay men, the party had stopped. The following year the first drug for AIDS was discovered, AZT, but it was extremely expensive.

Hugh continued to be an activist. He joined a new politically active group called ACT UP, for gays and lesbians. Now he and his group were lobbying the pharmaceutical companies to lower the price of AZT so more people could afford it. Hugh tried but couldn't make Teddy join, however—poor old thing so set in his ways. Teddy insisted he was too elderly to march. But one day he came to watch. Hugh was jubilant: Teddy, long since retired, nothing to lose anymore, coming out along with the young people, finding his pride in what he was.

People continued to notice Hugh. In a way, he had become to the AIDS cure movement what Dr. Spock, at eighty, had been to the Vietnam peace initiative. He didn't wear makeup in public anymore; he felt it was undignified in his new role, not to mention for someone of his advanced maturity. A touch of blush on freshly shaven cheeks on his missions of mercy was as far as he would go, and only because he thought someone in the room should look healthy.

Gay and straight, movie stars, celebrities, ordinary

people, were wearing the red looped ribbon on their lapels. It had become a symbol of honorable intent. How sad it was, Hugh thought, that something as terrible as this disease should be the force that finally united people in brotherhood.

At least, some people. There was a long way to go, but he had known that all his life, and now he was surprised to look back and see how far he had come.

FORTY-SEVEN

Research is like a galaxy, and every research lab is a different planet. Ginger's was in an old medical facility containing many other labs, only a block away from the one-bedroom apartment where she now lived, thus making her world smaller and smaller. She had a tiny office nestled next to a slightly larger laboratory—all hers. She had a tech, a young woman named Sheila Huang, who was her research assistant, with whom she met every day; she had a fellow, this year a young man from Pakistan, who was paid by the fellowship program and thus was sort of free labor; and one or two days a week she herself did hands-on bench work. At nearly fifty, and established, Ginger was no longer a "lab rat." She was the administrator. Her family, if they tried to understand her work at all, imagined her peering at a Bunsen burner, but it had been years since her fingers had touched anything like that.

Outside of her cluttered little unit, in the corridor, were files, and large machines filled with carbon dioxide that kept samples of tissue frozen—everyday cryogenics, really—until they were needed. A refrigerator held samples of blood. Across the hall and next door researchers were working on other kinds of cancer, following other leads. Three of those other labs were researching breast cancer, as she was.

Three afternoons a week Ginger worked at the oncology clinic in the hospital to help support her research projects. On weekends she was either in her lab or sequestered in her little office, struggling over the writing of articles for medical journals like *The New England Journal of Medicine*, describing her findings to keep herself known, and the rest of the time, during long days that ended at ten o'clock at night, she wrote applications for grants, to places like the National Institute of Health, or the Department of Defense. After all this time in medicine she was still working eighty hours a week, sixteen hours a day.

She told herself she was no different from the Wall Street types who put in those long hours; you had to be obsessed. After all, she was making $150,000 a year. She looked back at how she had begun her life's work, with so much altruism and starstruck fantasy, and now most of the time she felt she was slogging through it as a beggar and a clerk.

Detail overwhelmed her. The applications and the work proposals and the budget were complex. It took three months to write a grant application, and they were judged very harshly. People had multiple grants, overlapping in duration, so they spent a lot of time obsessing over getting the next one. If you didn't get the money you wouldn't be able to continue the research, or have a salary to live on. Some people liked the routine and the challenge, the paperwork and anxiety, and some hated it. It had taken Ginger this long to realize she hated it. But it let her do the part she loved, to follow her dream of discovering something no one else had found. The one thing she had always been was stubborn.

She still had friends and colleagues, many of them one and the same because colleagues became friends and there was little time to keep up with the others. The married male doctor down the hall worked from six a.m. to six p.m. and thought that was an abbreviated day because he could go home to have supper with his children. He remarked that he hadn't seen his children in the morning for years; not that it was a bad thing, he added, smiling. The young single people who worked in the labs, a transient group, amused her and kept her aware of the outside world, although she thought of them as an odd bunch, and she wondered if she had been odd too. Who would want to sit in a lonely room day after day doing repetitive work?

She was not sure now, looking back, if her lifelong dedication after polio had paralyzed her legs had been partly a way to remain hidden and to avoid being hurt.

She'd had lovers but not love; the love she'd had was so long ago now that she sometimes wondered what she had seen in him. Ginger was realistic, and she knew the chances of finding love now, of having a life's companion, were remote. Would it have helped if she were desperate, if she wanted a man so much that she made seeking and getting him as much a project as she did finding a cure for cancer? But even able-bodied women in their twenties, out and about, looking, trying, complained they could never find a man to marry. What could she expect?

She had her habits by now and she was attached to them. She was a workaholic, and, in her few spare moments, she was the new term, a Couch Potato. Sometimes it made her content, a reward after taxing her brain, and sometimes she realized that she felt about her solitary life the same way she did about the administration duties: She hated it.

Holidays were the hardest. What would she do without her mother, Uncle Hugh and Teddy, her sisters, her nieces and nephew, her extended family filling up her mother's house? They got her through Christmas, but New Year's Eve was unspeakable, with or without plans, because she was always without a date. Even three-day weekends were depressing (throngs at sales in the stores, families struggling to airports to get away for a mini vacation), so Ginger always worked and ignored them.

Sometimes she felt guilty that she wasn't trying to spend more time with her mother, who was getting older—eighty-seven, after all, was an age where you couldn't put things off—but Rose seemed almost as busy as Ginger was, and certainly happier. Even Rose did not live alone. Peter and Jamie and their menagerie were a fixture and showed no sign of planning to leave, although Peter and Jamie had finally gotten married, in Las Vegas, of all bizarre places. They expressed no desire to have children. Children, Peter and Jamie said, would interfere with their perfect symbiosis.

So Peggy had no grandchildren...yet. There would always be Markie and Angel to reproduce, whenever they settled down. But Peggy's voluntarily childless son, whom they all had underrated for so many years as a dilettante, had finally gotten his first novel published, to excellent reviews and a few weeks of exciting attention.

The other reason Ginger didn't visit with her mother alone was that she knew Rose would sense that she was depressed, and wondered if Rose would suggest she give a salon again. But it was too late, there was no time, and she was, at least for now but perhaps forever, no longer the hostess type.

That year, 1987, Harriette's husband, Julius, died of liver cancer. He had refused chemotherapy, which his doctors said wouldn't add much length to his life, and he said he wanted to go peacefully and quickly, which he did. Harriette, who had always deferred to him, didn't ask him to consider any other way.

After her husband died and she had recovered her good spirits, Harriette asked Ginger to come on a lecture cruise of the coast of Italy with her, which Ginger thought was like something out of a Victorian novel—the lively, elderly, rich, widowed aunt; the intelligent, crippled, spinster niece—and Ginger said she was too busy. "It will be good for you," Aunt Harriette said. "You can afford it. What do you do with your money? You should have some fun. Life is short and unpredictable. You never know if an opportunity is your last."

"Maybe some other time," Ginger said. Maybe never, she thought. Aunt Harriette went with a friend.

Of course I know life is short and unpredictable, Ginger wanted to say. I work in a cancer clinic. Every time I see those terribly sick people I feel thankful I'm not them. And sometimes I see one or another, a nice-enough-looking man, no wife, who is going to get well, and I wonder if under different circumstances we would feel about each other in a more personal way. It's unethical to date patients while they're under your care, and then they're gone, back to their real lives. Doctors marry patients, it's true. I've seen it. Your patients depend on you, they need you so much, and it becomes a kind of emotion very like a crush. Then sometimes it happens that you go out with each other afterward, while the closeness is still there.

As the song goes: "But not for me."

And yet sometimes she felt such a burst of joy, as if the unexpected love would sneak up on her if she only stopped thinking about it and let these things happen.

As the other song went: "*Que Sera Sera*."

FORTY-EIGHT

Joan's relationship to the adult Markie was as an older and wiser friend, nonjudgmental confidante, accidental aunt, and secret mother; and Markie to her was the person through whom she relived her youth in a better way. She had to admit Markie had healthier taste in men than she had at her age. While in the conservative fifties Joan had liked men she couldn't possibly bring home, and had probably liked them because of that, Markie's boyfriends were of the sort, *if* she had brought them home, that her parents would have welcomed. Markie had met them in college and law school, and later as a lawyer in a firm full of bright young men, and because besides being smart she was pretty and charming and had a dazzling and open smile, she was never alone for long. A few of those men had wanted to marry her, but she said she was too young. She was not too young; she was twenty-eight already, going on twenty-nine, but so were many of her single friends.

Peggy had never given up her resentment of the closeness between Markie and Joan, so they continued to underplay it. Now that Markie wasn't under Peggy's roof it was easy to keep her life private. Markie never thought it was odd that her mother was so jealous. Annoying, yes, but not strange. Possessiveness had always been part of her mother's nature. Poor Peggy, Markie told Joan, had lived only to have children; they were her raison d'être, her identity, her claim to fame. Nothing wrong with that, Joan said, it's perfectly normal; but she was still secretly gratified every time Markie put Peggy down.

It was old news, but everyone in the family knew that Peggy had been pregnant with Peter before she was legally married—she couldn't lie and say he had been premature because he had been such a bruiser—and they all knew his birthday and Peggy and Ed's anniversary. But it was clear that Peggy and Ed had wanted and eagerly welcomed their firstborn and had actually been engaged before he was conceived. One time Peggy had confided to Markie about the Rh babies who had died between Peter's birth and the birth of the now long-dead Marianne, and Markie told Joan it must have been very difficult for her mother to have had so many losses.

"Yes," Joan said. She didn't want to think about losses. She had put the memories away into a strongbox in her mind, and it was only occasionally that they came shrieking out like mad bats.

"All the same," Markie said, "I couldn't live only for my kids—I'm different."

"You don't know that," Joan said enigmatically. "You don't know anything until it happens." *You won't know until you have had a child.*

"Sometimes I still wonder who my real parents were," Markie said.

We're too close, Joan thought in alarm. You can read the inside of my head. But that wasn't true, it couldn't be.

She hated it when Markie started the business of speculating about her real parents. It would take one little sentence to reveal the truth and end her search forever. Look how happy we are, Joan could remind her after she told her. What difference does it make who your birth mother is? But of course there was an entire story to be told, not just a declaration of maternity. It was too convoluted and too crazy, and it was in the past.

Joan's relationship with Peggy was still so tenuous. She was wearily aware that they both tried to be civil, to pretend, but of course they did not fool each other. It had always been understood that if anyone were to tell Markie it would be Peggy, and Peggy did not want to. Once, when Markie had graduated from college, when she was twenty-one, when it seemed time, Joan had tried to broach the subject, and Peggy had flashed her a look of such hatred and fear that Joan had recoiled. "Don't ruin my life," Peggy had said.

"Would it be that easy?" Joan had responded. They didn't discuss it again.

Markie had a new boyfriend now, in this autumn of 1987. His name was David Laurent, and he had been her lover for three months, or, as they called it these days, they had been "dating" for three months. They hardly knew one another yet, they were in lust, not in love, they were learning, it was fresh.

David Laurent worked at Markie's firm, and he was four years younger than she was, which at their age was a big difference. She made more money than he did, and she said in many ways he was still a boy. But he was beautiful, with big, dark, yearning eyes and shiny dark curls, with lean, well-formed muscles and tendons moving seductively under his silky skin, and the sexual attraction between them was tremendous. "He's too pretty to be smart," Markie said, "but he's that, too."

Joan had met David Laurent twice. He didn't seem older with Markie; she seemed younger. She was flushed, vulnerable, laughing at nothing. They were always touching.

I remember that, Joan thought. She was nostalgic for the excitement and sad for the pain. After the first time she saw Markie and David together Joan surprised Trevor with her demanding passion, and even more with her tears, and she couldn't explain why. Those two are *breeding,* Joan thought. Markie would have been shocked at the very idea. Nature knows, Joan thought, even when they don't. They might as well be trying to make a child. They're programmed for it. The musk, the heat... For the first time, Joan felt fifty-six.

It was not enough, Joan thought, that sex and love could break your heart, but even the physical part was dangerous. Contraception was sometimes dangerous, as the Dalkon Shield had turned out to be. This IUD, which resembled a spiky piece of Native American jewelry, with a cord hanging down for testing, looked so frightening that Joan didn't know why any woman would have let a doctor insert it into her body. And childbirth was still occasionally dangerous too. And the woman had the responsibility. At least a woman didn't have to ask her husband for permission to have an abortion anymore.

Joan had greeted her own menopause a few years ago with a combination of relief and nostalgia. She had read in one of her feminist books that menstrual blood was power and that men were jealous of it and the fact that it represented women's magical ability to create life. Joan thought it was merely an unpleasant nuisance, and she was glad to have her body back for nothing but her own pleasure, and Trevor's. He had always thought of them as a childless couple, and he had never minded. She and Trevor hadn't been able to have another child after Markie, and now they never would.

But I have her, Joan thought. She is my direct bloodline. Fond as Joan was of Peter and Angel, she knew Markie would always be her favorite. She had stopped trying to mislead the family into believing that this was not so, because no one really cared. Some day, when the time is right, I'll have a grandchild through her,

Joan thought, and I'll be able to see the future. Somehow it made her feel serene to imagine this: her child's child, Rose and Ben's great-grandchild, the lineage continuing into another century, into the Millennium.

"Could we have lunch together on Saturday?" Markie asked. "Just you and me?"

"Of course."

Markie chose a tea room type of place on the upper East Side that didn't suit her at all, but she said she didn't want to run into anyone else she knew. She ordered chocolate cake and milk instead of her usual salad, and when it came she pushed it aside and her eyes filled with tears. "Life is just too difficult," she said.

"What particular part of it?"

"Everything. Sometimes I'm so tired."

"Maybe you're working too hard," Joan suggested.

"No..." She pulled the cake back and poked at it with her fork and then pushed it away again. Joan had noticed, when Markie walked in, that she looked a little bloated, as if it had happened suddenly. She wondered what had made her let herself go. "I need you," Markie said.

"I'm here."

"I'm pregnant," Markie said.

So that was why she looked different. Joan didn't know whether to be excited or upset; mainly she was numb. Suddenly there was a woman with a baby sitting here—her child carrying her grandchild, her fantasies come too soon—and she could almost see the mysterious floating creature, even though she knew it was too small to be seen. She put her arm around her daughter's slim shoulders and didn't know what to say.

"It's David's," Markie said. "I think it happened the first night we were together. I've only known him for three months! And I can't have it, of course. David isn't ready to help bring up a child. He isn't even ready for me. He's a kid. I can't do it alone. I'm having an abortion on Wednesday and I need you to come with me because someone has to bring me home."

"But so soon?" Joan cried. "Don't you want to think about it?"

"What would I think?"

"At least you should tell him."

"Of course I told him. He said he'd go to the clinic with me, but I want you. I'm angry with him, even though it's as much my fault as his."

"It's normal to be angry," Joan said. "Please don't have an abortion. If you want to keep it I'll help you bring it up." She had blurted out the offer without thinking, but as soon as she said it, it sounded practical—warm and cozy, exciting. In one instant she was already wondering about the best preschool.

Markie just smiled, as if the idea were beyond ridiculous.

"I have time," Joan said. "Trevor and I will help. Everyone will. And your parents…"

"Not my parents," Markie said. "They don't know and they're not to know."

"As soon as they look at that child they'll be thrilled," Joan said. "And then when you're ready you'll take over. It will be the family baby. You won't be alone. This is the eighties. People aren't embarrassed to have a baby without being married."

Markie shook her head. "It has nothing to do with what people think. This is what I have to do."

Of course Markie was right. A baby was not a toy. Joan began to wonder if everything she had believed all her life had been unrealistic, sentimental and mad. Mother's instincts? Familial adjustment? People who thought they *wanted* children often did not know how to bring them up, so what of people who knew they didn't? She had only to read the newspapers or watch television to see how people who should not have had children behaved toward their young; she had only to look at the difference between Peggy's full-time efforts and her own ignorance to see how difficult it was to bring up a child, and she thought about it frequently, no matter how ironically the results of Markie's upbringing had turned out for both her and Peggy.

Just don't think of it as a person, Joan told herself. If you don't think of it as someone you would have met, you'll get through this. "Are you upset?" she asked.

"Of course I am," Markie said. "I'll be twenty-nine soon, that's almost thirty, and I think about my biological clock. I should be looking for the right man. I want kids some day. But this is the wrong time and the wrong man. Not that I don't love him. I think I love him. But how would I know? This is something that should never have happened, but it did. After next Wednesday I can start pretending it didn't happen."

And I will never be able to pretend that, Joan thought.

On Wednesday, after it was over, Joan brought Markie back to her own apartment, where she slept for hours; and David, when he came by after work, with a dozen roses, bustled around trying to make tea and soup and being generally apologetic that he was well and Markie was not. Neither he nor Joan ever mentioned the reason for Markie's recent operation. But it was clear that he was concerned about her, and Joan couldn't help liking him for worrying and apparently sharing responsibility.

He and Markie weren't living together; he didn't even have a key, and there were only a few of his things in Markie's closet. He mentioned that he had a horrible apartment with two roommates, that he needed to move, that meeting Markie, who had become very special to him, had made him think they might find a new apartment together, or perhaps he would live here with her; how practical it would be if they shared the rent, then they would have money to go skiing. Perhaps it was too soon to make such a decision, he wondered, but then, perhaps not. A shared apartment wasn't a lifetime commitment, he murmured, but it was a step, wasn't it, toward getting to know someone, and he didn't want to end up like his parents, who had married each other as virtual strangers even though they didn't think so, and now were, of course, divorced, leaving two children to make the best of it.

As the trusted friend of this afternoon Aunt Joan was suddenly the recipient of his free-floating anxiety and his confidences. While he continued his stream of consciousness he showed her where he wanted to build bookshelves, and a partition for a small home office.

That would have been the baby's room, Joan thought. She wondered if David would have stayed all the same and made plans if Markie had had the baby, but now they would never know. Joan wondered if, despite his out-loud musing and planning, he would stay now. He was like a large child—enthusiastic, shy, mercurial—but of course this was a difficult moment for him, and Markie's drugged sleep made it worse. At least he was here today.

Markie turned twenty-nine before Thanksgiving, and had a small dinner party with some of her friends. "One more year before the dreaded three-oh," Markie said. "A significant year to cherish." How nice, Joan thought, to be so young that thirty seems old. But it was, in fact, the end of the confused twenties, the end of youth. You thought about mature good resolutions, even when you didn't keep them.

When the family gathered for Thanksgiving at Rose's house, Markie did not bring David with her. "He's with his family," she explained. Joan wondered if everything was all right. They were all in the living room having champagne, with spaces between their fragile bodies it seemed, in a room that had once accommodated many more. By now everyone had reluctantly grown used to the relatively meager number of their holiday group: it was Rose, Hugh and Teddy, Aunt Harriette alone for the first time in years, Ginger, Joan and Trevor, Peggy and Ed, Markie and Angel, Peter and Jamie: the family survivors. No one said they hoped that thirteen at the table wasn't bad luck, but Joan thought it, and she knew her mother did too.

Peggy and Ed had bought Markie a fur coat for her recent birthday, and Peter told her to take it off quickly and hide it because Jamie would have a fit. But it was too late; Jamie saw her hanging it in the hall closet.

"One should never wear what one cannot eat," Jamie said, looking very upset.

"Didn't you ever have a darling little roast mink on a toothpick?" Markie asked her. "They're delicious."

"That's not funny!" Jamie cried.

"Only if you were expecting a cocktail frank."

Jamie burst into tears and ran out of the house.

"My goodness, what's going on?" Rose asked, disturbed. "Peter dear, you should go after her."

He did. The others poured more champagne and pretended nothing had happened. "Poor Jamie wants a baby," Rose whispered to Joan. "She's afraid it will be too late, and Peter doesn't want one. She's threatened to leave him."

"And do what? Find a father?" As soon as Joan said it she realized how ironic that was. She had found a father for Markie, and run away from him and joined him again, and Markie had found a father and lost a baby, and for all she knew that father was on his way out.

"I hope she changes his mind," Rose said. "She and Peter do love each other."

"Yes," Joan said.

"I told him they could continue to live here even if they have two babies," her mother said wistfully. "There's plenty of room. We brought up you girls in this house."

"I know," Joan said. She wondered if her mother was getting forgetful.

"Just so you remember," Rose said with a smile.

"I do."

Peter finally came back with Jamie, who looked tearful and sullen, and Ed carved the turkey. Rose, diplomatic as always, had set out place cards. Joan and Peggy sat at opposite ends of the table and, although they gave each other pleasant looks and smiles when their eyes met, they hadn't exchanged a word after hello and how are you. Joan knew from experience it was possible for them to spend an entire evening this way, and she reassured herself that many other families had such tricky relationships too.

Nor did Peggy and Jamie act warmly to one another. Peggy was annoyed at her daughter-in-law's reaction to Markie's fur coat, although she had known before she bought it that Jamie would object. Peggy and Ed thought that Jamie was a left-over hippie, an eccentric, but had to admit that was what they would have expected their strange son to have married. It had always been Peggy's way, when she didn't like something, to withdraw, closing the wings of her household (what was left of it) around her, and so she did today, leaning over Markie and Angel with such devouring attention that Joan thought next she would cut their food.

Markie and Angel were seated between their parents. Ginger was with Uncle Hugh and Teddy, the eternal triumvirate. How old Uncle Hugh and Teddy are looking, Joan thought, and rightly so—although for years Uncle Hugh had dyed his hair. Ginger was going gray, with wiry silver strands, and she was wearing the same dress she had worn last year. She just didn't care, or perhaps didn't recall, but she seemed happy to be here; in fact, she was glowing at everyone.

We are all growing older, thought Joan, grandmother manqué. In all the years since she had returned to her family, Joan had attended Thanksgiving and Christmas dinners gratefully and never thought about the future, but this time, for the first time, she did. I wonder who will be gone next, she thought.

It did not occur to her to wonder until later who would be new.

FORTY-NINE

It was the end of the eighties. In Europe the Berlin Wall came down, while cheering onlookers grabbed pieces of it; in China tanks rolled through Tianamen Square, killing thousands of protesting students; and in New York City a young woman jogger was bludgeoned, raped, and left for dead by a group of Harlem boys in Central Park, making "wilding" the new urban fear as racial tensions rose. People who had believed they could have it all were beginning to think they couldn't; it was too expensive, too difficult, too exhausting, too time-consuming. Prozac was the new drug for depression and obsessive-compulsive behavior.

Sprightly Great Uncle Hugh was still going to ACT UP meetings to get rights for gays and lesbians, and Jamie, pregnant at last and huge, was at PETA meetings getting rights for animals. She was not as happy about her incipient firstborn as everyone had expected her to be because she had too many worries about this world her child would be born into. Peter didn't worry at all; he was one of the people on Prozac.

After her "procedure," it had been simpler than Markie had thought to go on with her life. David was still there, talking about moving in, changing his mind, putting more of his clothes in her closet. For all his complaints about his roommates he was still in that hovel—Animal House, she called it—refusing to grow up. Sometimes she thought she wanted to break up with him and look for someone better, more appropriate, and then she considered how easy it was to be with him just the way he was. She had enough free time for her career and her friends, and she had a Boyfriend so she didn't have to date. She had a man to bring to things, and she had her solitude when she needed it. Their appetite for one another continued undiminished, as did the tenderness afterward. Yet she also knew he could leave at any moment.

"How do you make them commit?" her unmarried women friends constantly asked, exasperated, as did Angel, although Angel didn't expect an answer—which was good because Markie had no answer to give.

Markie was thirty. She had felt a wrench at that birthday, knowing she needed to make something happen. Then she wondered why. After all, she was a well-paid attorney with an interesting career, a perfectly acceptable little apartment, living in New York, the city of her choice, and she was neither alone nor lonely. It could have been worse. To celebrate her birthday she and David went to Jamaica for a long weekend and stayed in a villa with another couple they were friendly with from the city, and four servants, who cooked for them while they went to the beach. It was a grown-up holiday, luxurious and quiet, and she felt as if she had the best of all possible worlds.

Why, then, did she sometimes feel that life was passing her by?

David was fond of saying that people lived several different lives in one lifetime these days because they lived so long. He said it was natural, and that they were lucky to have the chance. He was twenty-six now, but he was still, in many ways, a child. "There's school, and then the first career," he said. "There's the first marriage, and the children, and then there's the second marriage, and maybe the second set of children, and then the second career, and then..."

"Don't say any more," Markie would say, stopping him. If she had to think that the love she felt now would disintegrate with familiarity, that this beloved face she woke up next to would time-morph into the face of someone else, a total stranger at the moment, living his life, not knowing he would someday end up with her, not understanding that the woman he loved right now would bore him or go away or die, she would not be able to bear it. That was why one could not see the future. Who would want to?

Her mother had been in love with only one man her entire life. Aunt Joan had been in love with many. Her parents' friends, at least the ones they still saw, had stayed together for the long haul; many of Aunt Joan's had not. Markie wanted to be married only once, and because of this mental commitment, which seemed oppressive and frightening, she often didn't know how she felt about David. What could she think, when he believed in the freedom of serial monogamy and still did not know how he felt about her? Sometimes Markie thought Aunt Ginger was smarter than any of them, because she didn't need anybody.

That fall Jamie had the long-awaited baby, a girl she and Peter named Hannah. How retro, Markie thought. Hannah Glover: she already sounded like an old woman. The baby, Markie's first niece, was cheerful and pink and fair-haired and looked like her father. Jamie and Peter had redone the upstairs rooms in the town house where his aunts had spent their childhood, and this new family moved up there so the parents could be near the baby. The downstairs room was a den again, and an office. Peter, who was writing another novel, from which no one expected him to earn a living, had just taken a side job as a ghostwriter; and all day his computer screen glowed in the dimness, whether he was there or not, a symbol of his industrious intent.

Birth and death, Markie thought, when that fall, Teddy, who had recently been in failing health, died of a heart attack after attending a protest march with Hugh. Hugh felt proud of Teddy for going with him and guilty because he had let him. It had been too cold and windy, Hugh kept saying, it had been too much. Teddy had been eighty-two. He was two years younger than Hugh, it turned out, although no one had ever mentioned it, and probably no one but Hugh had known. Hugh had lied about his age when he was younger, always shaving off as many years as he could get away with, and only when being old had its own advantages did he tell the truth.

Teddy was cremated, as was his wish, and his ashes were scattered in a lake next to one of the nearby country inns where he and Hugh had spent many happy summer weekends. Hugh told the family he was going to do the same when his time came. Markie was surprised that he seemed calmer about the subject than she would have expected. The discussion seemed to her to be morbid and unsettling. There was a memorial service for Teddy in the city afterward, actually a potluck supper with little speeches in the mews house that had belonged to Hugh and Teddy, and now, through inheritance, was Hugh's alone.

When everyone but the immediate family had left, Hugh looked frightened. Grandma took his hand. "Come stay with us for a few days," she said quietly. "You can have your old room."

"But it's Peter's office," Great Uncle Hugh demurred.

"He can put his computer anywhere," Rose said. "Can't you, Peter? It's just temporary."

"Of course," Peter said, but it was clear he wasn't

pleased. Still, it was Rose's house, and this was his grieving great uncle. Peter faked a welcoming smile.

So now it had been two months and Hugh was still there, in the room that had been his so many years ago. He went back and forth to his mews house every day, to be sure it was still the same, as if it were his office. He went through Teddy's things, he sorted whatever one sorts when a longtime partner has gone, and he probably mourned. He checked up on the antique store and the new young man who was working for him. Then he came back to his sister's house faithfully in time for dinner, unless he had made plans with his younger friends. But even when he went out, he came back to the Carson house to sleep, just as he had in his youth. Everyone knew it. No one said anything, but they wondered how long this would go on.

It's too difficult to be solitary during the holidays, the family agreed. So Hugh remained for the holidays with his sister and grandnephew and the grand-nephew's wife and their baby, and then before any of them realized it, it was six months. It was not as if he didn't still have a life of his own outside that house. It was not as if he were senile or frail and had to be watched. It was not as if he had rented his empty mews house to strangers and made a decision. It was just that he was still there.

It's sad to be alone, Markie thought. People aren't really meant to be alone. It made her think about moving her relationship with David forward one notch, at least to declaring they lived together and getting him to prove it. And then perhaps the next notch…. After all, good sex didn't last forever. And she was thirty-one. Good looks didn't last forever either. She knew she and David would make a beautiful baby, and she had no idea how long young eggs would last.

"We need to talk," Markie said to David that Sunday. They had finished a run in Central Park, the brunch they prepared together with good things they had bought the day before, the reading of the *New York Times*, and later they would go to an early movie.

"Yes," he said. "I want to."

They sat side by side on the living room couch. "I've been thinking about this a lot lately," she said. "I think we should live together."

"I thought it was my place to say that," he said.

She was insulted. She hated it when he took on the stereotypical dominant role of the male. "Since it's my apartment," Markie said, "I am the one who should extend the invitation." As soon as the words left her lips she knew she shouldn't have said them. No man likes a castrator, she thought, or at least no man I would want.

David looked nervous but he didn't look hurt. "I wanted us to talk too," he said. "The reason I wanted to talk is, I think we should see other people."

"Other people?" She had always tried to be prepared for the fact that he might leave her someday, but now she discovered she was totally unprepared after all, and she felt as if he had punched her in the gut. He hadn't even acted suspiciously and given her any signs.

"Yes," he said.

"Why?" Well, that was a silly thing to ask, she thought. He wasn't interested in her anymore, that was why. Suddenly she felt chilled and she wanted him to stay and fall in love with her all over again. If he had been in love. If he had ever been in love at all.

"I need to be sure how I feel," David said.

"Oh."

"This is hard," he said. "We see each other at work so we have to be friends…."

"Well, how difficult will that be? I thought we *were* friends."

"We are. We are, absolutely. We're just…we're together too much."

"I thought too little. Apparently I was wrong."

"I've been with you longer than any woman I've ever known."

"And this is bad?"

He shook his head. "No. Scary."

"Love is scary. Being a grown-up is scary."

"I know that," he said. "And I'm not ready."

"When will you be?"

"I don't know."

Markie wondered if she should cry and beg, even though that was not her style. Other women, she knew, would have made a scene, but she wondered if it ever worked. Still, despite her best efforts, a tear trickled down her face. She wiped it away as fast as she could, but she knew he saw.

"I don't want to make you miserable," he said. "I care about you."

"But not enough."

"Markie, can't we stay friends?"

Could they? They couldn't be enemies, certainly, not when they saw each other every day at the office. She looked at him, at the shape of his dark and fleecy and childlike head, wondering about all the thoughts that were in it. It was only three o'clock, there was a whole evening ahead of them, and what should she do? Throw him out? Go with him to the movies? Take him to bed and hope to heal their relationship with the thing they did best? It would take him five minutes to pack his few things, and then what would she do afterward? All the Sunday nights she had been relieved to see him go disappeared. The special moments of being alone, of preparing herself for the work week, getting her identity back, seemed pointless and self-centered.

"Are you going out with other people already?" she asked.

"No," he said, but it sounded like yes.

"Oh," Markie said.

They had gone to a movie, finally, at his insistence, but she hadn't been able to see more than flashes of it and she couldn't remember it afterward. He didn't hold her hand. A movie where they didn't have to talk seemed preferable to a fight, and he, too, seemed reluctant to spend the rest of a Sunday alone and lonely. How cold are we? she thought. How sick are we? How expedient are we? After the movie they went to a cheap and fast Chinese restaurant, where he ate as if nothing was the matter and she could not. He left that night with his things. He kissed her good-bye and held her for a minute. She thought when he went home he would probably start calling women.

Men leave the bathroom so dirty, Markie thought, trying to hate him. She scrubbed it, removing every trace of him. She changed the sheets so she wouldn't have to smell him, because she knew it would set off a combination of yearning and rage. She put the happy, smiling vacation photographs of the two of them and their friends into the desk drawer so she wouldn't have to see them, then she pulled them out, then she put them back again and slammed the drawer shut. Then she called her sister, Angel, knowing she would be home by now, and when Angel answered the phone Markie at last allowed herself to cry.

FIFTY

Markie hated being alone even more than she had thought she would. Not only was there loneliness but there was the fear of AIDS, something you thought about even while you were in denial. She deeply resented David Laurent for sending her off unmoored to try again in a world where death waited under the guise and the bait and the promise of love.

She had been on the Pill ever since her one pregnancy disaster with David. She had decided then that any mistakes she made from that moment on would be her responsibility alone. Now that she was available again she also had a supply of condoms, for men she did not know well enough to trust, although they seemed to be men she knew well enough to have sex with. You could buy luminous condoms, or condoms in colors, but no matter what they looked like everyone hated them and often didn't use them. After all, the people they had sex with were from "their" world.

Life, she thought, was arbitrary, mean, and sad. Seeing David's familiar face at the office, not every day, but often enough to be disturbing, was both painful and reassuring. Of course they were friendly to each other, but "seeing other people" actually had meant not seeing one another anymore. At least, as far as she was concerned. She would not share him. If she had to be part of a nonexclusive relationship, it would be with a man she didn't care about.

She'd heard that most promising young men were too busy trying to advance in their careers to bother to go out with women, but so far she had not found that to be true, at least not for her. She supposed she exuded a kind of desperation that they liked because they misread it as a sense of adventure. She was too conscious of being thirty-one, of worrying that soon she would be too old for the competition. Having been with David for so long had been a sort of vacation, and now she had to work at her social life as if it were her second job.

Every bit of this mating game was fraught with tension. The third date was the crucial one. Either you refused to go to bed with him, and then he wouldn't call again; or you went to bed with him, and then he might never call again anyway because that was all he had needed, or he was frightened, or it was too close, or for whatever noxious reason; or, knowing that the third date was crucial he might beg off altogether before he had to see you, saying he had to go out of town on business and that he would be in touch, and then you never heard from him again. Of course you could call him, with some inducement like tickets to an event, but he knew what you wanted.

She and her friends were all such bright, accomplished young women, but when they were together somehow the conversation always quickly turned to men. How to get one, what was wrong with them, where to find them. One of Markie's friends was going to AA meetings even though she wasn't an alcoholic; she said she used to smoke pot and that counted, so she wanted to get over her "problem," while the real reason was she was looking for a recovering alcoholic bachelor. She said AA was full of men, and that a lot of them, deprived of their addiction to drink, were making up for it with an addiction to sex. You weren't supposed to date other members for a while, of course, but she did.

A connection between two people worked right away or it didn't, Markie believed. She was not here to be some loser's psychiatrist, or his mother, or the opposite of his mother if his mother was what he didn't like. She worked long hours, she needed her concentration, and she didn't want to be sidetracked by the anxiety of waiting for the phone to ring, or the fear that when she and the man were together she would say something to drive him away. Her mother liked to say that all relationships were the wrong one until the right one, but what did Peggy know, since she'd had only one relationship in her entire life and she was fourteen when it started.

You should have stayed, Markie told David silently; you should have stayed and we could have worked things out.

It was summer, and Markie took an expensive share in a group house in the Hamptons with some other single people she didn't know all that well, women and men. It was a move she hadn't planned to make, but someone had dropped out at the last moment leaving them short of funds, and they begged her to come along since she was free now. Markie was not attracted to any of the men, and as soon as they all spent their first weekend there some of the women were already showing her their worst side, but at least there would always be someone with whom to have dinner on those long, balmy Saturday nights when you were feeling sorry for yourself.

Angel, who had not been recently hurt and was less cynical than Markie, had a new boyfriend, a rich one, who had a house in the Hamptons too, and so Angel would be spending weekends with him. They would all see each other, give parties, go to the polo matches and to benefits, have fun; but under the hectic plans was always the knowledge that it would have been much more interesting with someone who made your heart pound. Markie didn't think she'd find him here. There were too many people in the Hamptons who were already couples, even if just for this summer, and there were too many gay men.

When fall came she was glad. She was tired of communal living; she was too old for it. New York was better in the fall, more alive, but even so, people were already planning to leave. Some of her friends had arranged to go to Aspen to ski over the Christmas/New Year's holidays, leaving the day after Christmas. They had rented a house, and Markie thought she would join them, although it was clear to her that she would just be chasing men in warmer clothes. She felt as if she had been single again forever. She wanted to have take-out Chinese food at home in front of a rented video with someone she loved. It was something so simple and yet so inaccessible. She wondered if David was enjoying his new life, but of course she couldn't ask him directly; she could only hope he wasn't.

And what if he had a real girlfriend? What if someone in the office were to find out he was engaged? The thought made her miserable. You have to go on with your own life, Markie kept telling herself. She smiled at him when she ran into him in the hall, she made small talk when they were trapped together by the water cooler or in the elevator. She pretended she was happy…and perhaps, so did he. But she was not going to be the one to ask to try again; she had too much pride. Markie wondered if there was something wrong with her because she had only discovered she was really in love with him when he was gone.

At least now that she was back in the city she was popular again, which was more than she could say about many of her women friends, who complained all the time. She had met a man at the gym, and another

one while running—take that, David, if I don't run
with you I do better!—and two others at parties. None
of them lasted very long; he was either going back to
his old girlfriend, or he hadn't yet gotten over his ex-
wife, or he was a self-avowed workaholic. Why don't
they tell you at the beginning, Markie thought, instead
of putting you through all this? She was beginning to
hate men, but she didn't like being alone either.

The low abdominal pain and slight fever, then accompanied by painful urination, sent her to her gynecologist, Dr. Brodsky, a young woman of her own generation who knew that good girls could get bad things
too. "You have chlamydia," Dr. Brodsky said.

Markie had heard of chlamydia, of course, had read
about it in her women's magazines along with the
slinky clothes, stiletto heels, and makeup tips. Usually
she shuddered and turned the page, but she was aware
anyway. Chlamydia was the most common bacterial
sexually transmitted disease in the nation. Dr. Brodsky
gave her an antibiotic called doxycycline and told her
she was actually lucky because four-fifths of the
women who were affected had no symptoms at all,
and of course if you had no symptoms you would not
get rid of it, and that was dangerous. "You should tell
him," the doctor added, "so he can get rid of it too."

Tell which one?

"And until you're both cured," the doctor said, "be
sure he wears a condom."

"I want an AIDS test," Markie said. She was grateful
there was no look of shock, no protestations that it
couldn't have happened to *her*, or questions about why
she thought she might be a candidate. Markie knew
that the reason she was asking to be tested was that in
her heart she was sure she would be negative. But during the ten days she waited for the results she thought
of nothing else.

She tried to reassure herself that she knew people

who were tested for AIDS all the time, they were always fine, they were just cautious. It was the people who thought they were infected who were afraid to find out. How much easier, she thought, it would have been to use protection and be done with it. But she also knew that her friends who were tested and found they were fine went right back to their old reckless ways, as if their escape were a validation, as if the same faulty instinct that told them it was going to be love this time would also tell them when it was safe.

The test results came back. She was negative; she would live. She hadn't told anyone, even her sister, and now she wouldn't have to. After her moments of great relief and celebration, to her surprise Markie suddenly found herself being very careful. She was celibate during her skiing holiday and then through the winter. It was as if her sex drive had vanished. She didn't even care. No man is worth all the aggravation he causes, she thought; there are other things in life, and fate will bring me what it brings. I am, finally, tired of other people and only interested in knowing myself.

Sometimes she still thought about the mystery of her real parents. She wondered what part of her came from them, if, after all this time, it did anymore. There were organizations that would try to find your birth parents for you, but she hadn't done anything about it. In a way, she was afraid. At long last, she was satisfied with the family she had. Now she was trying to become satisfied with herself. Oddly, this celibate and rather isolated period of her life did not make her irritable or horny; it made her serene and relaxed. She was even able to be friendly to David Laurent and mean it.

He sensed it was safe now and asked her to lunch. Markie agreed; why not? She still liked the things about him that she had liked all along. How strange it all is, she thought, sitting across from him at the little table with the thick white tablecloth and the tiny bunch of flowers in the upscale Italian restaurant near the office, smiling, daring to look into his eyes even though she didn't know if it would upset him, and noticing there a kind of apologetic affection.

"So how is it being free?" Markie asked.

He shrugged. "Exhausting and overrated."

"Exhausting?"

"The mental part. The games."

"Ah, yes," she said. "The game that no one wins."

He considered that for a moment. "You're right," he said.

They looked away then. It would be so much simpler if you just came back to me, she thought, and we could try again. You've had enough time to play. Grow up. I did.

"How is your family?" he asked.

She remembered he had liked her family. He had said it was unusual to find a family that was so good to each other, that wasn't dysfunctional, and that he wished they were his. They could have been, of course, Markie thought now.

"Uncle Hugh is still living with Grandma," she said. "I think he should just stay there. He refuses to sell his house. Peter and Jamie are having another baby. It's going to be a boy and they're naming him Henry. Henry Glover and Hannah Glover, it sounds like someone's grandparents; they'll be getting jury duty notices when they're four years old. And Peter is actually getting a job. It's at Webster and Dally, the publishing company where Aunt Joan works. He asked her to help him get it. It's not easy to support two children with nothing but freelance work. My parents are thrilled, of course. Oh, and Trevor is making a movie. He plays a bad cop who you don't know is bad until the end. It's shooting in New York so Aunt Joan is happy. And Angel is having a show next week in Soho. Maybe you'll come to the opening."

"I'd like to," David said.

"She'd like that too." She didn't ask him how his family was. Whatever ideas he had about dysfunctional families he had learned from them. He had never gotten over his parents' divorce and his father's remarriage, his mother's bitterness made him feel guilty, he didn't get along with his domineering sister, he was all alone. We would take you in and nourish you, Markie thought. I would. You and I could start our own family.

Thoughts like that were hazardous for your mental health, and when the following week David was sincere about coming to Angel's opening, Markie was a little sorry she had invited him. He was extremely solicitous, and of course everyone thought they were together again, or at least they wondered. Angel had reserved a table in a downtown restaurant for afterward, and Markie let David come with her as if he were her date, because she didn't know what else to do. When the dinner was over the two of them shared a cab uptown.

"Why don't you ask me in for a drink?" he said.

"No. I think it would be dangerous, and besides, it's late."

"Could we see each other again?"

"As what?"

"We could go on a date."

"I don't date," Markie said.

"How do you get to know someone?"

She didn't answer.

"Look, I'd like to try again," David said. "Slowly."

"Slowly is good," Markie said. "But I don't share."

"You're tough."

"I have to be."

"Leaving you was a mistake," he said.

Wasn't that what everyone wanted to hear? He probably knew it. "It was your choice," Markie said.

"I guess you're really angry."

"No."

"Would you have dinner with me Friday night?" he asked. "We could be alone and talk."

And it would segue so easily into the whole weekend, Markie thought, and then what? That was what she wanted, but Sunday night would hurt again. And what if it was only Friday night after all, and then he left on Saturday to go out with some other woman? People had previous plans. People had their own lives. "Dinner," she said. "No sex."

"No?"

"No."

"All right."

This time it's all or nothing, she thought. Let's see who wins.

FIFTY-ONE

Hugh knew more than the others did about when he was going to return to his own house. The answer was never. His life had come full circle; he had spent his youth with Rose and he would die with her, unless, of course, she died first, which was likely since she was older. He liked being in her home with the two babies, which reminded him of when his nieces were young. During those sad mornings or afternoons in the beloved mews house he had shared with Teddy he had thought a great deal about the past. Sometimes he spoke to Teddy in heaven, or wherever he was if there wasn't a real heaven, and asked him what he should do. If Hugh concentrated hard enough he could hear Teddy's voice, if only in his mind, and it always made him feel better.

The aged should not be alone, Teddy told him. Stay with Rose. I'm with you wherever you are. As for the house, if you don't want to live in it, do something useful with it.

But what? Hugh asked.

Leave good works as a testament to your life, Teddy said. Be of help to the less fortunate. It was odd how he sometimes sounded like someone in a Biblical movie.

I was going to leave it to my family, Hugh said.

To the young ones? How are they going to pay the inheritance taxes?

Have you been talking to Ben? Is Ben there? Hugh
asked. He imagined he could see Teddy smiling.

The world is your family too, Teddy said. And,
Hugh, please, that pink negligee with the feathers—
throw it away. It doesn't become you. It's dreadful.

Did the spirits of the dead sit on your shoulder to advise and comfort you? Hugh had read such a thing,
since occasionally he read spiritual books. He was sure
that Teddy, like the other departed, was waiting
around to be of help to him until he wasn't needed
anymore. Meanwhile, Hugh was packing, but he
didn't sell the furniture because he felt he might still
use it in some way. And one evening, after dinner, at
home in his comfortable room at Rose's, Hugh suddenly knew what he was going to do with his mews
house.

His gay activist activities had given him many con-
tacts. Through the Gay Men's Health Crisis he was able
to get the advice he needed, and then he gave the
house to them as a charitable contribution, to be made
into a hospice for people dying of AIDS. He told them
he wanted it to look nice, and therefore the furniture
would stay. Meanwhile they arranged for construction, for the changeover into a small medical facility
that would also look like a comforting residence, and
were building an elevator to accommodate stretchers
and wheelchairs.

His family was surprised at the news of Hugh's project, but not as stunned as he had thought they might
be. If anyone complained about their vanished inheritance, it was not to him—except, of course, for Peggy,
who, Hugh decided, had in her later years turned into
Celia. Funny, Celia had always been Peggy's favorite,
and vice versa. Maybe the spirits of the dead stayed
around longer than one thought.

Looking at him resentfully, as if he were an old fool,
Peggy informed him that Markie was living with Da-

vid Laurent again, in Markie's apartment, but this time they were talking about getting married. It was only a matter of setting the date and deciding where they might live. They wanted children right away, before Markie was too old, so they would need a larger apartment. "You might have let them buy your house," Peggy said. "There's a housing shortage, you know. You wouldn't have had to worry about financing; they would have gotten a mortgage easily, being well-paid lawyers, but you didn't even think."

Hugh was so annoyed he didn't speak to Peggy for a month, not that she noticed since he hardly ever saw her anyway.

When the Hugh Smith-Teddy Benedict Hospice opened in the spring of 1992 there was a little celebration, and photos were taken for the newspapers, since Hugh was always interesting news. "I only hope this is temporary and that there will be a cure soon," Hugh said. The next day patients began to be moved in. They were mainly young men, many of whose families were not willing to let them come home to die, or who wanted to spend their last days where they were, among their remaining friends in this city that had been their home for so long. There was a waiting list right away. It was devastatingly sad, and yet it was uplifting. If people had to die this horrible death, at least let them be surrounded by love, Hugh thought.

One of the best parts of this new endeavor was that he had been able to persuade Ginger to work there twice a week, as a doctor and also as a consoler whose heart was filled with kindness. He had even managed to see that she was paid. Of everyone in the family, it was Ginger who had been the most affected by Teddy's death. The three of them had been companions for so long, since she was a teenager, and he and Ginger were still taking care of each other, even now.

Hugh knew his project wouldn't have been the same without Ginger's being somehow connected with it.

Ginger had gone to work at Uncle Hugh's hospice with mixed feelings. Wasn't life bad enough; didn't she already see enough tragedy? At least at the hospital sick people often left well. But she knew how much the hospice meant to Hugh, and so she let him talk her into helping. She felt there was a certain kind of person who could regularly tend to the terminally ill, a Mother Teresa kind of person, and she was sure she wasn't that. Her knowledge of oncology did her little good here, since the purpose was not to cure, only to comfort. If she needed yet another lesson that her life wasn't so lonely, that her blessings were to be counted, then here it was. But how many lessons did she need?

The body was only a package for the mind and for the soul—such an imperfect package that people were constantly trying to patch it up, mend it, make it operate, make it last. Understanding the way genes worked made her more aware that this fragile and often defective organism was in many ways an unbelievable miracle. It created, it fought to survive, it evolved with a mindless tenacity. It made mistakes, it turned on itself. And through all this, the part that was cognitive just kept blundering along because the package it was in was the only one it was going to get, no matter what you did to make it look better, to keep it healthy, to make it feel good.

Organs could be transplanted, arteries and joints replaced, viruses killed until a resistant strain appeared—medical miracles that had happened in her lifetime—until now it was said that the largest growing part of the population was the people who were going to live to a hundred. Perhaps her own mother would. And yet, despite all the new knowledge and the frantic searching for more, people died too young all the time. The hospital had made her aware of this years ago, and now the hospice reminded her.

That summer Markie and David got married at Markie's parents' house in Larchmont. The couple had found a larger apartment without Hugh's help, on the upper West Side of Manhattan, not their first choice, but what they could afford. David seemed more mature now, in his attitude and somehow also his looks—a handsome young man, not a boy anymore—and they were both looking forward to having a family of their own.

It was a lovely wedding on a fine sunny day. Markie looked radiant, even triumphant. Angel, with a blue streak in her hair that matched her dress and annoyed her parents, was the maid of honor. Ed gave Markie away and Peggy wept, and Joan, when Ginger looked at her, seemed both proud and wistful. Well, of course she would, Ginger told herself. Ginger hadn't thought about Markie's origins for years, but Markie's wedding made her wonder if anyone was ever going to tell her who her real mother was. And who her father was, since only Joan knew that.

It's none of my business, Ginger told herself, and I was sworn to secrecy; and yet, Rose was getting older and so was Hugh, and when they died only four people would hold the answer to the mystery. It didn't seem fair. Ginger thought of a dangerous scenario: that Markie's children might fall in love with and marry their own first cousins without ever knowing. It won't happen, Ginger reassured herself, it's much too unlikely. Yet, in the fertility field, anonymous sperm donations were kept to four times so people wouldn't have to deal with the possibility of accidental incest—so doctors did worry about it.

Family secrets, no matter how interesting, die eventually and disappear if people won't tell, Ginger thought. She would have liked to discuss all this with

Rose, but she had kept silent for so long that by now she was almost afraid to talk about it. Peggy and Joan had made their pact long ago, a pact of which she had never been a part. If Uncle Hugh hadn't told her the story she would never have known. She felt rather like an outsider, and she supposed she was. It had been decided by the two principles that no one could tell Markie but Peggy, and by now Ginger could not imagine what would make Peggy tell her.

Maybe no one should, Ginger thought.

Markie's wedding made her think of something else too, of course: the joyful marriage of the next generation while she herself had no one and probably never would have. At the party after the wedding, even though she knew nearly everyone and they went out of their way to be nice to her, she had been so clearly alone. She sat with Hugh and Rose, who had each enjoyed a long lifetime with the one they loved, and now had lost those people, and Ginger briefly wondered who was worse off, herself or them.

The next day she returned to work at the hospice and forgot about her problems. There was a young man, Brian, dying on the second floor, and his family had come from Kansas to be with him. Apparently, Ginger was told by one of the nurses, the father and son had been estranged but now were reunited. There was a mother, she saw, a fair-haired, good-looking woman of about her own age, and occasionally another brother and sister came by. What was interesting about the mother was that she, too, was in a wheelchair.

The woman and Ginger met in the hall when the mother was coming back, nibbling at a sandwich she had bought for herself. They were on each other's eye level, which Ginger found refreshing. The woman peered at Ginger, and then her somber look was replaced by one of warmth. "You *are* Ginger Carson, you're the same one, I thought so!" she exclaimed.

"The same one?"

"From Warm Springs! You wouldn't remember me, I was Althea Crane."

"Althea…" Ginger looked at her more carefully. It had been years. But there was a resemblance, and now that she thought back she could see this was her old friend. "I can't believe it," Ginger said. "I'm so sorry about your son."

"Yes, it's tragic. Actually, he's my husband's son from his previous marriage. I'm only glad they got to reconcile. The young man and young woman you might have seen with me are my children from my first husband."

"You had two marriages?" Ginger asked stupidly.

"Oh, yes. Another casualty of our generation. My first husband left me for a younger woman, which happened to quite a few of my friends, and I suppose to yours. But Greg, my present husband, is a wonderful man. We've been married for ten years. His first wife died. And you, Ginger, you know I never forgot you and that cute boy you were in love with at Warm Springs…. What was his name?"

"Christopher," Ginger said.

"The two of you used to go off into the bushes and neck. Do you remember?"

"Yes."

"So what happened to him? Did you see him again?"

"I believe he became a doctor," Ginger said. "We lost touch."

"We had so much fun at Warm Springs, didn't we?" Althea said.

"I guess we did," Ginger said. You had *two* husbands? she thought again. Paralyzed legs and all? And I couldn't even find *one*.

"I admire you for doing this," Althea said. "And the nurse told me you're quite a respected oncologist and researcher. You're amazing. So intelligent and accomplished and doing so much good. I had dreams of being a doctor when I was at Warm Springs. I suppose many of us did, they were our heroes. But I was never that bright, or that academic, to tell you the truth. I became a housewife. I guess that term is out now, but that's what I was."

"Homemaker," Ginger said lightly. "Domestic engineer."

"And a mom."

"I envy you," Ginger said.

"Yes, it's been wonderful, but it wasn't easy. The divorce, feeling so badly about myself, and the years after, trying to feed my kids. Then Brian, my stepson, hiding his life from us, the estrangement from his father, a terrible thing. And the disease. You'd never want anyone in your life to have to go through something like that. When you love people you're open to tragedy."

Ginger didn't answer.

"And you, did you marry?"

"No," Ginger said.

"Well, you have other things. You and I were of that generation that still had to choose."

Did I choose this? Ginger wondered.

"Sometimes we're hardly responsible for the road taken," Althea said. "And sometimes we are. But for every one of us, every minute, it's choices and fate, whether we know it or not at the time. What a winding road it is, and so full of surprises. Whatever brought you here, Ginger Carson, thank you from the bottom of my heart for everything you're doing for Brian."

"You're welcome," Ginger said. She watched the woman wheel away. Sitting there looking after her, she remembered again who she was, and what she wanted. Her lonely inner world was, in some important ways, a mystery to others, and there was a world of struggle out there that she didn't even know about. Too often she forgot.

FIFTY-TWO

Markie and David had been married for a year, and marriage was almost everything she had hoped it would be. The missing part was that she had not yet gotten pregnant. A year of frequent unprotected sex—sex that was at first wonderful, and then sentimentally hopeful, and lately distractingly desperate—had produced nothing. If you tried, it was supposed to work in the first year. She knew couples who had hit the jackpot the very first month. She didn't understand why she had been so fertile when she and David first met and hardly knew each other, but now that they were encouraged by society and their families to procreate it wasn't happening.

She was thirty-four, not that this was old, but she was concerned. David was thirty. A husband, she liked to tell her friends, should be your own age or younger. But sometimes she worried that if she didn't cement her marriage by starting a family he might get bored and start to stray. Part of the deal when they decided to marry had been that they would have it all: the home, the job, the kid, no matter how difficult people said it was. Both of them wanted a baby, preferably two, to bring up, to be concerned about, to love; a child or children to make noise, to throw toys around, to take on vacations with them. The large apartment they had rented with such eager confidence in their future now seemed to be an omen of bad luck, an empty and too quiet symbol of hubris punished.

From time to time Markie couldn't help thinking about the abortion she'd had long ago—her baby with David—and she felt guilty. She wondered if he thought about it too. Neither of them was willing to mention it. Was she going to be punished for her abortion by not being able to conceive a child now that she was able to take care of it? Did something go wrong in the surgery? Was her body rebelling against her refusal to let it do what it wanted—telling her something?

Her gynecologist said that all of these were only her guilty fears, and that hers was a common feeling with no validity, but she would send Markie and David to a fertility specialist. It seemed so ironic Markie didn't even want to think about it right now. She and David went to Tahiti for their vacation, the quietest, most romantic place they could think of, timing the trip to the week she ovulated, but there were no results.

Back home again, they were involved in their daily lives. Getting involved with a fertility specialist would be a huge commitment of time, effort, and emotion, and then it could end in disappointment. So months went by, and then it was another year, and she was thirty-five.

In the *New York Times* there was news that the first test of a newer, more effective drug for people with advanced AIDS, called a protease inhibitor, had been successfully tested in a first trial, and that there would be a more intensive trial now, using this drug in addition to the drugs such as AZT that were already in use. Hugh often said he hoped to live long enough to see his hospice turned into something more pleasant, even a dispensary, since he would be happy with any kind of progress. Swords into plowshares, he said, but that day was still far away, and Markie doubted he would be here to celebrate it. It was strange how some very old people seemed to shrivel up overnight, she thought. Hugh was getting frail, as if a ghostlike hand had let all the air out of his face. He was nearly ninety, a good long run, and she was surprised he was here at all.

She wished he and Grandma were her real family so she could look forward to such longevity. Next year Grandma would be ninety-five. Her children and grandchildren were planning a party, a little nervously in case that was their own tempting of the fates, since you never knew what would happen to someone that age. But Grandma was an amazement; she ran up and down the stairs of her house and refused to use the staircase elevator. She had all sorts of outside activities, she remembered almost everything, and most annoying to Peggy and Joan, who'd both had plastic surgery, Grandma's soft, thin skin was still as smooth as cream.

This summer, there would be a wedding to go to, Angel's. Angel had recently become engaged to a performance artist named Juan, whom she had known for years and hardly even mentioned. After having been good friends they had decided they couldn't live without each other. Peggy and Ed, who had liked her rich boyfriend, and the banker she had dated before him, and the broker she had been seeing before that, were displeased. Juan's being Hispanic was the worst of it. Now it was Peter they liked, and Angel they deplored.

Peter, who had for so long resisted fatherhood, was thrilled with his two little kids, Hannah and Henry, and he and Jamie talked about them all the time, to the point where it was boring, at least to Markie. She and Angel made a pact that if and when they had children of their own they would never go on about them that way. But Peggy said Peter's lively family was a great comfort to Grandma, and, of course, to herself and Ed. Right on, Mom, Markie thought; rub it in.

There was a new coffeehouse that had just opened

near Markie's apartment on the upper West Side, called Starbucks, and now and then Markie went there alone and thought about her married life, and sometimes cried into her latte. Everyone was drinking coffee now, more than alcohol; it was the new addiction. On weekends everyone wore gym clothes in the street, even the women pushing baby strollers. What Markie saw, when she looked at these strollers, were how many of them were doubles, for twins, and how some even carried triplets. Fertility drug babies, she told herself. The mothers were usually her age or older. The twins were usually fraternal. These multiple births were exploding in every residential area, due to the new medical technology.

It had been years since people were able to adopt the kind of baby she had been—white, blond, blue-eyed; many people had so badly wanted babies who looked like her that they didn't even care if the child didn't look at all like the family it was going to enter. A family resemblance, of course, was a bonus to many others, and often adoption agencies tried to match. And then it didn't matter anymore. Markie felt like she came from the time tunnel. Today unmarried women were keeping their babies, even having them on purpose. Unmarried women were being artificially inseminated, lesbians too. Now the childless were adopting kids from Eastern Europe, from Latin America, from Asia—all those adorable little girls from China—and mixed-race babies from America, making her view from the sidewalk café that of a real melting pot.

Joan and Trevor had never had a child. Markie now wondered why not. And Daisy, back in Bristol, had had only one. Perhaps that had been choice, perhaps biology. Tampering with such a process as pregnancy, and actually succeeding, had seemed like science fiction. Medicine had advanced a lot since. I really *could* do something about this, Markie thought for the first time.

So now, finally, she and David were at the assisted reproduction center of Mt. Sinai Hospital, in a waiting room filled with women of a range of ages, some with their husbands, some alone. It was early in the morning, and some of these people had taken long drives to get here, and next they would go to work. There were photographs of babies tacked up all over the walls, sent by grateful parents: fraternal twins, a few sets of triplets, and a number of single babies, some of them with older siblings. The program here was supposed to be one of those with the best results.

She wasn't sure what she was expecting to see, but when they met their doctor, Dr. Leon Kuyper, Markie was pleasantly surprised. He was almost as young as she was, on the cutting edge of a new technology, an enthusiastic, cute young guy with photos of his own babies on his desk. He has a good job, Markie thought; he only has to make people happy. But then he described the many tests she and David would probably have to take and she started to get nervous. Dr. Kuyper took a detailed personal and medical history and, like a detective, asked a lot of questions about the things that might be causing their problem.

"Did you ever use an IUD?"

"No."

"Did either of you ever have a sexually transmitted disease? Chlamydia, for example? Or anything else?"

Markie and David looked at each other. "No," David said.

"No," Markie lied. "What would that have done?"

"An infection years ago might have given you blocked fallopian tubes," he said calmly.

"Oh," she said innocently. I have to get him alone, she thought.

She answered the rest of the questions as accurately

as she could, hoping there was some other reason and that he would find it. It was not that David wouldn't love her anymore if he knew she'd caught something once, she told herself, but it just wasn't something you told your husband, even if it was his fault for abandoning you and making you see other men. She was angry at him for his indecisive youth and at herself for her carelessness. It was all so unfair.

As soon as she got to her office where she could be alone, Markie called Dr. Kuyper.

"I had chlamydia a long time ago," she said. "I don't want my husband to know."

"A lot of women don't," he said calmly. "We'll take the other standard tests first, to rule everything else out, and I'll also give you a hysterosalpingogram, which is a sophisticated x-ray study to look for a blockage. If you have one we can do in vitro fertilization."

The thought plunged her into despair. She remembered when she was young, hearing of the first baby who had been started in a petri dish in England, Baby Louise Brown, who had been considered a miracle. Babies like that had been called test tube babies, and they were very rare. In vitro fertilization was known to be complicated. She'd heard of people even today who had tried for years, taken fertility drugs, spent a fortune, and it had ended in failure.

"But that's so hard, isn't it?" Markie said.

"You're lucky to be in New York," he said reassuringly. "Mt. Sinai and two other hospitals here in the area have the highest success rate in the nation, with a fifty percent success rate on the first try for a woman your age, and seventy-five percent by the second try. The rest of the country only has a twenty-five percent success rate."

It turned out that it was indeed her fallopian tubes that were the problem. David never asked why they were blocked and Markie didn't tell him. Now the two of them became involved in a proceeding so complex that they had to enroll in a three-hour class at the doctor's office, and went home with charts and literature and directions and vials of medications that had to be mixed and injected into her at specific times. There was a drug called Lupron to suppress her ovaries from producing eggs, because the procedure demanded more than she could make on her own, and later there was a drug called Pergonal to stimulate those same ovaries to produce as many eggs as possible for fertilization.

There were papers to be signed: Did Markie and David want to keep some of the extra fertilized eggs frozen for the next try if the first didn't work, or, if it did, so their baby or babies could have a sibling later? Or did they want to give them away? Would they prefer to have them destroyed? What if one of the parents died? What if Markie and David got divorced; who would own the embryos? Death seemed very far away, but the thought of breaking up some day and fighting over an unborn baby who would still be just a couple of cells in a freezer was very depressing.

David had to give her a shot every night, in the butt, after practicing on an orange, and he was so nervous and squeamish that Markie seriously thought of calling Aunt Ginger to come over and do it for him. The Lupron made Markie bloated and hysterical, like the worst PMS she'd ever had, and she gained five pounds of bloat in a week. Sex had to be kept going on a normal basis to keep the sperm count high, and then there was no sex allowed, and then there was mandatory sex, until Markie was surprised that, between her bad disposition and the medical necessity for him to perform, she and David could manage to have sex at all.

Every morning Markie had to be at the doctor's office at eight a.m., first-come first-served, waiting in a room with thirty other anxious women to have an ultrasound test to see how her eggs were growing. Day

Thirteen of the medication cycle was egg retrieval day. Markie had an anesthetic, and David had a copy of *Playboy* so he could masturbate in the doctor's office bathroom to provide the sperm. Why did they think *Playboy* always did the trick? If it did, then there was something about men that she would never understand.

After the procedure Dr. Kuyper told them he had retrieved ten eggs. They were injected with the sperm and then cultured in a dish with her own blood serum, and two days later he told her there were six that were successfully fertilized—embryos now—just tiny round dots with cells in them. Under a microscope you could see that some were more perfect than others. Two days later the three healthiest ones (three at the most so they could thrive in case all of them managed to "stick") were transferred into Markie's uterus. After the anxiety and the counting and the rushing to the doctor and the rules to follow it was hard to believe that this entire process had taken only one month.

But she didn't know yet how many would turn into her children, if any at all. Success rate to a childless person meant taking home a baby to play with, not what happened along the way. There could be a problem with the egg, with the uterus, or in the lab. Older women, Dr. Kuyper told her, often miscarried. He reminded her again, proudly, that for a younger woman her age the success rate was fifty percent, which Markie thought was a large number if you were looking at progress in the fertility field but a small one if you were the nervous patient. If a doctor told you that you had only a fifty percent chance of surviving you would be very upset. What should she say then for her child?

She had told her mother and Aunt Joan that she and David were trying to have a baby, but had omitted all the details. It seemed too clinical and private to describe everything she was going through, and besides, the others would either be too concerned or not concerned enough. She didn't want them asking questions, or being disappointed, and she felt so fragile right now that she was sure their concern would bring her to tears. The only one to whom Markie told everything that was happening was her sister, and she only told Angel because she had to share this with someone near her own age. Even so, she had the feeling that Angel really didn't want to know.

When Markie became pregnant she was excited, but didn't tell anyone but David because she didn't want to tempt fate. It was only when the pregnancy began to show, at Angel's wedding, that Markie finally felt confident enough to announce her success. By then she had been told she was carrying twins. "Twins!" Great Uncle Hugh exclaimed. "How nice, you can get it all over with at one time." They all smiled. Life, they knew, would no longer ever be the same. Everyone was thrilled, Aunt Joan as much as her own parents, as Markie had expected. No matter what Aunt Joan did to hide the fact, they all knew Markie was her favorite.

If Peggy and Ed hadn't really made peace with the idea of Angel marrying Juan, at least they were now pretending everything was fine. The thought of new grandchildren from Markie kept their minds off what their grandchildren from Angel would look like. Ed was over seventy and Peggy was old enough to qualify for Medicare. It was not so much a matter of age but of attitude; they would never be modern. Ironically, it was Grandma who was.

At the end of the year, near her own birthday, Markie gave birth to a perfectly healthy boy and girl. The boy looked just like her, and the girl looked like both her and David, but oddly also like Angel, and, Grandma told her, what Aunt Ginger had looked like as an infant. Everyone remarked on the family resemblance with enthusiasm, as if none of them remembered that Markie was adopted. She didn't bother to correct them. Perhaps they had forgotten after all these years.

Right away it was clear that David would be a doting and helpful father. He needed to be; she was exhausted. Markie had a three-month leave of absence from work, but secretly she thought she might drag it out to six, even if they fired her. Maybe she'd even quit. She could always find another job when the kids started school. Despite her former aversion to old-fashioned names, she and David had named the twins Abigail and Glover. It was funny how when you became a parent yourself all the ideas you'd had about other people's silliness went right out the window.

FIFTY-THREE

Her grandchildren! Joan had suspected but never really known to what degree these babies, Abigail and Glover, would cause her to melt into such a tender woman. She thought about them often, and missed them, and delighted in buying them presents, even the things they would not know about like clothing, which would be outgrown before they appreciated what it was or that it came from her. She tried not to give unrequested advice.

Unlike the protected and isolated infants of her generation, and even Markie's, Abigail and Glover went everywhere with their parents: to restaurants, to parties, to public places; in their stroller or in chest packs, no matter that it was late in the evening, or that people were smoking, or that there were probably germs. Joan pretended she wasn't concerned about it.

At Rose's ninety-fifth birthday party, which the family gave for her in an elegant private room at the St. Regis Hotel, with speeches and tributes, music and dancing, all the great-grandchildren were present, even Abigail and Glover. They watched everything, pacifiers in their mouths, and didn't even fuss. They were alert and socialized at a very early age, and Joan was constantly amazed at how intelligent they were, their minds like little computers, storing up everything.

She had free access to them as she had not had to Markie growing up, and although she didn't want to be a pest, she seemed to find herself visiting them more than she had imagined she would. If Markie and David did not take them to Larchmont on a Sunday to see Peggy and Ed, or if Peggy and Ed did not come in, then Joan would be at their apartment. If the twins were available on a Saturday instead, then Joan would be there. Trevor liked them and usually went along with her, quite willingly in fact, but he wasn't besotted the way she was. Of course not; he didn't know they were his too.

Trevor's grandchildren...

He was a caring man; he hadn't made an issue of their own childlessness (as he thought it was), and he had accepted Markie fondly as a niece by marriage, noticed how much Joan loved her, and had never in any way indicated that they should be jealous of Peggy and Ed. But watching him hold little Abigail, seeing the soft look on his face, which he wasn't even aware of, Joan suddenly had a shocking epiphany that made her throat clutch. Why had she never realized the enormity of her selfishness before? All these years she had cheated him.

First, he had been cheated of a daughter. At the time she hadn't even thought of what he might want, except as a possible threat; she had simply used him. Her pain had been so great that it had not occurred to her to think of him as anything but a means to an end. He had missed Markie's childhood altogether before he met Joan again, and she could only remind herself—to assuage the guilt—that he had been a different person when he was young, a footloose aspiring actor, and perhaps he would have found the situation of being a biological father much too difficult. If that were true, he would not be the first to feel that way. Then later, when they fell in love and he entered her family, she had simply told herself that Trevor didn't have to know. He had still been part of her long-ago scheme.

She could rationalize that she had spared him distress, that if he had known he had a daughter and Peggy had kept them apart, he would have been hurt. And Peggy *would* have kept them apart. Peggy would have been even more threatened than she already was, by seeing a father as well as a mother breathing on the boundaries of her life. Joan could also remind herself of the very real possibility that Trevor would be angry or reject her if he found out what she had done. But now it was more than only beleaguered Markie at stake; Joan knew she had, finally, cheated Trevor of his grandchildren, of his immortality, of his look into the future.

She could not compound her first crime with this one; she knew too much, she understood him too well, she had loved him for too long. At this moment it was as if finally she also understood herself.

She came from a family of strong, determined women—a domestic world of almost all women, in fact, except for her kindly father, who had been in a way overwhelmed by so much rampant estrogen in that house, and dear Uncle Hugh, who had been more like an aunt. So, Joan now suddenly realized, trying to repair Peggy's shattered life all by herself had been natural to her. The young Joan, the misfit, "bad Joan," had been a woman who could not dare to love a man, or accept love from him, who only saw him as a tool for what at the time had seemed her survival. The grown-up Joan saw what she had done as something that now caused her guilt and touched her with empathy.

She considered how far she had come from being that Joan of so many years ago. The pact of secrecy she had made with Peggy seemed odd now. Peggy's grief had given one person control of the entire family. Yes, grief and anguish had their own tyranny, over others as well as the one directly affected. And when the suffering seemed to be gone, there was still Peggy's hate, and her need to punish. All these years Joan, and the rest of them to a lesser degree, had waited and waited for Peggy to tell Markie, but Peggy would not do it. You've exhausted the statute of limitations, Peggy, Joan said to herself. It's over. Now it's my turn.

The other people who had known—the few there were left now—might tell her it was too late, that it was all over, that it was in the past. Joan knew Markie would not think so. Markie deserved to know that she had always been with her own family, that there was no mysterious "real" family somewhere out there in the world whom she would have to find. If the behavior of this family shocked and disturbed her, that was a gamble Joan would have to take. There was a whole story to be told, and it was long, but she couldn't hold it in anymore.

But first she would have to tell Trevor. Joan wondered if telling him would make her lose him. In expiation for her youthful betrayal she would be giving him his grandchildren. Knowing that, at last, how could he hate her, how could he refuse to forgive? Rose, Joan knew, would be on her side, as she always had been. She did not even have to ask.

So in the end, since revelations of old secrets were sometimes caused by unexpected events, it was Joan's understanding of what she had done to Trevor that made her decide to tell the story at last, not so much because of what she owed Markie, although there was always that too.

She waited for a day when he was not tired or busy, when he was feeling cheerful. She and Trevor were back in their apartment after having visited Markie and David and the twins. Looking around at all their familiar things, the photographs, the books, the record of their happy life together, Joan felt less afraid. He was not Peggy. She wasn't taking anything away from him; she was giving it back.

"Sit down," she said to him. "I need to tell you a secret. I have to begin at the beginning, so maybe you'd better have a drink."

She told him about the accident, about the way it had torn the whole family apart until she finally had to leave. She told him about Markie's conception and birth and adoption. She told him how Peggy, instead of forgiving her, had thought fearfully that Joan's gift was a weapon against her, and thus, that nothing had been resolved. She told him she was sorry for not having told him, and that she loved him. At the end, when she had told him everything, Trevor was silent. Then he reached over and took her hand.

"My poor, crazy Joan," he said. "How alone you were." To her astonishment his eyes were glazed with tears.

"Yes," she said. "I was."

"I would have loved her, you know," he said. "But when I think of who I was, I probably wouldn't have been a very good father back then. Ed seems like a very devoted dad to me; a little old-fashioned maybe, a little stiff, but he has always had a good heart. You're right, of course; you have to tell Markie. But I don't even know if she would want me at this point—she's an adult, with a family of her own. But when you tell her, tell her I'm there for her. And I'm delighted to have grandchildren. Don't you think Abigail looks like me?"

"She does," Joan said.

"I've always had that feeling." The tears were gone; he was smiling now. In fact, Trevor looked very pleased with himself. "And Glover's a little ham. I wouldn't be surprised if he became an actor like the old man, would you?"

"Not at all surprised," Joan said.

Now she wanted to give Peggy one final chance to end it herself. Joan called her to lay it out simply and decisively. Better to be abrupt, she thought, before she lost her nerve, and hope that at last, after all these years, there would be no fight.

"Peggy," she said on the phone to that voice that would never truly welcome her, "knowing Markie's children has made me think again about everything that has happened between you and me. I have decided that it's time to tell Markie who her birth mother is. *You* can tell her now, or else I will. Your shot."

There was a momentary silence, and then Peggy hung up. No scream, no cry of "No!" Just that soft click of the receiver being replaced, as if Joan were a lunatic making a crank call, someone to be gotten rid of.

Peggy thinks she can erase me, Joan thought. She doesn't think I'll do it.

Joan decided to tell Markie alone, without David there. Markie could tell him herself. If there were to be any retributions forthcoming, Joan wanted the encounter between her and her daughter to be one-on-one. Afterward, if Markie wanted to tell Peggy that she knew and have it out with her, it would be Markie's own decision.

Joan asked her to leave the twins with David for a while and come over for a late lunch on Sunday afternoon; she said it was important. Trevor was in an Off Broadway play—the pay wasn't good but it kept him busy and happy—and it was matinee day for him. Joan had told him to call her before he came home, in case the discussion took a long time, although part of her was afraid that Markie would run away in revulsion and it would not take long at all. Whichever was the case, Joan knew she herself would need a while alone to get over it. She had played the fantasy of the revelation in her mind innumerable times; sometimes it came out as a loving reunion, sometimes as a distancing shock. Now she did not know what to believe it would be anymore. She had hardly slept for the past several nights. The best thing was to get it over with.

"What's so important, Aunt Joan?" Markie asked curiously, poking at her salad.

Joan poured her a glass of wine. "I need to tell you a very long story about our family," Joan said. "Yours and mine. Everyone's. I'm going to begin with what happened to your sister Marianne."

She told the story rather differently from the way she had told Trevor. This version was not about him but about herself. It seemed to her that in explaining everything that had happened, somehow she was beginning to understand it more objectively. As she told it she was both the storyteller and the participant, and now it was the storyteller who had the wisdom for both of them. Markie kept looking at her sympathetically, if a little confused, until Joan got to what was really the point.

"That baby girl I had, Markie, was you."

Markie gasped. "You're my mother?"

Joan nodded. She waited to see if Markie might be glad, resentful, or simply relieved to see the end of the mystery.

"And Trevor's my father? And no one ever told me! Why not?"

"There's more." Joan went on, trying to explain what had happened through the years. How could you justify need—hers to be reunited with her family, Peggy's to stay normal? She told Markie how Peggy had refused to let Joan tell, how Ed had barely been able to speak to her, how they had never understood. When she had finally finished she waited, at last with more resignation than anxiety, to see the verdict in her daughter's eyes.

She could see she had been acquitted.

"Maybe that's why you and I were always so simpatico," Markie said thoughtfully. "I sometimes used to wish you were my mother. And all the time, you were."

"Maybe you wouldn't have liked me so much if I were the boring old disciplinary mom instead of the fun aunt," Joan said.

"Do you think not?"

"I don't know."

"My god, Aunt Joan, what do I call you now?"

"Joan would be good enough."

"The kids are your grandchildren!"

"Aren't I lucky?"

"It's just unbelievable," Markie said. "I feel safe now. There's nobody out there who's a part of me who I don't know, who I can't find."

"That's one of the reasons I had to tell you."

"I hate my mother," Markie said. "*She* should have told me."

"Then you should hate me too," Joan said, but of course she didn't mean it.

"No," Markie said. "You were a prisoner of your own ethics. I can't believe you all knew and nobody would tell me. This family is bizarre."

"We are."

Markie's eyes narrowed. "Joan," she said, "what would you have done if I had been a boy instead of a girl?"

"I prayed so hard I knew you'd be a girl."

"But that's nuts. What would you have done? Would you have kept me?"

"For myself?"

"For you, or just given me away to someone for adoption? I mean, you were replacing Marianne, you said."

There was no point to protest that if it had been a boy it wouldn't have been Markie but someone else. In Markie's mind it would always have been herself, and

Joan understood that. She thought for a moment, remembering what the young Joan would have done if biology had betrayed her. "Of course I would have given you to Peggy anyway," she said. "Infants look like infants. You can't tell if it's a boy or a girl right away. She would have fallen in love with you no matter what."

"Well," Markie said, "that's a relief. I would hate to have had you go to all that trouble and find out that no one wanted me."

"Everyone wanted you!"

"But you *would* have kept me if you had to?"

"Absolutely. You bet I would," Joan said.

Finally Markie smiled at her, and Joan smiled back. "I guess in a way you were sort of like a surrogate mother," Markie said. "Before they had such a thing. You always were modern, Aunt...I mean, Joan. You always were ahead of your time."

"Thank you."

Markie stood up. "I need to hug you now," she said. "Don't you need to hug me?"

They embraced as mother and daughter, the flesh of her flesh, the blood of her blood, the moment Joan had dreamed of for so long and then had finally abandoned. Of course they had hugged before, but never like this. My child, Joan thought, and felt released at last, light and free.

"What will I tell my mother...I mean, *Peggy?*" Markie asked.

"She's still your mother."

"I need to have this information for myself for a while," Markie said. "Later I'll tell her I know. After I see how I feel. After I figure out who I love and who I don't. She did a very bad thing to me."

"I didn't tell you this so you'd stop loving her."

"I know," Markie said. "But you can't control my emotions any more than you could control Peggy's.

And she can't control mine either. I don't think she has any idea what harm she did to me. I need to sort this out."

Why can't the legacy of what we do to each other ever end? Joan thought. What do we have to do to bring closure?

FIFTY-FOUR

Peggy finally, at sixty-seven—which she preferred to think of as middle-aged rather than as elderly—had grown into the person she had always meant to be. She was solid, like a tree, she thought, with the branches spread out wide: with children who had turned out pretty well, with four grandchildren and the hope of even more to come, and a husband who still loved her. She and her daughter-in-law got along well enough, although they often eyed one another with mistrust; Angel's Juan was a son-in-law she had never hoped or expected to see in her family, but he was nice to her and so she liked him; and Markie's David was a source of pride. Despite her face-lift and her professionally colored golden hair, Peggy had hardly a twinge of regret for her lost youth, since that would have been pointless; each event was meant for its own season. She had turned into a matriarch.

She and Ed had discussed selling their large Larchmont suburban home and moving into the city, but neither of them felt comfortable with the idea of change. Only a few of their friends were still here. Some had gone to warmer places, like Florida or even California; some had left to live nearer children and grandchildren; some of the wives, widowed now, had bought small condominium or cooperative apartments in Manhattan and only came to the country on weekends. But Peggy didn't feel lonely. She never had.

Ed was retired, although they would have let him stay on at the agency, and now he played golf and tennis regularly and volunteered as a Big Brother (big grandpa really) for poor inner-city kids. On her doctor's advice Peggy was in a group of women who did speed walking, and on Ed's advice, thinking that Angel must have gotten at least a spark of her artistic talent from her, Peggy was taking ceramics and gilding. She never had to worry anymore what to give someone for a present.

When Peggy looked at her mother and at Uncle Hugh she thought what good genes her family had. You could even see it in the faces of her sisters. Of course, who knew what she and Joan would have looked like if they hadn't had a little professional help? For years now she and Joan had looked much the way they always had. And so did Trevor! Of course, he was an actor; they had to stay young for their careers. Peggy was glad that Ed had aged gracefully, for she liked him the way he was now. She still kept her eye on him, in case any of the widows and divorced women had any ideas.

When Markie told Peggy and Ed not to drop by her apartment one Sunday as they had already planned, and said she and David couldn't bring the twins out to Larchmont either, since something had come up, Peggy thought nothing of it. Grown children had their own lives, and whenever you forgot it they moved away slightly to remind you. She and Ed went to see Peter's darling children anyway, and then she and Ed had dinner by themselves in a restaurant that Peggy had read a good review of, the way they had always liked to do.

She remembered how she and Ed had so seldom gone to the city to share their growing children with her parents, and how every time her own mother had given her a suggestion, no matter how mildly, it had made her feel there was a tug-of-war she had to win. Peggy had given up nagging Markie—and Peter and Angel, for that matter—about anything. Her children were entitled to their own social lives. Markie was a grown woman, and whatever mistakes she might have made secretly along the way, and Peggy was sure there had been some, she was fine now, a solid person.

When Markie made excuses again not to see her the following two weekends, Peggy began to wonder why she was so busy. And after a month the wondering turned into a kind of insecure and uncomfortable voice in her head. Then she was distracted because Aunt Harriette, who'd had many complaints, died of a heart attack. "Heart, the family curse," Rose sighed, although Aunt Harriette had been eighty-six and eventually you had to die of something. They all went to the funeral in Massachusetts, where a rabbi spoke, and afterward Aunt Harriette was buried in a Jewish cemetery next to Julius, her late husband. We are all scattered, Peggy thought.

Markie didn't go to the funeral. The children, she said, had colds, and so did she. Peggy was disappointed, but she understood. However, she determined to phone Markie and discuss the strange feeling she had that they were growing apart, an uneasiness that was exacerbated by the recent death of her aunt, Markie's great-aunt; not that they'd seen her so often, but she was the last of that generation except for Rose and Hugh.

"Can't you make a little time for me?" Peggy asked on the phone, hoping she sounded coy and not accusatory.

"I'm coughing my head off."

"When you're well."

"Fine," Markie said. Why did she sound as if this agreement was a sudden, rather angry decision?

"Fine," Peggy echoed, hoping she sounded nicer.

She understood that Markie was overwhelmed by the care of two small children, but she had been through that herself, with more, and Ed hadn't even helped her the way David did Markie. Of course, she'd had the housekeeper. But Markie had a baby-sitter, and a cleaning woman. Peggy had never thought her life was a burden, so why should Markie?

When everyone in the Laurent household was well, which took a long time because then David caught what the others had, and then Markie got it again, Peggy was at last invited to Markie's apartment for a weekday lunch. "Come alone," Markie said. "Don't bring Dad. I need to talk to you."

"Oh, good," Peggy said. "A girls' lunch. I'd like that." But she wasn't sure it would be the pleasure she was hoping it would be. There were too many undercurrents in Markie's voice, none of which she could attribute to strain. Markie seemed, rather, to be hostile.

The twins were napping when Peggy arrived. Peggy crept quietly into their room to look at them, to sniff their clean, sweet, baby scent. Markie and David had decided Abigail and Glover would share a room until they were older, because being together made them feel safe. Markie left the door ajar in case they awoke and needed her.

"*I left you alone to cry,*" Rose had said to Peggy so long ago. "I used to let you scream for hours. They told us to. I'm so sorry. I didn't know any better."

"I don't remember," Peggy had replied. Did she remember?

"Well, Mom," Markie said. She had bought take-out salads and put them on the dining room table, with a bottle of San Pellegrino. Peggy would have preferred a glass of white wine, but she didn't say anything.

"I'm very glad to see you," Peggy said. "It's been too long."

"Yes, well..." Markie said. Peggy ate, Markie picked, and Peggy smiled at her.

"Tell me what's new, what's been happening," Peggy said.

"Mostly I've been thinking," Markie said. "There were a lot of feelings I've had to deal with recently about my life. And now that I have, I want to ask you something."

"What?"

Markie looked straight at her with such intensity it seemed she was trying to see into Peggy's very soul. How blue her eyes are, Peggy thought, and how big. "Why didn't you tell me that Aunt Joan was my mother?" Markie said.

"Oh, my God!" Peggy felt the blood pouring into her face; her heart was racing. She put down her fork before she dropped it. "Who told you?"

"She did."

"I never thought she would," Peggy mumbled absurdly. Then, unexpectedly, she started to weep, trying to choke back the tears and unable to. She didn't even know why she was so overcome with sorrow; she felt threatened and alone. Markie seemed as surprised at her reaction as she was; both of them would have expected outrage, or at the least, excuses. After all these years, after worrying and then finally feeling secure, Peggy now found herself unable to speak at all.

"Why are you crying?" Markie said.

"I don't know." Certainly it was not from relief. Joan, who had always been the enemy, had betrayed her again. She should have expected as much. Joan sneaking around, trying to win over her child. Whose child?

"Did you know that Trevor is my father?" Markie said.

"*Trevor?* Impossible. She only met him when you were... How could that be?"

"They knew each other before. Years ago."

"Oh, my God," Peggy said. "Oh, my God. Did he know all this time?" Trevor in her house, Trevor laughing at her, Trevor and Joan…. Of course Trevor could be the father; Trevor looked like Ed. Peggy had always secretly thought that was why Joan had liked Trevor, because he reminded her of Ed, and Joan invariably wanted what Peggy had.

"No, but he knows now," Markie said.

Peggy wiped her eyes and blew her nose into the luncheon napkin as manners went completely out the window. At least it was paper. She felt now that whatever she did, Markie would be judging her. "I didn't expect you to be angry," she said.

"You didn't?"

"I was trying to protect you, Markie."

"From what? From who?"

Peggy didn't even have to think. It was so clear. Her antipathy toward Joan had little to do with it. Yes, Joan had always coveted what was hers, yes, Joan had been a beatnik, a hippie, a slut, an embarrassment, but that wasn't the real issue. "Markie, I didn't even know myself until you were ten years old. And afterward, how could you have lived in a family with both of us, knowing you were living with me and not your mother? What would you have thought on holidays, at get togethers? Think of the tug-of-war, the fractured loyalties, the questions about why she gave you up. You would have believed she didn't want you. Or you would have believed I couldn't be what she would have been. Every time you had a fight with me you would have run to her. Not that you didn't already. I couldn't tell you. Joan and I never liked each other enough to have made it work. Markie, I only wanted to protect you from conflict and questions. And…and grief."

"I'm not sure if I understand your logic."

"It's true."

"I know about Marianne," Markie said.

"I'm sure you do." The tragedy had happened almost forty years ago, but it was still unbearable to recall. Once again, just for an instant before she blotted out the picture, Peggy was on that driveway. "I'm sure Joan told you her rationale for bringing you to me," Peggy said.

"It wasn't a rationale, Mom, it was a sacrifice."

At least she's still calling me Mom, Peggy thought. "I suppose I should have forgiven Joan years ago," Peggy said. "What happened to Marianne was an accident."

"You never accepted that."

"Yes, I did! But it didn't make any difference in the way I felt."

"Aunt Joan knows that too."

"I couldn't tell you the story while you were growing up," Peggy said, "and afterward it was too late."

"You were unfair to everybody."

Was she? What was fair and what was unfair when whole lives were at stake? None of it had been fair. But it had seemed right at the time to keep their secret; even more than correct, the decision had seemed inescapable.

"I did the best I could," Peggy said. "Don't we all, all parents? Don't we try? Your father…Ed…was appalled when he found out you had been Joan's baby. He thought it was immoral what she did for us; trifling with life, he said, making one person interchangeable with another, playing God. It was I who was more realistic. After Joan told me, we couldn't go back, we couldn't go forward in the same way, everything was just so crazy after that. Markie, I'm sorry. I wish I had been…"

"Been what?"

"I don't know," Peggy said slowly. "I don't know

what I could have been. I am what I am. At least tell me I was a good mother."

"You were."

"Thank you."

"When are you going to stop hating Aunt Joan?" Markie said.

Peggy shook her head.

"Never?"

"It seems silly, doesn't it?" Peggy said. "These things happened so long ago. I suppose Joan hates me too."

"I don't think she does."

"Did she say that?"

"Why don't you ask her?" Markie said.

Ah, Joan… Those peaceful summer afternoons in the suburbs together were irretrievable; they had been smashed to bits the moment Marianne was. Peggy knew enough to know that she and Joan would never be sunning themselves and having ice cream together again.

"Just talk to her," Markie said. "She has things to forgive you for too—you deprived her of me."

I was angry at Marianne just before she died, Peggy thought. It wasn't right to be annoyed at a tiny child, only three years old, but her tantrum irritated me. I wanted her to shut up. And Joan, the look on Joan's face when she volunteered to go to the store for ice cream, was just like the way I felt inside. We wanted Marianne to *stop*.

And then she did.

Peggy started to cry again. People won't even let themselves be human, she thought. All these years I've been angry at Joan and also at myself. There were two people, not one, whom I couldn't forgive.

"You and Aunt Joan could be friends now," Markie said. "There are no more secrets. You could start afresh."

"You want that, don't you?"

"Yes."

"But we never had anything in common. Except for you, of course."

"Do you think it's too late?"

"Not too late," Peggy said. "Simply never meant to be. Believe me, Markie, I'm realistic. But when I see her I'll be warm, and we'll both pretend, and finally maybe we'll pretend so well that we'll actually think we *are* friends. That's all I can give you. Is that enough?"

"It's a start," Markie said.

No matter how grown-up they are, Peggy thought, your children still want to be told these little bedtime stories. She knew Joan was harmless now. She felt the relief of it. There was nothing more Joan could do. And thinking this, Peggy felt something that, if it wasn't close to tenderness toward Joan, at least it wasn't close to antipathy either.

FIFTY-FIVE

Rose, who had been born with the birth of the century, was often amazed not only at the many changes that had taken place in her lifetime, but that she was still here to see them in 1999. And Hugh was still here too, still living in her house, surrounded by his family's energy and love, and with a life's purpose, his hospice. He went there faithfully every day—a man who'd had a happy life and a second chance—all of which, she thought, was what was keeping him alive.

He was as feisty an old man in these dwindling years of the nineties as he had been a decade before, although he was over ninety years old. He carried a cane these days, claiming it was because he thought it looked dapper, but actually as a necessary aid for walking; he was glad to use the staircase elevator in the house (Ah, well, Rose had been using it regularly herself at last, *sic transit gloria mundi*); he had lost some of his hearing but could hear well enough when he recognized it as gossip; he'd had laser surgery and lens implants for his cataracts and said he could see like a young man; and his grasp on his memory was surprisingly firm. When Hugh turned ninety he had insisted on giving a big birthday party at the house, and then at the last minute he felt oddly guilty and turned it into an AIDS fund-raiser.

His idol was George Burns, who was older than Hugh. Burns had been planning to appear again on the stage on his hundredth birthday, if he lived that long. George Burns was funny, he remembered his lines, he smoked cigars. When he passed away in 1996, at one hundred, after not achieving his wish, Hugh was very sad, and felt almost betrayed. Hugh had read that during his long lifetime, George Burns still talked to his deceased wife, Gracie Allen, as Hugh still did to the departed Teddy. Sometimes Hugh mentioned this, as casually as if everyone spoke to spirits. However, he was one of the few to whom the spirits spoke back. "The other day, Teddy said to me…" Hugh would say.

"New Age Hugh," Rose called him, laughing. While she prayed to Ben's spirit in heaven, Rose never actually thought of talking with him in a normal conversation.

New Age Everyone, she thought often these days, watching the changes rush by so dizzyingly. She still read the newspaper with the magnifying glass she favored over her eyeglasses, she listened to the radio and watched television, she kept up.

Cloning of vital tissues and organs was being developed. Every fall she went for a flu shot. With the new protease inhibitor some AIDS patients had almost literally returned from the dead—it was called the Lazarus Effect. Kids who were once called brats were now said to have Attention Deficit Disorder, and were being given the drug Ritalin, which Joan said she had taken in her disco days, although she had taken it to stay up. And heart surgery had become almost routine, perhaps ending the "family curse" for Rose's own descendants.

Even now, Rose sometimes thought about her mother's mysterious early death. You never forgot such a trauma; a part of it remained inside you forever, even if it seldom emerged. If they had known what was wrong with her mother they might not have been able to save her anyway. Perhaps they *had* known,

Rose thought now, but they had been forced to be fatalists, and why would they burden a child with information about awful things?

Eventually there would be cures that one could hardly imagine for diseases. The government's Human Genome Project, Ginger had told Rose, was mapping every gene in the body: what it was, how it worked, what it did. For a while now it had been believed that breast cancer was caused by genes and could be inherited—mothers and daughters, sisters and aunts, all dying too young from their own "family curse." Now a woman could actually be tested for genetic defects that caused breast and ovarian cancer; gene mutations called BRCA 1 and BRCA 2, and if the news was bad she could opt for preventative surgery. In 1998 the drug Tamoxifen was approved. It had already been in use for women who had survived breast cancer, to prevent a recurrence, and now it was being given to women at high risk before they got the disease. This could benefit the family, since Daisy had died from breast cancer.

Angel and Juan had a baby now, a dark-eyed, adorable boy they had named Rafael, and the former Angelique confided with proud amusement to a rather appalled Peggy that everyone thought Angel was a Spanish name.

"We WASPS are a dying breed," Ed said ruefully. "The middle-aged white male has become an object of ridicule on comedy shows, shot down by female comedians. I never thought I'd live to see the day."

He was a little bewildered at what had happened in his lifetime, although he tried to adjust. He invited some of the black inner-city kids he worked with to come to a July Fourth picnic with his children and grandchildren on the lawn of his house in Larchmont, bringing them all in a hired bus, chaperoned by some of their mothers, and his next-door neighbor com-

plained. "Fuddy-duddy," Ed said, and invited them
again for the next year.

Peggy secretly agreed with the neighbor, but she'd
already had one argument with Ed before the event
(Who knows what they'll steal, she had said), and now
she thought it best to keep her opinion to herself.

It was interesting, Rose thought, to see Ed and Trevor trying to be friends now that Ed knew that Trevor
was Markie's biological father and had made peace
with it. "At least it's someone we know," Ed had told
Peggy.

Markie and David had struggled with the question
of whether or not to try to have a third child. Since neither of them could bear to destroy their frozen embryos
they decided to go ahead; after all, maybe it wouldn't
work, and if it didn't they wouldn't go through the
whole procedure again, particularly since at nearly
forty she didn't have so many eggs anyway. To their
surprise it did work: Their third and last child, a
healthy boy they named William after Markie's great-
grandfather and the future king of England, was born
in the beginning of 1998.

Peggy and Joan were being kind to each other again,
Rose had noticed, and although they didn't share a social life and never would, at family functions they
sometimes even made one another smile, in a way that
seemed totally genuine. Rose had despaired of ever
seeing the day when this would be, and now she was
relieved. She was glad Joan had finally told Markie the
story that had torn their family apart for so many
years. Now everyone knew, and so they could forget.

Joan had taken Rose to see the hit movie *Titanic*, and
afterward they both remarked that Rose was the name
of a survivor. Of course she hadn't had to deal with a
sinking ship, but she had always tried to be modern
and had always adjusted. There were some things she
couldn't deal with any longer, though. She had been

through classical music and jazz and the blues, popular music, ballads and swing, disco and rock, new age and alternative, but she couldn't understand that wretched hip hop and she didn't care if it was part of the mainstream now.

Rose had also decided she didn't need to learn how to use a computer. She was sure she was the oldest person seen taking money out of a cash machine—it was kind of an adventure, she wanted to keep her independence, and Peter always insisted on going with her so she wouldn't be mugged—but that was about as technological as she intended to get, and she thought, in a way, it was too bad that people had gotten so dependent on getting things done quickly. She had liked chatting in the bank.

With Rose's hundredth birthday coming not so many months from now, Trevor called the *Today Show* on NBC to ask them to have her be one of the people whose hundredth birthday Willard Scott announced on television—photos of their old faces framed by an ad for Smuckers jam. Trevor and Joan, and Hugh, and Peter and Markie and Angel too, thought it would be fun for Rose to become a momentary celebrity. Peggy and Ed were, as usual, a little alarmed. Ginger said, wryly, "Good luck." But Trevor reached only a recording, and to everyone's astonishment except Ginger's he was told that there were one hundred to one hundred twenty-five applicants weekly, from which the twelve were chosen.

"I could have told you there was a lot of competition," Ginger said. "And those are only the people who apply."

The show chose the oldest, the recording said; and men, because centenarian men were fewer. People whose birthdays fell on weekends were ineligible for the TV announcement anyway, since there was no show then. Looking at the calendar Peter discovered that January 1, 2000, would be a Saturday, so in any case Rose would get only a congratulatory letter. The family was disappointed; she was relieved.

"You don't think I want to tell the world how ancient I am," Rose said, her eyes twinkling. But the truth was, she didn't want to see herself on television. It was not her style. Besides, being so old was an accident.

She had settled things for after she was gone. She had gathered her three grandchildren together and spoken to them, and afterward she had left her house to them in her will; however, she had also stipulated that Hugh was to be allowed to live in the house until his death, and that Peter and his family could continue to live in it as long as they paid the bills. Peter had been very kind to her all these years, and besides, Rose didn't know where he could go. But if Peter didn't want to live in the house after Hugh was no longer alive, the three grandchildren could sell it; or if Markie or Angel wanted to move back in at some point with their own families they could, since it would be theirs too. Peggy and Ed had agreed to help pay the taxes.

The three grandchildren had all been civilized and generous at the meeting, and Rose hoped that after she was gone they wouldn't fight. Money had destroyed many families, she knew, and she just had to trust that their love would overcome their need to be rich. The house, she was now told, was worth two and a half million dollars. Maybe, ironically, it would be Peter who would want to sell it, since he could do a lot with his share, and he was the one who had the smallest income.

She was going to be buried in Bristol, along with so many of her family, and dear Ben. Rose wondered if any of the New York descendants would bother to go to visit her grave. It didn't matter; she wouldn't be alone.

But she still had one more thing to do.

The past and the present swam in her mind, so many memories of so many things. If you could cast away the terrible parts and keep the good, what richness there was in remembering! Although she still kept up with most of her activities, she needed nearly as many naps as Rafael and little William now. On Sunday family afternoons, the three of them slept in the same house, dreaming: the children looking forward, herself looking back. Lately part of her day was always spent in looking back.

Sometimes she told Hannah and Henry, her teen-aged and almost teen-aged great-grandchildren, stories about the past, about what their country was like. You had to tell stories to the children, how else would they learn? She told them about the two World Wars, about the Automat, about the Great Depression, about her favorite desserts that didn't exist anymore, about being able to walk into a movie at any time and stay through it all over again.

Rose thought she should have told those kinds of tales to her own children, even though they had been right there for the playing out of some of them; or to her grandchildren, in the role of family historian. But Peggy and Joan hadn't been curious about the old days, and while they were growing up, Rose herself had been young and too busy living her life to reminisce. Ginger had cared, but later she'd gone off to her own future and lost interest in the past. And Rose's grandchildren, from the elusive Peggy, had all been so inaccessible when they were small. And so these days, if they were willing to listen, Rose told whomever was around.

This was the one last thing she had to do, her last chore, although it was in many ways a pleasure because it allowed her to relive her memories.

Maybe later they would care enough to look up her stories in family photographs, in history books, in old magazines, would see them in old movies, might glance at objects at yard sales that had once been the admired and hard-won manifestations of people's daily lives. Or maybe they would be like her and pay no attention, until they looked back, as she now did, to see to their surprise that the past was still there, unrolling like a skein of bright silk, filled with shadows. She wanted to tell them about her rich and vivid and vanished world before it was too late, before she was gone, before it was all forgotten.

An artist's sudden blindness is diagnosed as psychological trauma—but what is it she doesn't want to see?

FOX RIVER

Fox River is a world where Thoroughbreds and fox hunting are passions, not pastimes. The community is rocked to the core when a beautiful heiress is murdered. The trauma has particular resonance for Julia Warwick—her lover has been charged with the crime. The result for Julia is that she plunges into a world without sight.

Blindness has darkened her world, but it has opened her eyes. Julia listens as her mother reads to her from her novel in progress. A story emerges, a forgotten memory returns and the secrets of Fox River are revealed.

EMILIE RICHARDS

USA Today Bestselling Author

Available June 2001 wherever paperbacks are sold!

A two-part epic story from *New York Times*
bestselling author

JAYNE ANN KRENTZ

*The warrior died at her
feet, his blood mingling
with the waterfall. With his
last breath he cursed her
spirit to remain chained in
the cave forever—until a
child was created and
born there....*

So goes the ancient legend of the Chained Lady
and the curse that bound her throughout the ages—
until destiny brings Diana Prentice and Colby Savager
together. Suddenly they are haunted by dreams
that link past and present...dark forces that can be
vanquished only by a passion that is timeless.

A Shared Dream

"One of the hottest writers in romance today."
—*USA Today*

Available July 2001 wherever paperbacks are sold!

DEBBIE

NEW YORK TIMES BESTSELLING AUTHOR

MACOMBER

MIRA®

"Thursday, 8:00 a.m.: Mocha Moments Café, Breakfast Club!"
These words appear in the calendars of four women. Four very
different women. Every week they meet for breakfast—and to
talk, to share the truths they've discovered about their lives. To tell
their stories, recount their sorrows and their joys. To offer each
other encouragement and unstinting support.

Thursdays at eight. A time for emotional sustenance. A time to
think about lives lived, choices made. A time for *friends*…

Thursdays at Eight

"Popular romance writer Macomber has a gift for evoking
the emotions that are at the heart of the genre's popularity."
—*Publishers Weekly*

On sale June 2001 wherever hardcovers are sold!

RONA JAFFE

66424 FIVE WOMEN   ___ $5.99 U.S. ___ $6.99 CAN.
66151 THE COUSINS   ___ $5.99 U.S. ___ $6.99 CAN.

(limited quantities available)

TOTAL AMOUNT	$_____
POSTAGE & HANDLING	$_____
($1.00 for one book; 50¢ for each additional)	
APPLICABLE TAXES*	$_____
<u>TOTAL PAYABLE</u>	$_____

(check or money order—please do not send cash)

To order, complete this form and send it, along with a check or money order for the total above, payable to MIRA Books®, to: **In the U.S.:** 3010 Walden Avenue, P.O. Box 9077, Buffalo, NY 14269-9077; **In Canada:** P.O. Box 636, Fort Erie, Ontario, L2A 5X3.

Name:_____
Address:_____ City:_____
State/Prov.:_____ Zip/Postal Code:_____
Account Number (if applicable):_____
075 CSAS

   *New York residents remit applicable sales taxes.
    Canadian residents remit applicable GST and provincial taxes.

MIRA®